Drekar in

MW01129187

Contents

Drekar in the Seine

Book 9 in the
Norman Genesis Series
By
Griff Hosker

Drekar in the Seine

Published by Sword Books Ltd 2018

Copyright © Griff Hosker First Edition

The author has asserted their moral right under the Copyright, Designs and Patents Act, 1988, to be identified as the author of this work.

All Rights reserved. No part of this publication may be reproduced, copied, stored in a retrieval system, or transmitted, in any form or by any means, without the prior written consent of the copyright holder, nor be otherwise circulated in any form of binding or cover other than that in which it is published and without a similar condition being imposed on the subsequent purchaser.
A CIP catalogue record for this title is available from the British Library.

Cover by Design for Writers
Thanks to Simon Walpole for the Chapter Headings.

Part One

The Curse

Prologue

I was Göngu-Hrólfr Rognvaldson, Lord of Rouen. I thought that title and the land which accompanied it would have been enough for me but it was not. I wanted more. Our family had been promised by the Norns that we would rule the land of the Franks and the land of the Angles. My grandfather, Hrolf the Horseman, was now old. He rarely left my hall and he knew that an ambition burned inside me. The witch who had spoken to him had planted the seed which I would see grow into a tree whose shadow would be a long one. I spoke to him each night for I did not know if he would wake up. He had lived longer than any man I had known. My wife, who was a Frank and a Christian tried to have my grandfather convert. She was certain that he would go to heaven if he converted. She did not understand our ways. It had caused a rift between us. That and the fact that she had borne me two girls since we had been married meant we were not as happy as in the first year. A warrior needed sons. She had yet to give me the son that would see the fulfilment of the prophecy.

My grandfather had a view on that. "Perhaps the curse that was on our family still remains. I paid a witch to remove it but it may be that the witch was not up to the task. You are a young virile warrior. You should have sons."

"You mean that we need to see a better witch?"

"You need to seek the best of witches. You should travel to the Land of the Wolf. You need Kara or her daughter Ylva. Ylva was such a

1

---

powerful witch that Urðr, Verðandi and Skuld, the Norns, tried to take her and make her a Norn. Only the courage of the Dragonheart had prevented that from happening."

"She lives in the Land of the Wolf?"

"She did but that was many years ago. Who knows? We do not have many dealings with the Land of the Wolf any longer. They have withdrawn into themselves."

When my wife was with child once more then I believed that I might have a son. It turned out to be worse than having a daughter. The child died inside my wife's womb. The witches of the clan then believed that it was the White Christ who had cursed my wife. I had taken a Christian wife. They believed that was the cause of the lack of sons. My father was not so certain, "Your grandmother was a Frank and a Christian. I was not cursed."

My wife became withdrawn. She cried and she wept. There were other Christian women who lived amongst us and she took refuge with them. The situation could not go on. My wife spent many hours in the church with our priest, Æðelwald of Remisgat. The followers of the White Christ believed that speaking to a priest would change their lives. I did not believe it. They did not know how to cast spells. In addition, some of my men were restless. They wished to be true Vikings. The sea was in their blood. We raided the Franks along the river the Franks called the Seine but they had learned how to stop us. They built walls around their halls. They added towers and, when we raided, they summoned helped from their neighbours. We had lost no ships but other Vikings had.

Sven Blue Cheek came to see me and my grandfather one night in the middle of Gói. "Lord, the men are unhappy."

"They have food. They have ale. They have women. What more can they want?"

"They want to be men. They want to sail to sea. The ones who are married and have wives tire of them and the ones without wives wish to sow their seed in pastures new."

"And the land hereabouts is not enough?"

He shook his head.

I finished off my horn of ale. I was drinking more ale than I once had. My wife denied me her bed. I would not lie with another and so I had no choice. My grandfather had told me that the Norns were complicated creatures. They had thrown Poppa before me and I had taken her. Now I

2

had to live with the baggage she brought. She followed the White Christ. I saw my grandfather watching me.

He smiled, "I am growing old. Each night you come to speak with me, Hrólfr. You come because I may not wake in the morning." I was about to protest and he held up his hand. "Do not lie to an old man. I see into your heart. Let us solve the problem of your men who wish to raid and your desire to have a wife who will bear you sons. I will come with you for one last voyage. We will sail to the Land of the Wolf and we will seek the witch. We can try to have the curse lifted." He looked at Sven Blue Cheek. "Will that suffice?"

He nodded, "It would. We could take '*Fafnir*'. She is a lucky ship. We take the best of the men. Aye, lord, that would do."

I looked at my grandfather, "One last voyage?"

"I have outlived all of my friends and all of those I held dear, save you. You are the last of my blood. What else is there to live for but you? If you are to have a son then a sacrifice must be made. I will be that sacrifice. When I searched for you and thought you lost, that gave me purpose. I now see that I have another purpose."

"Then I will have no son."

He laughed, "When I was in the cave with the witch I was told that my line would rule the land where we now live. If you have no sons then how can that be? There must be a blót. I will be that blót."

I felt a breeze across my neck. I knew that the Norns were spinning. I did not wish Hrolf the Horseman to die but I knew, deep in my heart, that he was right. I nodded. We would sail to the Land of the Wolf.

Chapter 1

Olaf Two Teeth steered my drekar. Although he ruled Djupr for me he would not relinquish the steering board of our favourite drekar. I took comfort in that for we would be sailing waters that were unfamiliar to us. We had replaced ropes and fitted a new steering board withy. The Land of the Wolf lay many miles away. On a voyage like that, you needed a ship that was well prepared. My crew were all happy to be sailing. I could have filled the ship many times over. Sven Blue Cheek, my Count of Caen, had chosen them for me. He was our oldest warrior and, I believed, our best. Bergil Fast Blade, Sámr Oakheart and Ragnar the Resolute were easy choices. They were my shield brothers. Sven, Bergil and Sámr ruled three of my towns for me. They led their own warbands but when I said where I was going and what I intended then they insisted upon accompanying me and my grandfather. They knew that we were all bound by the same threads. Others who asked to come, like Magnús Magnússon, Leif the Leaper and the Rus warriors, Næstr Dargsson, Habor Nokkesson and Thiok Clawusson, had shown themselves to be good warriors on whom we could rely. We took just sixty warriors and eight ship's boys. For most of the boys, this would be their first voyage. We had taken trade goods with us. The Franks produced fine pots. Our women had enough and the ones we had recently taken could be traded. We also had amphorae of wine and wheat. We would be sailing to places where such goods were as valuable as gold.

Although most of those who lived in my town came to see us off my wife did not. I was going to visit with a witch and she could not understand my reasons. Gefn and Bergljót came to wave tearfully as we left. They were fond of three of us on that ship, me, my grandfather and Bergil. But my wife remained absent as did her priest. My grandfather put his arm around my shoulder when he saw my disappointment. As the current and the breeze took us downstream he said not a word. He did not need to for I felt his thoughts. He felt closer to me than even my dead father. It was strange but I felt I could understand him without the need for words.

The words came as we headed out to sea and the wind continued from our larboard quarter. "You and I are beyond worries such as those which worry other men. We have a destiny. I was young when I led the Raven Wing Clan. My part in this journey was to bring the clan to the Land of the Horse. I thought that when I did my work was done but then your brother became a father killer. The Norns spun their web and I had to rouse myself and find you. When you took Rouen, I thought my work was done then but I was wrong. The Allfather will not let me die until you have a son and ensure that my blood courses through warriors long into the future. When I am in Valhalla then I will be able to talk of all the glory that we enjoyed. This is not a sad time, Hrólfr, it is a joyous time."

"But Poppa?"

"Your wife will either bear you children or you will take another wife. We are not Christian. You need a son. If she cannot bear one then find one who can."

I wondered at my grandfather then. Having lost so much, his son, his wife, his oathsworn all that was left to him was me and he was now becoming a different man. He was still my grandfather but I saw now, in him, a more ruthless side. It may have always been there. Perhaps it was in me too.

I stood with Olaf Two Teeth and my grandfather as we headed west. Olaf looked at the pennant flying from the masthead. "The wind is a fair one, Jarl. We do not need to hurry, do we?"

My grandfather answered for me. "You are not familiar with the waters between Wessex and Hibernia?" Olaf shook his head. "It is still early in the sailing season. Those waters can be treacherous and the weather can be an enemy. We have to sail close to Syllingar. There is a witch who lives there; some say she is a Norn. We sail as fast as we can for we are alone and there is much danger everywhere."

"You know these waters, grandfather." It was a statement and not a question.

"I did not until I sailed them with Erik Green Eye in *'Kara'* seeking you. There are beaches and moorings which are safe for us but we are well provisioned and with a good wind we can stay at sea. That is safer. However, Olaf Two Teeth, instead of having idle boys I would have them trail fishing lines. These seas teem with fish. Let us eat Ran's bounty and save the salted meat for harder times."

I could not help smiling. My grandfather was over sixty years of age and yet his mind was still sharp. Perhaps this purpose he had found had given him new life. Or, maybe, he knew he had a short time left and wished to make the most of it. His words still echoed in my mind, *'You are the last of my blood. What else is there to live for but you? If you are to have a son then a sacrifice must be made. I will be that sacrifice.'*

Almost as soon as the lines were thrown out the ship's boys began to pull in the shiny fish who seemed to be the simplest of fish to catch. They were also good eating. Dropped into a pail of seawater they would remain fresh until we were ready to eat them. By noon we had enough fish for the whole crew and we pulled in the lines. It did not do to be greedy. If we were then Ran would punish us. When we ate the fish then the guts would be thrown back to the god of the sea and all would be well. We had to sail along the coast of the land of the Horse. It had been our home but my brother had given it to the Bretons. It was now a dangerous coast for us. As a consequence, we risked sailing at night for we wanted to pass it quickly. I relieved Olaf and stood with my grandfather at the steering board. The Allfather must have smiled on our venture for he gave us, unusually for this time of year, clear skies and we had the stars to guide us. When dawn came I thanked the Allfather for the stars. Aldarennaöy lay to the south of us and that was good for south of Aldarennaöy there was a deadly current that had wrecked many an unwary ship. We now had open water and my grandfather and I left the ship to Olaf and Sven Blue Cheek. We would be able to keep this wind all day.

I slept by the dragon's prow. We had rigged a canvas and it was a comfortable place for my grandfather and me to sleep. When we slept at the steering board the crew felt obliged to be quiet. It was not fair. While we slept at the prow they could talk and they could laugh. As we made our way forward I saw that the more experienced men were using the time to carve delicate objects from wood and bone. Others were carving their wooden chests. The wind was a luxury and they each used their time well. At the masthead, Óðalríkr Odhensson kept a good watch. This was his third voyage. He was experienced. The newer boys would need to learn the ropes and the tackle first. Already Pái Skutalsson was working with the newer boys to teach them how to tie ropes and what they had to do aboard the drekar. We had no passengers. So long as the wind blew from our larboard quarter then this voyage would be simple. As I curled up beneath my cloak I knew that it would not last. The Norns were too close for that.

When I woke it was after noon. I saw that my grandfather was at the steering board eating some freshly caught fish. I made water on the leeward side and then headed down the centre to join them. Olaf, Sven Blue Cheek and my grandfather were having a discussion. "You are Jarl, Hrólfr, you can decide. Do we risk An Lysardh at night or find somewhere to lay up and wait for daylight?"

It was my grandfather who asked me and I saw the twinkle in his eye. This was a test. Would I pass? I took the fish which Pái Skutalsson offered me and bit into the dark red flesh. It gave me thinking time. I could see the smudge to the north which was the coast of either Wessex or Om Walum. I feared neither the Saxons nor the people of Om Walum but I feared the coast. It had rocks and shoals which could tear the keel from a ship.

"As much as I wish to get to the Land of the Wolf quickly I would not risk this drekar, nor," I smiled at my grandfather, "Hrolf the Horseman. Find us a beach Olaf and we will risk the wrath of the Norns tomorrow when we are all rested and can see what tricks those sisters wish to play on us."

My grandfather had already, in his mind, chosen a beach. He directed Olaf to the north and, as darkness fell and the sun dropped behind An Lysardh we saw the patch of lightness which indicated a beach. We used oars as had our sail lowered as we headed ashore. We had seen no houses and, as the ship's boys leapt ashore to secure us to the land, I could not smell wood smoke. We would keep a good watch but a night sleeping on a beach was not a bad thing. It meant we could light a fire. With a stew made from shellfish and some of our salted meat, we ate well.

We paid for our fine feast, for during the night the wind turned a little. Rather than blowing from the east, it had switched slightly so that it blew from the northeast. Olaf shook his head as we boarded the ship. "We should have risked Syllingar and An Lysardh at night. Now we will have a wind to fight too."

I laughed, "You would risk the Norns at night? You truly have courage. This way we can see the danger and our men need the chance to row."

"Aye Jarl Göngu-Hrólfr Rognvaldson but the wind means that we will need to row all day! We will be lucky to make the north coast of Om Walum and we will have to find another beach."

"Then we will do so. We will use shifts to row. That will keep the men fresh and I will take an oar too."

Olaf shook his head, "We cannot have the jarl rowing!"

My grandfather shook his head, "Why not Olaf? Do you think that my grandson might show up the others?"

It was decided and the crew took an oar. Sven Blue Cheek commanded the rowers and, to get us in the right frame of mind, he chose the first chant. It was a new one and commemorated the slaying of my brother. I felt honoured.

> *Ragnvald Ragnvaldson was cursed from his birth*
> *Through his dark life he was a curse to the earth*
> *A brother nearly drowned and father stabbed*
> *The fortunes of the clan ever ebbed*
> *The Norns they wove and Hrólfr lived*
> *From the dark waters he survived.*
> *Göngu-Hrólfr Rognvaldson he became*
> *A giant of a man with a mighty name*
> *Göngu-Hrólfr Rognvaldson with the Longsword*
> *Göngu-Hrólfr Rognvaldson with his Longsword*
> *When the brothers met by Rouen's walls*
> *Warriors emptied from warrior halls*
> *Then Ragnvald Ragnvaldson became the snake*
> *Letting others' shields the chances take*
> *Arne the Breton Slayer used a knife in the back*
> *Longsword he beat that treacherous attack*
> *When the snake it tired and dropped its guard*
> *Then Longsword struck swift and hard*
> *Göngu-Hrólfr Rognvaldson with the Longsword*
> *Göngu-Hrólfr Rognvaldson with his Longsword*
> *And with that sword he took the hand*
> *That killed his father and his land*
> *With no sword the snake was doomed*
> *To rot with Hel in darkness entombed*
> *When the head was struck and the brother died*
> *The battle ended and the clan all cried*

Göngu-Hrólfr Rognvaldson with the Longsword
Göngu-Hrólfr Rognvaldson with his Longsword
Göngu-Hrólfr Rognvaldson with the Longsword
Göngu-Hrólfr Rognvaldson with his Longsword

I saw my grandfather smiling as he heard the words. This was the first song that had celebrated his grandson. There were many about him. I changed places with Sven Blue Cheek when I saw that he was tiring. Others saw me and changed places with other rowers. With new arms pulling on the oars we increased our speed and I watched An Lysardh slip by our steerboard side. Olaf kept us as close as he dared to the coast for the alternative was to risk being blown towards Syllingar. The grey skies which had greeted us as we had begun rowing were a sign of a change and that change could be the work of the Norns. We rowed hard. By the time we were all exhausted, we had passed the stronghold of Tintaieol where the old kings of Om Walum lived. Sven Blue Cheek was rowing and I took the decision to pull in to the tiny spit of sand which nestled beneath the cliffs. Even if we could not land we would be sheltered in the bay which was little wider than the length of our drekar.

We slept well but I knew that, unless the wind changed, we would have a hard pull the next day. My grandfather saw my look and smiled, "You did not think that the Norns would make this easy for us, did you? So far they have sent an unfortunate wind. It could have been worse."

The wind was against us for the next two days and we barely made the tiny rock with the puffins and the monastery. The Saxons called it Bard Sey. We were all so tired that none even thought to raid the monks. It was as we were eating the birds that my grandfather showed us his experience. "Let us head for Dyflin. The wind will take us there without the need to row. We may find news of Ylva and Kara."

Although it was taking us away from the direction we would have chosen to take none argued with him and we left the lonely isle. The day was grey and filled with flecks of rain but we cared not. We did not have to row.

We arrived at the Viking port and trading centre in the middle of the afternoon. The last time we had been to Dyflin we had had to fight the men of Man. We had taken the drekar '*Hermóðr*' from them. This time we arrived without having had to fight. Even though we were not rowing we kept a good watch to the north and east as the wind took us north; it was a long day of sailing to Dyflin. The last time we had been there

9

Ragnar Lodbrok's sons had recruited many of the warriors to fight the Saxons and the port had been empty. I did not know who ruled there now, neither did my grandfather. This time there were four drekar in the harbour. We had no shields hung on our ship's side and they knew our intentions were peaceful.

Our arrival was something unexpected. The same ships used the harbour but our drekar was new. As we tied up other captains walked down the wooden quay to speak with us. My size meant that even men who had never met me recognised me. One captain, a Viking by his dress and speech looked up at me, grinning. "Unless I miss my guess you must be Göngu-Hrólfr Rognvaldson. If not, then there are two giants in the world."

I smiled back. I was used to such comments. Men meant nothing by them and I could not take offence. There were more important matters to consider. "I am. We have come from Rouen."

He nodded and held out an arm, "I heard that you had taken land from the Franks! Perhaps I should go there for there is little here to keep a warrior occupied. I am Finnbjǫrn Stormbringer."

I clasped his arm. He had a firm grip. "This is my grandfather Hrolf the Horseman."

"And the fame of both of you precedes you. They say King Harald Fairhair bears a grudge against you."

"He is king now?"

"As good as. Most of Norway bow the knee to him. He is the first King; who knows if he is truly the King. He has taken the title."

"I know not why he bears a grudge save that I would not bend the knee to him. That is every warrior's right." He nodded and pointed to the other three captains who had joined us. "This is Saxbjǫrn the Silent, Halfi Axe Tongue and Nefgeirr Haldisson." They nodded. "What brings you here to Dyflin? It is not a good time. The locals are becoming a little restless at the moment."

"The wind brought us. We were heading to the Land of the Wolf to speak with Kara or her daughter Ylva but the wind did not help us."

Naming the witches made each of them clutch their hammers of Thor. "Few ships travel there now. When the Dragonheart was alive and he had his galdramenn then it was a different place. His family fought after he died."

"Do you know what happened to his daughter and granddaughter?"

10

Saxbjǫrn the Silent belied his name and ventured, "Sámr Ship Killer is jarl there now. He lives in Cyninges-tūn. There is a rumour of a witch living in Myrddyn's cave north of there. You might try that to start with."

Finnbjǫrn Stormbringer said, "But first you had better speak with the Jarl of Dyflin, Ragnar Bonemaker. This is his port and he requires payment from ships which use it."

I looked at my grandfather. He shrugged, "We have goods to trade. Why not speak to him? It cannot hurt."

Leaving Sven Blue Cheek in charge of the drekar I went with my grandfather, Bergil Fast Blade, Sámr Oakheart and Ragnar the Resolute. We took our swords but we were not mailed. My sword hung down my back. I was more comfortable with it there.

After Rouen Dyflin seemed a little dirty and dishevelled. There were no stone buildings and the largest dwelling we saw was the jarl's hall. His hearth-weru were outside and stood when we approached. I had that effect on many warriors. I smiled for a scowl often made men fear that I meant violence.

"I am Lord Göngu-Hrólfr Rognvaldson. I understand Jarl Ragnar Bonemaker requires payment to use this port."

An older warrior stood, "Aye, Jarl. He does. I am Bjorn the Wanderer. Come and I will take you to him. If your men would wait outside."

"Aye but my grandfather comes with me." Bjorn nodded.

I had to duck beneath the door frame. I was used to that. After the brightness of the outside, it seemed both dark and oppressive inside. My hall was larger and airier. The jarl was speaking with a man who did not look like a Viking. They both turned as we entered and the jarl held up his hand. We stopped.

Bjorn the Wanderer seemed embarrassed. "I thought the jarl had finished with this fellow."

"He is a local?"

"Muirecán mac Dúnlainge; he calls himself a prince of this land but it seems to me that they have more princes and kings than they have warriors. None of them has any coin. They are brave enough but piss poor in a battle." He went to the table and poured two horns of ale for us. "The water on this island makes good ale. It has a soft taste."

He was right and the barley had been roasted well giving it a dark flavour. The Irish prince suddenly stood up and stormed out. He was not happy. Anger flared in his red cheeks. He had to pass us and I saw that

11

he was a little younger than me. He had a broad chest and tattooed cheeks. When he saw me, he stopped and stared. I just smiled. He left.

Bjorn led us to the jarl who looked annoyed. As we approached I saw that Ragnar Bonemaker had a shaved head. That was unusual and I wondered at the reason. His moustache and beard were plaited. Bones hung from the ends. He looked older than I was. Ivar the Boneless had ruled here until he had left to join his brothers in the land of the Saxons. I could see why. There was little evidence of wealth in this town.

Bjorn said, "Jarl this is Jarl Göngu-Hrólfr Rognvaldson. He wishes to trade here."

He stood and the scowl left his face. He looked at my grandfather. "Then you must be Hrolf the Horseman. I have heard much of you and your grandson." Sit. Bjorn, have food brought. You have a drekar?"

I nodded, "'*Fafnir*'."

"She is fully crewed?"

I wondered at the question. It could have had sinister implications. However, I could think of no reason why I should not answer. "She is. Why?"

"It is *wyrd* that you come here Göngu-Hrólfr Rognvaldson. You are a great lord who has defeated the Franks. Everyone speaks well of you. Guthrum who rules the East Angles is said to be your friend. The Franks and the Saxons fear you." I nodded. "The man who just left is a local leader. He came here because he wants me to help him make war on his cousin, Cerball mac Dúnlainge. He lives to the west of here and to be honest, there is little to be gained from it. The Irish have nothing worth stealing any longer. They are sometimes hard to kill."

My grandfather wiped the froth from his beard, "Then why stay here? Ivar the Boneless found greater rewards in the land of the Saxons."

"You may be right. But there are benefits. We can raid Mercia. They have cattle, women and treasure. It is close enough to raid easily."

"Why did you say it was *wyrd*? What has our arrival to do with this?"

"The Irish are easily insulted. He says he will make war on us."

"And can he?"

"He commands a warband of four hundred and fifty men. We have four drekar. We can muster three hundred."

The food arrived and my grandfather cut himself some bread and cheese. "Then you should be able to defeat him easily enough."

"If it was just his warband then I would agree but there is another, smaller one south of here. Their priests have stirred them up. They have been seeking an opportunity to attack us. If they combined then we would struggle."

I said nothing and joined my grandfather in eating the bread and the cheese. Neither was very good. My grandfather caught my eye.

The jarl waited while we ate. "I would pay you to fight for me."

"I thought you said the Irish were poor and there was little to be had in this land."

"I did but we raided the town they call Legacaestir. It is a rich city with many churches. We have gold and we have Holy Books. We can pay you well."

"We are not here long. We would sell some trade goods and then sail to the Land of the Wolf. We seek the counsel of Kara and Ylva."

He chewed his lip. "Stay here for three days. I will waive the port and trading fees. If the Irish attack then I will pay you to help us. If they do not then you can sail away and we will all be happy. If they do not come in three days then they are not coming."

I looked at my grandfather. He leaned over and whispered in my ear, "We have little to lose by staying here. The Norns sent us here for a reason. If we leave then who knows what trouble it might cause. Three days is not so much."

I nodded, "Very well, jarl, three days."

On the way back to the ship my three oar brothers questioned me about the events we had witnessed. "Why did the jarl not just hold the Irishman? It would have saved trouble."

"I know not, Sámr. There are few drekar here in the harbour. It may say much about Jarl Bonemaker. As my grandfather said, this looks like the Norns' work. As we intend to visit witches then we should not offend the sisters. Have the men prepare their weapons and their mail."

That was one of the strengths of my crew. Our success in battle meant that almost all of the men had a byrnie. Some were short ones but when we went to war we were protected. Finnbjǫrn Stormbringer, Saxbjǫrn the Silent, Halfi Axe Tongue and Nefgeirr Haldisson were still speaking with Sven Blue Cheek when we reached the drekar. That was not a surprise. Sven was a veteran warrior. He had fought for many jarls before joining Jarl Rognvald Eysteinsson and his crew. I knew that I was lucky to have him lead my warriors. Apart from my grandfather, he was the man on whom I relied the most.

The four Dyflin captains turned expectantly when we arrived. I smiled at Finnbjǫrn Stormbringer, "It seems you are all expecting trouble from the locals."

Finnbjǫrn Stormbringer looked down at the ground and then back up at me, "We did not mean to deceive you but, aye, we knew there was trouble. It is why we are here with our ships. We have families and if the Irish come in great numbers then we would take our families to Veðrafjǫrðr and Veisafjǫrðr. There are Vikings there too."

Bergil Fast Blade said, "Perhaps this Irish prince will not return. It seems to me that fighting us weakens his position. If he wants a crown then fighting his own kind makes sense."

Halfi Axe Tongue snorted, "And you do not know these savages! They live worse than pigs in a field and until we came they had no order to their lives. They were forever fighting amongst themselves. Yet they hate us worse than any. This Muirecán mac Dúnlainge, I will not give him the title of prince, will see this as a way of uniting the tribes against us. This might be his way of gaining a crown."

Sámr Oakheart shook his head, "Jarl Bonemaker should have taken his head. That would have ended the danger."

Finnbjǫrn laughed, "I like that attitude and you are right but we have emptied the water from the pot so there is little point in worrying. If they come we fight but I, for one, am pleased that we have Göngu-Hrólfr Rognvaldson and his crew. We now have six drekar crews."

Ragnar the Resolute looked down the quay. "I count but five drekar including ours."

Halfi nodded, "Jarl Bonemaker's ship sprang a leak. They have her on the beach further upstream. She is being repaired."

"We had best go and tell our crews that we stay and fight."

While I explained to Sven what we had spoken to the jarl about Sámr and Ragnar set about preparing the crew. "Get the trade goods out. We will sell them tomorrow at the market." I looked at the sun. It was sinking in the west. I wondered if we would get the opportunity to sell the goods without the Irish attacking. Two knarr arrived on the evening tide. They had brought goods to trade. We slept in a more hopeful frame of mind but we were prepared for war.

The market was a lively affair. Local Irishmen had brought animals and goods to trade. The two knarr had come from Orkneyjar and had seal skins, seal oil and pickled fish to trade. Our goods were the most exotic. I left the trading to Ubba Long Cheek. He had a clever mind and he would get us the best price. I saw my grandfather speaking with the captain of one of the knarr which had arrived. He waved me over.

"This is Nagli Naglisson."

The gnarled old Viking nodded, "Your grandfather tells me that you seek the witches?" I nodded. "The old one, Kara, she left the Land of the Wolf when her husband and father disappeared."

"I thought the Dragonheart and his galdramenn died?"

"They probably did but as no one found their bodies then the rumour is that they live still." He shrugged. "I do not believe that for Sámr the Ship Killer wields the sword that was touched by the gods. Kara left for the east. She went to Miklagård. Now her daughter, Ylva, lives in a cave. They say that it is she who protects the Land of the Wolf and not the warriors."

"Do they not raid?"

He nodded. "Ragnar Wolf Killersson, Ulla War Cry and Gruffyd, the Dragonheart's son are with the sons of Ragnar Lodbrok. They raid Wessex. Sámr Ship Killer stays in the Land of the Wolf."

When we were alone I asked my grandfather about the cave. He nodded, "I know the cave. I did not enter but I went there with the Dragonheart and the galdramenn. We can get to it by crossing the pass from the coast and heading down Lang's Dale."

"You would not visit with Sámr Ship Killer?"

He shook his head. "It seems to me that there is trouble in the Land of the Wolf. The Dragonheart would never fight alongside Danes unless he was desperate. We seek the witch and the witch alone. Better that a few of us travel to the cave in secret. It is Ylva that we seek."

We did well with the trades and our hold was empty. It was replaced by coins. I had promised Jarl Bonemaker that I would wait a further two days but, in truth, I wished to travel across to the Land of the Wolf as soon as possible. The wind was now from the south and we would make good time. However, I had given my word and I would keep it. My men enjoyed Dyflin for it was rough and it was crude but they found Vikings with new stories and tales. The captains we had first met were good men. My grandfather, Sven Blue Cheek and I ate and drank with them. We learned that Jarl Bonemaker was not popular. From the little I had seen of him I understood why.

We were in a strange port and so we kept a good watch. We used the ship's boys for the crew had consumed a great deal of the local beer.

Óðalríkr Odhensson woke me. I smelled burning as I came too. "Jarl, there is a fire upstream. I thought you should know."

I stood and looked. There were flames rising into the sky and the wind was blowing ash over the north bank of the river. It looked to be coming from the beached drekar. There was no reason for a fire to be there. I said, "Rouse the crew. There may be danger." If I was wrong then so be it but this did not feel right. I left the drekar and went to the next ship. It was Finnbjǫrn's.

The warrior on watch pointed to the fire, "What do you think that is, Jarl Göngu-Hrólfr Rognvaldson?"

"I know not but I have roused my crew. If I were you then I would wake your captain." The noise of my men donning mail woke some of the other crews. They were awake but only my crew was ready. I went back to my ship and said, "Sven Blue Cheek, I like not this fire. Have the men keep a good watch."

"Aye jarl." He held up my byrnie. "Here is your mail. Better not take chances."

I had just donned it when the air was rent by savage cries. A horde of wild Irishmen rushed from the dark. Halfi Axe Tongue's drekar was the closest one to them and his crew were not roused. I did not have time to don my helmet nor find my shield. I drew Longsword and leapt to join my men on the quay. We could not allow our new brothers in arms to be slaughtered.

"Wedge, behind me!"

Finnbjǫrn Stormbringer led his men from his drekar. Only a few wore mail. He looked at me, "A warrior cannot even sleep off a good drink without being woken."

"Halfi's ship is being attacked. Watch my flanks." I began to chant to help my men march in step.

A song of death to all its foes
The power of the clan grows and grows.
The power of the clan grows and grows.
The power of the clan grows and grows.
A song of death to all its foes
The power of the clan grows and grows.
The power of the clan grows and grows.
The power of the clan grows and grows.

I was the only one without a shield but with Sven on one side of me and Bergil Fast Blade on the other, I was protected. The Irish were racing towards us. Saxbjǫrn the Silent and Nefgeirr Haldisson had their men with their backs to their ships and were fighting off the Irish who swarmed over them like rats released from a sinking ship. Halfi and his men were desperately fighting on board their drekar. I watched the Irish charge us. They were half-naked. The ones who charged at us had helmets and long curved swords. I held my sword above my head. Timing would be all. I began my swing when the first warriors were three paces from me. My sword slashed across and down. The tip ripped across the throat of one warrior and continued to tear open the middle of a second. Bergil and Sven used their shields well and their swords found flesh. Behind them, Sámr and Ragnar found the flesh of half-naked men. Finnbjǫrn had said they were fearless and reckless foes. We saw the evidence of it. One of the warriors behind their front rank threw a spear at me. It had a bone head. It struck my mail and fell to the quayside. I whirled my sword. The length of the blade and my arms meant that only those with spears could get at me. My sword struck flesh, bone and the metal of swords. The swords were poorly made and bent.

Our attack had slowed but we were almost at Halfi's ship. Finnbjǫrn's men were joining with mine to hack through the wild Irishmen. Suddenly I heard a crack. Someone had severed the fore and backstays on Halfi's ship and the mast began to tumble. I shouted, "Halt!" The mast and yard seemed to take an age to descend. It cracked and crashed into the middle of the Irishmen. The ones who survived made the mistake of turning around to look.

"Finish them!" The mast had made a barrier and forty Irishmen were trapped on our side. The crews of four drekar made short work of them and then we clambered over their bodies and the mast to fall upon the others. I saw a bloody Halfi Axe Tongue lead the survivors of his crew over the side of his drekar. They had dead comrades to avenge. Belatedly, Jarl Ragnar Bonemaker led his men from his warrior hall. They attacked the rear of the warband. Attacked on all sides by mailed men the Hibernians were butchered and then they broke. They hurled themselves into the river; they clambered over dead and dying comrades to escape the vengeance of the Vikings.

When dawn broke it was over. Two hundred Irish warriors had fallen. One of them was the would-be prince, Muirecán mac Dúnlainge. There was little treasure to be had. The chiefs had golden torcs but the weapons were fit only for melting down. My crew had fared the best. We had lost none and suffered minor wounds. Halfi had lost half of his crew and the others had lost warriors.

Saxbjǫrn, Halfi, Finnbjǫrn and Nefgeirr all swore that they would repay me for our attack. Had we not led the assault on the enemy then all might have suffered the fate of Halfi Axe Tongue. Jarl Ragnar Bonemaker showed his gratitude with a small chest of silver. We stayed to bury the dead and left on the afternoon tide. We had kept our word and our honour was intact.

Chapter 2

My grandfather was eager to visit the Land of the Wolf. When the Dragonheart had rescued him from the Franks and brought him back to his stronghold in the north he had learned to be a warrior there. He had told me that had the witch on Syllingar not made her prophesy, then he would have stayed in the Land of the Wolf. I had seen the land but only from the sea. Thanks to the other captains we had met in Dyflin we had a better idea of our route. We would land at the small fishing village of Ravn Glas and head up the pass known as Ravn Hals, the pass of the raven. My grandfather took that to be a sign that Odin would smile on our venture. It was a long walk. I did not think that we could complete the journey there and back in less than three days.

We reached Ravn Glas in the late afternoon. The fishermen were Viking but their blood was mixed with the old people of the land. They were not warriors. We were welcomed but it was a cautious welcome. They were happy for us to moor our ship in the bay and even gave us advice on the journey. My grandfather and I were accompanied by Bergil, Sámr and Ragnar. We wore no mail but took bows and our swords as well as blankets and food. The next morning, as we left the village I looked up at the mountains which appeared to rise vertically. I glanced at my grandfather.

He did not look at me but said, "Do not worry. I can walk this road. It will do me good." And so we began the trek up the narrow track which led to the pass. We had been told that there was an abandoned Roman fort close to the summit. We found the fort, nestling against the side of the mountains, in the late afternoon. I think that while four of us could have gone on we had done enough for my grandfather. We lit a fire and put on a pot of water. We had some dried and salted meat. It always tasted better cooked. The men of Ravn Glas had given us some fresh fish. We ate well.

My grandfather looked at the Roman walls. Half had been robbed for their stone. I daresay there were houses with Roman stone as part of their structure. However, they were still a statement. "When we are all gone what will remain of us, Hrólfr? We build in wood and turf."

I smiled and patted myself, "Your blood, grandfather. This land will be ruled by those who spring from my loins. They will be of your blood. Where are the ones who built this? They are long dead and their seed spread but our seed will remain."

I felt at peace in the old fort. I had walked it and saw how the Romans had built it. I could use some of their ideas when I returned home. The next day was easier for we followed the trail downhill. It twisted and it turned but it led us to the valley below the Lough Rigg. I was in strange territory but, amazingly, my grandfather felt that he knew where we were. As the path rose towards the water of the Rye Dale my grandfather slowed. It was to be expected for he was old. As soon as we began the descent I was amazed by the vista which met my eyes. I had seen the fjords of Norway and they were beautiful but here we had high peaks and lush green valleys. The forests seemed to grow from patches of clear blue water. I could see why my grandfather had loved it so.

Once we had descended the pass and began to follow the twisting bubbling stream my grandfather began to consult the map which one of the warriors in Dyflin had drawn for him. It was crude but it helped us. When we saw the mountain known as Úlfarrberg to the north and east then we knew the cave was to the east of us. My grandfather pointed to a rock that stood out from the rolling fells behind. "That looks to be the Scar of Nab. If we head for that then the cave should be above us, to the north, on the Lough Rigg."

The Rigg became obvious. It was like the back of an animal that rose and headed north. The water of the Rye Dale glistened in the late afternoon sun and we knew we were close. It was then that the Norns intervened. Ragnar the Resolute took his eyes from the path. The scree beneath his feet gave way and he fell. Nothing broke but, even in seal skin boots, he had twisted his ankle. In the time it took to determine that it was a bad sprain and not a break the sun had started to set behind the mountains we had just climbed.

Grandfather nodded, "The Norns have set us a challenge."

We found a sheltered flat place below the cave where we left Sámr and Ragnar. We left our blankets and food. The place we sought the cave was above us. I saw a rocky overhang. There looked to be a sort of path leading to it. It might help us to find the cave but the sun was setting fast. As he headed up what we took to be a path Bergil asked, "Why do we not wait for daylight? Surely it will be easier to reach the cave then."

Grandfather said, "If you wish to wait with Ragnar then no one will think less of you."

"No, my oar brother is going and I will be with him. No matter what danger the cave and the witch bring." I could hear the fear in his voice. A man did not go readily into a witch's lair.

My grandfather put his hand on the ledge which was next to his head, "Unless I am wrong then I believe this is the place where the wolf leapt out when the Dragonheart and his son hunted the wolf."

I wondered how he could know and then I realised that close by us was the most powerful witch in the Viking world. We were now in a land that was ruled by the spirits and not by man. Anything and everything was possible. She may have planted the thought in his head.

Once we ascended to the ledge we saw that there were bushes that had grown from rocky fissures. There was just enough light to see them. The ledge was remarkably flat but as I looked at the gaping maw which was the cave I saw something glowing inside. It looked like a dragon's eye. To me, it appeared that a dragon had opened one eye and was peering at us from within his lair. Perhaps the witch had such a dragon to guard her. I was no Beowulf. Was it worth bearding a witch in her den? Was the curse that important? Perhaps grandfather was right. There were other women. I thought about turning around but two things stopped me. My grandfather kept walking and my body would not turn. It was as though I was being forced into the cave. I heard Bergil murmur, "Brother, I will guard the entrance I fear to go within."

I said nothing but nodded. I was afraid to speak. My feet seemed drawn into the darkness. The light had gone. Had the dragon closed its eye? My grandfather's voice, when it came to me, was both calm and reassuring. "We are safe here, Hrólfr. Do not be afraid of the darkness. You, who were at the bottom of the sea and reborn, should not fear a little darkness."

Then I heard a voice that sent shivers down my spine. It seemed to come from behind me and before me at the same time. It was almost a whisper yet I felt the breath on my neck, "The horseman is right Göngu-Hrólfr Rognvaldson. I am but a woman and you fear no woman, do you?"

I turned but there was no one behind me; there was just the gaping mouth of the cave but it suddenly appeared smaller. Had it shrunk? Was I bewitched already? I turned back and thought my grandfather had disappeared. I almost panicked and then I saw his back. He was seated before a glowing fire. I was a warrior. I had led armies. Why did I fear to go where an old man did not? I moved closer. I could not see anyone other than my grandfather. I saw that he was seated upon the stump of a hewn log. He patted another which was to his right. He said not a word. Perhaps we had been bewitched. Coming to see a witch no longer seemed a good idea.

A voice that seemed to be either in my head or on my shoulder said, "You were meant to come here, Göngu-Hrólfr Rognvaldson. The sisters sent you to me and it is *wyrd*. You must trust me as your grandfather trusts me."

I turned but saw no one. I sat on the log. I was grateful for the closeness of my grandfather. He would protect me. The sword which hung from my back seemed inadequate. How could I kill a spirit?

A figure appeared from the shadows. It was cloaked and hooded but I knew that it was the witch. When she spoke, it was the voice I had heard in my head, "Göngu-Hrólfr Rognvaldson, tell your men to come inside the cave. Tonight, there will be a storm and one is hurt. He needs to be healed." I stood and saw her throw a log onto the fire. It flamed up and I saw that the cave had a high ceiling. The fire made it easier for me to pick my way across the floor of the cave. I saw light reflecting from a large pool. Had we veered to the left when we had entered we would have had to wade through it. Someone had guided our feet.

I found Bergil hiding in the rocks by the entrance. He stood, "Fetch Sámr and Ragnar. She wants us within the cave."

"I am happy out here, lord."

"It will rain and do you really wish to risk the wrath of a witch?"

"No lord." He disappeared into the dark and I felt the first spot of rain on my head. Sámr and Bergil supported Ragnar when they neared the cave. They had our blankets and food with them. Sámr asked, "Are you certain about this, lord? A little rain never hurt anyone."

My smile was hidden in the darkness but these men who would board a drekar filled with enemies or charge with me into a horde of wild barbarians were afraid to face a witch. What had seemed easy in Ravn Glas now seemed daunting.

"She will not harm us."

As I turned I saw that the fire had been built up and its flames illuminated the cave. I saw runes and signs marked upon the walls. Some runes I recognised: wolf, hawk, a sword. Others were unknown to me. I saw the witch's back as she stirred something in a pot she had placed on the fire. She had put a tripod stand to hang the pot from it. Was she conjuring a potion? Were we about to be bewitched? Without turning she said, "It is a hearty soup, Göngu-Hrólfr Rognvaldson." I started and she turned. She had lowered her hood and I saw a woman who was beautiful beyond words and yet she was not young. She was smiling. "I read your thoughts." She waved a hand at my three companions. "I read all of your thoughts. Sit, Ragnar the Resolute. I will bind your foot. It is a long walk back to Ravn Glas." He did as he was told although terror was on his face. The witch took her bag and knelt next to him.

As I sat next to my grandfather I watched, almost mesmerized as the witch applied a salve to Ragnar's foot. I turned to look at my grandfather. He looked at peace. "This is a good place, Hrólfr. It is ancient. Witches and wizards have used this since before the time of the Romans." He smiled, "I have been in the Norns' cave at Syllingar. There you feel as though you are in a coffin. This feels comfortable. We are safe here. Ylva will help us." Just then we heard the rain as it began to fall even harder. I heard splashes and, as I turned, I saw that water was seeping through from the roof to fall into the pool. It was just a series of drops and it only fell in the pool. Was that by design?

"The spirits led the ancient seers to this place. It has water and it has shelter, Göngu-Hrólfr Rognvaldson. It is protected by those spirits. This world in which you live is kept safe by the spirits of the dead. You are a Viking. Never forget whence you came. Remember that you were saved from your brother's treachery. Who saved you? Why?" Her voice was mesmerizing. It commanded that you listen.

When she had finished applying a salve and binding Ragnar's foot she went to the pot and stirred it.

"You have bowls?"

It was as though we had been bewitched and her words broke the spell. Bergil said, "I will get them, lady."

She smiled, "You have honeyed words, Bergil Fast Blade. I need no title. I am Ylva Aidensdotter. I am of this land for my name means wolf and this is the Land of the Wolf."

Bergil handed us our bowls and Ylva filled them. My men hesitated but my grandfather and I ate. It was exquisite. I tasted mutton as well as fowl but there was another taste. There was a hint of heat beyond the cooking liquor. It warmed from within. I was aware that she was staring at me as I ate. It felt like she had seen me from within already and was now looking at the frame which held my thoughts and my spirit. I could not avoid the scrutiny. When she was satisfied she turned her attention to my grandfather.

"You are a brave man Hrolf the Horseman. I was but a babe in arms when you left but my grandfather often spoke of you."

"What happened to the Dragonheart?"

She smiled, enigmatically, "That is not your tale any longer, Horseman. Your thread is a different one. When Urðr prophesied your future then that thread was cut. The Norns wove a different life for you. It made the warrior who will become Rollo."

I misunderstood, "I will have a son and he will be Rollo?"

"You will be Rollo but you will have a son, eventually." I was confused. She turned to my three companions and pointed to some straw that lay in a corner of the cave. "There is your bed. There is ale there. Do not fear for your lord. He is safe in my hands." She laughed, "And if he were not then you could do little about it could you?" Like sheep being herded by a dog they allowed themselves to be led to the bed. They drank and Ylva returned to us. She smiled, "They will sleep and they will dream. They are loyal and they deserve to see a little of their future."

"And us?"

She looked at my grandfather, "You know your future already, Horseman. You promised the spirits and a bargain was made for they hear all. You cannot undo your words."

He nodded, "I am content."

She was talking about my grandfather's promise. She was talking of sacrifice, "I will not allow it! I need no son! I will find another wife! I will take a Viking bride!"

Ylva laughed, "You do not understand yet, do you, Göngu-Hrólfr Rognvaldson? This is out of your hands. When the web was spun for your grandfather then your course was made. You can do nothing about it. Why do you think your wife only bears you girls? It is because you are not yet ready to have a son. Your world has to change. You have to change. You lead a small clan perched on the edge of the world of the Franks. When you are ready to lead a world of drekar then you will be ready for a son."

She took some thread and a spindle and she laid them down. She walked over to my grandfather and took out a knife. I was frozen. Was she going to sacrifice him there before me? Was this to be the blót? Smiling she cut some of my grandfather's longer hairs and laid the tresses by the thread. Then she approached me. As she leaned in I smelled rosemary and thyme. She reached around me to cut some of my longer hair. She whispered, "Fear not it is not yet your grandfather's time but make the most of that which is left. He cannot undo the words that were spoken. The Norns do not forget such promises. He will join the spirit world soon. It is *wyrd*."

While the rain pelted down outside and the water dripped into the pool. Ylva cut some of her own fair tresses. We watched as Ylva used our hair, her hair and her threads to weave a spell. She chanted beneath her breath as she did so. I understood not a word for it was not in any language which I understood. When she had finished there was a small square of material that had been woven. I saw that our hair had been fashioned into the shape of a horse's head. She laid it before her.

"Is that it? The curse is lifted?"

She shook her head. "Curses are not so easy to lift. This spell and this web ensure that you will have a son." I reached for the material. "No, Göngu-Hrólfr Rognvaldson, I will keep this and I will guard it. When you become Rollo then you will know that the curse has been lifted. That is many years in the future. You will be greybeard before that happens. Now sleep. You have a long walk back to your drekar. Your grandfather is already enjoying the company of the spirits. This is a magical place. Enjoy your dreams." She came over and kissed me on the forehead.

I suddenly found myself tired beyond words and, with the fire before me, I lay down and slept.

I saw a sea of Saxons. They ebbed and flowed as though they were controlled by Ran himself. A wall of warriors stood firm. I saw Guthrum and I was next to him. We began to reap the Saxons like wheat and as they fell they were replaced by stacks of coin. All went black and I seemed to be flying high above the earth. I saw an island in the river. It was Paris. Filled with warriors it was surrounded by drekar. There were many hundreds of them. They destroyed a tower but they could not breach the wall. Once again, the warriors disappeared and their places were taken by chests of coin. All went black once more. In my dream I heard the cry of a child and the darkness cleared

to show Poppa suckling a boy child. As I leaned over the child grasped
my sword in his two tiny hands and raised it. All went black.

I heard my grandfather. He was talking. Then I recognised Ylva's
voice. I opened my eyes and saw them close by me. Ylva held my
grandfather's right hand between her two. She smiled, "You dreamed?"

I saw in her eyes that she knew the answer already. "You know that I
did but I do not understand it. I can see why I was in Paris but the
Saxons?"

"I do not send the dreams. The spirits do. I read them. You have been
sent glimpses of the future. When these events happen? Who knows?
Your grandfather has dreamed." She looked at him.

He smiled, "I have dreamed my death, Hrólfr."

"No!"

"You cannot change what is to be. I know it as does Ylva. I will keep
it here." He tapped his heart. "I dreamed your son too. He has a name
already eh?"

"You saw the same vision as I did? You saw the sword?"

"Not just any sword but Longsword. It is *wyrd*."

"And now you must head back. The weather will be clement for a day
and after that... wake your warriors, Göngu-Hrólfr Rognvaldson. I will
give you a hot meal before you go. Your grandfather has a long walk this
day. What took you two will now take you but one. I have two ponies
that you can use for your injured warrior and the Horseman."

I walked to the three warriors and shook Bergil Fast Blade awake.
"Rise, we eat and then we leave."

He looked up at me, his eyes wide. "I dreamed lord! We fought the
Franks! I have two sons!"

I smiled, "Then the visit to the witch was worthwhile eh?" I could not
help but feel dread. I would now be waiting for my grandfather to die.
How much worse would it be for him?

As I neared the fire and the bubbling pot Ylva said, "He will not be
dreading his death, Göngu-Hrólfr Rognvaldson, for he knows when it
will come. He will be ready. It will be a good death. His sword will be in
his hand and he will join your father. It is *wyrd*."

We ate and I saw the sky lighten outside as dawn broke. It would be a
grey day but a dry one. Ylva left the cave while we packed our
belongings. When we emerged, she had two hardy ponies. "You can
walk the last part of the journey to Ravn Glas. Leave them at the Roman
fort. They will find their way home. I have spoken with them."

My grandfather kissed her hand, "Thank you vǫlva."

She smiled, "I will see you in the Otherworld and in my dreams. You have had a good life and you have done all that was asked of you. The Allfather will have a place on his high table reserved for you."

He mounted one of the ponies and set it off down the track. The others followed. I waited. I felt that there should have been more. "Will I ever see you again?"

"The webs I spin I can control. The webs spun by the Norns are a different matter. We know not."

"And how will I know that what I do is right and is the way of the Sisters?"

She put her hand on my heart. "You will know in here." She smiled, "My grandfather taught me that. May the Allfather be with you but I do not think that you will need much help from any, Göngu-Hrólfr Rognvaldson, Jarl of Rouen and one day Dux Rollo of the Norsemen."

I headed down the trail to catch up with the others. We were all silent. Each of us was lost in the world of the dream we had had. The skies were grey and threatening and yet we had no rain. We made good time and reached the fort after noon. Ragnar and my grandfather dismounted. We gave the ponies some water and they turned and began to head down the Ravn Hals.

We did not have far to go and the road led down, not up. We would reach our ship before dark. "What of the Dragonheart, his galdramenn, Aiden and Ylva's mother, Kara?"

"Kara is on her way back from Miklagård." I gave my grandfather a surprised look. How could Ylva know that? He smiled, "She dreamed it. Her mother is old beyond years. Dragonheart and Aiden? They are in the Otherworld but she would not tell me how they travelled there. I will soon find out for myself."

"I do not want you to die. I especially do not want you to die so that I may have a son."

"And who says that is the reason why I will die? I said I would make a sacrifice. I dreamed and saw that my thread was ready to be cut but there are threads that bind us. Ylva used hair from both our heads. When I am gone then listen to that small voice inside your head for that will be me. The Norns weave strong threads, Hrólfr."

27

Map showing ÆSCEDŪN, WINTAN-CÆSTRE, BATTLE WITH THE SAXONS, HÆMWICH, CAMP, WIHTWARA, SEALS-EY, with a scale of 6 miles.

Chapter 3

Our men were relieved to see us. They plagued us with questions and were surprised at our reluctance to answer them. We had all dreamed. We did not share those dreams. Sven Blue Cheek was wise. He scattered the men, "Get to your oars. We have done that which we intended and now it is time to sail home. We have gold and we have our jarl. All is good."

The men moved away and my grandfather went to the prow. He was tired. The last part of the journey had been hard for him.

"Jarl, we do sail home do we not?"

"We do Olaf." I smiled and looked at Sven, "If the Norns allow it."

Ylva had been right the Allfather sent us a wind and we headed south. The crew had had three easy days and it was no problem to divide them into three watches. It allowed us to sail at night. The rain returned the first night and continued, off and on, for the rest of the journey to An Lysardh. We were philosophical about the rain. It filled the water barrels and we had spare sails we used for shelter. The fishermen of Ravn Glas had sold us a barrel of pickled fish and salted mutton as well as a barrel of beer. It was no hardship. Even though it was raining my grandfather braved the wet to look at the land as we sailed south. It would be the last time he saw it and he was making the most of it.

As we neared Tintaieol we prepared for danger. There were rocks and there were Saxons. The rocks were more dangerous than the Saxons but as we were halfway home it would be wise to be careful. The ship's boys ringed the ship and perched on the yard looking for danger. The wind was still from the north but was a little more easterly too. Our progress would not be as swift. Fortune favoured us or perhaps the Norns were being kind. We reached An Lysardh in daylight and Olaf Two Teeth took us around the treacherous teeth which threatened to tear out our hull and we made the southern coast of Om Walum.

Despite our care, we still suffered damage or maybe it was the Norns. Olaf found the ship to be a little sluggish as we headed into the open waters to the south and west. He rubbed his beard, "I would like to land, jarl. I fear we may have sprung a strake."

My grandfather had been listening. "I would head north and east if I were you. There are better beaches and fewer men there."

We heeded his advice. It was sage. As darkness approached we found a deserted beach. Sven Blue Cheek led a small warband up the cliffs and when he reported that there was no one nearby we hauled the drekar onto the sand. We would examine it the next morning. We did not risk a fire. We could not leave quickly.

As we ate cold rations and drank the last of the beer from Ravn Glas my father said, "When I was young this land was not Saxon. It belonged to the men of Om Walum. The men of Wessex have grown strong since then." I nodded my agreement. "Yet the land does not change. It cares not who owns it." He spat out a piece of mutton gristle. "Can a man ever truly own a piece of land? He can hold it until someone stronger comes to take it away from him."

I smiled, "Your dream has made you into a philosopher, grandfather."

"Perhaps or it may have just allowed me to see that which is important. Men will try to take Rouen from you. The Franks will regret allowing you to keep it. Charles the Bald made a mistake when he allowed us to stay. He will try to take it back."

"Then the sooner we are back the better."

He gave me a strange look, "That may not be as easy as you might think."

Olaf's instincts had been correct. One of the strakes just below the waterline had sprung. We had pine tar and we had nails. Along with sheep wool, they could be used to repair the hull. It just meant waiting for a day on the beach. The tar would need to harden and we would have to wait until high tide to float her off. We would have a long day to worry about enemies surprising us. The wind was cold and the day was wet. Winds from the south tended to be wet ones. In these waters winds from the north and east were drier. The joy of the journey south was gone. Worse the wind began to veer. Eventually, it changed to one from the south and east. Although that meant the wind was not as cold it was still wet. It also meant we could not sail directly home. We would have to sail east, along the Wessex coast. Once we reached Flanders then the men would have to row. I began to wonder if the voyage had been worthwhile. The curse was not lifted and although we had traded well and we had been rewarded by Jarl Bonemaker we had little else to show for it.

We left late at night. I did not want to risk another night ashore. Until Wihtwara we could sail due east in safety. When we reached the island, the Romans had called Vectis, we would have to row for we would need to sail into the wind to get around the island.

The crew took to the oars at noon. They had slept well and were ready for a hard row. Sven Blue Cheek led the chant.

Siggi was the son of a warrior brave
Mothered by a Hibernian slave
In the Northern sun where life is short
His back was strong and his arm was taut
Siggi White Hair warrior true
Siggi White Hair warrior true
When the Danes they came to take his home
He bit the shield and spat white foam
With berserk fury he killed them dead
When their captain fell the others fled
Siggi White Hair warrior true
Siggi White Hair warrior true
After they had gone and he stood alone
He was a rock, a mighty stone
Alone and bloodied after the fight
His hair had changed from black to white
His name was made and his courage sung
Hair of white and a body young
Siggi White Hair warrior true
Siggi White Hair warrior true
Siggi White Hair warrior true
Siggi White Hair warrior true

The song of Siggi was a popular one and I think Sven chose it for my grandfather. The two had been great friends. Perhaps the song was an omen for Pái Skutalsson who was at the masthead shouted, "A drekar to the north and east, lord. She is being attacked by three Saxon ships."

A drekar could easily handle one, or even two Saxon ships but three meant that both the prow and the steering board could be attacked at the same time. My grandfather said, quietly, "You must go to their aid."

I nodded. The Norns had spun and I think my grandfather had already dreamed this for he did not seem surprised. "Olaf, turn the steering board." As soon as we swung the wind caught us and I shouted, "Arm yourselves. We have a brother to save!"

Pái Skutalsson shouted down, "It is the *'Fire Drake'*, lord."

'Fire Drake' was the ship of Finnbjǫrn Stormbringer. When last we had seen him he had been in Dyflin. What was he doing in these waters? I did not bother with mail. I strapped on my sword and put a seax in each seal skin boot. I now saw the battle. The four ships had all lowered their sails but, even so, the wind was taking them inexorably towards the coast of Wihtwara.

I saw that two Saxons were on either side of the prow while the third was alongside the steering board. "Olaf lay us alongside the larboard quarter. We will go to the aid of the captain. The ones by the prow will have to hold. We have to win the battle at the stern before we can save the rest." I strode to the prow. I saw blades rising and falling. Finnbjǫrn was at the steering board and he had made a shield wall. I saw the rest of his warriors had made a shield wall around the mast and the mast fish. "When we board, Sven, take the larboard oars and relieve the men beleaguered at the mast. I will take the steerboard oars and go to the aid of Finnbjǫrn."

"Aye, lord." He grinned. "The Norns eh?"

"Aye! Steering board oars, to me!"

As we neared the four ships locked in a struggle of life and death we were spied. The crew of the Saxon at the steering board saw us. I saw their arms pointing. I could not hear anything but I guessed they were warning those on board the drekar that we were approaching. I chose not to wear my helmet. Most of my men adopted the same strategy. Whatever benefits there might be from a helmet there were more to having better vision. I confess that I had an advantage. It would take a mighty blow for a Saxon to strike my head. I pulled myself up onto the forestay. My sword would remain sheathed until I was aboard.

As we neared I saw three Saxons bring spears to fend us off. As they did so arrows flew from our yard as three ship's boys used their bows.

Olaf shouted, "Reef the sail!" Pái Skutalsson threw a grappling hook to secure us to the drekar. I leapt through the air even as we closed. There was a gap between the ships but I had long legs and I landed on the body of one of the Saxons slain by our arrows. One of the survivors pulled back his spear to ram it at me. I grabbed the spear shaft before the head reached me and I tore it from the Saxon's grip. I reversed it and skewered him to the deck. As the two drekar ground together the bump shook the deck. I had a wide stance but some of the Saxons who were turning to face the new threat did not. As they fell I stabbed forward at the backs of the ones who had not fallen. My Saxon spear found flesh. Then Bergil Fast Blade and Sámr Oakheart were with me. Their swords drawn, they fell upon those Saxons who were floundering like fish on the drekar's deck. I turned and hurled my spear at the back of a Saxon attacking the mast. Then, without waiting to see the result, I drew Longsword and swept it in a wide arc. Bergil and Sámr knew me well enough to stay behind me. The blade found three warriors. One died when the sword bit into his neck and the other two were wounded. As the three fell we leapt into the gap.

Finnbjǫrn shouted, "Allfather!" I saw his sword come down and split the helmet and skull of a Saxon.

I now had twenty-two men behind me and they were all good with a sword. Each had fought at sea before and our blades rose and fell with mechanical precision. They were carefully aimed blows that were intended to do serious harm to the Saxons. Longsword was a frightening weapon. Used by someone with long arms and great strength, such as me, it could slice a man in two or bend all but the best of swords. Helmets and mail were no obstacle to it. Bergil and his fast hands whipped, spun and stabbed so quickly that it was like a blur. When Sámr stabbed beneath the sword of the thegn who led this crew of Saxons it was all over for the rest hurled themselves back to their own ship. Someone on the Saxon vessel had already cut the ropes which bound them together and the Saxon was drifting north and east. Some of those fleeing us fell into the sea.

We had saved Finnbjǫrn but now we had to save the rest of his crew. Sven Blue Cheek and my larboard crew had contained the two Saxon crews but they outnumbered us. Finnbjǫrn joined me, "Come jarl. Let us rid this ship of these rats! They stink up my ship."

The two of us, with swords raised, ran at the Saxons. Three men had boarded with mail, full-face helmets and shields. They were either thegns or hearth-weru. Without hesitation, we ran at them. They had good swords but mine was longer. I was on the right of Finnbjǫrn and I was able to swing my sword from behind me over the gunwale of his drekar. Longsword smashed into the shield of the warrior on their left. My sword shattered his shield and ripped through his byrnie and arm. I pulled it back and it sawed into his side. With his lifeblood pumping away, he sank to his knees. The spraying blood had made the deck slippery and Bergil and Finnbjǫrn took advantage of two warriors encased in mail who could neither keep their balance nor see as well as they might. Both were wounded and when I swung again I took the head of one and Finnbjǫrn the other. With their three best warriors dead, the remainder of the Saxons edged their way back to their own ships.

We now had the advantage and as the Saxons slipped and stumbled over chests, ropes and dead warriors, they were slain. They were beaten before a single blow was struck for they were retreating. Their only aim was to get back to their ships safely. Twenty warriors were left dead aboard Finnbjǫrn's ship before the rest managed to escape. They fled north to their island home. My men cheered but I saw Finnbjǫrn's face. He had lost warriors.

I shouted, "Take what the dead Saxons have and toss their bodies overboard!"

With something to do other than cheer, both crews obeyed me.

"What happened, Finnbjǫrn?"

He shook his head, "Even as you left for the Land of the Wolf my crew and I decided we had had enough of Jarl Bonemaker. We decided to join the Danes. One of the knarr which came to trade brought news of a large camp at Readingum. It is said that Bagsecg and Halfdan Ragnarsson planned to attack Wessex. We were going to join them. The other captains were still debating."

We heard the splash of bodies as the Saxons were hurled overboard. "And now?"

He grinned, "And now? That is obvious. Before we came for treasure and now we come for vengeance." He looked at his ship's deck. It was both bloody and damaged. "I would be grateful if you would sail with me to Wessex for I fear my drekar might be damaged. If you do so then I will be in your debt once more."

My answer was an easy one. We would have had to sail north and east anyway. It made sense to help our fellow Viking. He had lost men. It would be dishonourable if we left him to face the Saxons alone.

"Aye, we shall."

We had been lucky. Aðils the Fearless had lived up to his name and had a badly gashed left arm. Petr, our sailmaker was already stitching him. Fifteen of Finnbjǫrn's crew were dead and another eight wounded. He would only be able to row with one man at each oar. It was another reason he needed us to stand by. If the Saxon ships saw us leave our consort then they might end the job they had started. Finnbjǫrn had been lucky too. They had had the wind with them and had been able to arm and mail themselves before the Saxons struck. If they had not then we might have arrived just to bury the dead. The Norns had sprung the strake and that had saved Finnbjǫrn. What else had they in mind?

"Olaf Two Teeth, keep three lengths astern of them. They do not have enough crew."

Sven Blue Cheek came along to speak with me. "Stormbringer said that we should keep the three byrnies and helmets. They are well made." He held up a bronze seal. "They were Eorls, lord. They had these around their necks."

"Then the Saxons are bolder than they once were. King Æthelred must have a new strategy. He is trying to defeat us at sea."

I had forgotten my grandfather. He had remained by the steering board during the battle. Now he nodded, "If that is so then he has miscalculated. Ylva told me that more than three hundred and fifty ships landed Danes in the East when the Great Raid took place. More than that have arrived since. Æthelred holds on to a tiny part of this land. It is the richest part, I grant you, but the smallest."

"What of the Dragonheart's family? Did I not hear that they had joined the Danes?"

"I had the truth of it from Ylva. They led their men in a raid on Mercia. I did not think that the Dragonheart's kin would fight for his enemies." My grandfather gave me another strange look, "And they were ever our enemies. When we were on Raven Wing Island it was Danes who made us leave."

I shrugged, "Guthrum is a Dane and I like him. I have pledged to be his shield brother."

My grandfather smiled, "And that is good. It is *wyrd*!"

Since his dream, he had been full of such enigmatic phrases. It was almost as though he knew all that was about to happen. What had he dreamed? Although the wind was behind us we were still slow for we travelled at the speed of *'Fire Drake'* and the collision with the three Saxons had damaged her. We could see her getting lower in the water as she headed towards the Wessex shore. The water in her hull was slowing her down.

We barely made the beach. The water was almost three quarters of the way up the side of *'Fire Drake'*. Finnbjǫrn found a sandbar which meant water was on two sides of his ship. Re-floating her would be easier. While we moored off the beach my men clambered over the side to help pull the stricken ship clear of the water. When she was safe Finnbjǫrn shook his head, "We are a burden for you. We cannot move quickly. This is Saxon country. When they know where we are they will come for us."

"And we will wait. If their numbers are too great then we will take you aboard our drekar and give *'Fire Drake'* a good funeral. I will fetch my men ashore and we will make a camp."

"Do you know where we are?"

"I have maps. I will look." I pointed south. On a spit of land stood a church and some Saxon houses. "That looks old and may be on my charts."

"There is no wall. We had time to look as we passed."

"And no signal tower. It does not look big enough to support more than ten or twelve warriors."

"Aye but if they send for help."

That was my worry too. The King's palace lay just a few dozen miles north at Wintan-Caestre. Worry would avail me nothing. I waded back to the drekar and consulted with my grandfather and Olaf. We would leave just Aðils the Fearless, the ship's boys and Olaf on the drekar. My grandfather had insisted on coming ashore. My men ferried their mail and weapons to the beach while I looked at the map.

Olaf said, "That looks to be Seals-ey and if it is then we are lucky for both sides of it is covered with hidden rocks. At high tide, it is cut off from the land. It is why they have no walls. It means that the burgh of Cissa-caestre is just five or six miles north of us." He was warning me that there were Saxons nearby.

I nodded and picked up my byrnie and my helmet. "We will be ashore. Keep a good watch. If you have to take her further out to sea then do so. Do not wait for a command from me."

Sven Blue Cheek had wisely set guards along the sand dunes. He had also ordered a fire to be lit. We could not hide from our enemies and we would enjoy hot food. We also needed a fire to melt the pine tar and repair the drekar. I went to inspect the damage. It was far worse than our single sprung strake had been. I was tempted to suggest burning the drekar but no Viking ever willingly burns his ship. It is the last act of a desperate man.

When Finnbjǫrn had examined his vessel, he came to speak with me, "It will take two days, Göngu-Hrólfr Rognvaldson, and then we will need to wait for the tar to set." He was giving me the opportunity to leave him.

I smiled, "Then we will see what the fishing is like hereabouts. We do not desert our shield brothers. This is the work of the Norns. Let us see what sort of web they have spun."

It proved to be a large one. With a good watch kept we slept well for no one came near. Finnbjǫrn Stormbringer was up before dawn and he and his men worked hard to seal their ship. The surprise was when there was a call from our drekar. It was Pái Skutalsson, "Jarl, there is a fleet of ships on the horizon. They are drekar!"

The only one who did not appear surprised was my grandfather. He smiled enigmatically. I walked to the shore and watched the sails as the ships drew closer. There were forty of them and they were Danish. I saw a beacon lit at Seals-ey. Obviously, we had not posed a threat but the Danish fleet did. The Danes lowered their sails and approached under oars. They ran them up onto the beach. I recognised Ivar the Boneless and, jumping from the second ship was Guthrum. Now I understood my grandfather's enigmatic smiles and his words. He had known the Danes were coming. He could not have known that they would land at this beach but it was *wyrd*.

Sven, Ragnar, Sámr and Bergil joined my grandfather and Finnbjǫrn Stormbringer. Guthrum held his arms open and I clasped his right with mine, "The Norns have woven well, Göngu-Hrólfr Rognvaldson. I did not expect to see you here but perhaps the Norns heard my prayers for a hero to join us."

"Then tell us why you are here, Guthrum for we are here by accident."

My grandfather said, "Perhaps but do not be hasty. Let us hear the Warlord out."

"It is good to see you Hrolf the Horseman. I will be brief for time is in short supply. There was a battle at Readingum. King Æthelred and his brother Alfred held the field. King Halfdan Ragnarsson and his men retreated south. They fought another battle and King Æthelred fled with his army. They went west to join Æthelwulf, the Ealdorman who has brought another army from Wintan-Caestre. We left by ship to reinforce him. If you join us it would put heart into our men."

I was about to refuse for this was not our war when my grandfather said, quietly, "Hrólfr, the Norns are at work. You have no choice. Your thread and that of Guthrum are woven together. You know that. As mine is too then we have to go with this army."

I looked at Sven and the others. They nodded. Finnbjǫrn Stormbringer smiled, "Then it seems we were attacked for a good reason. This will allow my ship to dry properly. We will come also."

Guthrum had learned well in his time fighting with the sons of Ragnar Lodbrok. He sent Karl Saxon Slayer and his men to raid Seals-ey and they brought horses. There were just twenty but it meant my grandfather did not need to walk. I had to for all of the horses were too small. I did not mind. I could walk as fast as the Saxon ponies. He also had scouts who knew Wessex and they were sent ahead of the forty-two Viking crews who marched towards Wintan-Caestre. I made sure that my grandfather was guarded. Magnús Magnússon was one of my most reliable warriors. He ran alongside my grandfather's horse. Guthrum rode with the other Danish lords. They were showing their men that they were the leaders.

I walked with Finnbjǫrn and he spoke of the warriors who had died in the sea battle with the Saxons. Like many of my men, they had been with him for some years. It was like losing a member of his family. He shook his head, "I have taken women. I dare say I had sired enough bastards to crew a drekar but they are not family. I envy you, Göngu-Hrólfr Rognvaldson."

"I have daughters only."

"Your wife will bear a son and if not then take another but you have a home and you have a clan. We wander the seas. When you are young then that is all that you want but when you get older you want roots. Is there room in your land for such as us?"

I nodded, "The King of the Franks is weak and cannot hold on to his own land. He is not a warrior. He has those who could fight and who would give us a battle worthy of us but he makes peace whenever he is threatened. The only strength they have is in their walled towns. They are made of stone and have towers."

"Perhaps when we have punished the Saxons I will return to your land with you. If nothing else it will give us the chance to raid those who have that which we wish to take. The Irish are too much trouble for too little reward."

We had travelled twenty miles when a rider came in to tell us that there had been another battle. The King's young brother had defeated Guthrum's allies at a place called Æscesdūn. Although many Danes had been killed it was not decisive and Halfdan and the survivors were heading for us. While many of the Danish leaders appeared to be indecisive Guthrum was just the opposite. He spied a gently sloping hill that was close by. I had seen it too for it was coming on to dark and I was looking for a campsite. This one looked ideal for there was a small wood and what looked like a stream. More importantly, it was large enough to be defended by the two and a half thousand men under Guthrum's command. I saw why Halfdan Ragnarsson was heading for us.

Guthrum pointed, "We make our camp there." He waved over one of the scouts and, dismounting, handed him the reins, "Ride to the King and tell him to bring the Saxons here. We will warm their feet for them." He walked over to my grandfather. "Hrolf the Horseman you can enjoy the shelter of the trees."

My grandfather shook his head. "I will stand with my clan and my grandson." He smiled and waved a hand at the scudding clouds. "Besides I think that there will be little sun to enjoy."

Each crew made its own camp except for Finnbjǫrn's. They had lost so many men in the sea battle that it was easier to combine with us. We were camped by the road in a dell. Some scrubby elder and alder bushes and trees gave some shelter from the northeasterly wind and we used our cloaks to rig a shelter. My grandfather was becoming a galdramenn for he had predicted rain. We had barely finished eating the stew the men had made when it began to rain.

We woke to even darker skies than the previous day and intermittent rain. After making water and breaking our fast Finnbjǫrn, my grandfather, Sven and myself huddled together beneath our sealskin cloaks. I knew that we were better off than most. Many of the Danes did not have sealskins cloaks. Their woollen ones would soon be soaked.

"So Göngu-Hrólfr Rognvaldson, we just wait?" Sven Blue Cheek pointed up the slope. Guthrum and the other Danish jarls had a shelter in the trees and I saw an animated conversation.

"We have enough men here to face whatever the Saxons throw at us. This is a good position. No matter what the direction the Saxons choose we can fight them."

My grandfather said, quietly, "It all depends upon when this Halfdan Ragnarsson arrives."

"You mean the King?"

Grandfather laughed, "King of what? He is not King of the Danes. The East Angles? He has given himself the title. It means nothing. It is men that Guthrum awaits."

I nodded and drank a little of the ale I had left in my skin. I offered it to my grandfather and he shook his head. "It is the men who follow Ragnarsson, the Saxon King and his brother, that Guthrum awaits. From what I have heard they have fought three or four battles in the last month. What we have here are fresh men who had walked but a little. It is why Guthrum chose to wait. He wants a fresh army. The Saxons will have a surprise when they find us."

The first of Halfdan Ragnarsson's army began to trickle in just after noon. One of Guthrum's men came for me. My grandfather was sleeping peacefully. I took Sven Blue Cheek with me. He knew how to read people. He could watch and he could listen. We would be fighting, whenever the battle commenced, with men who were not of our clan. You needed as much information about their quality as possible. When I reached the top, I saw that there was a line of men approaching from the north. It was not a defeated army. Their heads were held high. They marched in groups of oar brothers. They had their helmets and weapons.

"King Halfdan comes. The Saxons follow him. He has kept his best warriors as the rear-guard."

I nodded my approval. He was a good leader. "When will we fight?"

"From what his men had told me the King and his hearth-weru hold the advance guard of the Saxons at bay. Prince Alfred uses horsemen to harass." He smiled, "The King still has his spears. He hopes to break away in the night. By then the bulk of his men will have arrived here already." Pointing to the road below us, close to my camp he added, "That is the main road to Wintan-Caestre. King Æthelred will not want us to threaten it."

I could now see the cunning of Guthrum. This was the reason he had led us here. King Halfdan Ragnarsson had been north of us. Guthrum was forcing King Halfdan's hand. "Then this is where we will fight. Do you wish us to realign to face the threat from the north?"

He shook his head, "Your men are the rock which anchors our left flank. I am placing the ones who have just arrived on the north flank. I will have my standard here as a bastion. We will allow the Saxons to flow around our flanks for that will stretch them. When they become thin I will launch an attack through their centre."

"Will the King not want to make that decision?"

40

"He sent for me and my men for two reasons. He wants our fresh men and he wants my mind. I am his war chief. When he went to Readingum it was not to fight a battle. It was to hold the land until the new grass grew. Then we would have launched an attack. Readingum is close enough to Wintan-Caestre to reach in two days. The Saxons surprised him by their attack. The Saxons thought we would flee our camp and head back to Lundenwic. Their King does not know that we are here to stay."

I nodded, "Keep me informed Guthrum. I would hate to be surprised."

"I will, Göngu-Hrólfr Rognvaldson."

As we headed down the slope I said, "Well, Sven Blue Cheek?"

"It is a good plan. There is but one weakness."

"The road from Wintan-Caestre."

"Aye lord. Just as we threaten it so it threatens us. This Saxon King and his brother will not have emptied its capital of warriors to drive the Danes from his land. There will be some there. Two armies this close to him might make him risk all."

We spoke of how we might defend against such an attack as we headed down the slope. The hill was already becoming muddy. The rain and men walking to and fro had churned up the ground. We decided to make a defensive line thirty paces from our camp. That way we would have solid ground beneath our feet. As the road was a Roman one it was cobbled and had drainage ditches running alongside. We would use that to our advantage. Sven sent four men with axes to the wood which lay a mile or so south of the road. They were there to cut stakes and hew a couple of trees. We would make a barricade for the road. We had men who could use a bow. Petr Jorgensen led them. They would be able to stand behind the logs and harass the Saxons with arrows. The stakes would be a barrier to slow them down. If the Saxons used horsemen then the stakes would be a good deterrent.

My grandfather approved of our plans although Finnbjǫrn was a little less happy. He felt exposed. "We have to wait here at the end of the line. We will not know what is going on in the rest of the battle."

My grandfather smiled, "When I was younger, Stormbringer, I fought with the Dragonheart. We fought in some big battles. Each warrior and each clan will fight its own battle. We have to trust Guthrum. We have been given a place of honour. If we fall then the whole line collapses and the Saxons will win. My grandson is a rock and when the Saxons come then they will break against him."

41

The Saxons did not come for two days. Or, more accurately, the army did not arrive in full for two days. Their scouts came. They spied our lines and then they departed. Ominously two of them headed west to Wintan-Caestre. I had sent men out to forage for food. We found enough to eat. Had the Saxons not arrived when they had we might have run out of food or had to forage further afield but they had been campaigning for as long as the Danes. They were hungry. They were eager to end the raid.

Guthrum was right. They arrayed their men in a long crescent around the hill. Opposite us was the local fyrd. They were led by a thegn in a mail byrnie but the rest were the men of the land upon which we fought. Ill-armed and without mail they were nonetheless dangerous for they were fighting for their home. Men always fight harder for their home. They knew that if we won it would be their families who would suffer. Our fourteen men with bows were hidden behind the log barrier. The stakes would not be necessary for they did not have horses.

The rain which had briefly stopped now began again. My men with bows took the strings from their bows and covered their arrows. While we waited men used whetstones to sharpen spears and swords. My grandfather had insisted upon standing close to me. With Bergil on one side of me and Sven on the other, it was probably the safest place. He had, in his hand, the sword made by Bagsecg Beornsson. The old smith was dead but his sword was still one of the finest swords ever made.

My grandfather looked up at the sky and nodded, "It will stop raining soon. This is a good day, Hrólfr. I am honoured to stand by you and fight the Saxons."

"Grandfather it is I who have the honour. When this is over we will sail back to Rouen. We have done that which we intended. The curse may not yet be lifted but we have done all that we needed to do."

"Not yet, but soon."

I had no opportunity to ask him what he meant for we heard horns and, from the north, came a mighty shout as the Saxons began their attack. The thegns and their men opposite us did not move. I frowned. There was a plan here. Although there were almost three hundred fyrd just five hundred paces from us I was not worried for none were mailed save the ten men with the thegns. With few shields then they would fall to our shield wall. Why were they waiting? The rain stopped. We could hear the clash of arms to the north of us. The other warriors on our flank were also watching and waiting. Guthrum's plans were in danger of failing. They relied on the Saxon line being stretched thin.

A party of priests arrived and stood before the fyrd. The fyrd dropped to their knees. The chanting of the priests could be heard. Then the rains stopped. Sven Blue Cheek snorted, "I am guessing that their priests will say that was their doing!"

When the fyrd rose the leading thegn lifted his spear and waved them forward. The hundred or so who had shields made the front row. I saw a few leather helmets dotted amongst them. There was an occasional metal one but the thegns and their oathsworn were the only ones who posed a real threat.

"Stand to! Shield wall. Archers, you know what to do!"

"Aye Jarl Göngu-Hrólfr Rognvaldson."

The advance was measured. The fyrd normally used reckless abandon to charge. These were marching. There was order. Why? I saw that the whole of the Saxon line was advancing. I could still hear the battle around Guthrum and King Halfdan raging. I turned to Sven Blue Cheek. "I do not like this. Finnbjǫrn watch out for tricks! This is not the way that Saxons usually fight."

"Aye, I know. I have seen their tricks before now! They will not catch us a second time."

I picked up my spear and donned my helmet. I took my place in the line. The stakes were just five paces before us. The Saxons would not have enough time to form ranks once they had negotiated them. The Saxons with shields were banging them. That was a trick we often used. It might intimidate others but not us.

One of Finnbjǫrn's men shouted, "Come on you pretty little farmers, I have a spear here to make you a woman!" The rest of his crew cheered and laughed. It was not the wittiest of comments and the Saxons would not understand his words but the laughter and the cheers said enough. I saw some of the Saxons looking nervously at each other. That was not the right frame of mind in which to fight a battle.

I saw that the mailed men had formed a double line and were making for me. That was understandable. I stood out from the line. It suited me too. I would rather do the fighting than my men. I was their lord and it was my duty. "Brace!" Our shields locked and we presented our spears over the top. Mine reached further and was higher. My target would be the face of one of the thegns. Even though the three of them wore full-face helmets I knew that I had a target. I could strike down at their throats. They had no mail beneath the helmet, just an aventail behind.

I found myself smiling as they negotiated the stakes. My men had dropped their breeks and soiled the ground. Already slippery it now smelled like a dung heap. It was as the men looked down at their feet that my handful of archers began sending arrows at them. We had too few to cause a large number of casualties but those with shields raised them and that was what I wanted.

Sven shouted, "Brace!"

As they came through the stakes I heard a Saxon voice shout, "Form line!" That was easier said than done for those behind were pushing to avoid the arrows. They sought the protection of those with shields in the front rank. The result was that the mailed men were pushed onto our spears before they were ready. Along the line, I heard the cries and screams as Saxons who sheltered beneath shields were speared by my men.

The thegn I faced struck at the same moment I did. The difference was that I had a longer reach and my spear struck his neck first. As I tore into his neck his spear rattled ineffectually against my shield. I pulled my spear back and skewered the farmer behind who had a leather helmet, a short spear and no shield. A spear smacked into my shield. I saw one of the oathsworn of the dead thegn. He had an open helmet with no nasal. I swung my spear around and the shaft struck the side of his helmet. I then punched with the boss of my shield and caught him square in the face. His nose was broken. He lost teeth and I knew that his eyes would be streaming. I changed the grip on my spear and rammed it into the gaping maw of his bloody mouth. The spear came out of the back of his head and, as he fell, he tore the spear from my grip. Holding my shield before me I drew Longsword from my scabbard. We had cleared a space before us. The mailed men lay dead or dying. There were still many Saxons before us but they were warier now.

It was then I heard a shout from Petr Jorgensen. He commanded the archers, "Lord Göngu-Hrólfr Rognvaldson there is a warband approaching from the south. They have mailed men!"

I turned. My height allowed me to see over my men. This was why the Saxons had approached so slowly. They were pinning us to this front to allow men from Wintan-Caestre to march around and attack our exposed flank. The archers and their barrier would be of no use now.

"Petr, fetch your men here. Finnbjǫrn echelon your men to face the new threat! Single line!"

We had been in a double line but now it would have to be single. I turned. I would be the corner of our new line. Sven Blue Cheek was on my right and faced the fyrd. I was positioned to face both. Bergil Fast Blade was on my left and faced the new threat. There were no stakes there. The only obstacles they would have to negotiate were the two ditches.

My grandfather was still behind me, "Fear not Hrólfr, you can deal with this. I have seen this battle! I know how it ends! May the Allfather be with you." His words gave me hope. This was what he had dreamed.

Some of the fyrd became emboldened by the men who ran towards the road in a wedge formation. They rushed recklessly towards us. This was how I had expected them to fight. I swung my sword backhand as Sven Blue Cheek stabbed his spear forward. My blade tore through the cheek and jaw of one man and took the head of a second. Their bodies hit the next men and Sven and Ragnar slew them. Petr and his archers were now sending their arrows at the mailed men at the front, they were showering the ones without mail behind the front six ranks. The impact of the wedge would not be as powerful. Yet when they hit they struck Sámr and Bergil who were in a single line with none behind them. It was lucky that Magnús Magnússon, Leif the Leaper were there but they needed help. The fyrd had slowed down their attack. There was a wall of bodies and with the stakes and the mud, it was hard for them to get to us.

"Næstr Dargsson, Habor Nokkesson and Thiok Clawusson, go and support Bergil Fast Blade!"

"Aye lord." The three Rus warriors moved from Ragnar's side and joined Bergil, Sámr and Leif as they fought the tip of the wedge.

I turned to face the new threat too. I swung my sword from on high. I was above their shields which were there to protect the warriors from spear thrusts. My sword hacked into the shoulder and chest of the warrior in the second rank. Rather than pulling back I lunged forward and found the mail of a warrior in the third rank. It was little enough but it bought Bergil time to slay the tip of the wedge. The warriors to the left of Magnús Magnússon were being forced back. Some of Finnbjǫrn's men had poor mail and now they suffered. We were becoming beleaguered. I knew not how the rest of the battle was going but we were losing this one. We were no longer a cohesive line. Saxons had broken through. Their line was also disrupted but they had more men.

I swung my sword again. I was above their shields and I bit into mail. Then I heard a cry, "Hrólfr!" It was my grandfather. Even as I turned the

Saxon had stabbed him in the middle. I saw two dead Saxons nearby. He had killed the two of them. The third had done for my grandfather. I hit the Saxon so hard that I split his head and helmet in two. I dropped to my knee. He looked up at me, "This was my dream. I have my sword in my hand and you live. I did what Ylva told me I would do. I have made my sacrifice I..." His eyes glazed over. Hrolf the Horseman was dead.

I stood and turned to face the Saxons. Time seemed to have been frozen. I hurled my shield at the Saxons. It smashed into the face of one and then, taking Longsword in two hands I ran at the Saxon warband. I had my grandfather to avenge and I feared no death. If I died then I would be with him in Valhalla. Such was the force and power of my first blow that I took the head of a mailed thegn and bit into the shoulder of his companion. I stepped into the gap they had left and swung backhand. With two hands on the sword and no shield to encumber me, I could outreach their spears. Even so, spears rattled off my mail and my helmet. My long legs were striding through the dead and the dying. I swung at a spear thrust at my face. It shattered into kindling and I twisted my sword to stab the Saxon in the face.

Sven and Bergil had joined me. They still had their shields and they protected my side. As the next Saxon, I faced slipped and fell in the first of the roadside ditches I raised my right foot and smashed his face to a pulp. Using his body to spring forward I found myself on the Roman road. I was moving so quickly that I was almost running. The Saxons feared me. They thought I had gone berserk. I had not. I felt cold and ruthless. I swung backhanded and low at the next Saxon. My sword bit through his leg. Even as his lifeblood pumped away he fell. That was the point when the Saxons broke. The ones before me had no mail. As I ran some fell and tripped in the second roadside ditch. That saved many of their companions for we had to slay the ones in the ditch before we could pursue the others. Had I truly gone berserk then we would have run all the way to Wintan-Caestre to follow them but I had not? I stopped.

"Back to our original positions."

As I turned I saw the shock and horror on the faces of my men. My mail was now bloody. It was as though I had been bathed in blood. My sword was notched. I did not know it but my helmet was dented and scored. I had not even noticed the blows. I picked up my shield. It had hit a Saxon and rendered him unconscious. My sword still had a tip and I rammed it into his throat. When I reached my grandfather, I sheathed my sword and took his from his hands. "I will borrow this for but a short time and it shall be buried with you. I swear!"

My men left a gap for me. The fyrd stood on the other side of the stakes. Raising my grandfather's sword, I shouted, "For Hrolf the Horseman, the last of the Raven Wing Clan! Let us end this!" Outnumbered and tired we charged. Guthrum told me later that those on the hill could not believe the sixty men who charged four times their number. There was no order to our charge. My long legs, fuelled by the desire to kill Saxons, ate up the ground. The Saxons I caught had their backs to me but I cared not. I killed them anyway. Slashing left and right I carved a trail of bodies through them.

It was only when Sven Blue Cheek shouted, "Lord! Stop! They are fled! We have won! The battle is over!" that I stopped. We were a mile from our original position. My men held the field and it was covered in Saxon dead. I nodded and headed back. My grandfather had dreamed his death. He had known that he would save my life and in doing so would ensure that the Norn's prophesy would come true. Every conversation we had had since Ylva's cave now made more sense. Every look and every gesture had had a meaning and I saw it now. As we walked back I saw that one of the first men I had slain had been a thegn. He had a good sword. The Saxons made good swords. I took it as weregeld for my grandfather's life. It was shorter than Longsword but I sometimes needed a shorter one. I took the scabbard too for it was a well-made one. I held the sword and scabbard about my head and said, "This is Hrolf's Vengeance. My enemies will come to fear it!"

When I reached Hrolf the Horseman, I saw that those of my men who had been wounded had laid his body out. I put his sword in his hands. "Magnús Magnússon go to the hill and bring me eight horses. We will go and bury my grandfather."

"Aye Jarl."

I turned to Finnbjørn, "Command my men until I return."

"I will and it will be an honour. Men will talk of this day, long after we are dead. I am honoured to have fought at your side."

He waved over his men and they began to clear away the Saxon dead. There were many wounded warriors to be gathered, dying to be despatched and mail to be collected. We picked up my grandfather's body and headed for Magnús and the horses.

Of course, men did not remember what my men and I had done. All the talk was of the brilliance of Guthrum's plan and the courage of King

Halfdan. Guthrum knew the truth and he repaid my courage but I cared
not anyway. I would have changed it all for my grandfather to have lived.
I knew, deep in my heart, that there was nothing I could have done. As
soon as Ylva wove the spell with my hair and my grandfather's then his
fate was sealed. He had made his blót. He had saved me.

We took his body back to Seals-ey. The men of the village and their
families fled at our approach. I did not care. We found the largest fishing
boat they had drawn up on the beach. While Sámr and Ragnar fetched
kindling the rest of us laid out my grandfather. We had dressed him in
clean clothes and cleaned the blood from him. We put his sword in his
hands and laid his shield across him. Finally, we covered all with the
wolf skin cloak he had brought from the Land of the Wolf. Soon he
would be with the Dragonheart again and it was right that he greeted him
in a wolf cloak. With kindling around him Sven lit a fire. Magnús
Magnússon raised the sail and my men held on to the ropes to prevent it
from being blown away prematurely.

When the fire was blazing and each of us held a burning brand I
spoke. "Hrolf the Horseman, you came into this world as a slave and left
as a lord of a mighty land. The Allfather himself will welcome you there.
My father will be there to greet you with Ulf Big Nose, Siggi White Hair,
Rurik One Ear, Erik One Hand and all the others who helped you win the
land for me. I swear that I will not rest until the prophecy which cost you
your life comes true! Farewell, grandfather." I could barely speak. I took
my brand and threw it into the boat. The others emulated me and Magnús
and the others released their ropes. The wind caught it and the small boat
headed south and west. To the west, the sun was setting. The grey skies
had gone. There were clear skies. Ran would take my grandfather and his
ship west and thence to Valhalla.

As we rode back through the dark to the camp none of us said a word.
All of us had known my grandfather. All of us felt the loss. I had had
enough of the land of the Saxons. I wished to return to the Land of the
Franks. I had a land to win.

Chapter 4

Guthrum came to our camp the next day. "We owe our victory to you, Jarl Göngu-Hrólfr Rognvaldson. Others, jealous of your glory, may not say so but the warriors who fought know this to be true. I was already in your debt but now I am even more so. You lost a grandfather and we will not forget that."

I nodded, "I know not about Finnbjǫrn and his crew but we will be leaving for home soon. When the wounded are fit to travel then we will return to our drekar."

"Stay but a few days." I cocked my head to one side. "The Saxons know who was responsible for this victory. If you leave then we might have to fight again and the dead will have died in vain."

"A few days then."

Guthrum sent men foraging so that we ate well. Ale and beer were found. Our wounded were healed and I brooded. I needed to be home. My world was not on this island. It was in the land of the Norseman. It was Rouen and the land thereabouts. It was not just the piece of land perched on the edge of Frankia. It was the whole of Frankia and beyond. That was the prophecy given to my grandfather and I would do my part to see that it would be fulfilled.

The Norns were spinning; we had a message that King Æthelred had died. We knew not if he had been wounded or there was some other cause. The Saxon who brought the message just said that King Alfred would come to speak to us and that he wished a truce.

I headed up the hill to speak with Guthrum. He was speaking with King Halfdan. I saw smiles from many of the Danes jarls but not from the King. I did not waste idle words. "Do we fight this new king?"

Guthrum laughed, "Direct and to the point, Jarl Göngu-Hrólfr Rognvaldson. No, we do not fight. This new king thinks himself a holy and a learned man. He comes to talk about peace."

"Peace?"

King Halfdan laughed, "I can see that you are unused to these Saxons. He will buy us off. He will give us enough gold to make us leave. It buys him, quite literally, time. We lost many men in these battles so the weregeld will be expensive for them. When we have built up our numbers then we will return."

I nodded. I did not like this way of making war but this was not my war. I fought Franks and not Saxons. Guthrum said, "Fear not, Jarl Göngu-Hrólfr Rognvaldson, you will be given a fair share." He turned to face the King, "Is that not so?"

I could see that the King was not happy but his answer showed me that Guthrum held the power. "Of course."

I was invited to the meeting and so I met the King of Wessex. King Alfred proved to be more like King Egbert than his brother had been. Although pragmatic he knew how to fight and how to defend. He improved the burghs throughout the land. That day he came to negotiate a price to pay us to leave. Our ships at Seals-ey were a threat and he wished us gone. I noticed that he kept watching me when the King spoke. I must have interested him. After we had agreed on a price he turned to me. "I understand you speak our language."

I nodded, "I speak a few languages."

"And men say that you can read."

"I can read."

He nodded. He was ever a careful man and he took nothing at face value. He questioned everything. "I heard that you drowned and came back to life. Is that true or is it a tale made up by your saga singers?"

"I fell from a drekar in the Tamese. I sank to the bottom but I was picked up at sea."

"That is remarkable. Do you know why Christ saved you?"

I laughed, "It was not your White Christ who saved me. The Allfather has a purpose for me and the Sisters had woven a spell."

I saw his hand go to his cross as did his men. He shook his head, "And I thought there was hope for you but there is not. You are a pagan and until you embrace Christ and are baptised then you are lost."

I laughed even louder, "I would have thought that sinking to the bottom of the sea was baptism enough! I will stay with my gods and my beliefs."

"Then you are lost!" He waved his hands as though he was washing them. He had been intrigued that a barbarian could speak languages and read.

The chest of gold we were paid was a huge ransom. All of us would be rich men. I had plans for my share of the gold. We headed back across the sea to Frankia with Finnbjǫrn, his drekar and his crew. His depleted crew had been augmented with warriors who wished to serve him. Some had lost their lords in the battle. It was *wyrd*.

I knew that my men would wonder at my state of mind for I was quiet on the voyage back. I ran over every conversation I had had with my grandfather. It was so obvious to me now that I wondered why I had not realised earlier. When he could have stayed on the ship with Olaf Two Teeth he had come with me. When he could have been at the camp he chose to be behind me. I had been so obsessed with getting home as soon as I could that I had not been attentive enough. My men gave me the space to be alone. Ylva's words came back to me, '*Why do you think your wife only bears you girls? It is because you are not yet ready to have a son. Your world has to change. You have to change. You lead a small clan perched on the edge of the world of the Franks. When you are ready to lead a world of drekar then you will be ready for a son.*' What was the change I needed to make in me? I now knew that this was not the fault of my wife. The fault lay in me. The '*world of drekar*' I could understand. The forty ships Guthrum had brought had shown me the potential of a fleet. I could use Guthrum and his Danes to help me gain a fleet. There were others who would follow me. Saxbjǫrn the Silent, Halfi Axe Tongue and Nefgeirr Haldisson had told me that they would follow my banner. Drekar were not the problem. She had said we were a small clan perched on the edge of the world of the Franks. Was I meant to conquer the world of the Franks? I had much to do.

When we landed, we were assailed by questions. The absence of Hrolf the Horseman was noticed. Sven Blue Cheek knew that it would be distressing for me. "Bergil Fast Blade, take the jarl to his wife. I will deal with these questions and the housing of Finnbjǫrn and his men."

As Bergil led me through my town walls and into my home I knew that I had much to be grateful for. I had the best of crews and warriors. Our coin meant that all would be mailed. The money we had made in trade would be used to improve my town. Strong walls and towers meant that we could survive a determined attack by the Franks. However, I also needed to know more about the Franks and that I could not do. My size meant I would be known. I needed spies. They had to be men that I could trust.

When we entered my hall, my wife was not there. Sprota, her lady, told me that she was in the church confessing. I was annoyed but I did not let it show. "Tell her that I have returned and I would hold a feast tonight for my captains."

She bobbed her head, "Aye lord."

I turned to Bergil Fast Blade. "I know that you are anxious to return to Lisieux and your family but I would speak with you all this night. Tell the rest of my captains that I wish them to be here. I have words I need to say."

He smiled, "I have known this since the night in the cave. One more night away from my wife will not harm me." I nodded. He took my arm, "I am truly sorry about Hrolf the Horseman but you must know that it was the end he wished. On the journey back from the cave he was as happy as I had ever seen him. He told me, one night as we stood watch on *'Fafnir'*, that he had one last task to complete and then he would have fulfilled his oath. Few men get to know their death and it was a glorious one. He died with a sword protecting his grandson. What man could ask for more?"

"You are right but I still have much to do if I am to fulfil my own oath."

Rouen had a bath and I went to wash. A sluice down with seawater did not suffice. After bathing in hot water with soap I felt cleansed and refreshed and I was in my chamber changing when Poppa came in. Even though I was naked she threw her arms around me. "My husband, I did not know you were returning. I wanted to greet you when you arrived."

"And you have done so. I have washed and feel cleansed."

She kissed me and I felt myself becoming aroused. "I am sorry that I have not borne you a son!"

I pulled her to the bed, "It is not your fault. I know that now but let us see if we can make a son now while I smell like a Frank."

Later, as we lay in each other's arms, I told her of my grandfather. "It will be hard to tell Bergljót and Gefn. They were both fond of him."

She shook her head, "It is not just that. They are of an age with him. Both have lost husbands."

"Aye, you are right. I had better go and tell them"

Poppa shook her head, "I fear that all will know the news already. When I am dressed I will go and speak with them."

I shook my head, "I am Gefn's adopted son. That task falls to me. Tonight, we make merry but I have some serious words for my captains first."

Gefn did know but her concern was for me for he was my grandfather. She stroked my cheek as though I was a bairn who had grazed his knee, "You know that he was so proud of you and what you had achieved. He often said that you had had the odds against you your whole life and yet you never let it stop you. You were driven as he was. He will be happy now for he missed your grandmother much as I miss your adopted father. When I die do not shed tears for me. I will be in a happy place and my spirit will watch over you."

I felt the hairs on the back of my neck prickle. That was what my grandfather had said.

Even though it was short notice the cooks and servants had prepared a good feast. We were a rich people. We traded and raided well. The ale and the wine were the best. Before men became intoxicated I spoke with them. "You all know why I went to the Land of the Wolf." There were nods. "I have found out what we needed to do. My grandfather played his part. He dreamed his death and he promised to make a sacrifice. He did. He gave his life so that I may have a son." I was aware that my wife and Æðelwald of Remisgat both clutched their crosses for what I had said sounded remarkably like their story of the White Christ. I smiled and drank some ale to cover the smile. "A son will come." I touched my wife's hand. "But not yet. First, we have to make our land stronger. We need more warriors to follow us and I need a fleet with which to attack Paris and the court of Charles the Bald." I had their attention. Those of you who rule towns for me, Bayeux, Caen, Lisieux and Djupr; you have all made coin from the Saxons. I give you a command. You use that coin to make your walls stronger and to make your men better armed. You raid. Each time we raid the Franks and the Bretons we make them weaker and us stronger. When I am ready I will send to the land of the Angles for Guthrum and his Danes. He has promised ships and men. When we raid Paris, it will be the greatest raid by any fleet of Vikings and we will expand our borders so that this river becomes truly ours!"

I had judged the mood aright. Men cheered and banged the table. Only Æðelwald of Remisgat looked disturbed. He would need to be watched. I had not mentioned spies but I would have to seek out men I could trust to discover my enemies and their weaknesses. That meant at home as well as abroad.

From that moment I was driven. My whole purpose was to make my land stronger. Rouen had been strong when I had taken it and now I made it stronger with more towers and better gates. The ditches to the north were deepened and seeded with traps. A month after my return I took Ragnar the Resolute and some of our men to ride south. Stephen of Andecavis and my ten horsemen would have normally accompanied me but I had sent them to raid the farms north of us for horses. I needed more horses. I had seen, in Wessex, the necessity for moving quickly to war.

When we had taken Rouen, I had noticed a possible site for a stronghold. There was a village called Wellebou. It was just ten miles from my town and nestled in the bend of the river. I had had an idea to build something there. I took Ragnar as he had recently taken a wife. I rode the horse which Erik Gillesson had bred especially for me. Gilles was the largest horse in the land. I could ride him without my feet trailing along the ground. However, I found it difficult to ride him with Longsword over my back. I had a scabbard made for the saddle. I also carried a normal sword on the opposite side. The horse was strong enough to carry the weight. What he lacked was speed. He could ride for long periods and cover great distances but small horses could easily overtake him in a race. I needed him not for battle but for transport and the love of riding. I carried a seax in my sealskin boot and Hrolf's Vengeance in my belt. I would have felt naked without a weapon to hand. We reined in at the handful of buildings that made up the village. The fact that there were few people there appealed to me.

I said, "Well, Ragnar the Resolute, what do you think?"

"What am I looking at, lord?"

"How could we make this a place which could be defended? See how the river sweeps around on three sides. The only way it can be attacked is from the north."

He was a clever warrior. I hoped that he would see what I had already seen. He did. "Lord, it is not men who are the danger here. It is the river."

I nodded, "When we lived in the fjord the water was as close."

"Aye lord but the town was built on a rock above the fjord and the fjord never flooded. This would flood." I said nothing but just nodded. He dismounted and felt the soil. "This is good earth. With water flooding, it will keep it fertile." He looked around and then smiled. "We have rock which was too small for the walls of Rouen when we built them. We use that to make a good base and then build a mound on top so that even if the river rose it would not flood the hall. We could build a wooden wall around it and that would deter warriors. It could be done."

"Then I would have you build such a hall. Use whatever men you wish. They will be your warband. You will be Count of Wellebou. Encourage your men to farm. As you say it is rich soil. They will do well."

He nodded, "Thank you, Lord. I will make a hall which enemies will fear." I turned to ride away. He said, "Would you want us to accompany you, lord?"

"No, you have a hall to build and I have a land to explore." I headed for the river. Gilles was a powerful horse and even though the river was wide I was confident that he could swim it. I had no mail and just carried my sword. The river was two hundred paces wide but the current was strong. We ended downstream. I did not mind for it suited me. Erik Gillesson had a horse farm that lay on a higher piece of ground by a small river called the Risle. He supplied me with horses but he had married a Frank. His father had been Gilles who had been a young horseman who had served my grandfather. As his home was but half a day's ride away I thought to visit him.

His wife, Eliane, was with child again. I envied Erik; he had three sons and a daughter. I patted Erik on the back, "Congratulations, Erik. You hope for a son?"

"I hope for ten toes, ten fingers two eyes, a mouth and a nose." His face became sad. "If it is a boy then I shall name him Rollo for my dead brother."

"He was a good horseman. He knew his animals."

"Aye, my father taught us well." He shook his head for he knew mourning would not bring his brother and his brother's family back. He was practical and a horseman who loved the horses he bred. "And how is Gilles?"

"Your horse is everything I hoped. I am just sorry I do not get to ride him as much as I would like." He looked pleased. "I have bad news to bring. My grandfather, Hrolf the Horseman is dead. He died in battle with a sword in his hand."

"I am sorry for that, lord. He was the father of our people."

"He died happy but I miss him too. And your family?"

"My son Bagsecg is now old enough to help me although he prefers practising with his sword. I think he would be a warrior."

"How old is Bagsecg?"

"He has seen fourteen summers. He is strong too. Perhaps he gets that from my grandfather. He was a blacksmith. William has told me that he improves day by day."

"William?"

"When we fled from the land close by the Haugr we found him close to death. His left arm had been almost severed. My wife saved his arm but he cannot use it. He feels lucky to be alive."

"How did he come by the wound?"

"He was serving a French lord and they were attacked by Bretons. His lord left him to die. He hates both Breton and Frank in equal measure."

I felt the Norns spinning. I had come here to thank Erik for his horse now I saw that the Norns had spun this thread long ago. "I would like to speak to this William."

"He and my son are exercising and schooling two new young horses. They will be back here not long after noon. Bagsecg will be ready for food then."

I nodded and began to look at Erik's home. The river here, the Risle was not wide. There was a bridge but it could be easily forded. However, there were many streams and becks which criss-crossed the valley bottom and the valley was prone to flooding. Erik had built his hall on a higher piece of ground. To protect his horses, he had built a fence.

"Erik you know that the Franks do not like us and wish us gone from their land." He nodded. "They drove my grandfather's people from the Haugr. The reason they were able to do that was that we did not defend the land. We made the mistake of thinking that just by sitting there it would be ours. I would not make that mistake again." We were in the ring he used to train horses. There was no grass anymore and the weather had been dry for a couple of days. I took out my dagger and drew a map in the soil as I spoke. "Here is Rouen. It has a river and good walls to defend it. One hundred miles away is Bayeux. There Sámr Oakheart is building stronger walls. Fifteen miles away is Caen with Sven Blue Cheek. Twenty miles closer to us lies Lisieux and Bergil Fast Blade. Then we travel forty miles to Rouen. You see the problem?"

He shook his head. He was a horseman and not a warrior. He could fight but he did not have the wider vision a jarl needed. "I am sorry lord, I do not."

"If Charles the Bald ever shifts his carcass from his palace he could drive an army between Rouen and Lisieux. He could reach the sea and our forces would be divided. Before we could repulse them, we would be picked off one by one. I need a stronghold here." I swept my arm around." He looked dubiously at me. "Your father Gilles had a similar home not far from the Haugr. Had it been defended then it might have resisted. You have a home on a hill. You have fences. All that you need to do is to make those fences walls and dig a ditch around the outside. It will improve the drainage."

"But I have no men to defend my walls."

I pointed up the valley towards the sea. Smoke rose from farms. "There are farmers who live there. They will fight for you. You will be their lord."

"Some are Franks, lord."

"They were Franks but now that they live in my land they are my people. I dreamed when I went to the Land of the Wolf, Erik. This is the land that was promised to my father by the Norns. I will have more warriors come here and farm. They will give the steel which will hold the Franks at bay and when we are strong enough, they will be the sword that drives them back. All that I ask of you is for you to make your home somewhere which could be defended. If you need men then I will find them and they will help you dig and build."

"I am indebted to you lord and I believe this is where I am meant to be. I will do as you ask but I am not sure that I will be the lord you wish me to be."

"Let me be the judge of that. While we waited for William and Bagsecg I walked around his hall explaining how he could use the features he had to make it stronger. I had seen a couple of the burghs in Wessex. They were simple but effective deterrents against an attacker. I saw how to make them even stronger with a good gatehouse and a second wall close to the hall. It helped that Erik had an almost perfect place to defend. He had already cut back the trees to make his fences and to clear land for crops. By clearing more for his walls, he would improve his position dramatically.

William, when he arrived, reminded me of old Rurik One Ear. Although I had only seen Rurik in his later years when he was a bloated almost corpulent man I had seen the warrior within. That was William. He had a stocky build and rugged features. Like Rurik his face showed the scars of war and, like Erik One Arm, his damaged left arm showed why he was no longer a warrior. Before I could speak with him I was assailed by questions from Bagsecg who wished to be a warrior. I looked over to Erik who had a resigned look on his face. He had other sons. They would raise horses.

I turned to William before I spoke with Bagsecg. "Could he be a warrior?"

William grinned. I saw that he had lost teeth. That was another sign of a warrior. "Oh aye lord. He has the build. He will never be your size but he will be broader and taller than most. He has good hands and he loves the sword."

I nodded, "Then Bagsecg you can be a warrior but a warrior who serves me."

His eyes widened, "In Rouen? On the drekar?"

I shook my head, "No, here." He looked disappointed. "I have asked your father to make this a stronghold. He will be lord of this land. He is not a warrior but you can be. You can ride and William tells me that you can fight. If the Franks come then you would defend this land. If war came then you would ride with me to fight the Franks."

"Ride, lord?"

"Stephen of Andecavis leads my few horsemen. Just because Hrolf the Horseman is dead does not mean that his dream has died too. I am Jarl Göngu-Hrólfr Rognvaldson but even I ride. We are something new. We are Vikings who can fight aboard drekar and from the backs of horses or we will be eventually."

The idea appealed and he dropped to his knees. "Then I am your man."

"When William tells me that you are skilled enough to go to war then I will give you the blue cloak with the white sword. It marks my horsemen. Stephen of Andecavis wears such a device."

"Thank you, lord."

I nodded. "And now I would like to be alone with William."

Bagsecg looked curious but Erik put his arm around his son's shoulder and led him off, "Come, son. Let us see if the food is ready."

When we were alone I said, "William you can say no to what I ask of you. I know that I will be asking much. That is why I ask you alone. If you refuse then no one will know. No none will lose face. Do you understand?"

"Aye lord but know that I owe much to my master and his family and I know they are of your people."

"You are a Frank."

"I was but they deserted me. Your people saved me."

"War is coming with Charles the Bald."

William smiled, "He is a lazy king. He will not stir to war."

"He will if I poke him hard enough. I am a Viking, William. War is my business. This little piece of land perched at the edge of Frankia is not enough for me. I would have more. I would have more of the whole of the river valley and the land of the Bretons too."

He nodded and then tapped his left arm which hung from his side, "I would fight for you if I could lord but…"

"There are other ways of fighting. I would have you scout out the enemy. I would know his strengths and weakness. Who are the leaders I should fear? Where are the divisions I can widen?"

"You would have me be a spy."

I nodded, "You can speak the language. You can move around the land. Your wound makes you perfect for the role. None would suspect you."

I saw him debating within himself. From his face, I knew that it was not a question of would he but how would he succeed. His question confirmed it. "What would be my story lord? Questions would arouse suspicion."

"I see you are the right man for the job. I will speak with Erik and get you a horse. I will give you coin. I would have you travel as though you are a merchant looking to buy cloth. That gives you a reason to be in the towns east of here. You stay in inns and you listen. You were a warrior and you know that warriors like to drink and when they drink they are careless in what they say. Ride to Paris and then return. What say you?"

He smiled, "Like Master Bagsecg, I am your man, lord."

I did not reach Rouen until after dark and my wife was worried but I had had a most successful day. It was early days but I had, potentially, two more strongholds and a spy. It was a start.

I missed my grandfather and I missed Bergil Fast Blade, Sven Blue Cheek and the others. I had been able to talk with them. I had been able to talk through ideas. Now I was forced to do that inside my head. Poppa could advise me on matters to do with the people and the clan. There was no one better as a listener but military matters were not what she understood. More, she still confessed to her priest and I did not trust him. We needed time to build up our defences. Ragnar and Erik would take at least three months to have defences that were robust enough to fend off the Franks. William would need two months to do what I wished him to. I had to keep the Franks on the defensive.

It was Finnbjǫrn who gave me the answer. His drekar had been repaired and he had men willing to sail with him. His drekar stood idle on the river. One evening as we strolled along the river he said, "You are my lord now but I would not be as I was in Dyflin. Jarl Bonemaker was content to sit and squat on the profits from the port. I came here to raid. I beg permission to raid upriver."

"Be patient, Finnbjǫrn. I am as eager to raid as you are but I need to put Rouen in order. I have given commands to my lords and they are far away. If I leave before I am replaced then I may be storing up danger. Give me seven days to find someone then I will join you."

"Aye lord."

He was right we needed to raid. It had been more than a year since we had raided up the river. Finnbjǫrn had repaired his drekar and was eager to raid the Franks. I had a captain for my drekar but who would command while I was absent? The Norns provided the answer. Magnús Magnússon was practising with Petr Tallboys and he slipped. It was unlike him and normally would have resulted in laughter from those watching but this time something gave in his left leg and he could barely walk. Æðelwald of Remisgat told him that he would need to rest it for a month. That was perfect. He was reliable and could rule my stead. Once again, the webs were all around me and the Norns were sending me in the direction they had chosen.

I would take *'Wolf's Snout'*. Captained by Gandálfr she was a lithe ship. We had taken her from the Rus and her shallow draught meant we could sail up smaller rivers and raid places which thought themselves safe from our attacks. There were other ships that had called in at Rouen and all had asked permission to raid. One day I would lead them in an attack that would wrest control of the whole valley from the Franks. Until then I was happy for them to sail up the river and keep the Franks on the defensive. My raid would allow me to see their defences first hand.

When I approached him, Gandálfr was more than happy to be raiding. The two captains had good ships and their crews were not farmers. They were the young warriors who wished for adventure. Some of the crew of *'Wolf's Snout'* were known to me. I had taken them to the Land of the Wolf but others were new. This would help me to know the men I led.

I took Finnbjǫrn to pore over my maps with me. I had already chosen the place I would raid. Fifty miles upriver was Mantes. It was a prosperous town. More importantly, it was less than thirty miles from

Paris. I was keen to see how far we could get up the river and raid without incurring the wrath of the Franks. I knew that they had a wooden keep and wall but the town was largely undefended. We would have a hard row upstream but an easy voyage home.

I explained all to Finnbjǫrn and he nodded. He just wanted to raid. He wanted to see the mettle of his new men. We both had different reasons for wanting to raid. We stepped the mast so that we would be harder to see. We left in the early afternoon. It meant that we would be in Frankish territory after dark and stood a better chance of reaching Mantes unseen. We had to row and I joined my men at the oars. Our drekar had just fifteen oars a side. We had two men on each oar. When we rowed I rowed alone. Gandálfr chose the chant.

He chose the one which honoured my grandfather. It was right and I sang harder than any.

The horseman came through darkest night
He rode towards the dawning light
With fiery steed and thrusting spear
Hrolf the Horseman brought great fear

Slaughtering all he breached their line
Of warriors slain there were nine
Hrolf the Horseman with gleaming blade
Hrolf the Horseman all enemies slayed

With mighty axe Black Teeth stood
Angry and filled with hot blood
Hrolf the Horseman with gleaming blade
Hrolf the Horseman all enemies slayed
Ice cold Hrolf with Heart of Ice
Swung his arm and made it slice
Hrolf the Horseman with gleaming blade
Hrolf the Horseman all enemies slayed

In two strokes the Jarl was felled
Hrolf's sword nobly held
Hrolf the Horseman with gleaming blade
Hrolf the Horseman all enemies slayed

By the time we had reached Poses we had stopped singing and half of the crew had stopped rowing. Petr Tallboy took my oar. He was grinning, "Do not expect me to do as well as you, lord! I am a mortal man!"

"Do not worry Petr, I am mortal too. The day I cannot take an oar I might as well stay at home and tell tall tales."

Although we were smaller than *'Fire Drake'* we appeared to be faster. Arne Audunsson, the ship's boy at the stern said, when I approached my chest, "Lord the other drekar is struggling to keep up with us."

I looked at Gandálfr. He shrugged, "Finnbjǫrn does not know the river. You have to almost smell your way along it at night. We might not reach there at dawn."

"Then find somewhere to lay up. I would be as close to Mantes as we can be."

This was something I had not thought about. I had not raided Paris. When I had raided upstream it had been with those who knew the river. My planned attack on Paris would have the same problem. I wrestled through the night with a solution and the one I came up with was unsatisfactory. We would have to sail in daylight and they would know that we were coming.

We rested at a pair of islands close to Andelys. We tied up between the two. Even though we had slowed our rate Finnbjǫrn took some time to catch us up. He was annoyed with himself more than anything. "I am sorry, lord. This river is wide but the twists and turns at night test my skills."

I nodded, "The more you sail it the more familiar you will become. We have lost nothing. We will wait here. With no mast and the undergrowth then we may escape detection."

We managed to avoid detection. We left while the sun was still in the sky. We would have a short time to row in the twilight and then it would be darkness. So it was that I saw a perfect site for a stronghold. We were less than a thousand paces from Andelys. A huge rock seemed to rise from the river. It was too close to the French for us to consider building one but I wondered why Charles the Bald had not. It was his loss. We rowed without chanting. We had taken enough risks already. We were closing rapidly with our target and so we had an easy row. My men had donned mail while on the island. When we reached Mantes, we could attack instantly. There was a church there; almost every Frankish town had one but there were also warehouses with cloth and pots. Until we had taken Rouen and blocked the route to the sea ships had sailed from Mantes to supply the Saxons and those who lived along the river. Now they had to send them by wagon and cart north from Mantes to Bruggas. We would relieve them of that problem.

The further upstream we travelled the more settlements lined the river. We could smell them. It was a mixture of wood smoke, sweat and human dung. We tried to slip by them for we wanted surprise at Mantes. I had chosen my drekar because Gandálfr had travelled further up the river than any. He waved me over. "Soon, lord, we will be there. We have passed the last big loop. When we turn next there will be a long island in the middle of the river. The church is on the south bank and the warehouses to the north." We had decided that, with his bigger crew, Finnbjǫrn would attack the church and the town. They were all keen to impress me. We would raid the warehouses. Our ship was riding high for we had nothing in the hold save ballast. They were just stones and could be ditched overboard if we found great quantities of loot.

Finnbjǫrn had kept closer to us and I went to the stern and lifted the lid on the pot with the candle burning within. The light from the candle illuminated my face. It was the signal for which Finnbjǫrn was waiting. Gandálfr sent two extra ship's boys to the prow to keep a good watch.

Tostig came running down the ship. "Island ahead, lord." I saw, in the distance, the tiny glow of torches. They had a watch on the warehouses.

I signalled twice more so that Finnbjǫrn would know to take the southern channel while we headed for the north. I did not bother with my helmet and I left my sword in its scabbard. I joined Petr on the larboard side. We were in the middle of the channel with the island to one side and quays to the other when the alarm was raised.

"Vikings!" We might have stepped our masts but there was no disguising our dragons. There were ships there too. Hopefully, they would be laden and provide us with even more treasure.

Petr shouted, "Larboard, lord!"

Only half of our men were rowing and Gandálfr shouted, "Larboard oars in!" The steerboard oars forced us in.

It was not an elegant landing. *'Wolf's Snout'* pushed her dragon prow between two small ships. They came off worse. Even before we were tied up I leapt ashore and, as I landed, I drew my sword. Two night guards ran at me. They were brave men but perhaps they thought I was just one man. It was still dark and I would have been just a shadow to them. My sword ripped diagonally across the two of them. One fell dead for his throat had been cut and the other fell clutching his chest. I could see his ribs. I ran for the buildings I could see. I heard feet behind me. It was my men. Across the river, I heard the tolling of a bell as Finnbjǫrn and his men were spotted.

I turned and shouted, "Hurry. I would cross the river and join our shield brothers." I saw that Gandálfr and his ship's boys were emptying the knarr and the other two ships of their cargo. Taking the burning torch, I hurried towards the halls which contained their trade goods. They were not locked. I lifted my leg and kicked one open. There were wooden barrels already packed with goods. "Get these aboard!" There were people living nearby but they decided to flee. The goods in the warehouses belong to rich merchants and not them. Their lives were more valuable and they fled. Dawn was breaking and already our drekar was lower in the water.

Tostig ran towards me, "Lord, the other drekar is being attacked by warriors. When we raised the mast, I spied them."

I took a decision instantly, "What we have we take. It will have to be enough. Back to the drekar. *'Fire Drake'* is in trouble."

We ran for the drekar. Gandálfr had anticipated my decision and had left just one rope tying us to the land. We boarded over the prow.

"Land us to the west of the island. We will go to the aid of Finnbjǫrn." As the current took us west I could hear, in the distance, the sound of battle. "Ubba Long Cheek, we will make a wedge. Hopefully, we can catch the Franks unawares."

"Where will they be, lord?"

I pointed south, "I can hear fighting there so we head east along the river bank until we come to them. When they are aboard their drekar we fight our way back to ours."

He picked up my shield, "Do you need this, lord?"

"No. I will lead the wedge and use my Longsword."

Once we had passed the end of the island Gandálfr put the steering board over. There was no quay and so the ship's boys leapt ashore and wrapped the ropes around two trees. I cleared the gap easily as I jumped from the gunwale. I ran. My men would have to catch me. I could see, about a thousand paces from me, the Franks as they fought to get at Finnbjǫrn and his men. I wondered how they had caught *'Fire Drake's* crew. Perhaps there had been more men at watch on this side of the river.

Ubba shouted, "Slow down, lord. You have longer legs!"

I drew my Longsword and held it over my right shoulder. The Franks were so intent on butchering Finnbjǫrn's men that they did not see us. One at the rear started to turn as Petr Tallboy and Ubba Long Cheek and I ploughed into them. My sword took three men in one sweep. The surprised man who had turned lost half his face while my swinging sword sliced through the backs of two others. Petr and Ubba cleared a space on either side of me. I could no longer swing from the side and so I raised my sword above me and brought it down. This time it sliced through heads and shoulders. Blood spurted and spattered from one warrior whose neck was ripped open.

The Franks now knew that they were under attack. Finnbjǫrn and his beleaguered men took hope and the Frankish resistance crumbled. When they had outnumbered my men, their fight had been full of confidence. Now ferocious mailed men attacked their rear and they ran. Not all fled. Some warriors, we later found they were the oathsworn of the Count of Mantes, fought on and were slaughtered. They fought hard and they died hard. Four had mail and all wore good helmets. I saw a ring of bodies. Finnbjǫrn's men had paid a heavy price.

"Did you raid the church?"

He shook his head, "We were surprised by these mailed men. They seemed to have been in a guardhouse."

I nodded, "Ubba, Petr, have our men finish off any of those who resist. Finnbjǫrn, finish your raid. Our drekar is almost full. Let us fill yours."

"Aye, Lord. You heard Jarl Göngu-Hrólfr Rognvaldson."

As they hurried off to do his bidding I sheathed my sword. The ship's boys on the drekar had their bows in their hands. "Put your bows away and fetch our dead to their ship. We will not leave them here to be mutilated and abused."

Grateful for the chance to do something, they chorused, "Aye Jarl."

I saw that there was a bakery and baker's house by the river. It was empty but they had fled so fast that they had left the bread in the oven. It was on the point of catching. I pulled the bread out. This was a joy. The smell of fresh, hot bread, took away the smell of blood. With two loaves in my hand, I walked outside and shouted, "Gandálfr, send boys. We have bread!"

As I bit into the loaf I reflected that warriors needed simple things to make them happy. It took until noon to clear the town and take all that there was. By that time riders were seen approaching. The raid had not been the total success I had hoped it would be but it was a success and we had learned valuable lessons. With full sails and a healthy current, we set off for Rouen.

Part Two

Frankia

Chapter 5

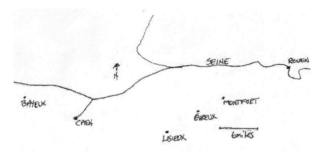

When we reached Rouen, I sent for Finnbjǫrn while his ship was being unloaded. "What went wrong?"

He shook his head, "Had you not been there then we would be dead. The Franks were organized. We did not expect that. They had better arms and weapons. When we were in Dyflin we raided the wild men of the islands, Hibernia and the Pictii. They wear little armour and have poor defences."

"The Franks are a different proposition. They are more like the Saxons. They have stone walls and know how to defend themselves. Perhaps this was my fault. I should have given you the task of taking the north shore."

He shook his head, "I had the larger drekar. It was right that I should go but ten of my crew have died. I will have to learn to lead quickly."

That was all that I could ask of my lord. They had to learn to lead. This was what Ylva had meant. I was used to leading a small band. What would happen when I led many drekar? What about the captains I did not know? How would I ensure that they did as I wished?

"When my lords have improved their defences, we will return to Mantes. We took what they had but left their defences intact. We did not try to attack their stronghold. With more men, we can hurt them. It is a short distance from Mantes to Paris." I saw him nodding. He would be able to atone for what might have been a disaster. "Do not worry too much about this raid. We all have to learn. I was lucky. I raided with my father and he had first raided with my grandfather. He, in turn, learned from the greatest Viking, the Dragonheart."

I spent the next few weeks watching Ragnar's stronghold at Wellebou take shape and then I visited Erik to see how the stronghold he had named Montfort developed. It was not far and I rode alone.

"Why Montfort?"

"It is French. It means strong hill and that seems appropriate. More than half the people who live around here speak the language of the Franks. My son likes these defences that we build and is happy that his father is becoming more warlike."

"And has William returned from Paris yet?"

"No lord."

"Then I will visit Sámr and my other lords. I am anxious to see if they have progressed enough for me to lead another raid."

"I will have some of my men accompany you."

I shook my head. "It is but a day's ride at most between each of them. I have a good horse. The Franks are still licking their wounds after our attack on Mantes. I will be safe." The Norns were spinning. I should have known that but my mind was on other things. Bergil Fast Blade was the nearest to Erik. He had built good walls and a fine ditch. His gatehouse had two small towers. He had done exactly what I had wished. He had used Alfred's gold well. I told him of the raid and the two strongholds being built to the east of him.

He smiled and poured me more ale, "When we fished you out of the sea I did not think that you would change our world as much as you have. Look at me now. I live like a Frank in a hall surrounded by a stone wall. My wife is a Frank and I am happy to drink wine. You have even given me a title!"

"It was the Norns who spun, Bergil. Always remember that. They can take away as well as give!" I could not dampen his enthusiasm. His wife was with child and the dream in Ylva's cave had promised him sons.

Sven Blue Cheek had built the most impressive home. Caen had a naturally strong position and Sven, the wisest of my lords, had improved it well. He had built a small keep from stone. He smiled when I asked where he had got the stone. "There is a quarry close by. My men were more than happy to cut and drag it hither. If you need stone, lord there is a great quantity just waiting to be dug from the ground."

"Rouen is well provided but Erik might like some."

"Then he shall have it."

"Any trouble from the Bretons?" Caen and Bayeux were the closest places to the Land of the Horse. My grandfather had told me of warriors who had come to his land seeking a home. They had been the first to test Caen's defences. Then it had been Frank. After my father was murdered the Bretons spread east and Caen became their eastern border. They still saw it as theirs. That meant there was always a threat from the Bretons.

"No, lord. We have seen their riders. They approach and when I send men to investigate they flee. I am guessing they wonder what we are about. We do not behave as Vikings."

"And your ship?"

"It is moored on the river with Bergil's. When you need us to raid then we will be ready. Come, I will show you the quay. We have improved it too." I spent the morning admiring Sven's men's hard work.

I was feeling full of confidence as I left, at noon, to ride the eighteen miles to Bayeux. If Sámr had done as well as my other two lords then we could begin our next raid. Gilles was enjoying the ride and I was, I confess, distracted by plans which raced through my head. I was within a few miles of Bayeux. The afternoon was heading towards dusk. I would just make Sámr's stronghold before darkness engulfed the land. I saw the wood ahead and thought no more about it. I was working out how many ships I could take upriver. This would not be the great raid I had planned. I would just destroy Mantes. The rough handling Finnbjǫrn had received meant that I had to eliminate the stronghold before we raided Paris. Guthrum was still busy fighting Alfred. When Alfred was defeated I would be able to draw on a fleet of Danish ships. At that moment I would be able to fulfil my destiny

I was approaching one of the many woods through which the road passed. They were all very similar. They spread out for a couple of miles

69

on either side and were, perhaps five or six miles long. The farmers were cutting them back and I knew that over time they would disappear. I enjoyed them for they brought relief from the sun.

Gilles alerted me to the danger but, by then it was too late. I had fallen into the Breton trap. There were ten Breton riders ahead. We spied each other at the same time. Gilles' legs were open and he was galloping. That was my only advantage and I would have to use it. He could get to his full speed quickly. I had been taught enough about riding from my grandfather to know that you keep up the speed if you have it. I drew Hrolf's Vengeance and kicked him in the flanks. I only had one chance against such numbers. I had to break through them and disappear. Gilles could not outrun them and there were too many to fight. Longsword would be of little use and so I would rely upon Hrolf's Vengeance. I kicked my horse in the flanks and galloped towards them. They saw me and gave me a chance for they galloped towards me. They must have known who I was. I wore the blue cloak with the white sword emblazoned over the heart. I rode a huge horse and I was a giant. Who else could I be? I had no time to speculate about the reason for their presence. I had to deal with the problem they posed.

They were gathered together in a knot of warriors as they galloped up the road towards me. Like me, they wore no mail and had no helmets. They had swords but, unlike me, their weapons were still in their scabbards. I also saw that they did not use stiraps. If they struck me hard they risked falling. As we closed they began to draw their weapons. It was only a slight distraction but when you are fighting odds of ten to one you took any help the Allfather sent your way. They were a hundred paces from the woods when I struck the first of them. As we closed with each other they spread out to surround me. Perhaps they miscalculated the speed of Gilles for the first two were slow to react to my rapid approach. I veered to the right of the two of them so that only one would be a threat. I brought my sword across the top of the first horse's head and my sword ripped through his unprotected middle. As he fell he knocked his companion from his horse. The third man managed to hit me with his sword but it was neither clean nor hard. It did not break flesh. It just hurt for it was the flat of the sword which struck me. I lunged at the next Breton and, thanks to my longer arm, was rewarded by flesh. I was halfway through the column of men. Two were down when I ducked beneath the sword of a Breton who thought he had me. He over swung and fell from his horse. That was the problem with not using stiraps. As I passed the last man I swung backhand and my sword bit through his back. Four men were down and two might be hurt or dead. I found myself in the wood. Turning I saw the Bretons turn to pursue me. I had hurt them but now the advantage lay with them. They could see me. Their horses would gradually overtake Gilles and they would now be more cautious. They had seen what I could do. I sheathed my sword.

The road turned once we entered the woods and I disappeared from Breton eyes. I did not have long. Their smaller, faster horses would catch up with me in a short time. Already Gilles was labouring, if I wanted to ride a long way I would have to slow down. When I had fallen to the bottom of the sea I had not panicked and I did not do so now. I tied the reins on the saddle and rode with my knees. I sheathed my sword and I looked ahead. There was a branch overhanging the road. Most men would have been able to ride beneath it upright. I would have to duck. I could hear hooves behind me but when I glanced over my shoulder I could not see them. The twisting road and overhanging branches hid me from sight. In my head, I said, *'Grandfather, I need the help of the spirits.'* I kicked my feet from my stiraps. Nearing the branch, I raised my arms and grabbed the limb which was as thick as my leg. Gilles continued to gallop. When he had passed I dropped to the ground. As soon as I landed I dived to my left and rolled beneath the low branches of a hawthorn tree which lay just six paces from the edge of the road. I was scratched and cut but I made it to the bole. I barely fitted but I kept my face down. My dark cloak would disguise me. I heard the hooves thunder down the road. I kept my face down and when they had passed, only then did I look up. I could barely see through the branches of the hawthorn. The horsemen had disappeared.

Gilles would be caught and they would know that I had left him. They would find my two swords and think that I was unarmed. They did not know about the seax I had and Hrolf's Vengeance. If I was the leader of the Bretons then I would backtrack and see where I had left the road. If I left my sanctuary then I would make footprints. I realised that I might not be seen beneath these branches. I had not made any prints to get here. I had landed on the road and I had rolled. Already the grass and weeds over which I had rolled were springing back up. I pulled myself further under the branches. My hands were scratched as I pulled myself under but that was a small price to pay. Darkness would soon be upon me. If I could evade them until dark then I stood a chance. I was on foot but I could walk to Bayeux. I pulled the hood over my head and picked up some of the dead leaves and branches which lay around me. I scattered them over my back and I waited. With my face down on the earth, I could see nothing but I had my ears and I had other senses. I heard the hooves coming back towards me and the mumble of words. They were too far away to be distinct. As they neared me I gradually made them out.

"We have lost him, Alan of Nantes!"

"We have lost him when I say so! He was the giant! The one who took Rouen! We have his long sword. How can we have lost him? Fulk, ride and fetch our brothers and their horses. Episoe and Jean might be alive. The rest of you search the edge of the road. Find where he left it."

"It is getting dark."

I heard the one called Alan of Nantes laugh, "And are you afraid of one man in the dark? The Vikings in Bayeux keep within their walls. He will get no help from his men. We are safe so long as we are mounted. Now search."

They were so close that I could smell them. The sound of the horses' hooves on the road gradually faded. Then I heard the clip-clop of hooves coming from the east. Hooves galloped from the west. They were near to me but not close. "They are all dead?"

"Aye, Alan of Nantes. The giant's sword slew three and Jean's neck was broken when he fell."

Another voice shouted, "We cannot find any sign, Alan of Nantes. It is as though he has disappeared from the face of the earth."

"That is impossible."

"Lord, it is getting too dark to see! How can we find his tracks when we cannot even see our own feet?"

There was silence. Then I heard the leader. His words gave me hope. "Fulk, take your two brothers and go to the western edge of the forest. If he breaks from the woods then you will see him. Keep a good watch. It is too late now to make our home. Besides, I would have this Viking leader. Our King will reward us if we bring him his head. Make a camp and keep a good watch and listen for him. He is hiding somewhere just waiting for us to leave these woods. He is a giant. He cannot move quietly. We will find him. I want one of us on watch all night!"

"And the dead?"

"Bury them. We will keep the giant's horse and camp by the stream. The horse may let us know if he is near."

The noises faded. Alan of Nantes's voice had moved and, as he spoke his last words, appeared to have come from so close that he had to have been beneath the tree branch I had used. The spirits had hidden me. Human noise faded and I heard the sound of the woods. There was scurrying as the woodland animals resumed their activities which had been halted while the men and horses moved around. Birds returned. My pursuers had gone. I waited a long time until I risked raising my head. It was dark. Night had fallen. I sniffed. I could smell smoke. They had lit a fire and that meant that they were close. I was getting stiff. The blow from the sword now ached. I would have to move soon. I waited a while and then rolled as silently as I dared, from beneath the hawthorn tree which had saved my life. I slowly stood and stretched. I checked my boot. I still had my seax. Hrolf's Vengeance still hung from my belt. I was thirsty but that was the least of my worries. There were three men close by and if I evaded them then I had another three at the edge of the wood. I could have turned around and walked back to Caen but a voice in my head told me not to. They had my sword. Longsword was part of me. It was part of my unborn son's heritage. I would take back my sword and my horse and then I would go back to Caen. I lowered my hood so that I could see better and I drew my two weapons. I would not be taken without a fight.

Watching the ground, I made my way back to the road. The road would be the safest way to move for I would be silent. I had walked barely forty paces when I spied a glow in the woods. I kept walking until I was level with the glow. My dark blue cloak made me invisible. I stepped next to the elm and peered around its trunk. At first, I saw nothing and then I spied the sentry. Alan of Nantes was taking no chances. They were by the stream he had mentioned and it was below me. I heard the horses as they moved. I used their noise to head closer to the camp. I prayed to the Allfather that Gilles would not smell me and whinny. The ground beneath my feet was hard and without leaves and branches. I was lucky to have found a hawthorn with undisturbed dead leaves and branches. Here the winter rains had swept the leaves down to the stream. It took me some time to get within sight of the camp.

I saw a sentry with his back to me. I slid my sword silently back into its scabbard. My seax would be a better weapon. Two forms lay sleeping. I was wondering how to get close when the sentry rose and came towards me. Had he seen me? I dismissed the idea for I was hidden by the bole of an ash tree. He was coming to make water. He passed me and then lowered his breeks. This was too good an opportunity to miss. In two long strides, I was upon him. Holding him around the chest I pulled back his head and ripped my seax across his throat. Blood spurted and flowed down onto my hand but I ignored it. I lowered his body to the ground and slid my sword from its scabbard. There were now just two of them and they were asleep. With luck, they would both die silently and I could ride back to Caen. I stepped carefully back towards the fire. Even if they were half awake they would take the noise as their comrade returning from the woods.

I saw that one of them had my long sword by him. That would be the leader, Alan of Nantes. I had to kill him first. The other lay curled around the fire. I made not a sound. The woods and the horses were silent and so it could only have been the Norns which awoke the other sleeping Breton. His eyes opened and widened. He had seen me and shouted, "Alarm! Viking!" I turned and brought Hrolf's Vengeance across his body. It ripped through his chest.

In the time it took to turn Alan of Nantes faced me and he held Longsword in his hands. He was no fool and he shouted, loudly, "Fulk! We have him!"

I did not have long. Alan of Nantes had made a mistake. He had chosen the wrong weapon. He should have used a sword he was familiar with. My sword was long and it was heavy. I was the only one who could wield it one handed and most men found it hard to swing two handed. As he lifted it above his head I knew what would happen. As he brought it down to split me open the tip caught on a branch. I stepped close and held Hrolf's Vengeance above me. I held the guard against Longsword and ripped my seax across his middle. His entrails tumbled out like a nest of vipers.

I heard hooves. That would be the men he had sent to the edge of the wood. I sheathed my seax and Hrolf's Vengeance. Picking up Longsword, I ran back towards the road. It did not matter about noise now for the horses' hooves would drown out any sound I made and my long legs ate up the ground. There were three of them and they were forewarned. The edge of the wood must have been closer than I had thought. I stepped behind the trunk of a large elm. There was enough room for me to swing my sword. I used the night to hide myself. My choice of cloak had been inspired or perhaps I had my grandfather and Alain of Auxerre to thank for it. As the horses approached I resisted the urge to see where they were. I would use surprise and risk all. The horses stopped. Silence fell. They were listening.

I heard the one called Fulk call out, "Spread out! I can hear nothing."

Drekar in the Seine

Their hooves became muffled as they left the cobbled road and walked on the softer earth but I heard the neigh of a horse and it was close. I began to swing without a target. Most men would have hit the horse's head with their swing but I was taller than any man and their horses were small ones. My sword brushed the ears of the Breton horse and then its edge hacked into the Breton. He managed a scream which alerted the other two. They were on either side of me but, thankfully a few paces away. I stepped back to the tree as they came at me. That way my back was secure. Two to one were odds that I could handle. I saw that two had spears and one a sword. In a perfect world, I would attack the one with the spear but the world was imperfect and the Norns were spinning. The one with the sword would reach me first and he knew his business. He was leaning to the side. I could not take a chance. I swung Longsword at his horse. It pained me to do so but it was his life or mine. My sword was angled down and it hacked through both forelegs. Its head went down and the rider flew from the saddle.

I felt a pain in my right shoulder. I had been speared. As I turned, and with the spearhead still in my shoulder, the movement tore it from the Breton's grip. I swung my sword blindly and was rewarded by a scream as my sword hacked through the Breton's thigh. The rider who had fallen rose to his feet. I was in pain thanks to the spearhead embedded in my shoulder and I just ran at the Breton with my sword held before me. He seemed mesmerized and did not move. The sword came out of his back and I tore it out. I looked around to see the third Breton, the one I had wounded. He was galloping up the road in the direction of Caen. If he had had a little more courage then he might have slain me. As it was I was hurt and I needed to get to Bayeux while I could.

I put my hand behind my back and I could not feel torrents of blood. The broken spearhead, still sticking from my shoulder, was actually helping me. It prevented the blood from flowing freely. I headed back to the camp. I sheathed my sword in my saddle and tied the five horses in a line. I tied the halter to Gilles' saddle and rode back to the road. I was going to stop to pick up the last two horses and realised that they had wandered off. I left them and headed down the road. Within a mile or so I was in the open. Behind me, the sun was beginning to rise. I kicked hard and Gilles began to canter. It hurt more than any pain I had ever experienced. The spearhead was grating on a bone. The Norns had sent a rigorous challenge for me. In my head I heard grandfather's voice, 'You are of my blood. You can do this!' I gritted my teeth and endured the pain. I now felt the blood trickling down my back and was wondering if I would even make Bayeux when I saw the walls ahead. I gripped Gilles with my knees. I could not rely on my right hand any longer. I almost made it. I saw the gates ahead as the sun finally broke behind me and then all went black.

I do not think I was out long for when I opened my eyes I was looking into the face of one of Sámr's guards. I recognised him but could not put a name to his face. "Jarl Göngu-Hrólfr Rognvaldson, what are you doing here?"

It was on the tip of my tongue to say dying and then I realised the man would not know I was wounded. "I was attacked by Bretons in the woods. I have a spearhead in my back."

"You have a..." was all I heard and I passed out again.

I dreamed.

My grandfather was reaching down to me to pull me up. I wondered why I could not move. I was in a pool of blood. It was thick, viscous blood and it was sucking me down. I felt a fire as though I was in the middle of a funeral pyre yet I could not see flames. I just felt the heat. Then I spied Ylva. She seemed too frail to help but she reached down and pulled me from the bloody mire. She lifted me up into the air and my grandfather disappeared. We rose beyond the earth and the clouds and then we fell. We fell like a hawk diving to catch its prey. The earth loomed up quickly and then we suddenly stopped and I saw that we were above Paris. Ylva spoke but her mouth did not move. It was as though her words were in my head, "I have woven the spell, Rollo, the Norseman. You cannot ride alone! Choose warriors as you would a bride." I turned to speak to her and she was no longer there. I began to fall. I tumbled over and over. The ground raced up to me then all went black.

"Lord I saw him move. Jarl Göngu-Hrólfr Rognvaldson lives."

"Thank you, Brother Paul. Fetch ale, he will need it." I recognised the voice of Sámr Oakheart.

I opened my eyes and smiled. I tried to speak but only a croak came out. I coughed and the priest said, "Wait until you have had a drink before you try to speak. You have been in the land between life and death for three days."

He disappeared from my sight and Sámr said, "You had us worried, lord. When you were brought here your kyrtle was as wet as though you had been swimming in a sea of blood. Brother Paul saved your life. He used fire to seal the wound but you had lost so much blood that we thought it impossible that you lived. Brother Paul said that it was your size which saved you. You will need to rest for another seven days, or so my priest tells me."

The priest returned and he supported my head while I drank the ale. My mouth was parched and I drank long and deep. "No more, lord. If he drinks more it may undo the work I have done. Water for the rest of the day."

I waited until he had gone before I spoke, "You have told my wife that I am safe?"

"I have and Stephen of Andecavis and four of your horsemen are here as your escort. You ride alone no longer." His voice was commanding. My dream came back to me. "We found the other horses and the Bretons you had slain. They are the men of Vire. Their Count fancies himself a future ruler of this land. We have had to deter them before now."

I remembered the words of the Breton leader. "Horsemen. You need horsemen. They know that men on foot cannot stop them. You need horsemen!"

The effort was too much for me and I coughed and spluttered, "Peace, my lord! You are right. Had we had horsemen on the road then you might not have been hurt. You gave me this land to rule and I have let you down."

"No, I should have explained better." I smiled, "I was on my way here to tell you to use more horsemen. Erik Gillesson is already breeding better horses. Most of your men can ride. You need to have someone teach them to be horsemen."

"Rest, lord. I will speak with you again in the morning."

"Morning?"

"It is the middle watch of the night. I have sat by you for three days. I can now sleep. I will put a man to wait with you." He rose. "It was when we thought that we had lost you that we realised we could not survive without you. There have been messages from Caen and Lisieux. You have had all of your lords worried, lord."

I dozed but I did not sleep. My wound ached. I had not asked if the damage to my right arm was permanent. If it was then I was no longer a warrior. I thought about Ylva's message. She had been right. I needed horsemen to protect me. I had thought I was immortal because of the spell. That was not the case. Erik had bred me a horse to use and use it I would. I saw now that I needed to do more. Sámr and my men could ride the roads and keep them safe but we had to make the Bretons, as well as the Franks, fear us and keep well away from our land. We had to hurt them. Vire had chosen itself as our messenger. We would destroy Vire. The message would spread. If you hurt the Vikings then they would destroy you.

I dozed and the wound must have woken me for I started. The man watching me, Petr Æbbison, had come with us from Norway. We knew each other well, "Are you in pain, lord? Should I fetch the healer?"

"No Petr. It just aches that is all." I was awake now. "Do you like this land we have taken?"

He smiled, "Compared with the rocks we farmed in Norway it is a paradise. I still miss the fjord and the mountains but when I think about it I cannot see why. You cannot eat beauty. I have a wife who is a Breton and five children. This is my home."

"What do you make of the Bretons?"

"I prefer them to the Franks." He grinned, "And that is not just because I married one. They have more honesty and they are better warriors. My sons will not let you down. I have a fine farm. I can grow apples and raise pigs! What more can a man want?"

I lay back and thought about Petr's words. If he was typical of those who had come from Norway then we were meant to rule this land. The Bretons had shown me that we needed to fight to take and keep it. It was a land worth fighting for.

Sven, Bergil and Ragnar all arrived in the next few days. Sven Blue Cheek pointed an accusing finger at me, "I knew I should have forced you to accept men to guard you! In my heart, I knew there was danger."

I smiled, "Have you forgotten that I am the lord of this land?"

"You were nearly the lord of the largest grave in this land! Just because a witch has spun a spell does not mean you are immortal. Your grandfather discovered that."

I nodded, "Consider me chastened. I swear I will not do it again. And you need not fear for me riding alone again. Stephen of Andecavis and the other horsemen will be my hearth-weru. Each of you must have at least four horsemen who do the same for you. I would have them wear the same blue cloak with my Longsword upon it."

"Why?"

I smiled, "Because it saved my life and I believe it is lucky. Besides, it will confuse our enemies. They will see these horsemen all along the border. They will not know where we will strike."

Sven seemed appeased, "But you know eh, lord?"

Sámr nodded. We had spoken of the men of Vire. He said, "Vire. It was their lord who sent men to harass us. I have already sent men to scout it out."

"But we will not attack until I am healed and they think that we have forgotten them. Revenge is a dish best served cold."

We left six days later. I had a heavy escort which only left me at Lisieux. I had just Stephen of Andecavis and four of my horsemen for the journey to Montfort but we were close enough to Erik's farm for us to be safe. The Franks were not as aggressive as the Bretons. Erik had heard the news and was solicitous, "Lord you should not take such chances."

"I have more mothers than enough. Peace. I will not ride alone and you need to breed or capture more horses. I want each of my lords to have ten good horsemen."

"If it will stop you from being so reckless then I will breed hundreds for you!"

"And William?"

"He has returned. He is out with Bagsecg. They will be back soon and then he can report to you."

"Then we will stay here overnight for his intelligence is vital to us."

The news was worth waiting for. William was a good spy. He had been both diligent and thorough. "I travelled to Paris, Lord, as you commanded." He smiled. "No one questioned my reasons for being there. The coin you gave me meant I could pay to stay in inns and I was not suspected. King Charles the Bald is not a well man. He spends most of his time in the east. Count Odo of Paris, the man who rules Paris is, however, a warrior that I would fear. As the King is unwell there are many men vying for the crown. That helps you, I think." I nodded. "Charles the Fat is King of Germany and Italy. I heard rumours that if anything happened to Charles the Bald then Charles the Fat would take the crown." He shook his head, "It was a rumour lord."

"And the land between here and Paris? How stands it?"

"They fear you. They are building two bridges across the river. One is made of stone. It is almost completed. The one on the north arm of the river is wooden and is finished. They have towers at the ends of the

79

bridges. You can no longer get beyond Paris. They have yet to fortify their border towns. They do not seem to think that the Vikings can take their towns." He shook his head again, "You took Rouen!"

"Thank you, William." I handed him a purse of coins. We had taken them from the dead Bretons. "I would have you return in six months."

"It will be an honour, lord."

My wife was watching for me from my walls. She raced to greet me when I entered as did Gefn. Poppa threw her arms around me, "You could have been killed! What possessed you to ride alone?"

"I survived, I am alive and I will take riders with me in future." I kissed Gefn, "It was a minor wound. The Allfather was watching me and Hrolf the Horseman was by my side." While my wife frowned, Gefn clutched her amulet and smiled. I looked at Poppa, "Am I to be a father again?"

"Not yet, husband."

"Then let us go and remedy that situation."

Chapter 6

It took a month for me to heal sufficiently to practise with my men. In that time, we had cloaks and shields made for the horsemen of each town. My brush with death had put everyone on edge. My lords all built up their armies. The Norns had, indeed, been spinning. Men and drekar had been arriving all year. Halfi Axe Tongue, Nefgeirr Haldisson and Saxbjǫrn the Silent all arrived with their drekar and their men. They were more than welcome. I prepared for my attacked on Vire.

It was getting on to winter and they would not expect an attack. Vire was far from the sea. It was more than thirty miles from Bayeux and they did not know we had horsemen. Alan of Nantes words had told me that. We had more than enough warriors to watch the walls of our towns and yet could field a good army. We had one hundred horsemen and three hundred warriors. My plan was a simple one. I would gather my army at Bayeux. With a forced march we could move the men on foot to Vire in a day but we could have the horsemen surround the town in half a day. I had the army camp north of Bayeux so that none could see our numbers. Sven Blue Cheek would lead the men on foot, the army and I would lead the horsemen. My lords and I ate in Sámr's hall and I told them my plan.

"We take everything they have. We destroy their town and its walls. The Bretons will learn the hard way of the folly of attacking us. After we have returned home then they may threaten you, Sámr. If they do then do not attack, send a rider to Sven and he will send to me. I will bring another army to punish those who dare to attack you. We are sending a message to our enemies. Let us make it a harsh one."

Magnús Magnússon was healed and he came with us. I was pleased for he was a good warrior. Petr Jorgensen had been training archers and sixty of the men we took were archers. They could fight with a sword, spear and shield but as archers, they might make the difference. With Stephen of Andecavis and Erik Gillesson, I led the horsemen. We left before dawn and headed south. The men on foot used the main road and the horsemen rode in two fast-moving columns.

Although my wound had healed the true test would come when we fought. My wife had rubbed a salve on the scar but when I stretched I could feel it. Those warriors, like Lars Three Fingers who had lost limbs, told me that eventually there was no discomfort. I had hoped it would be the same for me. That was another reason I was going to war on a horse. I would not have to raise my arm as much. I had seen that the Bretons did not use stiraps. That gave us an advantage. We had spears and could push the Bretons from their horses. I hoped that we would have surprise and they would not have time to mount a counter-attack but I was ready. This time I had my helmet and I had my shield. Fighting from a horse meant that it was unlikely I would use Longsword but it was ready in its scabbard.

Those were the early days of leading armies to raid deep into French and Breton land. We made mistakes. As events turned out they did not harm us but we just headed for Vire almost like a horde. The two columns of horsemen split up as soon as we left Bayeux. We rode the smaller roads and crossed the open fields. Our task was to encircle the town. I wanted as few of their warriors leaving as possible. Gilles' relatively slow speed worked in our favour. The rest of our horses did not tire as quickly as they might have done. Stephen of Andecavis' column would be regulated by our most experienced warrior. He was also the oldest.

It was after noon when we spied the town to the east of us. There was a wood we would have to pass to reach the far side. It helped us for it kept us hidden. It was as we turned to head east that we heard the sound of battle. A horn sounded and then I heard a roar and the clash of metal on metal. I dug my heels into Gilles and he lumbered forward. Clearing the wood, I saw that Stephen of Andecavis' column had either attacked early or been seen by the men of Vire. They were surrounded and under attack. I waved my spear and shouted, "Spread out in a long line." Using just my knees to guide Gilles I donned my helmet. My brush with death had shown me that I was mortal. The Bretons had bows and slings. Any of those could kill me. I needed my mail and my helmet. I pulled up my shield and held my spear ready. Even as I approached I saw Stephen of Andecavis fall. He was a magnificent horseman but he was surrounded by Breton horsemen. First, a horseman hit him with his spear and even as Stephen fended off the blow a man on the ground thrust up and under his spear. My horseman still fought on but when a Breton rode at his rear and skewered him with a spear then I knew he was dead. I saw all this as Gilles' hooves ate up the ground. Some of my horsemen were faster than I was and they had already struck the Breton line. I aimed Gilles at the two horsemen who had killed the last of my grandfather's horsemen.

The two were obviously leaders for I saw them shouting orders. How they could have failed to see me I know not but perhaps Erik Gillesson and the rest of the men who had ridden with Stephen of Andecavis distracted them. It cost one his life immediately. Gilles barged his way towards them and I pulled my arm back and rammed my spear deep into the back of the nearest horseman. He wore mail but my spear came out of his front. The weapon was lost to me and I let go to draw Hrolf's Vengeance. This was not the time to risk my Longsword. The other horseman turned. He too had lost his spear and he had a sword in his hand. My stiraps saved me. A warrior on foot rammed his spear at my shield as the horseman swung his sword. I blocked the blow with my sword but the two blows had almost unseated me. I pulled Gilles head around for him to snap his teeth at the warrior on the ground as I swung my sword horizontally across the Breton's horse's head. The Breton horseman's shield was on his other side and even though he lunged at me my longer arms and quicker reactions meant that my sword won the race. It bit into the Breton's middle. My choice of blow minimised the pain in my shoulder. Continuing my turn, I brought my sword down onto the head of the Breton who had tried to spear me.

It was a confused battle. I think that they still outnumbered us but many of the men who were fighting had been trained by Stephen of Andecavis and they were Vikings. We knew how to fight and we did not know when to stop. I saw other Vikings who had ridden with Erik and Stephen close by. They had not been willing to lose their lord and we ploughed, as a mounted wedge, into the heart of the Breton horses. I continued to use the sweeping blow. I was tall enough not to need to bring the sword down against horsemen. The power of my arms and their length made me an irresistible force. I knocked two horsemen from their saddles. Our horses trampled them to death. Our bigger shields protected us from the enemy blows. More than half of my men wore mail and we had better swords.

The end, when it came, was dramatic. The men of Vire fought bravely until six horsemen decided that they had had enough. They turned and rode north to the town. It was as though a strake had suddenly sprung on a drekar. The trickle became a flood as the remaining Bretons ran. My horsemen were still fighting the few who remained. Our horses were tired. I shouted, "Hold!"

I saw that Erik Gillesson and his son Bagsecg were still alive. I waved them over. "I am sorry lord, we were surprised. They spied us as we approached and attacked us!

I nodded. "We will speak of that later, Erik. Have the men form a long line. Leave the wounded here. By now Sven Blue Cheek should be approaching the town. Let us hold their attention so that they prepare their defences on this side."

"Aye lord."

The Bretons had reached their town. The wooden wall was there to keep animals safe and would not stop us but they lined it anyway. The ditch which ran around the wooden wall was there to drain water from the town. As we approached at a walk I saw more men lining the walls. We had less than eighty horsemen who would be able to charge, however, I had no intention of allowing our valuable horses to be slaughtered in a pointless attack. I relied on Sven Blue Cheek and my men. We halted beyond the range of their hunting bows. Some of Petr Jorgensen's men had bows that had a longer range. They would be approaching with Sven Blue Cheek.

I began to bang my shield and I chanted, "The Norse are come, fear our blades, The Norse are here, your blood will flow!"

My men took up the chant. I doubted that the Bretons would understand the words. They did not need to. My purpose was to fix their attention. When I saw heads turn I stopped chanting and we listened. We could hear a roar. Sven Blue Cheek and my warriors had arrived on the other side of the small town. We rode towards the walls with our shields held before us. More than half of the defenders had left the walls. The few stones and arrows which came our way did little damage. We stopped just forty paces from the walls.

"Dismount! We fight on foot." I left my Longsword in the scabbard. I left Gilles. He would graze. Those who were not confident about their mounts hobbled them. The result was that we were a ragged line who approached the walls. I had learned a lesson. We needed men to hold the horses. Stones rattled off my shield. I felt the thud of an arrow as it hit the leather covering of my shield. A stone pinged off my helmet but we continued our steady approach.

The wall came up to the shoulders of a normal man. I was not a normal man and I punched my shield at the face I saw on the other side of the wooden wall. As he fell I swung my sword horizontally and took a second man in the side of the head. I turned, "Audun, Bjorn, Leif, with me. Let us breach this wall."

With my three men behind me, I ran at the wooden wall. We burst through, trampling over the two Bretons who lay there, one dead and one stunned. My men poured through the gap. I left them to clear the wall and I ran with Audun, Leif and Bjorn. I could hear the battle raging in the town. This time it was the Bretons who were outnumbered. I arrived in time to see the Count of Vire falling to Sven Blue Cheek's sword. With his death, all resistance ended. We had taken Vire.

"Gather the women and children together! I would speak with them."

I took off my helmet and drank from the ale skin Bjorn had found. He grinned. Bjorn was young and this had been his first battle. He was a good horseman and had not come with me to the Land of the Wolf. "That was easy, lord. Is it always that easy?"

I shook my head. "When they have good walls to defend and towers then it costs us good men. We have paid a high enough price with Stephen of Andecavis."

Sven Blue Cheek had his helmet in his hand and his mail was bloody, "I am sorry we were a little late, lord. Some of our warriors have forgotten how to march!"

"It matters not. Use the horses and wagons to take everything of value. We start to send them back now."

"And the women and children?" All of the men, save the priests, lay dead.

"I will speak to them."

They were all gathered. They looked at the priests for comfort and at us with terror on their faces. I spoke in their language, "You expect slavery but I am in a benevolent mood. Know that this attack was to punish your men for their attack on me. That is why they are all dead. I give you your lives and the clothes on your backs. Go now. Any who remain, choose to be the slaves of my men."

They did not move. One of the priests said, "You give us our lives? This is not a trick, is it? Will you slay us when we move?"

"I could slay you now. Do not try my patience priest! Go!"

They needed no further urging and they fled. I sent Bjorn and Audun to fetch the horses, our wounded and our dead. As we ate in the dead Breton lord's hall Sven asked me, "How is the shoulder?"

"It is fine but I am still wary of raising it above my head."

"That will come in time."

I nodded. "We have more of that now. With what we have taken from here and the losses we have caused, the Bretons will not be a threat. We can continue to build up our numbers."

"Was it a mistake to let the people go?"

"We could have ransomed them but then we would have had to feed and watch them. This way they become a burden on whoever takes them in. There will be less food in the other towns and villages. We have rid ourselves of every man who might have fought against us. There are other towns close by that we could take but we need to improve our strategy. Stephen of Andecavis died because our attacks did not coincide."

"We have time now lord."

We headed back the next day. We left a town engulfed in flames. It would have to be completely rebuilt. The column of smoke rising in the sky told the whole of the surrounding land that the Vikings were here and here to stay.

As we had raided the Bretons, the ones who had slain her people when she was younger, my wife was not saddened by our killing of Christians. Her priest, however, frowned and scowled at me. That did not worry me but if he continued to annoy me I would banish him. He stayed in Rouen only because my father and grandfather had approved of him. I did not. My wife was delighted about the pots and wall hangings we had brought back. The Count of Vire had some finely woven wall hangings and my hall needed them. That would have been the biggest change my father would have seen. The hall in which I was born had changed little from the hall in which I had dwelled in Norway. With just two doors and a high roof, it had been covered in turf. The hall in Rouen was made of stone. The roof was made of slate. There were windows that allowed light to make the rooms bright. In times of inclement weather, we used shutters to keep out the cold. We did not have an open fire in the middle of the room. We had a stone fireplace at one end and the smoke was taken up a chimney. There were some things I would not miss about our old life.

Drekar in the Seine

We were changing. When I went to war I still looked the same but when I walked around my town I looked more like a Frank than a Viking. Most of my men did. Our beards and moustaches, not to mention our hair were shorter, groomed and neater. Our clothes were made of finer cloth and were more colourful. We still drank ale and beer but we would have been fools to ignore the wines which were made so close to us. The biggest change, however, was in the way we organised ourselves. Only a few men still called me jarl. When we met other Vikings then I was accorded that title. Jarl was the wrong word for the leaders I had. They were of my clan and yet they ruled towns. The towns they ruled were many times bigger than the largest town in Norway. Even Dyflin was tiny by comparison. Bergil, Sven, Ragnar, Sámr and Erik were all called lord and yet they acknowledged me as their leader and their lord. In Norway, the only ones with more power than a jarl were the older members of their family. Here I made them lords and I was the lord who commanded them. My father had been a jarl amongst other jarls.

Poppa had also changed the way we ate. When we were at sea we ate more pickled fish but it was a rarity in Rouen. We ate more beef. That had been unheard of in Norway. There you did not eat beef because if you did then you would not have milk and cheese. We now also ate sweeter foods. There were more bees and honey was plentiful. The women made biscuits and sweet breads. Dried fruits from further south enriched them. We ate more game. My men would ride into the forests and hunt. We shared what we hunted and we still ate together whenever possible but most of my men did not live in a warrior hall. They had homes within the walls of Rouen or they had their own farms. Those farms had more in common with the Franks than anything in Norway or even the Land of the Wolf.

Our towns also reflected the changes in the way we lived. The communal bread oven was gone. There was a baker who sold bread. We held a market two or three times a week so that farmers could come into town and sell their goods. Our knarr traded in Lundenwic and Bruggas. They sold goods in our markets. Since the Danes had taken over half of the Saxon lands we were more prosperous. It seemed to me that the ones who were unhappy were the priests, the Franks and the Saxons. We were pagans and we were winning. We were the ones with the coin. I did not indulge in ornamenting myself with gold and silver but I knew of Danes who did that.

As another winter passed and a new year began we heard that my friend Guthrum was now King of the Danelaw. He had come a long way since we had rescued him. I now had a powerful ally. That alliance was reflected in the ease with which we could trade in Lundenwic which was now Danish. We also found that warriors sought to join us and be part of our clan. This had happened before but now we were more likely to trust them and rely on them. We were not land-hungry yet. The raids before we had conquered this land had emptied it of most of the Franks. The ones who remained were not farmers, they were the ones who lived and prospered in the towns. They realised that they could be of service to us and would make money. However, I wanted secure borders and that meant pushing the Franks and the Bretons further back.

I was contemplating organizing another raid. We did not need the coin. King Alfred's weregeld was still untouched and we had emptied the coffers of Vire. I was thinking more about the young men who would wish to raid. I did not have enough ships yet to launch a serious attack on Paris but I had enough to hit Mantes again and this time destroy it. It would show me the problems with raiding Paris. Sven Blue Cheek had journeyed from Caen to discuss the idea with me.

We were enjoying some wine when one of the guards from the main gate came to speak to me, "Lord there is an emissary from the King of Aquitaine to speak with you."

"Send him in."

Sven asked, "King of Aquitaine?"

"Louis the Stammerer he is the son of Charles the Bald. His lands lie to the south of the Bretons and he guards the southern part of Frankia."

Sven Blue Cheek did not understand the complicated families of Frankia. Thanks to William I was becoming more familiar. Three men were admitted. One was obviously a lord and the two his bodyguards. I smiled. The Franks ever feared Vikings.

"I am Lord Göngu-Hrólfr Rognvaldson of Rouen."

"I am Charles of Tours and I serve King Louis of Aquitaine." He was an older Frank. Flecks of grey were in his beard and he had a slight frame. I did not think he was a warrior.

"Sit. What does he want of me?"

"He would buy your land from you. The King has gold to spare and he would have this land you have taken returned to Frankia." I cocked my head to one side. "Aquitaine is rich, Lord Göngu-Hrólfr Rognvaldson. His majesty has just given the counties of Barcelona,

Girona, and Besalú to Wilfred the Hairy. He has received much gold in return. It is simple enough. His majesty will do as King Alfred did with the Danes. He will give you gold and you will quit this land. He does not wish it polluted with pagans. He is a devout man. The Pope has just crowned him at Troyes and His Majesty sees this as a way of thanking the Pope." The way he spoke it was as though I had no choice. The familiarity of his words suggested that he thought me below him. I think Louis the Stammerer expected me to take the money and run.

I did not know whether to have him thrown into a cell or laugh. His suggestion was outrageous. "This is my home. My people are settled here. Why should we leave? What makes you think your King has enough gold in his treasury to buy us off?"

"But you are little more than pirates! There are other lands for you. Go to Wessex."

I had enough. "You call us pagans and think that we are barbarians. Go back to your King and tell him that we are here to stay. More than that we are here to grow. His father might be Emperor but that does not frighten me. Go!"

The man was shocked but he left. After he had gone I spoke with Sven. "I cannot believe that anyone thinks they have enough money to buy us."

"It worked with the Danes, lord"

"You may be right. I need to send to William. I may need his services again."

"And the raid on Mantes?"

"We will delay that until we have dealt with this new problem."

While I waited for William to arrive my wife showed her great knowledge. She had been the daughter of an important noble. She knew how the royal families of the Empire worked. "King Louis took over the crown from his brother, Charles the Child, after he died. From what I remember of him Louis is a simple and sweet man, a lover of peace, justice, and religion. I cannot see why he should think he could buy you off. His land is to the south of us."

"But it borders Brittany?"

"Yes, husband."

"But its borders are a hundred and fifty miles from us."

"I believe so."

"Then this must be prompted by the Pope's coronation of him. He wishes to be seen as a man who rid the land of pagans."

89

When William arrived the next day, I questioned him and then gave him orders to ride to Tours. While he was away I sent for all the horsemen from my land. I would ride as far south and west as I could get. I wanted to probe the land south of us. If King Louis was worried about us then it might be because the land close to us was unprotected. The Bretons had wrested huge swathes of land from the Franks. They spoke of an Empire but it seemed to me it was a series of clans loosely held together by an Emperor who barely clung on to power. Perhaps we had not been ambitious enough. Ylva had said a small piece of land. Did she know more than she had said? Was Frankia a plum that was ready to be plucked from the tree? We needed to ascertain the forces to the south of us. That would tell us the state of the fruit! By taking horses we could travel fifty miles in a day.

Erik Gillesson had scouts who knew the land and they rode ahead of us. We reached Dreux at the end of the first day. It was the only place we had passed with defences. They had walls that were twice the height of a man. When we neared it, they barred the gates and manned the walls. In one day we had seen what we faced. If I had had my Vikings then I could have easily taken it. We camped outside.

That night, in our camp, I spoke with the leaders of my horsemen. I now had one hundred and fifty thanks to the horses we had captured at Vire. "We will divide into three groups of fifty. I want you to ride back to your towns and raid on the way there. Let us make this land a wasteland so that the men who live here, Bretons, Franks, Gascons, I care not, vacate it. That way we can see an enemy army approaching. We have seen nothing that can stand against us."

The idea appealed to them. It was almost harvest time and there were many animals in the fields and crops to be taken. I now saw why the Franks were trying to buy us off. They feared us!

We reached Rouen two days later. We had eight wagons laden with the goods we had taken. We had not lost a man because we were able to surprise those who might have fought us. They did not expect it. This was even easier than raiding with a drekar. Horses allowed us to close quickly with a village or a farm and take the men before they could defend themselves. If the other two columns had done as well then we would be even richer.

William arrived three days later. The news he brought was surprising. "Lord, King Louis is raising an army to come and chase you from his land." His voice was incredulous. "He has decided that he must rid

Frankia of pagans. He sees it as a crusade. In the towns, they talk of pagan blood polluting Frankia. Lord, he sees himself becoming a saint!"

"How many men can he muster?"

"More than fifteen hundred, Lord, but they are mainly farmers. Warriors like myself? Perhaps two hundred."

"And when can I expect him?"

"It will take at least a month for him to raise his men and then march north. I would guess two months."

"And from which direction?"

He smiled, "I passed through Dreux and heard of your visit lord. They were terrified. That is where they will come. The men of Dreux will happily follow King Louis."

"Good, then we will give them a warm reception."

One of our knarr also brought welcome news: not only was Guthrum King of the Danes, but he had also defeated King Alfred and the Saxon King was forced to flee and hide with his oathsworn in a swamp to the west of his lands. The Danes had almost conquered the island of the Saxons. We would be able to summon help to take Paris sooner rather than later. Following this news, I sent messages for my men to gather at Haustmánuður. We would muster at Évreux. We had destroyed the town on our ride north and it was on the main road from Dreux. I did not know what King Louis intended but he would have to pass through Évreux to reach Rouen. We could wait.

I was getting used to taking Gilles to war. My shoulder felt better and I thought that I would try to use Longsword again. I was eager to leave and see how my shoulder had healed. We left Rouen with half of my men mounted. My men were the closest to the muster point and we reached the blackened stumps of Évreux first. I was not a fool and I had my men find wood to fashion into stakes. The Franks were moving slowly. They were using the levy. Even so, I did not want to be engulfed by an army many times the one hundred and twenty warriors I had brought. I had no intention of fighting from the back of a horse. We were not yet ready to face the Franks on horseback. Stephen of Andecavis' death had shown us that. I would use our strength; a shield wall backed by archers. We would fight them beard to beard. No matter how many they had we would win.

Over the next four days, my men arrived. Erik Gillesson and his horsemen would be our only mounted men. I wanted them behind us as a threat. Half of our men were mailed. Every warrior had a helmet, a shield and a spear. Many slingers, boys mainly, had accompanied the warriors.

Some were barely ten summers' old but all wished to fight for their lord. I was touched. The scouts reported the ponderous advance of King Louis and his army. They were at Dreux. They were twenty-seven miles from us. That night I summoned my lords to explain my plan. It would involve deception, horsemen, archers and an attack at night.

"They will take one whole day to reach us. They will be tired and they will camp. We will be fresh. We fight a battle at night. Erik Gillesson, you take your horsemen and ride around them to drive their horses away. Petr Jorgensen, you take your archers and you also go around their rear and send your arrows towards their standard. The rest of us advance in a boar's snout with five points. Bergil Fast Blade, Sven Blue Cheek, Sámr Oakheart and Ragnar the Resolute, along with my men, will drive into them. The five attacks will confuse them and protect those of our men who have yet to fight in a shield wall.

None could see any problem with the plan and we waited for the Franks of Aquitaine to arrive. They were numerous and they were noisy but they lacked any order. As soon as they came upon us they stopped. They had not bothered to use scouts and our formation came as a shock to them. I had to smile at the confusion for their King was no leader. Eventually, they decided to make camp. Had no one told Louis the Stammerer that Vikings do not follow rules? Our campfires burned and we ate. We allayed their fears. We did not attack them. As soon as it was dark Erik led his men to the north to encircle the camp. Petr led his archers south. We armed and we prepared. Finnbjǫrn Stormbringer and his men were with me in my wedge. Having been there for a few days we had had the opportunity to examine the ground and we prepared our lines. The Frankish camp was noisy. That was to be expected. I raised my sword and we began to march. We did not chant and that did not help us as we marched over the uneven ground but surprise was more important. They had guards and sentries on the perimeter of their camp. They would spy on us first but if that was their only warning then it would be too late.

I carried my helmet. My shield was over my back. I would have time later to don my helmet and swing my shield around. I had to see them for I was one of the five points of attack. We were in the centre. It was Bergil Fast Blade who slew the first Frank. Even as he was spotted by the sentry he lived up to his name and killed the Gascon. The horns sounded and I donned my helmet and swung around my shield. Using Longsword, one handed, I ripped it across the middle of the sentry before me. My shoulder did not ache. I was healed and I felt the confidence course back through my body. My five-pointed attack, even though we were vastly outnumbered worked. I heard cries from ahead of us and knew that my archers were raining death on the Franks. The fact that they were releasing blind did not matter. Confusion and chaos ruled. They plunged into a camp of tired men who had marched all day. King Louis' army had shed their mail and every arrow found flesh. When I heard the wild neighing of horses I knew that Erik Gillesson had reached the horse herd. With those driven off the enemy would be on foot.

The Franks were organizing but it was too late. My sword sliced through the neck of a lord. Even though he had managed to don his mail Longsword made short work of his byrnie. It was pitch black except for the glow of the Frankish fires. This was where we were comfortable and the Franks and Gascons were not. As we neared them I saw their confusion. Men ran to and fro reacting to the threat of our wedges, archers and horses. My wife's assessment had been accurate. He was a simple and sweet man and he was leading his men to be slaughtered. As we ploughed our way through the men of Aquitaine I saw, by the glow of the King's campfire, Erik Gillesson led his men to attack the standard. King Louis had many men around him but Erik and his horsemen in their dark blue cloaks with white swords made short work of most of them. Their spears rose and fell. The bodyguard died. Erik hurled his spear and the King fell. It took some time for the news to permeate the ranks but, when it did, then the men of Aquitaine fled. We were their worst nightmare. We were barbarians who attacked at night. Their god had forsaken them and they ran. It was hard to see it at first. It was when I realised there were no more warriors to be hewn that I knew they had routed.

It was a night battle and, as such, confusing. As soon as I realised that the enemy was fleeing I slid my shield around to my back and I shouted, "Hold fast!" My voice was recognised and the order rippled through the battlefield. The enemy was broken and had fled but that did not mean that the fighting had ended. The ones who had not routed fought in huddles of men. The King had oathsworn who had survived and did not run. These were warriors in mail. They had managed to don armour when we had attacked.

It fell to Sven and myself to lead the two wedges which encircled them. Using Longsword two-handed I smashed my sword across the middle of them. One shield and the arm which held it were shattered and another warrior fell with his thigh torn open. Sven's sword struck another warrior a glancing blow to the head and he fell. Bjorn was behind me and he slew the warrior who had fallen. I raised my sword and, thankful that my shoulder had healed, brought it down to smash through the helmet of the warrior with the broken arm. And then it was over. None remained alive.

It took until dawn to completely seal the camp. We had captured their herd of horses intact. They were good horses. The King had brought his crown and jewels as well as the coin to pay men. His priests had brought religious artefacts and regalia. We had much armour. Although we had surprised our enemy there had been many of them and we had lost warriors. We buried them and then made a pyre and burned the enemy dead. As the heavily laden wagons and captured horses trudged north the air was filled with the smell of burning flesh. The column of black smoke rose high in the air and Aquitaine needed a new King. We had let the Franks know that they had a dangerous beast close to them and if they prodded it then it would bite.

Chapter 7

This one battle secured our borders. We had won and lost fewer men than one might have expected. Our horse herd had been doubled and there were few men without a helmet, good sword and mail. The coin and treasures we had taken and sold meant that we had quadrupled our treasury. These were the good days. More men sought to join us as a result. We were victorious. We were rich and the combination of the two made us powerful attractions to Vikings who sought both.

Our battle with the men of Aquitaine meant that we did not need to raid. Nefgeirr Haldisson and his men had fought well. He begged to make a stronghold. I agreed and he led his men to Évreux. He would build his hall there. Many of his men had taken wives and had families. Finnbjǫrn Stormbringer and his men asked to follow Nefgeirr. Both crews had seen that life was easier and more profitable in this land than raiding. Their drekar remained at anchor in the river at Rouen. We spent half a year enjoying the fruits of our victory and preparing for the raid on Mantes. My life should have been perfect except that my wife bore me another child and she was a girl. As much as I loved my daughters none could lead the clan. None could fulfil my grandfather's prophesy. Ylva had promised me that when I had raided Paris then I would sire a son. We were not yet ready for such a task.

William had been to Paris a second and third time. He was becoming known and accepted. He even traded with the men of Paris. I learned that Count Odo of Paris feared us and was making his island into a fortress. If we were going to take the city then we would need four hundred drekar. I now commanded fifteen. I had sent word to other leaders and to King Guthrum that when time allowed I would need them to raid the Franks. The Norns were spinning. King Alfred had returned from his swamp and was fighting back. My old ally was not having an easy time of it. A year to the day after we had killed King Louis we heard that King Alfred and his ships had destroyed a Danish fleet to the west of Wihtwara. The King of Wessex was learning to fight back.

One positive result of the Danish disaster was that some of the survivors of the battle sought refuge with me. Ten drekar had escaped and they joined me. Siegfried Sharp Sword and Sinric Steady Hand led them. Both were older warriors who had sailed with Guthrum for many years.

"We have not abandoned Guthrum, Lord Göngu-Hrólfr Rognvaldson but we use our drekar to raid. We heard that you wish to raid down the river of the Franks and that suits us. We would serve alongside you."

I noticed that Siegfried Sharp Sword did not say under. "Then you are welcome to sail with us but I give the commands. I have ruled this land for many years. It is our home and we strive to make it stronger. When we raid the Franks, it is to make our homes more secure and to take that which is close to us."

I could see that my idea was not the one they sought. "King Guthrum allowed us to lead our men and ships."

I smiled, "And how did that result? King Alfred, a Saxon, defeated you."

I saw the hurt and humiliation in their eyes. The Saxons were no sailors. Their ships were not the equal of a drekar and yet they had defeated a Danish fleet. "We will sail with you on a raid, Lord Göngu-Hrólfr Rognvaldson. Our men need a victory. Then we will return to Lundenwic and discover if our King has wrested victory from the men of Wessex."

I could almost hear the Norns spinning. I could raid and destroy Mantes. That would open the gateway to Paris. They could return to Guthrum and when Alfred was beaten then they would join me. I smiled, "That is good. I will send for my other ships. We will raid Mantes."

Finnbjǫrn, in particular, had been keen to return to raid Mantes. He had lost some of his crew there. My other lords were also anxious to make another raid. The gold we had taken from Alfred and Louis had been, largely, spent. It had not been wasted. Most of our men now wore mail. Our walls were stone and higher. We had towers but the gold was almost gone and the Franks were the best supply that we had. Before the Danes had gone to the Land of the Saxons then that had been a rich source. Siegfried had told us of many Danes and Norse who raided the lands to the north of Bruggas but I did not see that there would be as many riches there. My river filled as drekar came to join us. We had twenty-five drekar. That was over a thousand Viking warriors.

My lords and I led the fleet up the river. There were so many of us that we would be seen from a great distance. Even with masts stepped we could not be missed. We had fifty miles to row and we stopped just ten miles from the town. Vétheuil was a small village by the river and when we approached the people fled. They left their livestock and we ate well. Leaving Vétheuil in the middle of the night I led my fleet around the last bend to Mantes. It was a hard row for the river was flowing swiftly. Rains had added water to swell the flow of the mighty river. That would help us when we reached Mantes but, as we rowed towards the rising sun, my men had to strain at the oars.

We had half of the ship's boys ready with bows. Half of the rowers were already prepared to land. We had our shields and our helmets. Of the ones who remained the steerboard oars would ship them first and that would give me thirty-seven men to land and fight whoever waited for us. I stood at the prow and, as the sun rose I saw that they had built a tower on the island. Although made of wood and no deterrent it would warn the Franks of our arrival. There would be warriors waiting for us. My crew would have to fight to gain a foothold.

I turned to the crew, "Men of the *'Fafnir'*, there are warriors waiting for us. There are Franks who thought that our last raid was the best that we could do. We are going to show them what Vikings can do when they mean it. When we land, we form a wedge. We march to their hall. If the other crews can keep up with us then they can have some of the glory. I know that this crew will not need their help. What say you?"

The ones standing began banging their shields and chanting, "Göngu-Hrólfr Rognvaldson, Göngu-Hrólfr Rognvaldson, Göngu-Hrólfr Rognvaldson!" As we neared the tower a few arrows were sent in our direction. The boys of three drekar sent their arrows at the tower and when the four bowmen fell there was a cheer from the ships behind. It was a good start.

Siggi Siggison was at the steering board and he shouted, "Steerboard oars in!" As soon as he said that we veered towards the bank. The rowers having vacated that side the ones who would land with me lined up and the steerboard oars donned helmets and grabbed their shields. Óðalríkr Odhensson leapt ashore. He had courage for he only had a seax for defence and two Franks ran at him. One was hit by an arrow and I sprang from the drekar to land next to Óðalríkr. My shield took the sword thrust which was intended to take his life. I had no sword in my hand and so I grabbed the Frank and pulled him towards me. I threw him behind me and he fell between the drekar and the quay. As the rope was pulled he screamed as he was crushed to death.

"Thank you, lord!"

I grinned at Óðalríkr and drew my sword, "We are all *'Fafnir'* crew! One day you will join me with a sword and a shield!" The Franks were running down the quay towards us. I held my shield before me and my sword over the top. Petr Tallboy and Ubba Long Cheek locked their shields behind my back and they began our chant. It helped us to move in time.

> *Clan of the Horseman*
> *Warriors strong*
> *Clan of the Horseman*
> *Our reach is long*
> *Clan of the Horseman*
> *Fight as one*
> *Clan of the Horseman*
> *Death will come*

The ones at the rear of the wedge banged their shields. Those of us at the front prepared to meet the Franks who ran at us. Vire and the battle of Évreux had shown them that we were ruthless. The men who charged us were trying to save their families and they would fight hard. The first two Franks ran at me with their spears. They saw a giant and made the mistake of going for the head. In their position, I would have gone for my legs. Holding my shield before me meant that their spearheads slid harmless up the metal-studded leather. I used my long arms and Longsword to stab down at the one on my right. The tip of my sword entered his mouth and I drove it down through his body. At the same time, I punched with my shield at the other Frank and his face became a bloody mess. Petr Tallboy and Ubba Long Cheek stabbed and slashed at the men facing them. The Franks had so many men that some were pushed into the river by their own warriors. Our formation meant that we would not suffer that fate.

The Franks had sent all of their men to try to drive us into the river. Behind me, I heard Sven Blue Cheek ordering his crew to use the side streets and narrow alleyways. They would flank the men we were fighting. Our one disadvantage was that our shields were on the left, the riverside. It made it easier for the Franks to attack our sword side. I heard cries from behind as some of my crew fell. When Ubba killed the man he was fighting, I was able to use the length of my sword better. I swung it in an arc. The Franks suffered wounds from it and that allowed the men behind to close up with us. Ahead of me, I saw Sven Blue Cheek and his men burst from between two large houses and fall upon the Franks. Assailed on two sides they died. These were their best men. More of my crews emulated Sven and they ran up the deserted streets, roads and alleys to attack the mass of Franks in the side. As more men joined them so the mailed Franks were forced into the river. They drowned.

Ahead of me, I saw the open market area before the stone hall of the Lord of Mantes. People were fleeing. They wished to be anywhere so long as it was away from the Viking warriors who had poured ashore. The women and children, the old and those who could not fight chose to escape. The warriors fought on to allow their families to live. My mail, helmet and shield saved my life on more than one occasion that day. This was not an open battlefield. It was a town. We were pressed close together. There were buildings that were used as refuges for the warriors we had defeated. Inside them, I could not use my Longsword. I realised I would have to sheathe it. Even as I lifted my arm to sheathe it a sword was swung at my side. It was not a good sword or I would have been hurt. It struck my mail and broke a link but my padded undershirt absorbed the impact. I swung the edge of my shield around and it hit the Frank on the side of the head. He reeled and I punched him in the face with my right hand. As he tumbled backwards I drew Hrolf's Vengeance and stabbed him in the middle of his stomach.

A stone was dropped from the roof. It was the size of a fist and hit my helmet. The padded protector I wore beneath it and the metal cross reinforcers on the top of the helmet meant it made my ears ring but that was all. What it did do was to make me angry. I ran into the house. Two Franks stood there. I filled the doorway and they ran at me. One ran into my sword and I punched the other with my shield. Their swords hit the metal boss on my shield. I despatched the one I had hit with my shield. I saw that there was a ladder to the next floor. I kicked it to the ground. Taking a burning log from the fire I dropped it onto the ladder. I took another and threw it at the wall. Finally, I took the table and laid it on the fire. Flames began to leap up towards the ceiling. As the smoke began to pour upstairs I went back to the battle. It had moved on. Already there were screams from above me as the fire took hold. I ran to join my men. I passed dead Franks and a few wounded Vikings.

When we reached the hall, I saw that they had a stone tower attached to it and the survivors had fled there. I spied Sámr Oakheart. "Sámr, take men to the hall. Take anything of value and then fire it! I will not waste men trying to take it."

Aye lord."

"Bergil Fast Blade, take as many men as you need and find the church before the priests strip it of all that we would have."

"Aye lord."

This time I had sent Finnbjǫrn and two other crews to take the warehouses. It meant that Siegfried Sharp Sword and Sinric Steady Hand were with me. I took off my helmet and held up my shield in case they had any archers in the tower. Already the smoke from the burning house was drifting in front of the tower to obscure it. I turned to them. "Take your men and search the north side of the town. We will wait here."

Sinric pointed to my helmet. There was a large dent in it, "The Allfather was watching over you, Lord."

"And I had a well-made helmet."

Most of the fighting had finished. Siggi and the ship's boys had brought up my drekar to the centre of the town. The other drekar were following. We would load our wounded upon our ships. My men were busy emptying the houses for the fire I had started was now spreading. I saw Sámr ordering his men from the hall and then I watched him and his oathsworn throw burning brands inside. I realised that they had used oil and wax to help accelerate the fire when the flames roared skyward. The tower was made of stone but one entrance faced us and the other led to the hall. They had made their own tomb. As the fire took hold some men tried to flee out of the door. They were cut down by my waiting warriors. I do not know why the rest did not try to escape that way for the alternative was a fiery death. I am not sure if it was an escape attempt or suicide but three warriors fell from the top. When flames began to leap up from the inside of the tower then I knew it was all over.

It took until the middle of the afternoon for us to empty the town of all that was valuable. Even if it was not we would have had to leave for the fire had engulfed the whole of the town. We sailed our drekar to the north side of the river. We disembarked and watched the inferno destroy the southern side of Mantes. Finnbjǫrn had emptied the warehouses and we made a camp by them to eat and enjoy our victory. As we sat around a fire enjoying the beef from the butchered cows and enjoying the red wine which had been intended for a lord somewhere in Frankia, Sinric and Siegfried asked me about Paris. Both were in a happy frame of mind. They had lost few men and become rich in one raid.

"Why not push on to Paris Lord Göngu-Hrólfr Rognvaldson? We have lost few men."

"Because Paris is better defended. It is an island and they have two bridges which will stop us from surrounding it. We need ten times the number of ships we had today. We need a better plan."

Sinric shook his head. "The plan worked!"

"If Sven Blue Cheek had not had the wit to flank the Franks then it might have gone badly for us. I should have planned for that. This is the first time I have commanded so many men and ships. I have learned lessons. When we go to take Paris, I will be a better leader."

Even though we had defeated the men of Mantes I still had sentries keeping watch. It was a good thing I did. They reported, the next morning as we prepared to leave that a Frankish army was approaching. We could have rushed to our ships and fled downriver but that would have ruined what had been a successful raid. I wanted to destroy the warehouses. When the Franks returned to Mantes I wanted them to have to rebuild completely. If they were doing that then they could not be preparing to destroy us. Louis the Stammerer had shown me that the Franks hatred of us was religious as much as anything. Our religion offended and frightened them. They could not understand that it was unlike the religion of the White Christ. It was a way of life.

I quickly organized my men. The ships were loaded and, with sails ready, we could leave whenever we chose. I had the wounded men make the warehouses into fire traps. We would fire them before we left. We marched east to meet the men of Paris who had come to punish us. They had not brought many horses. They had brought large numbers of men who would fight on foot. Count Odo of Paris led them. This was the first time I had fought him and he was a competent commander. He had organized his men well. His mailed warriors were interspersed with the levy, the ordinary men of Paris. His small number of horses guarded his flanks.

They were still five hundred paces from us and advancing slowly. I walked out from the shield wall and addressed my men. "We meet them beard to beard but listen for the horn. When it is sounded three times we fall back to the ships. We do this rank by rank. The front rank will pass through the second. Then the second through the first. We walk! They will think that we are trapped but our men are already preparing the buildings. We will set them alight. Kill as many as you can but survive. This is but the beginning. We will fight with the men of Paris again and when we do we will have an army far bigger than this one!"

As, "Göngu-Hrólfr Rognvaldson, Göngu-Hrólfr Rognvaldson, Göngu-Hrólfr Rognvaldson!" rang out I rejoined my men.

Leif carried the horn and he was in the third rank, "Leif, you know the sound of my voice?"

He laughed, "Aye, Lord."

"Then when you hear me shout, '*Now*', blow the horn three times and lead the third rank back!"

"Aye lord."

"You will order the buildings to be fired."

As we waited Bjorn chuckled, "And we may well get a singed beard!"

"If that is the only price we pay then I will be happy, Bjorn."

The Franks were marching steadily. Their mixed formation meant that we would be facing either unarmed men or mailed warriors. Count Odo was clever. He was relying on the Viking warriors who faced his farmers advancing and allowing the rest of us to be outflanked. That would not happen. I had no intention of advancing. I had a spear in my hand for the Franks did and I knew my long arms would allow me to strike first. I saw that they had sent mailed men towards me and my warriors for we were in the centre. The ones who faced me wore a high domed open helmet without a nasal. Their leader had a plume in his.

When they were twenty paces from us the warrior with the plume raised his spear and shouted, "Charge!" That was a mistake. The ones without mail ran quickly towards us while the mailed men had more discipline and came more slowly. There was a crash of metal on wood and screams as the levy hit mailed men. The Franks died. Our warriors did not. I rammed my spear forward as the plumed helmet came towards me. I held my shield before me knowing that, as I was taller, the Frank would have to stab upwards. His spear caught on my boss. His helmet deflected my spear but it struck him just below the helmet. I scored a long ragged line along his skull and knocked his helmet from his head. He was stunned and I punched with my spear to take advantage. I quickly pulled back my arm and rammed it through his mail and into his stomach. I twisted as I pulled it out and he fell writhing to the ground. The next Frank seemed mesmerized by the entrails dangling like worms.

He flailed his shield at the spear and that allowed me to step forward and ram my knee between his legs. He fell backwards and I skewered him.

From my right, I heard a cry from Finnbjǫrn Stormbringer, "Lord they are breaking through!"

Some of the mailed men had managed to create a hole in the shield wall of one of Sinric's crews' shield wall. It was time. "Leif! Now!" The horn sounded three times. I shouted, "Thrust and retire!" I stabbed at the Franks with my spear. I hit a shield but even as the Frank responded I had stepped back through the gap left by Bjorn and my other men. The Franks found themselves facing a fresh line of men who were ready with sharp weapons. We walked back five paces and held our shields and spears before us. "Fall back!" As our men stepped back towards us, Petr Tallboy moved to the right and I moved to the left to allow Bjorn to walk back between us. As soon he had passed us we closed ranks and presented spears. We repeated the manoeuvre three times until I felt the wall of the warehouse behind me. I could smell smoke. My men had fired the buildings. "Back to the ships!" I hurled my spear at the nearest Frank. It hit him in the shoulder and he fell backwards. Others charged the Franks to make them reel and then they turned to head for the river and safety.

Leif had organized bows and as we headed for the drekar a shower of arrows descended to strike the unwary Franks. Suddenly a wall of flame leapt into the air. Leif was right, we were singed by the flames but some Franks were engulfed as oil caught fire. We boarded our drekar and took our oars. With a wall of flame close by we had to keep our sail furled but the wall of fire kept the Franks at bay. We began to row. I took an oar and joined my crew as we sang. They sang the song of the death of my treacherous brother. It was *wyrd*.

> *Ragnvald Ragnvaldson was cursed from his birth*
> *Through his dark life he was a curse to the earth*
> *A brother nearly drowned and father stabbed*
> *The fortunes of the clan ever ebbed*
> *The Norns they wove and Hrólfr lived*
> *From the dark waters he survived.*
> *Göngu-Hrólfr Rognvaldson he became*
> *A giant of a man with a mighty name*
> *Göngu-Hrólfr Rognvaldson with the Longsword*
> *Göngu-Hrólfr Rognvaldson with his Longsword*
> *When the brothers met by Rouen's walls*

Warriors emptied from warrior halls
Then Ragnvald Ragnvaldson became the snake
Letting others' shields the chances take
Arne the Breton Slayer used a knife in the back
Longsword he beat that treacherous attack
When the snake it tired and dropped its guard
Then Longsword struck swift and hard
Göngu-Hrólfr Rognvaldson with the Longsword
Göngu-Hrólfr Rognvaldson with his Longsword
And with that sword he took the hand
That killed his father and his land
With no sword the snake was doomed
To rot with Hel in darkness entombed
When the head was struck and the brother died
The battle ended and the clan all cried
Göngu-Hrólfr Rognvaldson with the Longsword
Göngu-Hrólfr Rognvaldson with his Longsword
Göngu-Hrólfr Rognvaldson with the Longsword
Göngu-Hrólfr Rognvaldson with his Longsword

Chapter 8

Siegfried and Sinric stayed a few days in my town. They had wounded men who needed to be healed and they had goods to sell in our market. They intended to sail back to Lundenwic. We too had goods to sell but I wanted some time with my wife. I had neglected her of late. Perhaps that was why she could not bear me a son. My lords returned, much richer now, to their strongholds and I rewarded those who had fought with me. Bjorn and Leif were given the two suits of mail we had found in the hall. They each had a byrnie but it was a short one. I made certain that those who lived in my town, like the smiths received coins. I gave my wife the fine linens we had liberated. As we lay in my bed and she had tended to the bruises I had suffered we coupled. She snuggled in to me, "If I cannot bear you a son then you should take another woman. Perhaps it is me."

"You want me to take another woman?"

"Of course not, but I know that it is something you need."

"Ylva told me that you would not bear a child until we attack Paris. I am not yet ready to do so. I have not enough men nor do I have enough ships. I will go to Lundenwic and speak with King Guthrum. When he has conquered Wessex, he will be able to join us."

The Norns were spinning. I did not get to sail to Lundenwic, not for some time. That which I had not expected to happen, happened. The Bretons attacked. They surprised us and attacked Bayeux and Caen at the same time. By the time the messenger reached us, it was nightfall and we had to delay our departure until the next morning. I fretted. I left Ragnar the Resolute to guard the approach to my town. I went to Caen first. As we approached, with the men of Évreux and Lisieux as well as Erik Gillesson's men from Montfort sur Risle, the Bretons saw us and fled south.

Sven Blue Cheek was contemptuous of the Bretons. "They had many hundreds of men but they had no idea how to deal with our defences." All the hard work he had done had paid off. The Bretons had thought they were attacking barbarians. They would learn that we were anything but.

"Then tomorrow we head for Bayeux and hope that Sámr is as fortunate."

This time we were not even needed. The siege had ended and the Bretons had fled before we even arrived there. They had destroyed farms and taken livestock but that was all. The next morning, we headed for Brittany. We would punish them for their attack. One of the men who had led the attack was a lord who lived at Guiberville. Sámr had recognised his banner. While Erik led his horsemen to gather every animal we could find we marched to his town. As we arrayed before his wooden walls an emissary rode forth. I took off my helmet and nudged Gilles forward to meet him. Sámr Oakheart and Sven Blue Cheek flanked me.

The emissary was accompanied by a priest. I know not why they thought that would make a difference. The emissary said, "My Lord Raymond would avoid bloodshed. He apologises for any misunderstanding."

Sámr snapped, "Misunderstanding? You tried to reduce our towns, my town! You slew our people who farm close by and you took our animals."

"We were ordered to do so by King Alan. Our lord had no choice."

"And now he will pay for his town will be destroyed and all of his men blinded."

The priest said, "My lord, I beg you, show mercy."

"We are Vikings. We do not understand the concept."

The emissary threw an angry glance in the direction of the priest. He had not needed help. "My lord we will return all of the animals that were taken and my lord will pay you gold."

"We can take all that he has now!"

"And we will pay the same amount each year that you do not attack us."

"And what of your King?"

"Our King lives far from here. He knows not the danger you represent."

"Return in the morning and I will give you my decision then."

As we headed back to our camp Sven Blue Cheek said, "You intend to take him up on his offer do you not, lord?"

"I do."

"Then why wait until the morning?"

"Two reasons, I want him to sweat and wonder if we will attack and I want Erik to collect as many animals as we can. I do not think that King Alan will allow his lord to pay regularly but when they do not and we attack then we will have right on our side."

Sven gave me a strange look, "Right? We are Vikings. When did we become concerned about right and wrong?"

"As much as I would like to impose our will on this land, at the moment we do not have enough men. Until we do then we have to pretend to play by their rules. Be patient Sven, we are becoming stronger each day. Soon we will have King Guthrum and his Danes to help us and then this land will be ours."

After I had met with the Count of Guiberville and agreed to his request I went back to Bayeux with Sámr Oakheart. I stayed long enough to make sure that King Alan did not send more men to try to retake his towns. Then I headed back to Rouen. Instead of heading directly for Lundenwic, I used the coin we had received to make my walls stronger and to make Ragnar the Resolute's new stronghold even stronger. He had the fewest men on his drekar. They manned his walls as did his farmers. He was important to me for we had built stone-throwers so that we could bar the river. We had learned how to make them and also how to use fire. The greatest danger to any ship was fire. As a result of the delay, it was Þorri when I headed for Lundenwic.

As we sailed north in *'Fafnir'* I had good reason to be happy. We had thwarted the Bretons and the Franks. The men of Aquitaine were no longer a threat. We were richer now than at any time. My people were happy and safe. The only cloud which spoiled my blue sky was the lack of a son. My grandfather had sacrificed himself to give me the chance of having a son and heir. It was always on my mind.

There had been a time when the Tamese was Saxon. It was in the mouth of that river where my father had been murdered by my brother. That had been the last time I had visited. Then we had raided with Danes and taken great treasure. The treasure was not worth the cost for my father had died and I had almost died. As we rowed west I reflected on that day. If my brother had not killed our father and I had not sunk to the bottom of the sea then I would not have been rescued. I would not have learned to be a warrior. The Norns had spun and there was little point in bemoaning what might have been. I had to live with the reality of what was.

There were many Danish ships tied up and we struggled to find a berth. I left Bjorn and Petr Tallboy to trade and I went alone to the old Roman fort where I knew that King Guthrum resided. As I entered the gates I noticed the downward glances of the men who were there. They not the faces of victorious warriors. I recognised one, "Einar, how is life treating you?"

"It could be better lord." His voice sounded dull as though they had lost all.

"Better? Your master is King of this land and Alfred hides in his swamp fearing his wrath."

Einar shook his head, "That might have been true lord but the Allfather has deserted us. We were defeated by Alfred when he starved us out at Cippanhamm." He shook his head. "We should have fought them. We might have been defeated but this..."

My head reeled. This was not what I had expected. "But he is still King."

Einar looked distraught, "Lord, Guthrum has become a follower of the White Christ. He is now King Athelstan. He bends the knee to Alfred!"

I was bereft of words. It felt as though my world had ended. How could I have a son when the ally upon whom I depended was now a vassal of Wessex?

"I am sorry, Einar."

"Will you take me for one of your men, lord. You are a Viking. You would not have surrendered. Guthrum has lost his purpose. He has been bewitched!"

"If your lord allows then you can but if you are oathsworn..."

He almost spat his words out, "How can I be oathsworn to a Christian and a lord who has abandoned the Allfather?"

I was admitted to the chamber where Guthrum, I could not call him Athelstan, sat with his jarls. When he saw me, he stood and strode over to me. "Sinric said that you would come. A shame it was not earlier. We could have used you and your men. Then we might have won." He saw my face. "You know?"

"That you took the cross? Aye. Why?"

He shrugged and swallowed off the ale in his horn. "I had water poured on my head and I took a name I will never use. In my heart, I am still Guthrum."

"You are foresworn and the Allfather does not forgive that." I shook my head, "The spirits know. The Allfather knows. The Norns know. You had everything Guthrum. I envied you. I would have changed places with you."

"You are the legend. I am a warrior who is lucky to be alive. Had you not saved me that day in the north of this land then I would have died in the icy waters with my oathsworn. Perhaps that would have been a better end."

One of his men said, "But you are still King!"

I looked into Guthrum's eyes and saw sadness. He would rather be the warrior who had defeated Alfred. "So, Guthrum, you cannot fight Alfred for you would break your oath." He said nothing. I felt my dream of a son fading. "Then I would beg you to encourage your men to come to my land. You should come. I do not fight Alfred I fight Charles the Bald!"

He looked like an empty shell of a man. He had been defeated and his men were abandoning him. He seemed to have given up on life. He had made a covenant with a Christian. No good could come of it.

"I might wish to but many of my men seek to raid the Frisians. Others have left to join Hastein on the Liger where they fight for the Bretons."

"Then warn them that if King Alan sends them north they will have to face Longsword, Lord Göngu-Hrólfr Rognvaldson, and I do not cow to enemies. I fight with my last breath. When my sword is torn from my dead hands then I will be defeated; until then, fear me!"

I saw his men look at Guthrum but my arrow had found its mark. "You are right to speak thus, Göngu-Hrólfr Rognvaldson, I have failed you and for that, I am most sorry of all."

We stayed for seven days. I did not intend to do so but we had trades to make and I had many warriors who sought my advice. Guthrum was being deserted. I had never seen the like. Guthrum was correct. Many were sailing to Frisia and others to the Liger. Guthrum could not attack Alfred again. His army was deserting him but some chose to come to my land. I offered hope. I was able to choose the best of the warriors and the best of the jarls. Guthrum advised me. He was honest. He had lost everything. By helping me he could regain just a little of his honour.

The seven days proved useful in many ways. Not only did we manage to trade well and recruit warriors who wished to come to my land, but we also learned more about the threats. Many of the Danes were concerned about the burghs which Alfred was building. The places we had raided before such as Hamwic, Haestingaceaster and Cantwareburh were now being made into strongholds. We would no longer be able to scale low wooden walls or hack through wooden gates. We would have to assault ditches and towers. Wessex was no longer an easy target and a good source of gold. We had been bought off once but that well was now dry.

We also learned that ships had sailed into the Blue Sea to raid there. Some of the towns of the Caliphate had been taken and the warriors had brought back great quantities of treasure. When I had heard that news I had smiled. It had been my grandfather's friend, Dragonheart who had first sailed that sea. He did cast a long shadow. The world was changing and it was Vikings who were changing it.

It was on the last day, just as we were about to leave on the late afternoon tide, that a drekar arrived. The berth next to us was vacant and she took it. I was on the quay paying the fees to the official Guthrum used. The warrior who had given the orders on the drekar landed and came to speak with the official. He suddenly seemed to see me, "You must be the one they call Göngu-Hrólfr Rognvaldson."

I nodded. I was no longer surprised when I was recognised. "I am. I am Lord of Rouen."

"I am Ulla War Cry. You came to our land to speak with Ylva."

Wyrd! "You are of the blood of the Dragonheart!"

"I am. They tell me that you are carving out an Empire in the Land of the Franks."

"I have a land which I protect. It is little bigger than the Land of the Horse."

He looked at the official, "How much is it to land and trade?"

"Five silver pennies a day. It is more if your men cause trouble."

"These are men of the Land of the Wolf. They cause no trouble unless I command it." The official wandered off. "We were raiding on the Liger. We fought the Bretons and the Franks. They fought hard and protected their treasure with walls. We did well enough but many crewmen died." I nodded. "You intend to raid Paris." He must have seen the surprise on my face. He laughed, "Drekar captains talk. You raided Mantes, or so I heard. That is not far from Paris. Outside of Rome, it is the richest city a man could take."

"You are right. I need more than three hundred drekar and their crews to do so."

Drekar in the Seine

"You are not ready yet?"

"Guthrum has converted to Christianity and was defeated by Alfred. I do not think I can rely on as many ships from this land as I had hoped. My plan was to raid this year but until the Danes return from the Liger and Frisia then there will not be enough ships."

"That suits me. I am on my way home to the Land of the Wolf. I will speak with Sámr Ship Killer, Mordaf ap Gruffyd and Ragnar son of the Wolf Killer. We have good drekar and you are known to be a true leader. Your grandfather Hrolf the Horseman was well respected. My kin are in Dyflin for we were asked to help the Vikings who lived there. The Irish have risen. When that is done we may be able to join you for a raid which would make us all rich."

The voice from behind me was urgent, "We are ready, lord. If we are to catch this tide we should leave soon."

"Aye Gandálfr."

Ulla War Cry clasped my arm, "I will try to come to Rouen. My kin may come too. May the Allfather be with you."

As we headed down the Tames I reflected on the visit to Lundenwic. The Norns had indeed spun a prodigious web. Their web went to Miklagård and back. It covered the Liger and Frisia, the Blue Sea and Dyflin. They linked Ulla War Cry's great grandfather and my grandfather. My black humour when I had realised that Guthrum had become a Christian was now replaced by hope. I might not be leading Guthrum's ships but there would be warriors and drekar who would follow me. There was hope. In that hope lay the promise of a son. Without a son then all was without a point.

My news about Guthrum was greeted with disappointment for Sven and the others had been anticipating a great raid on Paris. I had been back for two months when I summoned my lords to Rouen. My wife had ordered the building of a new hall. It had taken a year to complete and she wished to show it off to my lords and their ladies. I often forgot that Poppa was the daughter of a count who had had the ear of the King. She was used to a grander life than I had given her. Our home was now one of which she could be proud. We had chambers rather than a large communal sleeping space. Gefn was now old but the life she now lived was a total transformation from her life in Norway. It had been for her that I had allowed Poppa to spend the gold we had taken from Alfred, the Franks and the men of Aquitaine.

Our feasting hall was large enough to accommodate all of my lords and their families. Poppa showed that she understood how to arrange such things. She had one table for our family. Two other tables were attached at right angles so that every face looked to us. I would not have arranged it thus. I would have had my men closer to me but this was Poppa's first feast and the look of joy on Gefn's face made the arrangement acceptable. I sat between Gefn and Poppa. Our four daughters sat next to Gefn and Poppa. I was the only man at this table save Æðelwald of Remisgat who was between two of my daughters. My wife had spent much coin to obtain delicacies. They were designed to impress the ladies of my lords. In the main, they were Bretons or Franks and it was understandable. Norse ladies would not have known the difference. Gefn was close enough to Bergljót for them to talk.

My wife was busy chatting to Sven's wife and I was quietly sipping the heavy red wine. Gefn turned to me and said, "You have a good wife, my son. I know that this is not enjoyable to you. Hrolf and my husband would have felt the same. To the three of you, a feast is something for warriors to enjoy. The ale would have flowed and the talk would have been of battles. We have come to a new land and we are starting anew. This is not Norway. We do not cling to the side of a fjord." She smiled and turned her palms over. They were rough and calloused, "Here the wife of a jarl does not gut fish and sew leather for her husband. She is like your wife with soft hands and servants who do her bidding. You and your grandfather chose this life. Do not be unhappy that it is not the life you left. Would you return to the fjord?"

I leaned over and kissed her on the cheek, "You are wise and I needed your words. I miss my grandfather. At night when I sleep then I hear his voice and I see his face but it is not the same."

"He is ever-present for I have dreamed of him and of my husband, your adopted father. They both watch over you." She patted my hand. "Soon I will join them"

"You are ill?"

She smiled, "No, I am just old. Bergljót and I have outlived all of the old ones from our home in Norway. The Allfather has sent me granddaughters and for that I am grateful. I have raised a son and watched another become a great warrior. Your daughters will not die in battle. When I am in the Otherworld I will see them and be content."

My wife understood that my lords and I needed to speak. When the food had been finished she clapped her hands. "Ladies, the men will need to be men now and talk of war. I have a smaller chamber next door. There is a harpist there who will sing us songs of love for he is a Frank and not a Viking!" If she thought we would be offended then she was wrong.

As soon as the women left my lords all gathered around my table. Sven Blue Cheek sat on one side of me and Bergil Fast Blade on the other. "Well, lord. We heard a rumour about Guthrum, is it true?"

"It is Bergil. Alfred defeated him and he became a Christian." I saw the shock on their faces and held up my hand, "He says that he has not forsaken the old ways but he has given his word."

Sven Blue Cheek shook his head, "Then we do not want to sail with him. A man who swears an untruth is a nithing. He would bring bad luck."

I nodded and touched my horse amulet. "Many of his men feel the same. He holds on to what he has but no more. Many of his men have gone a-Viking on the Liger and Frisia. They will return and, I believe, follow my banner. Siegfried and Sinric have promised to do so but it will not be this year."

Ragnar the Resolute said, "Lord our men grow restless." The others nodded their agreement.

Olaf Two Teeth said, "Lord what about the land north of Rouen and east of Djupr. The Franks cling on to that land. If the Danes are raiding Frisia then this might be the chance we seek to make that land secure." Djupr was the domain of Olaf and I was his nearest neighbour. There were many miles between us. I saw nods of agreement from most of my lords.

Sámr was not as convinced as the other men around my table. "I now have a young son and a daughter, lord. If we leave my home then I fear the Bretons may take advantage of our absence. I am the furthest from Rouen and the most in danger."

This was another sign that we were changing as a people. When Sámr had saved Gefn in Norway he had been wild and reckless. He had followed me to the cave of the witch and yet now, just a few years later he was cautious. Were we Vikings any longer?

"We do not all need to go. The land to the north of us has one major town, Anmyen. If we raid that then we can control the land between us. I will not command any to come with me. That is the choice of each lord."

Ragnar said, "But you are Lord of Rouen. You can command us to go."

113

I laughed, "And when have I ever done that? No, you choose. I had thought that this year we would be raiding Paris. That will not happen. When we have taken Anmyen then we will cast our eye to the west. Perhaps we retake the land that was the Land of the Horse. The Bretons have not yet eradicated all traces of my grandfather. Sámr, you can scout the land. Find where our enemies are strong and where we could exploit their weaknesses. That would be as useful to us as coming to Anmyen with us."

Sámr Oakheart looked happier, "Aye lord, I will do that. I am not afraid to fight but I would not lose my family."

That settled, we planned our attack. I knew that we had consumed much wine and ale. The plans would have to be modified when we had clearer heads but the basic strategy was decided that night in my wife's new feasting hall.

Olaf Two Teeth and Sven Blue Cheek would lead their men from Djupr, eastwards. Sven could sail to Djupr with his drekar. He now had three under his command. The rest of us would strike northeast from Rouen. Olaf and Sven would have fifty miles to travel while we would have sixty. I was aware of the problems we had had the last time we divided the army. This time we would use riders to keep each other informed. Thanks to our victories over the Bretons and the men of Aquitaine, we had many horses.

It took a month to organize properly. The wine had made us overestimate how far we could travel in one day. Ragnar had been convinced that the journey would take but two days. In the cold light of day, we realised that it would require three or four. Erik now led the horsemen. They were distinctive for all wore the same blue cloak over their mail. While some of those who fought on foot had helmets with face masks or open helmets all of my horsemen had adopted the same conical helmet with the nasal. Their shields were still round but slightly smaller than the ones my men who fought on foot used. They would be used as a screen and as scouts. When our two main armies arrived, I wanted it to be a complete surprise.

It was high summer when we left. The days were long and they were warm. The land through which we travelled was rich farmland with many rivers and streams. We did not need wagons to carry our supplies. We would take what we needed from the Franks. By the end of the first day of marching, we were beyond the last Viking farm. Those who lived in the village of Héroult fled when my horsemen approached. The speed of our advance meant that they fled without their animals. We ate well that night. We ransacked the church.

We found our first opposition the next day. De Forgis was an old town. The Romans had used it for there was iron nearby and the town was renowned for its metalworking. It had a wall and a tower. It also had men who were mailed and had good helmets. They were not a large number but they did not flee. They were willing to fight for their land. I sent Erik to blockade the road into the town. They were effectively trapped within its walls. Olaf and Sven had sent me a message to tell me that they were twenty-five miles from Anmyen. The Franks were contesting the river at Sennarpont.

I did not want to waste time building siege machines. The wooden walls could be reduced by axes. We had a drekar crew of Danes. Many of them had the two-handed axe. Along with Petr Jorgensen's archers, I believed they would gain us entry. We still had food we had taken from Héroult. My horsemen had also captured horses and cattle. As we did not need to eat them I had them sent back to Rouen. We prepared for our attack. We had enough leaders for me to have an attack on five different points around the walls. That would spread the defenders out. I had Gurt the Dane and his men with me. With my drekar crew and Petr's archers, we were the largest of the warbands and so we took the main gate. It was wooden and had two wooden towers.

Petr and his archers advanced and sent a hail of arrows at the towers and the gatehouse. I am not sure if they hit many of the defenders but they kept their heads down and allowed Gurt and his Danes to race towards the gate. I led the rest of my men behind raised shields. The crack of axes on wood soon filled the air. I saw defenders attempt to throw rocks. Petr's archers ended that threat. All around the walls my other men, Finnbjǫrn, Ragnar, Bergil Fast Blade, were all attacking the wooden walls of De Forgis. It would be a matter of time before we broke through and we had plenty of that. We had begun the attack at dawn. It would be many hours until darkness fell. My horsemen had prevented the men of De Forgis from sending for help. We did not need to risk our men.

"Shield wall. Wedge formation."

Gurt and his men would just break through the gate. Then it would be up to me and my men to exploit the breach. He and his men attacked the gate with a determination I admired. Perhaps they were trying to show me that he and his Danes were made of sterner stuff than Guthrum. There was a crack and a crash. Gurt raised his axe. The gate was broken. The Franks would have braced it with wood but that would not stop us.

I raised my spear and began the chant as we ran towards the gate.

Clan of Rouen
Warriors strong
Clan of Rouen
Our reach is long
Clan of Rouen
Fight as one
Clan of Rouen
Death will come
Death will come

I held my shield before me. Bjorn and Audun had their shields in my back. I hit the gate and heard a loud crack as the wood bracing it shattered and the gates burst open. One disadvantage of such long legs was a tendency to overbalance. As I began to go I felt Bjorn grab the scabbard of my sword to stabilize me. It was good that he did for a Frank lunged at me with his spear. I barely managed to block it with my shield. The wedge behind rammed me bodily into him and he overbalanced and fell. I trampled over him and Einar, in the third row, skewered him.

The charge of the brave Frank had allowed other Franks to form their own shield wall. I saw that it was just two men deep. "Keep going. We charge." I lowered my spear and Bjorn and Audun did the same. There were many men facing us but the three of us would hit the centre. We would be fighting two men with two more behind. Our seal skin boots pounded on the cobbled road surface. I tried to imagine what the Franks would see. There was a wall of Vikings led by a giant. The ones on the flanks might feel secure but the ones we would strike knew that they would have to take the impact of many times our number. Even as we ran I saw Bergil Fast Blade and his men clamber over the walls. Soon we would outnumber the defenders. My long arms meant that my spear struck the Frank before his spear could reach me. I was able to stab down over his shield for Bjorn and Audun had spears at his eye level. My spear struck his chest. He was dying when his spear hit my shield and the impact sent the spear upwards and back towards the Frank who was behind him. The Norns were spinning! The spear clanged off the Frank's helmet and my shield hit him in the face. Audun speared him and we were through!

"Break wedge!"

This was a manoeuvre we had practised. Bjorn and I went right. Audun and Snorri went left. We peeled around and Bjorn and I stabbed two Franks through their mail before they had the chance to turn. Bergil Fast Blade led his men from the walls to fall upon the flanks of these mailed Franks. Everyone died before I could even shout for them to stop. I turned and looked at the tower. Would they defend it? I saw a lord on the top. He was leaning over and looking at his dead men.

I took off my helmet and shouted, "Yield or we will burn you alive!"

I believe that they had expected their forty men to hold us. They had good mail and fine swords and spears. We had had good fortune but the Franks did not see that. They just saw a shattered gate and dead warriors. Their leader took off his helmet and shouted, "We yield!"

Clodion was an old warrior. We learned that his son had been the one I had slain when I had burst through the gate. That had destroyed his will to fight. "What will happen to us Viking?"

"I am the Lord of Rouen. You can continue to rule here but there will be a tithe of a tenth of all that you produce."

"Crops, animals?"

I smiled, "And the iron that you make. If you do that then you may keep your arms. Your women and children will not be enslaved and you will not be raided by Vikings."

"King Charles may not be happy about that."

"King Charles is many miles from here. Whom do you fear most Lord Clodion, me or Charles the Bald?"

The answer was clear, from his face. "You lord!"

Gurt and his Danes were surprised by my clemency but we had not lost many men and I saw an advantage in having somewhere close which would provide us with a regular supply of mail and weapons. After sending a message to Olaf and Sven we enjoyed the hospitality of a town relieved that it was not burned and its men slaughtered. After sending back our wounded with the first of our tribute we left to head north. We were close now. Anmyen was less than forty miles away. We were halted once more. This time it was at Poix-de-Picardie. It was slightly smaller than De Forgis had been. This time it was their horsemen who caused the delay. They charged Erik and his horsemen as my men approached the town. There was a stone tower and Erik's men had been spied when some distance away. It allowed the townsfolk to flee towards Anmyen. It was a serious setback. They would know we were coming. The Frankish horsemen all died but they had bought their folk the time to flee.

When we reached the town, my men ransacked it. We stripped the church and found all the treasure which they had hidden. They had escaped with their lives but little else. By a stroke of good fortune, or perhaps the Norns' web, Olaf and Sven were just eight miles away and I sent for them. We combined our men and planned the last part of this raid. We had lost horsemen and my men took their deaths out on the town. Before we left for Anmyen they destroyed the church and burned the houses. As we headed northeast a towering black cloud was a warning for the Franks that a Viking army was coming.

The river which flowed through the city was an important one. It had been raided by Vikings before, almost thirty years earlier but the ships had come up the river. The bridge was heavily defended. They did not need walls for the river barred an enemy's approach. They had two towers guarding the bridge which had been built by the Romans. The bridge, however, was to the north. The Frisians had been a bigger threat. As a result of the first Viking raid, they had thrown a wall up around the most valuable of their buildings, the Cathedral and the hall of the lord. The rest of the town was open.

As we neared the town we knew that word of our approach had spread. We passed empty farms and houses. Every animal had been taken. They would all be north of the river. The houses which lay outside the wall were also abandoned. I sensed frustration amongst my men as they searched them and found almost nothing there. I was not, as they were, unhappy. I had a plan. We camped in their town. My leaders and I occupied a house that had belonged to a merchant. It had a fine table and chairs. We still had food from De Forgis and we ate well.

"Olaf Two Teeth, you are a sailor. You know the weather and the wind. From what direction will the wind blow tomorrow?"

"You would have me as a galdramenn?"

"Humour me."

"It is shifting but I would say that it will be from the south and the west. But how does that help us? We are not sailing there. We march!"

"You say it is shifting then the Allfather is aiding us." I stood and tapped the wall of the house. It was made of the same material as the other houses in the town. It was lath. There were wooden beams and the roof was made of straw. "They have obligingly emptied their houses for us. We set fire to them. The wind will take the flames towards their wooden wall. It will burn. Erik, you and your men can ford the river tomorrow at dawn and get close to their bridge. Capture as many of their animals and their goods as you can. When the fire begins to burn their walls then they will flee."

Sven Blue Cheek began to laugh, "The Franks would be as well to bow the knee to you now Göngu-Hrólfr Rognvaldson for they have none who can match your mind. We let the wind fight our battle for us."

I nodded, "I am mindful that Sámr wishes us to take on the Bretons. We all know that they are a more serious foe than the Franks. Let us finish this quickly

Every home was made into a potential pyre. The wood in each house was piled together by the north wall. Kindling was placed beneath it. Oil was poured upon the kindling and then, as I had the horn sounded fifty warriors all took a burning brand into their designated house and set it alight. The effect was spectacular. It was as though a wall of flame all erupted at once. The wind quickly took it and it spread to the next houses. Our fifty fires became a hundred and then it reached the walls. They had a river but there was no way that they could extinguish the flames. The pall of smoke was so thick that we could see nothing. It was evening before the flames died down and the smoke disappeared. There was no wall any longer. There was a just blackened line in the earth where it had stood. The defenders had gone. We were able to march into the city during the hours of darkness. The ground was still warm. Blackened bodies littered the city but none remained alive. The candles and holy books from the cathedral were all burned but the metal was there to be reclaimed. We were able to salvage the twisted objects. As we moved north to the gate and the river we found that some of those fleeing had been trampled to death by others trying to escape the inferno. The bridge was unguarded. On the other side, Erik and his men guarded the valuables the people had tried to take. The sight of my horsemen had helped them make their choice. Valuables or their lives? Most had chosen their lives. The ones who had chosen treasure lay dead.

When we headed back, two days later, we took wagonloads of goods and many animals. We had lost a handful of men and taken five towns. At least one town served us and the Franks had done nothing. I silently thanked the spirits for I knew that they had intervened with the Allfather. Now we could turn our attention to the Bretons and when the Haugr and Ċiriċeburh were Viking once more then I would have done what my grandfather wanted.

It was some months after this that we heard of the death of Charles the Bald. The King of the Franks was now the Emperor, Charles the Fat. Would that bring a change to our fortunes?

Part Three

The Breton Threat

Chapter 9

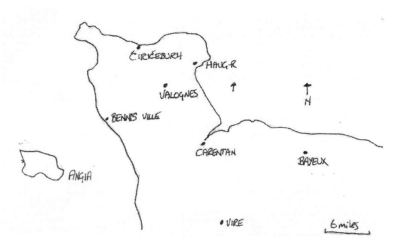

Word spread of our raid and drew more warriors to our land. The raid on Frisia had not brought as much treasure as the Danes had hoped. Warriors liked success and I had shown that I knew how to win. Those who had raided with us returned to Lundenwic and Bruggas with coins to spend and treasure to sell. With the new land to the north of Rouen, the new warriors had farms they could take. The displaced Franks moved further east. Already our frontier had spread further south. Despite Sámr's fears, the Bretons had not retaliated after our last raid. From what we had learned the raids along the Liger had made the Bretons look south

121

and not north. While my wife and her priest were not happy about us making war on Franks she was happy about the income it generated. Rather than slaves we now employed servants. Our newest daughter, Isabelle had her own wet nurse. We had more wall hangings. Already we had craftsmen who sought to work in Rouen for they knew they could sell their wares easily. Poppa's choice of furnishings was reflected in the other ladies who were married to my lords. Our town grew. The new animals improved the bloodlines of both horses and cattle. Life was good. The only cloud was the lack of a son.

I visited with Sámr. He was less anxious about attacks from the Bretons. We sat in his new tower which looked south. "If your grandfather was alive, Göngu-Hrólfr Rognvaldson, he would have known where my men ought to have scouted. We discovered a number of strongly defended towns. Coutances and Valognes look to be the hard places to take. That was as far as we went."

I nodded, "The Haugr was well built but my brother allowed it to fall into disrepair. The hard place to take will be Ćiriċeburh. That one may need our ships and our horsemen." I finished the beaker of wine he had offered me. "I wish to wait until the new grass for us to attack the Bretons. We have horses and we have ships. What we need is to be confident about the men we use. My grandfather was wary of Danes. They let him down more than once. I would have the winter to see the mettle of these men."

"Lord, the Bretons are quiet. We can leave them for a while. I confess that I worried over nothing. I am sorry."

"You have a son now and that means your world changes. Do not relax your vigilance. Send for me at the slightest hint of danger."

It was not danger which came our way but an emissary from the King of Frankia. We were approaching Christmas. My warriors did not celebrate the birth of the White Christ but our women and our children did. We celebrated the winter solstice. However, we accommodated our families. They went to church and we drank! It worked out well for all. Seven days after the shortest day our sentries reported the arrival of a ship downstream. It was not a warship but contained a mission from Paris. There were four lords and four priests. They risked my wrath for they had not asked permission to land but Poppa pleaded with me to hear them, "Husband, it is Christmas! This is a time of peace. For once behave like a civilised man and not a pagan!"

122

Ignoring the insult, I acceded to her request. If I did not like the message I would take the ship and have the emissaries put to death. The Archbishop was the most senior figure. As they entered my hall I wondered at that. Were they relying on my wife's faith to ensure the safety of such an important cleric? The Count of Reims was the most senior warrior. They were emissaries but the face of the Count of Reims told me his opinion of me quite clearly. He despised me and feared me at the same time. He had not come here of his own volition. Although his land lay over a hundred miles away, our raid on Anmyen had clearly unsettled the Franks or why else would he be here?

I deliberately sat on my chair. As it had to accommodate me it was bigger than any other. It felt like a throne and while I did not wear a crown it made men who were not Viking feel as though they ought to bow. I spoke and I did so with a smile, "What brings such eminent men to my humble home?"

The Archbishop spoke and he also did so with a smile, "This is a fine home and I can see that the Lady Poppa has made it palatial."

"It suits us. And what brings you here for I have much to occupy me?"

I think the Count of Reims was going to speak but a subtly raised finger silenced him. "Know you that the Dane formerly known as Guthrum has now been baptised and taken the name King Athelstan?"

"I had heard."

"His Majesty, the Emperor asks you to also become a Christian and leave your pagan beliefs behind. It would make you more acceptable as lord of this land and if you did so then he would consider allowing you to continue as Count of Rouen."

I nodded, as though I was weighing his words. "The fact is, Archbishop, that you cannot shift me from Rouen. If you could have done then you would have tried already. Mantes and Anmyen are both destroyed. You now fear that I will do the same to Paris." I saw in their eyes that I had hit the mark.

The Count of Reims could not remain silent, "Paris is a stronger city. You could not take it with a hundred ships!"

"I agree!" I had stunned them as I had intended. "But what if I had two hundred, three hundred, who knows, perhaps four hundred? What then Count?"

I saw the fear on all their faces. The Archbishop leaned forward, "I must press you for an answer. Will you become a Christian?"

"I will not give up my religion for this worship of a weak god who turns the other cheek."

"Your wife is a Christian."

"So?"

They had no more arguments and I thought that they would end their embassy and leave. They did not. They looked at each other. The Count of Reims was not enamoured of the visit. I could see it in his face and his body. His hands clenched and unclenched.

"Then will you agree not to raid Paris?"

That was the real reason for their visit. They had heard that I had a raid planned. Had I agreed to become a Christian then they would have had some sort of leverage over me. This was the real purpose. How far would I be able to push them?

"I will not make that promise. Unlike you Christians when I give my word I keep it. If that is your purpose in coming here then you have wasted your time and it is a long hard row back to Paris."

"What if we were to pay you coin not to attack us?"

"My men are warriors. It is what they do. They need to fight. It is in their blood."

I saw the light in the Count of Reims' eyes as he suddenly said, "Then fight the Bretons."

I nodded as though I was considering that which we had already planned. "And you would pay me to raid the Bretons?"

"And not to attack Paris."

I drank some wine, "This year."

The Archbishop said, "This year? But…"

"I either take Paris next year or you pay me to fight another enemy. You have many, I believe."

I saw the Count and the Archbishop exchange a look. They had anticipated my answer but not my price. The Archbishop nodded. "We have a chest of gold." He hesitated, "If you were a Christian then I would ask you to swear on a Bible."

"Then it is lucky for you that I am Göngu-Hrólfr Rognvaldson. When I give my word then you know it will not be broken. I will not attack Paris for one year. Is that good enough for you?"

They nodded and the Count of Reims said, "It will have to be."

The chest of gold was a surprise and all the more welcome for that. I had planned on fighting the Bretons and now I had a good reason to do so, gold. To assuage my wife's disappointment at my rejection of the

Archbishop's offer I gave her a quarter of the coins to spend as she saw fit. Her priest persuaded her to spend it on his church.

When I visited with my lords, escorted this time by my horsemen, I told them of the arrangement. It amused all of them. Sven could not stop chuckling, "We have not enough ships yet anyway. You have deceived the Franks and made money out of doing so."

"And more ships arrive each day. I am sending them to Caen. When we attack the Bretons, we will wage two wars, one by sea and one by land. We blockade the Haugr and Ćiriĉeburh. With the bulk of our men marching from the south, we will cut off the Cotentin. I do not expect it to be easy but we have a year to do so. Then the Franks will either pay us more coin or we will attack Paris." In my heart, I wanted to attack Paris sooner rather than later. Only then could the curse be lifted and Ylva's spell would begin to work. I would have a son.

We gathered at Bayeux while Olaf and Sven Blue Cheek took our small fleet around the coast to blockade their harbours. The Bretons did not have many warships and the ones they had were inferior to ours. We could outsail and outfight them. I was confident that they would have neither trade nor fish. My mother's people had been fishermen but they had left the troubled Cotentin during the battles with the Bretons. I knew not where they had gone. I doubted that I would even recognise them. It had been almost thirty years since I had left the Haugr to sail with my father and fight with the Danes in Lundenwic. It was more than that since I had fought in the land my grandfather had conquered. He had died too soon. I needed his advice.

Sámr had not been happy about his decision not to follow me to Anmyen. To make up for it he had scouted out the lands thoroughly. I remembered some of the towns. He had made a map and that helped me to understand the location of the harder targets. My grandfather and I had travelled the land visiting Folki and Rurik in their strongholds. We had stayed in Benni's Ville. I knew where the strongholds were but Sámr knew which ones would be hard to take.

The night before we left Bayeux he took out his map to show us the land and the route he suggested we take. "Carentan and Valognes both have lords and they have maintained their ditches. Carentan has a stone tower but the walls are made of wood. The walls of Valognes have not been maintained. They are made of stone and topped with wood but the mortar has crumbled in places. Those two places have horsemen and mailed warriors. The rest do not."

"Then first we take Carentan. It is the gateway to the Cotentin."

Sámr smiled, "I know I need not tell you, lord, but the land thereabouts is boggy and damp. Siege engines, even if we had them, would be bogged down."

I shook my head. "We do not waste time building machines. Our war against the Franks showed me how we fight. Erik and his riders cut off the town. We approach during the night and attack the walls under cover of darkness. Once we have Carentan then we take Benni's Ville, and the Haugr and Bárekr's Haven for they do not have good defences."

Bergil Fast Blade said, "Not Valognes?"

"Sámr said that it still had stone walls. Even if the mortar is crumbling they would still resist our attacks. We surround and isolate it. When we take Benni's Ville in the west and the Haugr and Bárekr's Haven in the east the people who live there will flee. There are two strongholds open to them. Valognes and Ċiriċeburh. Once they are filled with hungry mouths we sit and wait for them to surrender."

"And if the Breton King sends an army to relieve them?"

"That is where our brothers in arms have aided us, Ragnar the Resolute. There is a Viking fleet along the Liger. His eye is there. If he does send an army then it will not be a large one. Besides, I think he may regard this as just another raid. When we fought King Louis we did not stay."

Finnbjǫrn nodded, "And this time we stay?"

I waved an arm at the four Danes who had recently joined us. "We have warriors who seek land and seek homes, Ċiriċeburh, Benni's Ville, the Haugr and Bárekr's Haven are all good places to berth a drekar. My grandfather chose the land for a reason." They nodded. "Saxbjǫrn the Silent, you and Nefgeirr have your drekar in Caen. I would have you take your ships and sail up the river to Carentan. If you leave now then you will arrive at the river during the night and we will be there."

"You wish us to attack?"

I shook my head, "I wish you to stop the Bretons from escaping by sea. Folki improved the channel there. They may have ships capable of taking men and treasure from the town. When we have taken it then your crew can occupy the town and drive the Bretons who live thereabouts towards Valognes."

My plan was a simple one. We were hunting game and the game was human. We hunted the larger game and drove the smaller into a net. The net would be Valognes.

We had thirty miles to walk and the road was a good surface. We did not rush for Erik and his men were already galloping around the town using the roads to the west. Saxbjǫrn the Silent and Nefgeirr would be rowing along the coast later in the morning. Timing was all. Everyone knew that we had to arrive after dark. We could not hide our numbers. I led fewer men than when I had attacked Anmyen but the targets I had chosen were not as strong. As an incentive for my captains, I had shared out the Frankish gold. There would be more when we captured the Cotentin but the coins in their purses was an added inducement.

I found myself recognising landmarks as we headed west. I had ridden this land with my grandfather. He knew it well. I had thought I had forgotten it but the memories came flooding back. With the memories came the ghosts of warriors long dead: Folki, Erik Green Eye, Rurik One Ear, Harold Fast Sailing, Alain of Auxerre. It was as though their spirits were still in this land. We had conquered it briefly and then lost it. When I won it back I would not lose it so easily. Lords like Saxbjǫrn the Silent, Nefgeirr, Bergil and Finnbjǫrn, would hold on to what they had. My father and grandfather had made the mistake of being complacent. When this was mine I would visit on a regular basis and be ever watchful. I knew how to play games with Kings. I was not in awe of King Charles or King Alan. I had slain one King. If I had to then I would kill more.

Sámr's scouts had found somewhere we could wait for darkness. It was hidden from the Carentan walls. There we ate and prepared for the attack. The scouts had ensured that the farmers who lived close by and had tried to flee to Carentan had not made the walls. Their bodies lay along the road. Those in Carentan might wonder why no one had come north through their town for half a day but they could not know the reason. A river and a patch of boggy ground lay between us and the walls. Perhaps that was a reason they felt secure. As soon as the darkness was complete we forded the river and made our way across the ground. At best it was spongy and at worst, in a few places, it threatened to suck off our seal skin boots. Our scouts had done a good job and they took us on the driest paths. We stopped two hundred paces from the walls.

The Bretons had added a couple of wooden towers. At the corners and in the towers, they had brands burning. They helped us to see the sentries. There were four on the walls closest to us. I had archers who would use the light from the burning brands to eliminate that threat. Sámr

127

had told us that the walls were my height. The ditch was far enough away from the walls to allow us to stand there and boost men over the walls.

I raised Hrolf's Vengeance and my archers moved forward. As they passed through us the rest followed. I was attacking a gate and one wall. That way we had a better chance of complete surprise. Erik was watching the north gate. It was impossible to avoid noise for at least two of the sentries who died did so noisily but we ran quickly towards the walls. I might not have needed a boost but Bjorn and Audun held a shield for me to step on and they raised me up. They did not have to lift me far and I stepped over the wall and swung my own shield around. Inside the town, I heard the sounds of alarm as warriors were woken. They would either have to take the time to don mail or rush out and face us without.

I ran down the fighting platform. There had been a couple of sentries down by the gate and they had climbed the ladder to the walkway. I did not stop. Holding my shield before me I ran at them. Both were knocked to the cobbled stone of the road beneath. I heard the crack of a skull and the scream of a man who had his leg broken. I slid down the ladder and, sheathing my sword I lifted the bar on the gate. When I opened it Finnbjorn led his men through the gate. I put my shield around my back and drew a seax and Hrolf's Vengeance. Town fighting did not need Longsword. I needed quick hands and two blades.

I followed Finnbjorn's men as they raced through the town. As men emerged sleepily from houses they were cut down. Panic ensued. Everyone ran for the north gate. I saw Bretons trampled by their own people. The warriors did not do as the men of De Forgis and Anmyen had done. They fought but it was to save themselves and not their people. It was hard to make progress. I would not strike women and children and they were mixed up amongst the warriors. There was little point in moving. Erik Gillesson would kill the warriors.

"Hold! Search the buildings. Slay any warriors you may find. Sámr Oakheart, take your men along the fighting platform and clear it."

I took off my helmet and sheathed my seax and sword. This was not what I had expected. We had a victory but I was dissatisfied. We were warriors and we wanted to fight warriors. I saw the trampled bodies of a young mother and her baby just twenty paces from me. That was not our doing. It was the Breton warriors who had behaved without honour. Once I was able I walked through the town. It had been totally abandoned. Nothing had been taken for they were so afraid of us. When I reached the north gate, I saw the dead warriors slain by my horsemen. They were dispatching the Breton wounded.

Erik saw me and walked over, "We let the women, children and the old go. They headed north. I was right to do so was I not?"

I nodded, "They trampled and hurt some of their own people when they tried to flee. Have your men come inside the walls. We will eat and then rest. There is no hurry now."

"Those who escaped will spread the word that Vikings are loose."

"And that is what I want. They will panic. Remember that they had the men of my brother fighting for them. Men like Ailmær the Cruel had no honour. They think we are worse than we really are. That will work in our favour. The fear will fuel panic when next we approach one of their strongholds. We are planting an enemy in the heart of every Breton town and village. I will divide the men into two columns on the morrow. One half will go to Benni's Ville and the other to the Haugr. Neither have the defences that Carentan had."

By the time dawn broke, we had food ready. The Bretons had obligingly put their bread into the ovens to bake and some of my men found it before it burned. We ate hot wheat bread washed down with cider. Saxbjǫrn and Nefgeirr arrived with their men when they saw that we had taken it.

"We will take the horses. It means we can mount more men. I leave you two to divide the treasure. Each crew gets an equal share."

"You are generous, lord."

"I reward those who fight for me. I expect this to be a stronghold for the Bretons may well try to take it back."

Saxbjǫrn nodded, "We can improve the channel of the river even more. We should be able to tie up by the walls. To take it they will have to turn the land red."

Nefgeirr said, "And I have learned much about defence having improved Évreux. I will help my brother."

I divided my men in two. Erik led half the horsemen and his son, Bagsecg led the other. Sámr went with Bagsecg to Benni's Ville. I led the rest towards the Haugr. I realised that I was taking the one which held the most danger but I knew it. I had sailed, along with my grandfather, to inspect it when we had returned from Norway. I knew that they had fortified the church my grandmother had used. On a spit of land protected on three sides by the sea, it would be hard to take. However, Sven Blue Cheek was blockading it and I hoped that my sudden arrival might cause the defenders to surrender. They were a mixture of those Vikings who had followed my brother and Bretons. They would be a dangerous combination. We had less than eighteen miles to travel and the land was flat. To Erik, it was a poignant ride. His father's horse farm lay just a few miles south of the Haugr. It now lay abandoned. I saw my leader of horsemen ride up to the walls and peer at the farmhouse where he had been born.

When we had passed Gilles' old farm we saw the masts of three drekar. Two would be ours, Sven's and Halfi Axe Tongue. The third would belong to the men who lived in the fortified church. Even as we headed north I saw people flocking to the spit of land. Some still lived in my grandfather's old home but the tower which had defended it had fallen in a storm. The more people crammed inside the fortified church the better for they would only have the fish that they could catch for food. The Vikings could survive on such fare but not the Bretons.

When we reached the stronghold, I saw that the enemy drekar was tied up at the jetty. Our ships could not get closer without risking an attack from the walls of the defences. Harold fast Sailing had helped to make the entrance difficult to stop us from being attacked. I had no intention of risking my drekar. I had impressed upon Sven that he was there to blockade and not to attack. Time was on our side.

"Erik, ride north to Bárekr's Haven and see if it is defended. Return here and we will have a camp ready."

"Aye lord."

Since my grandfather had first built the Haugr the coast had changed. When he had lived there the sea had been a hundred paces from the walls. Now it lay just fifty paces away. The storm had scoured away a large part of the beach. I saw that another spit was growing further south. My grandfather's hall still stood on the rock. The sea would not take that away but the tower which had been built by Father Michael had tumbled down. Most of the stones had been taken to build the new defences by the church.

I pointed to the hall, "We will camp up there. Finnbjǫrn and Leif, come with me and we will speak with the defenders."

I put my shield over my back and hung my helmet from my sword. It was a sign that we came in peace. There were treacherous men and I would not get close enough to be taken. We walked along the causeway which had been built. Some of the sand which had washed from the beach had been blown onto it and the Bretons had added more stones to make it sturdier. Over time it would grow. What had been an island when my grandfather had come would soon be attached to the land. Ailmær the Cruel had been the lord there but he was now dead. I had slain him. He had been a clever man who had made this church a stronghold and I saw that at the end of the spit was a stone gatehouse with two small towers. An attack would be suicidal. We stopped two hundred and fifty paces from the gate. Beyond the church, I saw the masts of my two drekar. They were just out of bow range but I knew that if there was danger then Sven would bring them closer and unleash his own arrow storm.

"I am Lord Göngu-Hrólfr Rognvaldson. You know my name. Carentan is now mine. I would have my grandfather's home returned to me too. You have two choices: board your drekar and leave this land or stay and fight for it." I waved a hand behind me. "I have real warriors behind me who will slaughter every warrior we find if you fight."

Silence greeted my words. I did not mind. They were discussing what to do. They were weighing up their chances. Two drekar crews lay to their seaward side. They had counted our men as they had marched into the Haugr and they knew that we outnumbered them.

A voice shouted, eventually, "I am the lord of this sea, Robert of Rennes, how do we know you will keep your word?"

"I am Lord Göngu-Hrólfr Rognvaldson and I am never foresworn."

Silence.

"We have people here who took shelter with us. We do not want them!"

"Women and children can go to Valognes. I have not taken that yet or any who wish can submit to my authority for I will rule this Land of the Horse. It comes back to my family."

"How long do we have?"

"If you are here by morning then you die and we burn your drekar."

They must have realised that with just three of us we were not going to take their stronghold and the voice shouted, "Those who wish to travel to Valognes and those who wish to submit are coming out now."

We waited and a priest led out families who huddled together. "If you wish to submit then go to the Haugr. We will feed you. For the rest, the road to Valognes is open.... For now. We will be coming to take back old Rurik One Ear's town."

The priest made the sign of the cross and then they headed down the causeway. I turned to Leif, "Go and hail Sven Blue Cheek, tell him what we have agreed."

As we walked back Finnbjǫrn said, "Where will they go?"

"They are allies of the Bretons. They will sail around the coast and go to Nantes. If King Alan did not know already that we were here to retake our land he knows it now."

"Was it not Breton land? I thought it was the Breton Kingdom."

I laughed, "The Breton King has given himself that title. I do not think the Emperor would accord him the title King. This was Frankia land. It was raided by the Bretons and the Franks who were here welcomed my grandfather for he protected them from the Bretons. Why do you think they fled so quickly when we came? They have no roots here. I was born in this land and then it was Viking."

When Erik came back it was with the news that the only ones at Bárekr's Haven were those of Bárekr's family who had never left. It was now in our hands. Leif returned to tell us that he had passed on the message. Sven and Halfi would join Olaf at Ćiriċeburh when he followed the drekar from the anchorage. The two ships following him would be intimidating.

While my men began the food, I walked into the hall. It felt as though it was filled with ghosts. I could see my grandmother's touch all over it. Whoever had lived here had not changed anything. There was the wall hanging she had made with my aunts. It was faded but it still made me swell with pride. It was a drekar with Hrolf the Horseman at the prow. She had subtly used the cross on my grandfather's cloak as a symbol of the White Christ. I had often asked my grandfather why he had chosen that design for his horsemen. He told me that was the choice of Alain of Auxerre. *Wyrd*. I went up the stairs to the chamber my grandfather and grandmother had shared. Next to it was a smaller room. When I had lived here with my grandfather, learning to be a horseman, that had been my room. Even when I had lived there I had outgrown it. The bed was still the one my grandfather had made. I went to the mattress. It was the one my grandmother had stuffed. There were goose and duck feathers mixed with owl.

"Lord, the food is ready."

"I am coming."

As I descended, Ragnar the Resolute said, "The drekar has left. I sent men to occupy the church. Sven followed the drekar."

"Good."

My grandfather's hall had never been a large one but now, with my leaders and captains inside it seemed tiny. I found my head brushing the low ceiling. When I had been growing up it had seemed huge. I was quiet while the others were full of three relatively quick and easy victories. Finnbjǫrn turned to me, "Do you think Sámr will have such an easy time of it, lord?"

"Perhaps. It is best not to anticipate what the Norns will do. I am grateful that we managed to take this without bloodshed." I noticed that Erik was quiet too. "Do not forget, Finnbjǫrn, that Erik and I have many friends who died in this land. When my brother turned traitor, it was our people who paid the price. The easy time you speak of came at a cost."

Ragnar nodded, "And I can see why you wanted this land back. It has great potential. When we marched north I saw many abandoned farms. This is a rich land but the Bretons have not used it as they should."

Erik said, "One of them belonged to my father. With the Lord's permission, I will return here." I cocked an eye, "My son is not yet ready to be a lord but I have many men who can advise him until he grows. He can rule Montfort for you. Besides, you will need lords here. This can be a stronghold once more."

Finnbjǫrn smiled, "Are you reading my mind, horseman? I would like to be lord here if Lord Göngu-Hrólfr Rognvaldson allows it."

"This Haugr is precious to me, Finnbjǫrn Stormbringer. I am not saying that I would live here but if I allow you to be lord then you would be protecting my most valuable possession."

"And I would treat it as though it was a son to me, lord."

"Then you are Lord of the Haugr."

Ragnar the Resolute nodded, although he looked a little disappointed, "And tomorrow?"

"Tomorrow we send riders to Benni's Ville to see if Sámr has taken it. If not then we join him. If he has we march to Ċiriċeburh. When we take that we can use every warrior we have to capture Valognes and then this land will be ours."

Erik knew the Bretons as well as any. I could see that he was not as optimistic as we appeared to be, "I still cannot believe that King Alan will sit idly by and watch us take his strongholds one by one."

"You are right to be cautious, Erik Gillesson but look at it from the viewpoint of King Alan. When would he discover what had happened at Carentan?" He looked blankly at me. "The ones we defeated fled to Valognes. They would have sent a messenger to the King. He might be receiving it now. What would that tell him? We have taken a town. When Robert of Rennes reaches An Oriant then a rider will be sent to Rennes and another to Nantes. Nantes is a two-day ride from An Orient. The King will not know for a couple of days that we have taken this coast. When he marches, it will take him five days. I am not saying he will not come but we have up to seven days to capture as much of this land as we can."

That night, as I lay in my grandfather's bed, I found sleep hard to come. It was a number of things that prevented a much-needed rest not least the fact that we would be stretched thin until we had taken Ċiriċeburh. That had to be our priority. Valognes was stuck in the middle of a web of Vikings. We had learned from the Norns and we had spun our own web and it was a web of steel.

Eventually, I fell asleep and I dreamed.

My grandfather was riding a white horse. In his hand he held his sword and he was leading my horsemen. I had no horse and I ran to keep up with him. A mist rose from the ground. Gradually I lost sight of him and I was floundering in a fog. I looked down and I was on the deck of my drekar. When the fog lifted I was in the river and behind me were hundreds of ships. It seemed as though every Viking was following me. I heard a voice and when I turned it was my grandfather. He was behind me, "Beware the Danes and beware the Count." He pointed ahead and I looked at the Franks lining the walls of Paris." Paris is not the prize the land you rule is. Take what you can and you will have a son." As I turned to speak to him he had gone and in his place was a mewling infant. It was a naked boy and even as I picked him up he turned into Longsword. I looked for my grandfather and my son. They were gone and the mist crept up towards my head. I was engulfed in mist. When it cleared I was in a lush valley and my men were chanting my name, over and over.

"Lord Göngu-Hrólfr Rognvaldson!"

I opened my eyes and Bjorn stood there, "I am sorry to disturb you lord but a rider arrived before dawn. Sámr and Bagsecg have taken Benni's Ville. He has left men to guard it and marches north to meet with us."

The Allfather has smiled on us. We had managed to do in four days what I had thought might take seven. If we could take Ċiriċeburh as quickly then we had a chance.

I summoned Erik, "Take your horsemen and watch Valognes. Stop the warriors from leaving. If I do not need them then I will send your son and the rest of the horsemen to help you. Let any, save warriors, into the town. There will be many people seeking refuge within its walls. The more they have to feed the quicker will the siege end."

"Aye lord. I am sorry that I was so pessimistic last night. It was the sight of my father's farm that did it."

"I know. Erik. and I felt the same when I saw the Haugr. It is good that you will be lord there. Your father's spirit will watch over you and I know that you will care for the land. These new lords are brave warriors but I have not yet seen into their hearts. Will they protect the land as well as the people? You and I both know how one bad heart can cause disaster."

"I believe they will but only time will tell."

Finnbjǫrn left just twelve men to guard his new land. The refuge by the church remained undamaged and his men could hold out there for a few days even if they were attacked and that seemed unlikely. We would need as many men as we could get. We headed north and west for Ċiriċeburh. This was familiar land but only to me. Erik knew it but he was heading for Valognes. I had some scouts ahead. They were not to find our way, I knew that they were there to give us warning of an enemy. We joined the main road north just five miles south of Ċiriċeburh and we had not been on it for long when my scouts ran back towards us.

"Lord Göngu-Hrólfr Rognvaldson there are twenty horsemen coming down the road."

I knew horses. "They will be upon us before we know it. Shield wall. Petr Jorgensen, hide your archers in the flanks. Let none live!" I swung my shield around as my men spread out on either side of me. We would be presenting a wall of spears three men deep and fifty men wide.

The horsemen turned the bend and spied us there just two hundred paces from them. They made the fatal error of reining in and discussing what they should do. Petr shouted, "Release!" and forty arrows fell from the sky. His archers kept releasing as fast as they could. Eight of the horsemen decided to try to force their way through and two turned to head back to the port. The two heading for the port fell with arrows in their backs.

I held Longsword before me and my men presented their spears. The Bretons had panicked. A horse will not ride at a man with a spear. They are not stupid creatures. They all stopped when they neared the spears. Three of them stopped so sharply that their riders were thrown onto spears and impaled. I shouted, "Charge!" and we ran at the stationary horsemen. Longsword hacked so deep into the side of one that I struck his spine. All of them died.

We took their horses and gave them to our scouts. Ragnar asked, "What do you think they were doing?"

"I think they saw their drekar heading for An Oriant and discovered that we had more drekar. The lord there will have realised that he had more to contend with than a couple of drekar. He was sending for help."

The gates of the port were barred but I saw that they were just wooden. There were no metal studs. The walls were topped with wood and the stones neglected. When Bertrand had ruled there, he had had walls with stone and wood. Where had all the stone gone? The walls were, however, manned. We would have to fight. The fact that they were wooden walls helped.

"Make a camp and dig a ditch!"

We had the last port on the Cotentin within our grasp. What had seemed unlikely less than three months earlier, now seemed possible. The Norns had woven well.

Chapter 10

We had learned how to besiege a town. The men with axes went to cut the stakes which would be planted behind the ditch my men dug. The whole purpose of the ditch and the stakes was to stop them from attacking us. They did not know it but this would be their best chance to defeat us. Until Sámr and the rest of my men arrived we would not have enough numbers to attack. Once we did attack then Olaf and my drekar crews would land and attack the sea gate. They would capture any ships in the port and set fire to the empty ones. I took off my helmet, shield and Longsword. The enemy showed no signs of trying to shift us. There would be no fighting this night. As the afternoon became evening so the camp took shape. The ditch and stakes were soon completed and fires were lit to cook the food. We had taken animals which had been deserted and we cooked them. There would be time to build up herds but first, we had to take the land.

Ragnar the Resolute sat with me. "You have been quiet since we came to this land, lord. What bothers you?"

I smiled, "I had not planned this war with the Bretons, Ragnar. My mind was set on a raid on Paris. I need a son and the witch told me that Paris would achieve that. We could have captured this land last year or the year before. I did not and I should have. Now that I am back here I see why my grandfather and the Raven Wing Clan took it. I think that I feared to see what it had become. I wondered if my grandfather's work had been undone."

"And has it?"

"In part but not as much as I might have feared. When I heard the Bárekr's clan still lived then that gave me hope. The exodus when we first took the land around Rouen made me think that all of my grandfather's people had come but they had not. There are small numbers of the old Raven Wing Clan who still eke out a living. If I am silent it is because I am annoyed with myself. Paris is not the end, it is a means to an end. The witch told me that I would rule a large land. That is the end. This land is more important and we must hold on to it this time."

"I chose to follow you, lord, from the time we were in Norway and I have always been there to guard your back. It is why I was honoured when you gave me the stronghold on the river but you need me here. Sámr holds Bayeux and Olaf, Djupr. Sven has Caen but here you need someone who comes from the fjord. We were bound in blood, fire and ice. I had a young family and I would deem it an honour if you would let me bring them up here. This is as far from Rouen as anywhere. It will be exposed and it will need a strong hand to rule it. I have learned from Wellebou. Let me be the hand of iron. There are others who can guard the river. The stronghold of Wellebou could be held by a dozen men."

Ragnar had read my mind. Finnbjǫrn was a good warrior but I needed someone I knew as well as myself. I needed an oar brother. Ragnar, Sven and Sámr were closer than a blood brother. "Then when we have taken this land you choose your hall. I owe you that."

He shook his head, "You owe me nothing. If you had not been fished out of the sea then Sámr and I would be serving an ill-deserving jarl in Norway or following Finehair to build a kingdom and to flatter his flowing locks!"

We both laughed. King Harald Finehair was an arrogant and self-obsessed man. I had been one of the few who had rejected his offer to join him and he had never forgiven us. The fact that he had done nothing about the perceived insult told me that he feared me more than he showed.

I rose before dawn and after donning my mail I sharpened my swords. My wife had said that as I was a mighty lord I should have servants to do that for me. I did not want to delegate such a task. When I sharpened my weapons, I touched them. I inspected them. I could see weaknesses. I listened to their song as the whetstone slid along them. When I went to war, I knew that the blades I used were stronger and better than those I fought against. The simple action of sliding a whetstone down the blade helped my mind to become clear. I could plan and I could think. When I was satisfied I sheathed them both and then went to eat and have some ale. This would be a long day.

My leaders were gathered around the fire. None had disturbed me while I prepared for they knew that it was something I did each morning before we went into battle. When we sailed the drekar I did the same, standing at the prow. Ragnar handed me some bread and Finnbjǫrn the horn of ale. They waited while I ate and drank. They knew that when I finished I would tell them my plan.

"Sven and Olaf are waiting for the sound of our horns to tell them that we attack. The rest of our warriors will be here later today. We will hold off our main attack until he comes. Petr, your archers will advance to within arrow range. We will clear the walls of Bretons. They have poor bows. You have, amongst your archers, seven men with Saami bows. Use them well."

"Aye lord."

"The rest of us will form a long, single line of warriors behind shields. I want them to wonder when we will attack. Fear is a weapon and we will use it. They will see me. They will know why I have come. I wish them assailed by doubts. They need not know that we are awaiting reinforcements. When Sámr comes and Bagsecg Eriksson it will suck any hope they have left. Then I will demand their surrender."

Ragnar nodded, "And if they fight?"

"Then we take the walls. While the archers are getting in position cut down trees to use as bridges over the ditch. We just need four crossings and the ditch is not as wide as it should be."

Soon there was the sound of axes on trees and I walked with Petr and his archers. Petr stopped two hundred paces from the walls. Nocking a carefully chosen arrow he raised his Saami bow. As he did so four archers standing on the walls released their own arrows. The four men were spread out along the wall. Two were on the gatehouse and the other two in the towers at the end of the walls. Even though they were elevated their arrows fell twenty paces short of us. Petr walked forward picked one up and brought it back. He showed it to me. It was poorly fletched and was a hunting arrow. Contemptuously throwing it to the ground he said, "Lars you have a war bow. See if you can hit the archer on the gatehouse."

Lars' arrow struck the archer in the shoulder. The defender had thought he was beyond our range as we were beyond his. The men on the gatehouse took shelter. The two archers in the towers were further away and they did not move. Petr took aim and his arrow flew straight and true into the head of the archer in the west tower. My archer nodded, satisfied, "March forward to their fallen arrows. Do not waste an arrow. Any bowman whose arrow fails to find flesh will be fletching all night!" His archers smiled. They made their own arrows but it was not a chore they enjoyed. They would be frugal with their missiles. Petr knew that we were in no hurry. Patience was all. The Bretons would be careful and keep under cover but they would have to spy over the walls to see what we were up to. When they did that they would die.

Leaving them to their work I went back to our camp. Already the pile of logs was growing. Behind me, I heard a cry from the walls as Petr's men found flesh. The sound of hooves told us that Bagsecg was here. They stopped by the trees so that the Bretons would not see them. I walked to speak with them. He told me that Sámr and Bergil were a few miles down the road. I wanted their appearance to come as a complete shock to the Bretons. Arriving piecemeal would not achieve the effect I wanted.,

By mid-morning the logs were ready and my shield wall arrayed behind the archers. There were gaps in the walls where we could be observed and I knew that they had been watching what we were doing. What they did not know was the purpose. We could have been building a ram. They anticipated an assault on the gate for we heard hammering. They were strengthening the gate. When we were all in a line I began to bang my shield and we began a chant. It was to buy time until Sámr arrived.

Siggi was the son of a warrior brave
Mothered by a Hibernian slave
In the Northern sun where life is short
His back was strong and his arm was taut
Siggi White Hair warrior true
Siggi White Hair warrior true
When the Danes they came to take his home
He bit the shield and spat white foam
With berserk fury he killed them dead
When their captain fell the others fled
Siggi White Hair warrior true
Siggi White Hair warrior true
After they had gone and he stood alone
He was a rock, a mighty stone
Alone and bloodied after the fight
His hair had changed from black to white
His name was made and his courage sung
Hair of white and a body young
Siggi White Hair warrior true

Siggi White Hair warrior true
With dying breath, he saved the clan
He died as he lived like a man
And now reborn to the clan's hersir
Göngu-Hrólfr Rognvaldson the clan does cheer
Göngu-Hrólfr Rognvaldson warrior true
Göngu-Hrólfr Rognvaldson warrior true

My men had changed some of the words but the rhythm was still the same and the banging of the shields was hypnotic.

When we had finished and silence reigned I stepped forward. I walked to stand in front of my archers. I raised Longsword, "I am Lord Göngu-Hrólfr Rognvaldson. My father was Ragnvald Hrolfsson, my grandfather was Hrolf the Horseman. You live in the citadel built by the Clan of the Horse. The traitor Ragnvald Ragnvaldson usurped it after he slew his own father. You have one opportunity to live. Open your gates and leave. Go to Valognes, go to Rennes, go anywhere but leave. If you do so then I give you my word that you shall live." I spoke their language so that they all understood. The response was that eight of their archers stood and pulled back on bows. All eight fell. Four arrows fell three paces from my feet. I nodded, "That is your answer? Then know that every warrior within your walls will die. Make your peace with your god for you shall meet him soon!"

I did not know it but Sámr Oakheart, Bergil Fast Blade and their men had reached Bagsecg even as I had begun to speak. Now their numbers would swell my ranks and we could assault the town. I heard the keening of women inside Ćirićeburh as the news was passed around.

I walked back through my archers, "Thank you, Petr."

He shrugged, "My son is just ten summers old and he could have done better than those Bretons."

I clasped Sámr's arm and then Bergil's. "You have lived up to your name Sámr Oakheart and you, Bagsecg the Swift have justified your father's faith in you. Have your men dismount. They will not be needed today save to swell our numbers. When darkness comes I would have you join your father at Valognes."

"Aye, lord."

I shouted, "Now we will attack. Finnbjǫrn, your men will protect those carrying the logs. Lay them across the ditch. I want two bridges on either side of the gates."

"Aye, Lord."

"Ragnar, your men will carry the logs. All of you will wait for the horn to sound before you advance."

As the two warbands hurried to do my bidding I turned to Sámr, "Have you come far this morning?"

"Six miles. We marched late until it was dark." He knew what I was thinking. "Bergil and I can fight this day."

"I would have you and Bergil Fast Blade lead the attack with me. What say you?"

He and Bergil grinned, "We have barely whetted our blades. It is time for warriors to earn the right to live in the Land of the Horse."

I pointed Longsword at the eastern side of the gate. "Sámr you lead your men there. Bergil I will join you on the other side of the gate. They have strengthened the gate. We attack the walls. See how the mortar has crumbled on the stones at the bottom of the wall. We do not ascend, we will dig our way in. If we loosen the mortar we can pull out the stones. If we pull out enough then the walls will fall."

I heard Finnbjǫrn shout, "Ready Lord."

"Then attack!"

The defenders knew what was coming but they were powerless to do anything about it. My archers won the duel of the bow and only two of our men were wounded as the logs were carried and then dropped to make four bridges over the ditch. The two warbands then formed a double shield wall with four gaps.

"Leif, sound the horn three times!" The horn would signal our drekar to close with the walls and land their men. I hoped that the Bretons would have to divide their defence.

I raised Hrolf's Vengeance and we marched. I held my shield before me but it was not needed for their slingers and archers were sending their missiles blindly. It would take a lucky hit to do me damage. I had a good helmet and fine mail. The Bretons did not use good arrows. They were lazy and used barbed hunting arrows. They could not penetrate mail. One arrow clanked off my helmet and a couple of stones struck my shoulders. The padding I wore beneath my mail and my helmet absorbed the impact of the stones and the arrow. The trickiest part was crossing the roughhewn logs. They were not secured. For a man my size, they could have been dangerous. The ditch had been allowed to fall into disrepair. The sides were not steep and they had used it to deposit rubbish. Even so, a fall might have resulted in a broken limb. Once across it was just four paces to the wall. When Bertrand had had the ditch dug he had been careful to avoid the foundations of the walls. The walls were older than I was. The sea and the elements had worn at the stones. The mortar had seashells in it and birds had pecked at the mortar to get at them. The defenders should have refurbished the mortar twenty years ago. They had not done so and now they would pay the price for their indolence.

I slid my shield around to my back and took out a seax. I began to gouge out the crumbling mortar. Bjorn and Leif joined me and they took two of the sides of the stone. The defenders realised what we were about and I heard a cry as an arrow struck one who was on the fighting platform with a stone. He landed on my back. The shield spread the weight but it still drove me to my knees. I heard Petr shout, "Defend Lord Göngu-Hrólfr Rognvaldson!"

I returned to the gouging. When we had sailed back from the Land of the Wolf my grandfather had spoken of how they had built the walls. The stone I was trying to dislodge was the width of two of my hands. Inside that was the infill of small stones. That had been placed in last between the two outer walls. When I could no longer get my seax under any further I began to take the mortar from the top. Leif and Bjorn joined me. I heard Petr shout, "Get him!"

I braced myself by dropping to a knee and I heard a cry from above. This time it was not a warrior who fell it was his spear. The head was flatter than my seax and I put the seax back in my boot and began to rasp the head along the mortar.

Bjorn said, "Lord, I felt the stone move!"

We worked a little longer and then I turned and took the sword from the dead Breton who had fallen. It was a short sword. "Here Bjorn use that. We will try to lever the stone out."

At first, I thought it would not move but Leif shouted, "It is working!"

"Shift to the other side."

By alternating where we used the levers, the stone, little by little began to come out. Bergil, just two men away was having equal success. In fact, as I looked down the line I saw that a whole series of stones were now standing proud from the wall. Ours and Bergil's were a handspan further than any other.

"We have nearly done it." When the stone came out it simply slipped and tumbled to the ground. We pushed it behind us and the slope took it to the ditch. Inside were the stones which had made the infill between the outer and inner walls started to trickle down. Using our bare hands, we began to pull them out. Bergil and his men gave a cheer as their stone fell and a moment later another stone came loose. All along the wall stones came out and the infill tumbled and was torn out. I heard a creak. Without the infill, the outer and inner walls could not stand. They had not been maintained. The creak told me that the wall was doomed.

"Fall back beyond the ditch!" Even as we raced back I saw a crack in the wall above us. It moved up to where the wood met the stone. The Bretons had many men on the fighting platform. The weight was too much for the remaining six courses of stones. We had just made the other side when there was an almighty groan and thud as stones fell from above. One fell and then another. On the other side of the gate Sámr and his men were still scraping away but I knew that our wall would breach. The men on the fighting platform tried to flee and that accelerated the destruction of the wall. When it went, the wooden structure went with a crack like Odin's lightning. The dead Breton who had fallen upon me was buried by the wood and stone which fell down. Columns of dust rose like mist. There were screams and cries from the Breton warriors who had fallen with the platform. I raised the Breton spear, "Charge!"

I led Bergil and his men back across the causeway and we clambered over the stones, wood and corpses through the gap which we had caused. I stood on the top of the pile of rubble and leapt down towards the Bretons who were belatedly racing to seal the breach. I hefted the spear above my shoulder and hurled it. It embedded itself in the chest of a Breton. My shield was still over my back and so I used Longsword two-handed. It hacked across the shields and shoulders of three Bretons. One was felled and two stepped back. Bergil Fast Blade joined me and he lived up to his name as he slew the two who had stepped back.

"Form wedge!"

Sven and Olaf would be attacking the sea gate. We had to relieve the pressure on them and a wedge was the best way to move quickly. I remembered the layout of the port and recalled that there was a direct route from the south gate to the river gate. Even if the Bretons held the east and the west parts we would have them divided. As my men formed up behind me those defenders who had been racing to send us hence thought better of it for Bjorn and Leif had opened the gate and all of my men, more than a hundred and fifty, were already pouring through. The Bretons turned and ran to join the shield wall forming near the lord's hall. I began to chant so that we could run at them. It seemed right to sing the song of the Raven Wing Clan which had first landed just a few miles from where we fought.

Raven Wing Clan goes to war,
A song of death to all its foes
The power of the raven grows and grows.
The power of the raven grows and grows.
The power of the raven grows and grows.
A song of death to all its foes
The power of the raven grows and grows.
The power of the raven grows and grows.
The power of the raven grows and grows.
A song of death to all its foes
The power of the raven grows and grows.
The power of the raven grows and grows.
The power of the raven grows and grows.

We were moving at a good pace when we hit them. I held Longsword before me. I had no shield before me, it was on my back, and I relied on Bergil Fast Blade and Ubba Long Cheek to stop the Breton spears from hitting me. Bergil's sword hacked through the ash shaft of one spear as Longsword was driven into the skull of the man who wielded it. Ubba had a spear and he took the man next to the warrior I had slain. I could not have stopped even had I wanted to. I had a solid column of men behind me. I almost tripped over the man I had killed. My sword was torn from his skull and found the gut of the man behind. It split his body from the crotch to the throat. I had to take longer strides to avoid falling and I found myself ahead of my men and behind the Breton shield wall. I swung first right and then left. Longsword sliced through the spines of the men who were there and that allowed Bergil, Ubba and the rest to widen the breach.

The wedge had done its work and I shouted, "Break wedge! Kill them!" Without a shield to encumber me and fighting men whose swords were much shorter than mine I was able to swing my sword in wide arcs. I used a figure of eight action, much as the Danish axe men did. The result was that none could get close to me. Few tried for I was a giant wielding a sword which was almost as long as some of them. As in all battles where there was no King involved the best warriors were at the fore of the fight and when they died the rest fell far quicker.

145

I could see the gate ahead. I stepped forward and, while swinging my sword in a circle to clear space behind me I shouted, "Ragnar! Get your men to the gate! Open it!"

"Aye, Lord." Ragnar was keen to show that the men he led were as good as any. In addition, this would be his town when we took it. They flew ferociously at the men who had fled to the side to avoid my scything sword. They tore through the terrified Bretons. Some of those who were close to me and being attacked by Bergil and Finnbjǫrn's men tried in vain to surrender. My men were having none of it. They would have been as well to fight to the death for they were slain in any case. As soon as the sea gate was thrown open then Sven and Olaf led the rest of my warriors to fall upon the warriors who remained. We found the women, children, old and the priests, hiding in the church. As my men went around catching and despatching warriors who were still alive I spoke to the survivors.

"I am Lord Göngu-Hrólfr Rognvaldson. My father was Ragnvald Hrolfsson, my grandfather was Hrolf the Horseman. I am Lord of Rouen and now I am the lord of this land. I spare you because I have mercy within me. You will leave. The nearest Bretons are in Valognes. You may travel there unmolested but you take only that which is on your back."

I saw the priest looking at the church.

I shook my head, "That includes your holy books and that which you use for your services. Go!" They needed no further urging and they fled. I turned to greet Olaf and Sven. "Did you lose any men?"

They shook their heads. When we heard the horn, we landed. We crossed using their own ships. They had few archers. Some were wounded but only a few. And you, Lord Göngu-Hrólfr Rognvaldson?"

"I am not certain."

Bergil Fast Blade shook his head, "He led! How would he know? Since Hrolf, the Horseman died I think we have a berserker amongst us."

I smiled, "Let us say that I am keen to father a son and there is much which needs to happen before then. Secure the town. Ragnar the Resolute will be lord here. You can leave your drekar in the harbour. The ships' boys and the forty men I leave with Ragnar can defend this place."

Ragnar said, "I will not let you down, Lord."

I looked down and saw my bloody mail. It looked as though I had been working in a slaughterhouse. "Have food prepared. I will go to the sea and bathe."

"You can leave all with us."

I took off my helmet and shield. I left them by the door of the church and I headed through the gate to the sea. There were four Breton ships in the port. One was a warship and the others were knarr. From the way they were riding I guessed that they were laden. I walked down to the end of the jetty which curved around to form a breakwater. I stripped off my swords and mail. When I took off my kyrtle I dived in the sea, naked. It held no fear for me. The shock of the cold refreshed me and I dived as deep as I could go. When I came to the surface I swam back to the drekar and clambered aboard '*Hermóðr.*' I laughed as Arne Three Toes almost fell overboard in shock. I strode across the deck leaving giant wet prints on the deck. When I had dressed I felt refreshed. I did not don my mail. It would need cleaning in a bag of sand.

Picking up my swords I headed back to the gate. I saw that they had put a smaller gate in the side. Walking through it I saw that it came out in the cemetery of the church. I remembered my grandfather telling me that Bertrand and his family were buried there. I walked over to look for their grave. Bertrand had been a Frank and a follower of the White Christ. It was right that he was buried here. I found the grave almost immediately. The stones, which had marked them, had been wrecked and the bones emptied. I knew that it was Bertrand's grave for one piece which remained and could be read had the letters '*Bertr*'. The Bretons had despoiled it. The good humour I had had after my swim disappeared in an instant. I regretted my clemency. Valognes would not enjoy such clemency. They called us barbarians but we would never damage the resting place of a warrior, even an enemy.

That evening, as we ate in the lord's hall, I said nothing to the others. They did not know Bertrand. He had been the one who taught me how to be a mounted warrior. Gilles had taught me to ride but my grandfather had brought me to Bertrand to learn how to fight from the back of a horse. I became the horseman I was thanks to him and I would have my vengeance. I smiled and was happy with my captains and their banter but in my heart, I was seething with rage.

Sámr told me how the defenders at Benni's Ville had been warned by those fleeing Carentan. Most had fled west to Angia. Half of the warriors had remained thinking they could hold off barbarians. They were wrong. The attack had been both swift and successful. Sámr had been delayed while he made the walls secure and ensured that there was a good garrison. Sven Blue Cheek asked, "Who will be lord there? It needs someone strong for it is close to the Breton Sea."

I was still thinking of Bertrand. I shook my head, "Who would have it?"

Haldi Axe Tongue said little normally but he stood and spoke, "I have not seen it, lord, but if there is danger and I can serve you then I would be your lord. It is by the sea and I am a sailor. If it were not for you and your clan we would have perished in Dyflin. Mr crew and I owe all to you. I would be lord there."

"Then it is *wyrd*."

"And Valognes?"

"Let us take it before we give it to a warrior. We will need all of our men to take it for its walls are made of stone and higher than here."

"Are the walls all made of stone, lord?"

"No, the outer wall of the town is made of wood but they have a tower with a hall attached and there is a stone wall that runs around that."

The conversation moved to the taking of walls as well as a heated discussion about the merits of this land as opposed to our river valley and the land of Norway. Sven Blue Cheek joined me. "Is it your grandfather makes you thus, lord, for if so then old Hrolf would be angry with you? He did not want you to mourn. He wanted to give his life for you. We both know that."

I shook my head and smiled. He was right to chide me thus. "No Sven, I found that the Bretons had wrecked the grave of the man who made me a horseman. The bones of him and his family lie scattered around the graveyard. It was done since we came. It was a petty and vindictive act."

"And it shows that they fear you. This is a good place and Ragnar will rule it well."

"If you wished it…"

"No lord, Caen is perfect. It is close to Rouen and is a mighty fortress. I have an idea for Valognes."

"You do? Who would you have as lord there?"

"Ubba Long Cheek. He does not captain a drekar but we both know that men look to him in battle. He is a natural leader and he recently married. This would please his wife and you would have a leader upon whom you could completely rely."

I lowered my voice, "You do not trust the Danes?"

"They are good men but Guthrum let us down when he converted. I trust those who are Norse but the ones who have joined us from the land of the Angles have yet to prove themselves to me."

The dream and my grandfather's words from the spirit world came into my head, '*Beware the Danes and beware the Count.*' Perhaps Sven Blue Cheek was right.

We left the next morning. There had been horses in the town and we rode those as well as the ones we had captured further south. They were good horses and we could use them to breed better beasts. This time we needed no scouts. There might be Breton warriors loose in the land but they would be avoiding us and not seeking us. We left the farmers and small villages alone. When Valognes was ours then we could turn our attention to them. I had told my lords what our plan would be. We would offer them the chance to swear allegiance to their lord, and ultimately, me or they could leave the land. Most were newcomers to the land. They had come when our people had been evicted. It would be interesting to see how many stayed.

Erik and his son had established camps at each of the gates. Beyond the range of the archers in the town, they were in a good position to stop any from leaving. I headed for the camp on the road north. The walls of the town could just be seen over the top of the trees. Erik and his son were talking when I arrived.

"Have you spoken with them yet, Erik?"

He shook his head. "When I approached, bareheaded and with open palms, they sent arrows and stones at me." He laughed, "It is fortunate that they are such poor marksmen but they might have hurt my horse."

Bagsecg said, "But none have left yet. Ten horsemen tried but we slew four and the rest ran back inside the town. Had we had more men we might have risked following them."

"You have done the right thing. I have told my men to spread themselves around the walls. Tomorrow we will have a show of force and I will speak to them. I will go mailed. After what I saw in the graveyard at Ċiriċeburh I almost hope that they reject my offer of clemency."

"What happened?" I told him of Bertrand's grave. He shook his head. His father and Bertrand had been good friends. "Aye the ones whom your brother let into this land were both cruel and reckless. It is good that we scour the land of them."

"And have you told your son of our plans?"

He nodded, "He is happy to be lord of Montfort but worries that he might be too young." I saw Bagsecg's smile. It was a nervous one.

I laughed, "Age has nothing to do with leadership. My grandfather led the Raven Wing Clan when he was little older than you, Bagsecg, and when I was in Norway I was the same age and men followed me. You are a leader and I am close enough so that you can ask my advice. I do not bite."

With more men to watch the walls more of the horsemen were able to get some rest. Erik and his son, however, were more interested in the animals we had liberated from their Breton owners. "These will make good breeding stock. When we go to war we can mount more men."

"Aye Erik but remember they will just be warriors riding a horse to war. They will not be horsemen. Our warriors are too valuable to throw away. Until the two of you have trained more men then we just use the extra horses to reach places quicker."

As I curled up next to the campfire I reflected that few of the new men had shown any desire to become horsemen. Finnbjǫrn, Haldi, Saxbjǫrn, all of them and their crews preferred ships. Those that had come with me from Norway preferred ships and fighting on their own two feet. The horsemen had come from those who had been born in this land. They were the ones with the blood of the Norse and the blood of the Frank. Bagsecg would have to wait until the new boys became men and then they might be warriors.

We all rose early. There was an air of anticipation in the camp. As we no longer needed them as guards I sent the horsemen to scout the borders of this new land. I had them ride between Carentan and Benni's Ville. I still did not believe that King Alan would be able to bring an army quickly but my mounted men would warn us. Bjorn had cleaned my mail and it was now burnished as was my helmet. This was not the helmet that had been dented. I had had a new one made. Rather than having a face mask, I had a mail hood beneath it. My lower face was protected. Men who stabbed upwards had a better chance of hitting my chin and jaw. The well-made mail links would slow down a blade or a spearhead. I had my shield around my back and, thanks to my mail hood, I was able to carry my helmet and still have some protection against treachery. As well as giving me a powerful body the Allfather had also given me a powerful voice. I could be heard even in the fiercest of storms. My men and I marched to the walls and we stopped out of bow range. Now that we had

Petr and his archers we could discourage the enemy from using bows and stones when we spoke of peace.

I stood before the main gate. If there were those from Carentan and Ċiriċeburh within then they would have heard part of it already, "I am Lord Göngu-Hrólfr Rognvaldson. My father was Ragnvald Hrolfsson, my grandfather was Hrolf the Horseman. I am Lord of Rouen and now I am the lord of this land. I make you an offer and I make it once. Reject it and you suffer the same fate as Ċiriċeburh. Accept it and like the men of the Haugr, you can march away with your weapons. Surrender the town that was ours through Rurik One Ear and was betrayed by Ragnvald Ragnvaldson. There will be no negotiation. Take it or leave it."

I waited. A man who was, perhaps thirty summers old, with a well-trimmed beard and polished mail stepped closer to the edge of the wall over the gate. "I am Count Erispoe, Lord of the Cotentin. You do not frighten me, Viking monster. You are a freak of nature. You are an abomination before God and King Alan will strike you down. Until he comes we will defy you. You have no engines of war and you are barbarians. You will tire and you will go away but before then a mighty army will march from the south and you will all be destroyed. You are Norse. Go back to the cold land of the Norse. It is enough for savages such as you!"

I waited until he had finished and then I said, "You like the sound of your own voice. I will say that. A simple no would have sufficed. If your King is foolish enough to come to your aid then we will destroy him. Who knows, we may decide to take the whole of Brittany!" I was going to offer free passage for the women, children and old and then I remembered Bertrand. They need not have come to Valognes. They could have carried on to safer places deeper in Brittany. I led my men back to our camp.

Halfi Axe Tongue asked, "Do we not fight them this day? My men are eager for a fight."

"I care not. They fight when I say. We are well-rested. Petr, have your men make fire arrows. Tonight, we keep them awake with an arrow storm. Use the hunting arrows we found in Ċiriċeburh. They are little good for anything else."

He nodded, "We have little chance of burning down the town lord."

I nodded, "You do not need to. Just start a few fires, which they will put out."

Finnbjǫrn frowned, "How does that help us? Is that not a waste of arrows?"

I saw Petr hide a smile. Finnbjǫrn did not know bows. "Firstly, the hunting arrows are little use against men in mail. Secondly, what will they use to douse the fires?"

"Water of course, lord." He said it as though I was simple.

"And the water they use they cannot drink. We have driven many mouths into the town. They need food and water. If they put out the fires with water then they will be thirsty sooner. Thirdly, it will make them lose sleep and they will live in fear that we might succeed a second time. When they have stood to all night we will attack in the morning. We choose the section of the wooden wall which is furthest from their hall. You have fine axes which will render the walls into kindling. Once we have breached the wooden wall we let them retreat within the stone wall and the hall of Rurik. I have been in that hall and they will be cramped and crowded. They will have to live in their own waste and stink. The women, old and the children will beg to be released from this prison."

Finnbjǫrn dropped to one knee, "Forgive me, Lord. Next time I will remain silent."

"That is not necessary. I do not mind questions. It shows that you are listening and thinking about what I say."

While the archers made their fire arrows I had other men collecting kindling. As well as using axes to hack through the wooden walls I would also use fire to burn them. Half of my men walked the walls to keep the Bretons on their toes. They would anticipate an attack that would not materialize. Although Petr was not confident about starting a major fire with his arrows he was also an archer who was proud of his skill. He would do his best to do what I had asked of him. He checked every arrow personally. I went with him to the walls. We had pots of fire. They would only be opened once we were in position. There was a risk that the Bretons might react but they were more likely to be conserving arrows and archers for our daylight attack.

"It is in your hands now, Petr."

He shouted to his archers, "We light, draw and release on one command." There was a murmur of assent. They were worried for none had done this before. "Open the pots. Draw!"

When the ten pots were opened it was as though the sun had begun to rise. There was a glow of light from the ground. Then the fifty arrows sailed high. Some hit the stone of the walls and buildings. A few hit the wooden walls and burned briefly before dying. We did not see the effect of the rest. Each archer had twenty arrows and they released them until they were all gone. The night went dark again. The arrows which we could see all appeared to be extinguished but then I saw a glow. Arrows had started a fire somewhere. Flames licked into the sky and I heard screams and cries from within. It took some time but the fire was brought under control. The smell of burning filled the air and palls of thick smoke drifted towards us.

"Well done, Petr. That went better than either of us expected." We could hear the panic in the town as they sought to douse the flames.

I curled up next to our fire feeling content.

There was still a tendril of smoke rising from Valognes when we rose the next day. Although we could not see the damage the smell of charred and burned wood filled the air. Petr and his archers were already awake and eating. I waved him over, "Today you support my attack on the north gate. You and our archers did well last night."

"The Allfather guided our arrows. We were loosing them by instinct."

"And your instinct worked. Today you can use your skill."

My captains and lords were waiting for me by the fire. Sven had livened it up with fresh wood. He looked up as I approached, "Your plan is working lord."

"Today we try our first assault. Halfi and Finnbjǫrn, I want your men hidden by the south gate with the kindling. Our horns will tell you when we attack. Give us a count of a thousand and then have your men pile the kindling around the gate and fire it. Retire to the woods. We will need your men for the final assault."

They nodded. There would have been a time when they would have questioned me but no longer. I had explained my plan to all of them. Once the south gate was weakened we would make a nighttime attack on it. The stone wall and the hall lay close to the north gate. There would be little to stop them. Once we surrounded the stone wall our real attack could begin.

"Then let us prepare!" Sven led them away to don their mail.

Once again Bjorn had made certain that my helmet and mail were polished. When I put on my mail I also put on my cloak before fastening the scabbard of Longsword over my back. With Hrolf's Vengeance on my left and shield on my arm, I was ready. I carried my helmet to the walls. Sven was organizing the men. He saw my cloak and frowned, "Why the cloak, lord?"

"I have neither standard nor bearer. This marks me for all to see."

"They can hardly miss you, Lord Göngu-Hrólfr Rognvaldson."

"It will draw more men to this wall. They will think I intend to make this attack succeed. Finnbjǫrn and Halfi need a major distraction to do what they intend. Remember that today is a distraction. If we can weaken their gate and kill some of their men then all well and good but I do not wish to be profligate with our men's lives. We have a larger land to guard and until we have more men we must be more cautious than any of us would like."

I donned my helmet. We had a column of men forty wide and three deep. The ones around me in the centre were all armed with an axe rather than a spear. Behind our three ranks came the two ranks of archers. We began banging our shields and chanting. We had adapted one of our old chants. The words of Count Erispoe which had been intended as an insult had inspired us. We were Norsemen and we were proud of it.

> *The men of Rouen go to war,*
> *A song of death to all their foes*
> *The power of the Norse grows and grows.*
> *The power of the Norse grows and grows.*
> *The power of the Norse grows and grows.*
> *A song of death to all their foes*
> *The power of the Norse grows and grows.*
> *The power of the Norse grows and grows.*
> *The power of the Norse grows and grows.*
> *A song of death to all their foes*
> *The power of the Norse grows and grows.*
> *The power of the Norse grows and grows.*

I unsheathed Hrolf's Vengeance and swung my shield. "March!" I knew that Bjorn was behind me. "When next we stop then sound your horn three times."

"Aye, Lord."

When we were just within the arrow range of the men who lined the walls I shouted, "Halt!" As Bjorn sounded the horn Petr and his men loosed their arrows. Our shields were held tightly before us. We did not need to lock them. We would not be facing men; we would be facing stone. "March!"

> *The men of Rouen go to war,*

A song of death to all their foes
The power of the Norse grows and grows.
The power of the Norse grows and grows.
The power of the Norse grows and grows.
A song of death to all their foes
The power of the Norse grows and grows.
The power of the Norse grows and grows.
The power of the Norse grows and grows.
A song of death to all their foes
The power of the Norse grows and grows.
The power of the Norse grows and grows.

As Petr's arrows hit the men on the walls so the enemy sent their hunting arrows in our direction. They had boys with slings and their stones began to join the Breton arrows in striking our shields and helmets. Out of the corner of my eye. I saw a warrior to the right of me .tumble to the ground. The chant we used helped not only keep the rhythm but also helped to put steel into our stride. Each man knew he was not going to battle alone. He was going with his clan, his shield brothers. Gradually the arrow and stone storm thinned. Our archers were targeting the archers and slingers. They were aiming for us and we had mailed and armoured men protected by shields and good helmets. I knew not what the Breton business was but ours was war and we did it well.

We had chosen the north gate for it had the widest approach. There was a ditch but it ran around the walls and not the gate. I saw no faces on their wall. They had shields above their heads to protect them from the arrows which fell like rain. These would have rocks. If Count Episoe had any sense he would have boiling water and oil ready. We were prepared for that. The gate was recessed beneath the stone lintel which gave the gate its strength. When we reached the recess, I stopped and held my shield above my head. The eight men with axes slipped their shields around their backs and took their axes to begin to hack into the gate. The gate was not Breton it was Norse. Rurik One Ear had made it and he had made it well. I had seen it being made. The tree trunks which had been used had been my handspan wide. With sturdy crosspieces, they would not be reduced easily. They were old but they had been coated in pine tar to preserve them. All that we had to do was weaken them. My intention was not to break them down. We would need a ram for that.

As the axes struck the oak so the stones were dropped. The Bretons were limited. They could only drop stones that they were able to carry and these were not oarsmen with shoulders that were broad and muscles like knotted oaks. They were dropping them the six paces that separated the fighting platform from our heads. In my case, it was nearer to five paces. They hurt but they did not harm. We endured the stone storm. When their men dropped the stones, they were exposed to our archers and at least one body fell onto the shields.

Ubba Long Cheek led the axemen and, after a while, he said, "Lord, our axes are becoming blunted. We are almost through to the cross pieces and braces."

"Try a little longer. When we smell smoke then we know that our oar brothers have succeeded at the south gate!"

"Aye lord."

It was not long after that I heard a cry from above me, "Fire!" I did not need to smell the smoke and the flames to know that the south gate was afire.

"Fall back!"

Men had fallen and their bodies were collected and taken back with us. Most of the wounded had been rendered unconscious by stones. They would be tended by our healers. As we moved back I was able to see the effect of the axes. Raw cuts showed through the weathered wood. There were gaps that allowed us to see the cross braces. If we had had a ram then we could have used it and gained entry. A ram took time to build. If my plan succeeded we would have breached the defences by the next night.

When we reached our camp, I assessed the damage. Eight men had been hurt and one killed. Arne Halfisson had been unlucky. Petr Jorgensen explained how my warrior had died. "They had a giant, lord. He was almost as big as you. He had a huge rock. We hit him with six arrows but, with his dying throw he hurled the rock and it hit Arne."

"It could have been worse."

Sven pointed towards the gate. We could hear hammering, "They are repairing it, lord."

"And we both know that will not save it but it is more important that Halfi and Finnbjǫrn succeeded."

A short while later they arrived. They had as many injuries as we and two dead men. They had not had the protection of archers. They seemed in high spirits. "The gate is burning, look."

We could see a thin column of smoke rising in the sky on the other side of the town.

"Will they be able to douse it?"

Halfi shook his head. "They were using soil to smother the flames. They are short of water. We heard the sentries shouting for water. We do not know all the Breton words but we recognised that one."

"Then have all our men rest. Tonight, we reverse our roles. You lost men today. You begin a fake attack on this gate and I will lead the rest of our men to attack the south gate."

We waited until it was dark to march around to the south gate. It was still standing but I could see, in the darkness, the glow of burning embers. It was still afire. Now I knew why they had not used boiling water on us, they did not have enough. This time our attack would have to be just ten warriors wide for the entrance was narrow. When Rurik had built his wooden wall, it was deemed that this would be where the greatest danger would lie. South of here were Franks, or they were when he had been Lord of Valognes. The ditch was deep and the entrance narrow.

The Bretons had sentries; we saw them on the wall. Our archers were not with us. They were with the others at the north wall. They had the horn and this time we would await their signal to begin our attack. Alongside me, I had Sven, Ubba Long Cheek, Sámr, Bergil Fast Blade, Ragnar, Bjorn, Leif and Habor the Rus. We were the biggest men. We would be the human battering ram. We waited in the dark. The gate was just two hundred paces from us and our approach would be silent but we had to listen for the horn. When the horn sounded it almost made us jump. We heard our men chanting as they approached the north gate and we heard the cries from within the walls. We gave them enough time to shift more men to face the attack and then I raised Hrolf's Vengeance and led my men at a fast walk towards the gate. My dark cloak helped to mask me. We were a hundred paces from the wall when we were seen and the cries of alarm rippled around the walls.

A spear was hurled from the walls when we were just thirty paces from us. It fell short. Bergil Fast Blade had to hurdle it. I heard a shout from further back as one of our warriors tripped over it. That was the problem with a night attack. "Brace!" We all lifted our shields before our faces. I could still feel residual heat from the charred gate but the fire had done its work and the integrity of the structure was gone. As we hit it the blackened wood burst asunder and we were in the south side of the small town. Already those who lived in the houses close to the gate were fleeing towards the safety of the stone wall and the lord's hall.

Some of the men who came from the halls tried to slow us down but we were an unstoppable force. They were slain. When the mass of people reached the gate to the hall it was barred. There were women beating at the door with their bare hands. It remained closed. As I neared they began screaming and begging to be allowed in. Count Episode would not do so. If he did then the siege would be over for we would capture his hall.

I took off my helmet and said, in Breton, "Leave! Go out of the south gate. I am kinder than your lord! I give you your lives!"

They turned and beat on the door once more. From above the gate came the Count's voice, "Do as the pagan says. We have neither food nor water for you."

Thus spurned, they fled. As they passed us they cowered but none of my men raised a finger. I turned to Sámr and Sven, "Quickly, while it is dark and before they know how many are here find anything which will burn and pile it by the gate. We will burn their gates down."

With men attacking two sides of the inner ward there was confusion within and we exploited it. By the time they realised what we were doing Sámr's men were tossing in burning brands and the fire began. As it was dark and we were mailed we were able to feed the fire with the furniture which was in the Breton homes. Jars of oil made the flames lick ever higher. The defenders sent arrows and spears in our direction but we had houses for shelter and mail and shields for protection.

Sven Blue Cheek came to speak with me, "We have lost few men. Do you think they will surrender?"

"If they had any sense then they would. It would save their women, children and the old being harmed accidentally." I pointed to the body of the old woman trampled by her own people. "I think he will try to save himself."

As dawn began to break my captains began to report to me. There were no Bretons left in the part of the town we had captured. The fire had cleared the gatehouse and, as the sun began to light the walls we saw cracks appearing. The fire had done its work.

"Form a shield wall. The moment that the fire dies down we charge it down. We end this today." As it turned out, even before the fire burned itself out we had won. One of Halfi's men ran around, "Lord we have gained entry to the north gate. The Count and twenty of his horsemen have escaped."

I turned to Sven, "We charge the gate now!" Without waiting for my men, I held my shield before me and ran at the burning gate. There was almost nothing left to burn and when I hit the flaming wood it seemed to crumble before me. My cloak, beard and hair were singed but I was in the inner ward. Ahead I saw Halfi and Finnbjǫrn leading their men. As Sven and Sámr led the rest through the remnants of the gate I knew that we had won. We had captured the Cotentin. Now the question remained, could we hold it?

Chapter 11

Finnbjǫrn and Halfi were disappointed in themselves. The Count and his men had opened the gate and when our men had poured in, thinking they had won, the horsemen galloped over them. Ten warriors were slain either by spears or by horses' hooves. I knew that it could have been worse. We could have lost a leader. We had sent the women, children and the old, south as soon as we had secured the hall. Then we began to prepare its defences. King Alan would come. We had to be ready.

Ironically, we had done more damage to the Bretons than they had to us. The two gates to the south were destroyed. The stone around the outer ward gate was badly damaged. I walked the walls with Sven and Ubba Long Cheek. He had gratefully accepted my offer to be lord of Valognes but was not certain he could do the task as well as I believed. "Ubba I have stood beside you in a shield wall. Just do as you do when commanding warriors and you will more than do me justice."

Sven came up with a solution. "Dig a deep ditch where the outer wall gate stood so that they cannot use that. Pile logs in the gate which leads to the outer ward and fight him. We force him to attack where we want. We have men on the walls and men in the woods. They can attack his flanks. We put Petr and his archers on the walls and make a shield wall."

Ubba and Sámr were dubious. Sámr vocalised their worries, "But what if King Alan does not do as we wish? He may well try to use the half-destroyed buildings. It is what we would do."

"Sven Blue Cheek is right. When he comes we make him do that which we wish. I can think of no better solution."

As Ubba organized the men to dig the ditch and Sven took men to hew trees Sámr and Bergil tasked me about my plan. "Lord, I do not understand. How can you make this Breton King do that which we want?"

"I am the one he wants to either kill or capture. He has heard my name. He knows of my brother and my grandfather. I am sorry but he will see the rest of you as seafaring pirates who will move off to the next place to raid."

Sámr smiled, "A few years ago and he would have been right but I have put down roots. I am still a pirate but a pirate who likes this land." I laughed, Sámr had changed more than anyone since I had first met him. "So how do you make him come for you?"

"I find the biggest horse which Erik has and I ride with my horsemen. I taunt him. I insult him. I challenge him. Count Episoe will be with him as will Robert of Rennes. There are two men who will see the vaunted Viking sitting on a horse that is too small for him with just a hundred or so horsemen for protection. They will come and you and the rest of my men will be waiting. There will be archers on my walls and men in the woods with bows. The rest of you will be behind stakes and a ditch. There will be a narrow path through the defences through which we will ride. I will dismount and we will fill the gap."

"You make it sound easy."

"Everything is easy... until the Norns begin to spin a new web. We make our plans and if they do not work then we adapt them." I still trusted in my dead grandfather and in the witch's prophesy.

The Bretons did not come for two more days. Bagsecg sent back two riders to tell us that they were approaching from the direction of Avranches. We had found four horses in Valognes. None were particularly big or very good. It explained why they had been left. Taking Leif and Bjorn with me I rode south to my horsemen. I was confident that Sven would know exactly what to do. The town was prepared. My men had made traps in the deserted part of the town and cleared the houses, many of which were already damaged, that lay close to the stone wall. With embedded stakes and a ditch, we were as prepared as we would be. The weapons we had taken from the Bretons and found in their armoury were also used to augment our defences. What we had not done was to send for men from our other strongholds. I did not know this King Alan. He might be as tricky as I was. I had to ensure that all of our acquisitions were protected.

The two riders Bagsecg had sent to us were amused at the sight of me with my feet trailing along the ground but they were fearful of laughing at Lord Göngu-Hrólfr Rognvaldson. I did not mind. I knew how ridiculous I looked. "Does Lord Erik have bigger horses with him?"

"He does, lord, but I am not certain that they will be large enough for you."

"And how far away are the Bretons?"

Another twenty miles and we will find our camp. They were another ten miles further south. We have just a screen of twenty riders watching them. Lord Erik is resting the rest of our herd."

"And he is wise to do so."

The two were young riders. These were not yet horsemen. I knew that for they just had a helmet, small round shield, short sword and a spear. My most experienced horsemen all had a blue cloak, a helmet with a nasal and a short byrnie. Their shields were also bigger. My grandfather had known that making a force of horsemen who could fight the Franks would take time. Ragnvald, my brother, had robbed us of that time. When he had killed my father and tried to kill me he had put back the training of young riders by years. Perhaps that was another reason why my grandfather had made the sacrifice he had.

We reached the camp after dark. I saw that they had foraged for their food. This was Breton land and any farm was fair game. When I dismounted I saw that both Erik and his son were surprised. "We did not expect to see you, lord."

I stretched. I had not had a comfortable ride. Taking the proffered horn of cider, I told them of my plan. "We need to draw them twenty miles up this road. I know that you were keeping hidden from our foes but tomorrow I want you to let them see your scouts. Let us appear fearful. The two leaders who fled to King Alan have never seen our horsemen in action. They think that we are Vikings who ride horses to war. Our men with the blue cloaks are the equal of any Breton." I saw the two of them swell with pride. "When we are ten miles from Valognes I will reveal myself. I will offer a challenge to them."

"What if they accept?"

I saw the worry on Bagsecg's face. His father laughed, "Lord Göngu-Hrólfr Rognvaldson will be happy to fight any who accept his challenge but I doubt that they will. There is no warrior within a thousand miles of here who could face Lord Göngu-Hrólfr Rognvaldson in battle and win."

"Thank you for those words but I wish you had not spoken to them. The Norns have been spinning. Let us not encourage them."

My two escorts insisted upon taking it in turns to stand watch over me. Bjorn shook his head when I said that I was safe. "We thought you safe when you went to Bayeux. We will watch. You are the father of our clan. Who would not watch over his own father?"

When we woke, we cleared the camp. Their scouts would be leaving. Erik had told his men what they needed to do. He used the ones without the blue cloaks, the younger, more inexperienced riders. "Ride as though you are afraid of them and head up the road. They will stop chasing you and you can watch them again."

"And if they follow us all the way to the rest of you, lord, what then?"

"Then we will fight them and hurt them. It will anger them."

Erik was a confident leader when it came to horses and horsemen. He knew both limitations and the potential of each.

I think the horse he found for me had been a horse which had pulled a plough. It was bigger than the rest and my feet were off the ground. More importantly, it was strong enough to carry both me and my weapons. I had left my mail at Valognes. We headed slowly north. The place we had chosen for the challenge was at the bottom of a slight rise. The road emerged from a small wood and stand of scrubby trees. They masked the slight rise and the place where we would camp for the night. The land through which we had passed had been open but we had emptied all of the farms as we had ridden north. The farmers had fled east and west. The Bretons would only know what their scouts told them. We made a camp halfway up. Our young riders galloped in after dark.

They addressed Erik, "Lord we did as you said. They followed us but did not close with us. They seemed content to chase us off. They have camped just four miles away. We managed to count them, Lord Göngu-Hrólfr Rognvaldson."

"Good. And how many are there?"

"They have two hundred horsemen. Half of them are mailed. There are more than five hundred on foot."

Bagsecg shook his head, "That is far more than we have!"

I ignored him. "How many of the ones on foot wear mail?"

"Just the leaders, lord, and each of the leaders rides a horse."

"Then it is good. We have warriors facing farmers. They will break their camp at dawn and send out their scouts. We will let them see us. We will break camp before dawn but make it look as though they have surprised us. We will have the men playing dice and sleeping."

I slept little for I knew that I was gambling and yet the Norns seemed to be spinning a web which entrapped the Bretons. I had to trust that Ylva's spell was working. My grandfather had woven his life thread into that spell. Part of me was in the spell. The Norns might cut my thread but it would be in Paris if they did. They had sent those Bretons to kill me for a purpose. My path was as inevitable as the sun which began to rise in the east. There lay my home, my wife and my daughters. When I had fulfilled my side of the promise then they would deliver me a son and all the deaths would be worthwhile. My blood would go on.

We had our own scouts out but they were well hidden. The sun was rising in the sky when they galloped in. "Their scouts approach lord." Einar Sharp Eyes shook his head, "They do not know what they are doing. They ride up the road. Had you commanded it then all six of them would be dead."

"Good, then when they come you and your men attack them. Chase them back to their King." I smiled, "Make sure at least one gets back to report."

"Aye lord."

I turned and cupped my hands, "Let us play at being barbaric, pagan pirates with no discipline! Our prey comes but they do not know yet that they are dead men walking!" Their cheers told me that they were in good spirits.

I was the exception to my men. I stood with Erik and Bagsecg. The scouts had to see me and by standing next to two men it was obvious who I was. We needed the scouts to report that Lord Göngu-Hrólfr Rognvaldson was with a handful of horsemen and that we had been caught unawares. We stood in the middle of the road as though we were discussing our plans. In fact, Erik and I were telling Bagsecg of the wars we had both fought when we were young men. Then Erik had been his father's horse holder and I had carried my grandfather's banner.

The road which wound up to where we waited was not Roman. The Franks had built it and it followed the natural curves of the land and passed through woods and the small stands of scrubby trees. We heard their hooves before we saw them. They came around the corner and saw us, just two hundred paces away. Einar was right. They did not know their business. They had found the Vikings they sought but they sat talking. Einar and his ten scouts mounted their horses and galloped towards them. Panic ensued and the Breton scouts turned. Even so, one was slain before they disappeared from sight. I hoped that Einar would heed his orders.

Erik turned, "Mount!" I saw the men, who had been awaiting the order, run for their horses. "Bagsecg, you know what to do?"

"Aye father. I take half of the men and hide in the woods halfway up the slope. When their horsemen pursue you, I attack them and follow you back to Valognes."

Leif and Bjorn brought our horses. I said, to Erik, "Your son will acquit himself well. He understands what you have to do."

"I know but I am a father and I worry. I know that is not a Viking thing but my father was a Frank. Perhaps I inherited some of his traits."

I knew what he meant. Most Vikings, those who were not jarls, would give their son a sword when he became a man and old enough to fight. He would then show him the door and he would forget him. In the harsh world of the Norwegian fjords that was the only way to avoid having too many mouths to feed. That was why so many young Vikings went raiding. It was that or starve to death. I slid my shield behind my back, over my Longsword and then donned my cloak. My helmet I hung from my saddle. I did not think that I would need it.

Einar and his men galloped back to us by the time that our men had formed up behind us. We looked like an ill-disciplined mob but each of the fifty warriors behind us knew what they had to do. He was grinning when he rode up. "We killed three of them. We did not take their horses, lord, for that would have made us appear as though we were good riders! We turned when they reached their army. Their horsemen come."

The Bretons would now determine our action. If they charged us then we would flee and Bagsecg would ambush them. What was more likely was that they would stop and talk to allow their army to close with us. That was why I had ordered our men to mill around as though we were just a warband raiding.

It was the Breton mailed horsemen who emerged from the woods. They rode towards us and then stopped just a hundred paces from us. The slope meant that if they charged us we would be able to escape. We wore no mail. I counted more than a hundred of them. I saw that they had standards with them and I recognized one of them as the King's standard. I also saw the standards of Robert of Rennes and Count Episoe. I had seen them at Valognes and the Haugr. They waited.

Bjorn asked, "Why do they wait, lord? They outnumber us and they should attack."

"They are looking for the ambush, Bjorn. It is why I chose here. The woods are well to the north of us. They cannot see Bagsecg and his men but they are wondering why we wait. They could be awaiting the arrival of their army."

Just then the standard-bearer and another horseman, after taking off their helmets, detached themselves from the column and rode towards us. "Come, Erik, let us see what they want."

As we headed down the slope Erik said, "You knew they would do this."

"Let us say I hoped that they would try to seek a peaceful solution. This King was barely a baby when my grandfather ruled here. Since he and his family have ruled they have only seen the likes of my brother. They do not know us. They think that we are like those who raided the Liger." We reined in and waited for the two horsemen. We were just forty paces from our men.

"You are the one they call, Lord Göngu-Hrólfr Rognvaldson?"

"I am."

"King Alan the Great would like to speak with you before you are all slain. Do you give your word to a peaceful talk?"

I nodded, "It is a pleasant morning and we have not yet decided where we shall raid. We will speak." The two turned and rode down the hill. "Erik, I do not put it past these Bretons to try something treacherous. Watch for danger and be prepared."

"Aye lord. My shield is over my leg and I have a seax in my right boot."

It was the King, his standard-bearer and Count Episoe who rode towards us. If there was treachery then it would come from the Count of Valognes. I waited for the King to speak. He was younger than I was. I knew that Judicael had also had a claim to the throne and the title. I wondered what had happened to him. This was the first I had heard of the title King of the Bretons. The fact that his standard-bearer had given him the title, the Great, told me much about the King. He was ambitious.

He came directly to the point. His tone was commanding as though he expected me to say I was sorry and give back that which we had taken. "You are the one who has raided my towns and driven my people from their homes."

I smiled, "So it would appear but you are mistaken when you say your people were driven from their homes, they were not. Those homes belonged to the Clan of the Horse, my grandfather's clan, I merely reclaimed them."

Count Episoe could not remain silent, "I have lived there the past five years!"

"And Rurik One Ear lived there for more than ten years before it was taken from his people. You were not strong enough to hold on to it Count and you fled quickly enough, abandoning your people. I showed clemency. Be careful or next time I will not."

"Count, be silent!" The Count of Valognes nodded. "Your clemency is the reason I speak with you Viking. I will give you the chance to quit Brittany and take your warriors back to Rouen. You will pay us one thousand crowns for the damage you have done and you will swear to stay north of your river."

In that moment I saw his ambitions. The men who had tried to kill me were a scouting party. He was looking to take all of the land west of the river. He wanted Bayeux, Caen and my other towns. This was an empire builder. I nodded, "Then I will make a counteroffer. Pay me a thousand crowns and we will swear to keep this frontier for at least a year."

The King coloured but he held his temper. "Know you that we have already slaughtered great numbers of Vikings in the southern part of our land. The army I bring is but a fragment of that which I will bring to wreak vengeance on more Vikings!"

"You seem to think that all Vikings are the same. Are all the Franks the same? When King Louis came north he and his men were slaughtered. Are they the same as you? When we went to Mantes and Anmyen we destroyed those towns completely. Were those Franks the same as you? You call yourself King but I suspect that the Emperor would not accord you that title. I give myself the title Lord of Rouen. If you think that you are strong enough to wrest Valognes from me then try and the crows will feast on the flesh of your men!"

I could see that he was angry now. He raised his hand and then pointed it at me. I knew it was a signal for his standard-bearer and the Count slid their hands towards their swords. "I will have you crucified when I catch you and I will slaughter every Viking I find! I will ride to Rouen to bring ruin to your family and your followers!"

He backed his horse down the slope as his horsemen galloped towards us. The Count Episoe and the standard-bearer drew their swords. In one motion I drew my Longsword from the scabbard on my back and brought it down to cleave the standard bearer's head in two. The Count of Valognes looked in horror as he was spattered with blood and Erik rammed his seax into the Count's thigh. We turned our horses and galloped up the slope. I was grinning as I sheathed my sword, "I think that should make them chase us. Remember, Erik we do not want to outrun them. Their horses have ridden five miles more than ours and when your son attacks them they will wait for the rest of their army."

We had reached our men and they followed us up the slope. We could hear the thunder of hooves behind us. "Lord Göngu-Hrólfr Rognvaldson I like not this. I should be at the back and not leading my men!"

"I want them to see me and think that they can catch me. He will see this horse labouring up the slope and it will encourage him. This King will see it as a quick way to end this war. It is good."

Nodding he dug his heels into his horse and galloped to lead his men. Bjorn and Leif flanked me. Leif glanced over his shoulder, "They are a hundred and fifty paces from us."

"Good. Keep it that way!"

When we reached the top of the hill and the wood Bagsecg did exactly as I had asked. He and his men charged the flank of the Bretons. The Bretons were watching us and they did not see the horsemen who tore through their ranks. Bagsecg and his men were fast and they were skilled. Ten men fell from their horses and then they formed ranks expecting us to continue the attack. Bagsecg led his gleeful men. He rode next to me for a while. "Did we do what you wanted, lord?"

"You did. Now join your father. They will be watching for ambushes all the way to Valognes."

I was satisfied. I had not wanted them too close. We had a twenty-mile ride ahead of us. My aim was to tease them along the road to where my army awaited them. It would be a long day. I had to warn Bjorn and Leif about constantly turning around. "We will hear them if they close with us. Keep a steady pace. If they are going to catch us they will gallop. They are trying to avoid us escaping."

"But we do not want to escape, lord."

"Exactly."

We used the bends in the road to turn and view the progress of the horsemen. The King had rejoined his army but the men who had followed the Count of Valognes were at the fore. If the others ceased their pursuit then they would carry on. They had a master to avenge. We had the advantage that we had passed along this road recently and we knew what to expect. The men of Valognes knew it too but they were blinded by the hope of vengeance. We reined in our horses when we knew that we had an incline and opened their legs on the flatter parts. The result was that our gait was smooth. The Bretons had to keep reacting to us. Despite my instructions, Bjorn continued to look around and he suddenly said, "Lord, we have lost them. They are no longer following."

We were less than five miles from Valognes and the sun was getting lower in the sky. Were they camping for the night? A small stream passed beneath the road and I shouted, "Halt! Let us water the horses."

I dismounted and allowed my horse to drink. Erik rode back through his men. "He did not do as you expected, lord?"

"I am not certain. They have begun to become strung out. Perhaps he is allowing his men to rest. Have one of your men ride ahead to Sven Blue Cheek. Warn him of our position."

"Aye lord."

To be honest, the rest and the water were welcome. This horse was not as comfortable to ride as Gilles. I drank from my water skin too. I did not need food but I saw Leif and Bjorn eating some dried venison They were young and the young were always hungry. I had just hung the skin from my saddle when I heard the thunder of hooves. I had been wrong. The men of Valognes did know the road and they knew of the stream.

"Mount and ride! This is a trap."

I barely had time to mount my horse when the mailed Bretons galloped towards us. I drew Hrolf's Vengeance. We still had an advantage. We had stiraps. Not all of the Bretons did. We must have looked like a routing army as we galloped the last few miles to Valognes but each of us was confident in the men with whom we rode. I glanced over my shoulder. The men of Valognes were less than twenty paces from us. The rest of the horsemen were in a column behind them. I wondered about donning my helmet and then thought better of it. I could hear them closing with us. They were risking irreparably damaging their horses to get the prize that was Lord Göngu-Hrólfr Rognvaldson. They had spears and they were leaning forward like hunters on the chase. The three of us were riding abreast but, as I was the heaviest, my horse was slowly slipping back. The leading warrior made an error. He tried to spear me in the back. It hit my shield and the head broke off. As soon as the spear struck my shield I knew what he had done. Pulling hard on the reins with my left hand I swung Hrolf's Vengeance in an arc. It connected with his chest and knocked him from his horse. He fell beneath the hooves of the next men and they had to slow to avoid their horses falling foul of his body. By such narrow margins are battles won and lost. I dug my heels into my horse's flanks and he galloped after the others. When I looked over my shoulder the Bretons were thirty paces back. They were still close but we had the legs to outrun them. There was no point in teasing them any longer. My men were waiting three miles ahead. The road was flat and we had them where we wanted them. I now knew that their men on foot would be some way down the road but their dangerous men, their horsemen, were all being towed along behind us.

I knew where my men were and yet I struggled to see them. Sven had used his time well. He had disguised our positions with branches and leaves. I did see the gap through which we would pass. Bjorn, Leif and I were the last through and as soon as we were then Sven's men pulled two tree trunks to block it. I reined in, along with the others.

I spoke to Erik and Bagsecg, "You have all done well, now rest. You will be needed on the morrow. Walk your horses to the south gate."

"Aye lord."

I sheathed Hrolf's Vengeance, donned my helmet and drew Longsword. With Bjorn and Leif flanking me I walked back to the logs. Even before I had reached it the archers and slingers on the flanks sent stones, javelins and arrows into the Breton horsemen. I know not if the Count of Valognes lived but his men did not for they were the first to be slain. Fifty horsemen fell before a horn sounded and the survivors fell back to the main army. Another twenty were hit before they escaped.

Sven shouted, "Collect any horses, mail and weapons. Despatch the wounded!"

He was grinning when he turned around. "That will hurt them, lord."

"More than you can know, Sven. We slew three others and they only had two hundred. The men who follow do not have mail!"

My plan had appeared to work but I still needed them to attack my defences. It was why I had sent my horsemen to the south gate. They would deter an attack and allow us to send more men there. I must have looked worried for Sven Blue Cheek said, "Lord, you are tired. Go and eat. We have done nothing save wait for a couple of days. We need you fresh in the morning when they attack."

He was right and I trusted my men. "Aye, Sven but wake me if anything untoward occurs."

I slept remarkably well and that was probably because of the hard ride. The next time I rode from dawn until dusk I would ride Gilles.

Sven had had the sense to send out scouts and they returned with the news that the Bretons had not moved from their camp and, from the talk of their sentries, they were going to attack us. The men he sent spoke Breton and they were good scouts who could hide and listen. My plan had succeeded. After I had eaten I left Sven to prepare our defences and I went through the town to meet with Erik.

"Today, I need you to ride around their rear and make attacks on their baggage. I want no one lost. You are there to hurt them and to worry them. They will be attacking us and I want them to fear that they will be surrounded."

Erik and his son nodded, "We can do that, lord."

As I headed back I heard Bretons' horns. They were attacking. By the time I reached our lines, the Bretons were advancing. They had seen our defences and they were approaching cautiously using their men on foot. They would keep their horsemen for the final charge. They would wait until their men who fought on foot had blunted our weapons and bled us dry. That would not happen. My men made way to accommodate me in the front rank. That was my place and all knew it.

The front ranks were made up of their mailed men and men with shields. My archers let them pass and then showered the ones who followed. Their attack was weakened already but they did not know it. I was in the front rank with my mail and helmet. Longsword was in my hand and my shield hung around my back. I would swing the sword two-handed and harvest Bretons. The men in the woods to my right used javelins and they were able to hurt the men with mail. The result was that those who were closest to the walls of Valognes reached us first. I heard the clash of steel on steel and metal on wood to my left. I awaited the attack for those in the centre were still some paces from us.

In the centre of their line were ten warriors with byrnies, good helmets and spears. I was unworried. With my oathsworn around me, I was as safe as in a tower. I would rely on Bjorn and Leif to deal with the spears they would thrust at me. I would teach them the dangers of fighting a giant. I swung my sword from right to left even as they jabbed their spears at me. My height meant I used a downward angle and I smashed through their spear shafts. As their weapons were shattered, my men thrust their own spears and most found flesh. Around us our men had less success but, in the centre, and on the right, we were hurting them.

I heard Petr Jorgensen shout, "Archers, switch targets!" Now that the mailed men had passed them they could send arrows at their backs. The walls of Valognes were less than a hundred paces from the men who were attacking us and Petr's arrows drove through the mail into the backs of the Bretons. I swung backhanded and this time I hit a mailed Breton.

171

My sword bit into this neck. I think that some of the Bretons might have
fled but the press of men was too great. They were forced onto our spears
and my swinging sword which seemed to sing a song of death as it
descended into Breton flesh. I had the rhythm of a Danish axeman. I
swung in a figure of eight. I was not even looking at the men I was
slaying. My sword just scythed men like wheat. Still, the Bretons were
forced forward but when I found my sword hacking into warriors without
mail then I knew that we were winning.

I heard horns sound. I did not know then what it meant but I later
learned that Erik and Bagsecg had done as I had commanded and
attacked the Breton camp. They had captured many horses and taken a
chest of treasure from King Alan. The Bretons pulled back. They feared
a stronger attack on their rear. Some of my men were eager to follow and
to finish them off. I looked down my line and saw the dead bodies of my
warriors who had died.

"Hold! We wait here for their next attack. Clear away the dead. Be
ready to fight again!"

They did not come again that day. Nor did they sue for peace. I
wondered when it became obvious that they would not attack again if
they were waiting for reinforcements. "Sven Blue Cheek, make sure we
keep good sentries watching this night. I would not have them try a
night-time attack."

"Aye lord but I do not think these Bretons relish the thought of risking
meeting a Viking at night time. They fear us enough in daylight as it is."

"And have the men well fed. The Bretons are in the open and they
will be hungry. The smell of our cooking food may dishearten them."

I went into the town. Petr met me. He and his archers had the best
view of the battle. "How are you for arrows?"

"When this battle is over we will need to make arrows but we have
enough. I have sent some of the boys out to collect undamaged ones.
They lost more than a hundred men this day, lord."

"Then we only have five hundred more to slaughter and we will have
won!" He laughed.

When I reached Erik, I saw the horses he had captured. Bagsecg was
so excited that he spoke to me before his father, "Lord, we drove off their
horses and look, we have a chest of treasure."

I smiled at his enthusiasm but spoke to his father, "Did we lose men?"

"Four but we slew twenty and wounded others. They were the servants who watched the tents and a few Breton warriors. We also drove off two of their cattle. The Bretons will be hungry this night."

"Have they tents?"

"Some but when we drove off the horses they damaged some."

"You have done well," I turned to Bagsecg, "you have all done well but always remember, Bagsecg Eriksson, that we do not have great numbers of horsemen. The four men who fell were worth more than that chest of coins."

After checking the rest of the defences, I went into the hall where men had prepared food. It felt strange to be in a town without women and children. We were a town of warriors. Ubba Long Cheek and Sven were waiting for me in the hall. Ubba said, "Sit lord, you have done more than any. It is not right."

"It is necessary, Ubba, for we are on the edge of something. The battle is poised on the edge of a sword. They outnumber us but we have better men. Tomorrow will determine who rules this land. A little effort from me and we might hold on to what we have. When that day comes I can return to Rouen and begin to plan for Paris. I still have a dream and a prophecy to fulfil. My grandfather died so that I might have a son."

I am sorry, lord." He shook his head, "I still cannot believe that I am to be lord of Valognes!"

"And you will have the hardest task for yours will be the only stronghold which cannot be reached by drekar. Saxbjǫrn might be the closest to the Bretons but yours is the only stronghold which the Bretons can surround. I have not given you the easiest of tasks. You bring your family here. If you wish to reconsider your promise to hold this for me I will understand."

"Lord, when I followed you from the fjord I was a young boy. I was barely able to hold a sword let alone use one. All that I have I owe to you. I have followed your Longsword and learned from you. I have seen that which I can become. You have a land to hold. I have but one town. If I cannot do that then I do not deserve to be called a warrior. I will choose men whom I can trust and we will make this a stronghold which will break the Breton hearts!"

Sven and the others insisted that I slept in the hall. Although I slept well I was still awoken by the sudden storm which erupted in the middle of the night. It was the kind of storm which comes from nowhere and is as though the gods are punishing men. Thunder crashed and lightning flashed. The rain was so loud on the roof above me that it woke me. This was the sort of storm which made ships, far out to sea, disappear. It was a storm sent for a purpose. Restless I rose and went to the walls. The sentries had wisely taken shelter. Recklessly I stood on the walls and watched the sky lit by Thor's bolts. I wondered if it had been such a storm that had touched Dragonheart's sword. I was tempted to go for my sword and raise it. Perhaps I would have a magic sword. Then I realised it was not meant to be. When Dragonheart had had his sword touched by the gods he and his oathsworn had been about to be slaughtered. We were not in such danger. The storm had been sent to help us. The Bretons would be out there in this wild storm and they would have to endure it. They were Christians and they did not believe in Thor and Odin. We understood such storms and they did not. I went back to my chamber and took off my soaking wet clothes. I dried myself and dressed.

I built up the fire in the hall and found some cured pig meat. I cut two thick slices and placed them on a metal skillet. While they heated through I sought out some bread. There was some but it was stale. I cut some and placed them in the skillet with the pig meat. The rendered fat would soften the bread. By the time I had found ale the food was ready and I was eating it when Ubba found me.

"You are up early lord. Were you hungry?"

"No Ubba but the storm woke me. The gods have sent it. On this day we defeat the Bretons. It has given me an appetite. There is more meat as well as bread. It is good. The Bretons know how to cure meat."

The smell of the cooking meat woke others and soon men were arriving to cook their own food. The result was that, when dawn broke, we were all awake. We were all fed and dressed. Dawn brought brooding skies but the rain had stopped and the storm had passed. I led the men to the battle lines. The night sentries were relieved, "Go to the hall eat, sleep and rest. If we need you this day I will summon you."

Sven Long Strider who had commanded the night guard said, "That storm made me worried, lord. Had I not had my hammer of Thor I might have fled. Trees were struck close to the Breton camp. Thor wishes us to win. Perhaps he does not like the White Christ."

"Perhaps. We will see what the day brings."

There was damage which we had to clear. Broken branches and debris created hazards. We left the hazards on the road but cleared them from our lines. We waited. If they were going to come then it would be sooner rather than later. Any reinforcements which were coming would now be slowed. I knew from experience what such a storm would do to a road. Debris and mud would slow up an army coming to the aid of their King. If the Bretons did not attack us then we would attack them and end this battle.

We heard their horns not long before noon. They were coming. From the walls of Valognes I heard Petr Jorgensen shout, "Lord, they are advancing. They have their horsemen dismounted and marching with their men."

"Thin out the others with your arrows. We have the mettle to meet their metal this day!"

Bergil Fast Blade began to bang his shield and to chant.

Hrólfr and his Vikings march to war
See their spears and hear them roar
The Hrólfr and his Vikings with bloody blades
Their roaring means you will be shades
Hrólfr and his Vikings our best men
Hrólfr and his Vikings death comes again
Leading Vikings up the Breton water
They brought death they brought slaughter
Taking slaves, swords and gold
Hrólfr and his Vikings were the most bold
Hrólfr and his Vikings our best men
Hrólfr and his Vikings death comes again
Fear us Breton we are the best
Fighting us a fatal test
We come for land to make our own
To give young Vikings not yet grown
Hrólfr and his Vikings our best men
Hrólfr and his Vikings death comes again
Hrólfr and his Vikings our best men
Hrólfr and his Vikings death comes again

As Petr and his archers took up the chant, and, in the horse camp Erik and his men, the song seemed to roll around the town like the thunder of the previous night. It mattered not that they could not understand the words; it was the intent which would put fear in the hearts of the men advancing towards us.

The rain had spread debris on the road. The ditches along the side had flooded and mud now covered the surface along with puddles and pools.

They were trying to come at us in a straight line but they could not maintain it. Some fell in the ditches. Others tripped and slipped when they walked in the mud and the puddles filled with hidden obstacles. We had not cleared the bodies and their own dead hampered them. They neared us but it was not the formation their King had envisaged. It was a ragged line. We, on the other hand, had a solid line of spears, swords and shields. I was the only one who did not use his shield. I would rely on my Longsword and Bjorn and Leif. The more we had fought together the more accomplished they had become. My height meant I could swing above their heads and my two warriors' shields protected most of my chest.

The leader of the Bretons had a plumed helmet. His shield had a red boar upon it. He shouted, "Charge!" They ran at us. That in itself was a mistake for the surface was too slippery and their boots inadequate. Some fell while others slipped and, when they tumbled, were close enough for my men with spears to skewer them as they lay writhing at our feet. The leader and the men around him struck us together. My sword was already swinging as Leif's shield took the first warrior's spear. My sword hacked deep into his left shoulder. Bjorn stabbed the next Breton in the face with his spear but he, too, was struck by a spear. I swung backhand and smashed my sword through the shield of a third Breton, breaking his arm and knocking him to the ground. Ubba Long Cheek finished him off. All along our line men were engaged.

Sven Blue Cheek and Bergil Fast Blade were fortunate. They were close to the ditch next to the road and they had fewer men to fight. Sven Blue Cheek was a master of strategy. He could have led the clan had he chosen to. "Charge!" He led Bergil Fast Blade and his men into the flank of the men we were fighting. They were attacking their right sides and they had no shield there to protect themselves. In close combat, their spears were a hindrance and Sven and his opportunist attackers wreaked havoc. From the walls of Valognes Petr and his men rained arrows on those behind the mailed warriors but what decided the battle that day was the charge, through Valognes north gate, of Erik and his horsemen. They exploited the gap created by Sven Blue Cheek.

All the pressure was in the centre. As I had expected King Alan had wanted me dead and the Bretons who charged at us were determined to kill me. Our spears were shattered and Leif, Ubba and the rest had to use swords. Sámr Oakheart and Ragnar the Resolute used the woods to our right to infiltrate around the other flank of the Breton attack. As Bjorn was struck in the helmet and fell I swung my sword in a wide arc which made the attackers before me recoil. Two were too slow and died. In that momentary breathing space, I saw that King Alan had defeated himself. By sending his best towards me my horsemen, Sven's attack, allied to Sámr's, had destroyed the rest of their army. As the farmers and levy fled my men turned to surround the hundred or so warriors trying to get at me. They had nowhere to go. They could have surrendered but they feared our vengeance and so they fought on. It was to no avail. Their circle shrank and the Breton bodies mounted as we whittled their numbers down. It took time for they were mailed but when the last one was slain my men cheered and called my name.

"Göngu-Hrólfr Rognvaldson, Göngu-Hrólfr Rognvaldson, Göngu-Hrólfr Rognvaldson!"

We had won. Erik and his horsemen rode after the men we had routed. They returned at noon with bloodied blades. "The Bretons have fled, lord. We slew many but their King and his horsemen evaded us. This land is now yours!"

Part 4 The Siege of Paris

Chapter 12

It had been half a year since we had returned from the battle of Valognes. We had not been able to return as swiftly as I would have wished. King Alan had, despite his defeat, not accepted it gracefully. He had sent emissaries demanding the return of the captured towns. I had invited him to take them. The delay helped us for we had an army of warriors who had little to do. They rebuilt the defences of the towns we had captured. Saxbjǫrn had not been idle in Carentan and it was now stronger than it had ever been. It would become the rock in the centre of our defences. The lords who had joined me and had been given towns were more than grateful to me for the opportunities I had given them. They each now had a home which they could defend and a port from which they could raid. Eventually, after the Bretons had sent raiding parties which we had slaughtered, they seemed to accept the situation but I knew that King Alan had not forgotten us. He chose, instead, to raid the Franks and that suited me for it would make our own raid on Paris that much easier. Leif and Bjorn had both been wounded but not seriously. I gave them both the mail from the Breton leaders as well as names. They would be Bjorn the Brave and Leif Shield Bearer. It was typical of the men that they valued the names more than the mail and weapons of the rich Breton lords.

We returned with great quantities of treasure and booty. We had captured all of the towns so quickly that the Bretons had only managed to escape with their lives. They had left, hidden in their homes and farms, all of their coins, jewels and seals of office. With the horses, mail and weapons we had captured every warrior was richer. That had an immediate effect. The Danes who had gone to Frisia to raid had not been as splendidly rewarded as we. The ones who had raided the Liger were also not as comfortable as the men who followed me. Every day more drekar arrived. Some wanted land and a home. I sent them to Valognes and Carentan. We needed the land filling up with Vikings. The Bretons would not shift us a second time. Others wished to join me on my raid to Paris. The Viking world all knew of my plan. That meant the Franks would know too. I would not be able to surprise them. Those drekar were moored upstream from us. All traffic down the Seine ceased. Paris was cut off from the sea to the west. They had to send goods they wished to trade with the north down the Rhine. That journey added five days and many wagons. The Franks were now being hurt by our presence.

I was ruthless when it came to accepting men who wished to follow me. My grandfather had taught me the dangers of blindly trusting other Vikings. My father had died because of a brother's treachery and perfidious Danes. I spoke with all who came. Those whom I knew had served Guthrum were, generally, accepted. Others did not meet my eye or they did not give the right answers to my questions. Those I sent hence. I made enemies rather than friends but at least I knew who those enemies were.

Back in Rouen, I busied myself with organizing my land. I had warriors who could fight but I needed men I could trust to run my town. My wife tried to persuade me to have Æðelwald of Remisgat serve as steward. I did not trust him and I refused. Relations were strained between us. I cared not. My wife had borne me another daughter. This one was born dead. The curse still remained. While I sought men who could serve me, I made sure that my walls and towers were improved. We had taken the Breton strongholds too easily. I had bridges over my ditches. I had my gates studded with iron so that they would not burn as quickly and would resist axes. I had a second gate built behind the first. If we could use fire then so could our enemies.

Guthrum made a visit to speak with me. It was at Mörsugur. I wondered why he had chosen that time. With short days and violent seas, it was the worst time of year to sail. He came with Siegfried and Sinric. There were four drekar in all. Now that he was King of Danelaw and a Christian he was more acceptable to my wife and her priest, Æðelwald of Remisgat.

As we walked my walls I discovered the reason for his visit. "Hrólfr, I know that you are disappointed that I took the cross. Yet I did so because Alfred is a cunning King. He would have defeated us. His burghs are impossible to take." I did not believe so but I said nothing. "I came here because I was invited to Wintan-Caestre to celebrate the birth of the White Christ. It is a dreary feast. They drink little and pray too much. I said that I would come here to try to convert you." I glared at him. He laughed, "I know that I cannot. And I came here too because Siegfried and Sinric, along with other jarls, refuse to convert. Alfred is not happy. They are here because they will be safer with you. I fear that their short tempers will resurrect the war."

"But you are a Viking. War is in your blood."

"You know not how many of my men were slaughtered. I lost many men who had followed me for years. Men you can trust are hard to replace. No, I make war in the north."

"The Land of the Wolf?"

He shivered and clutched the hammer of Thor which lay, hidden, beneath his cross, "They are safe for they have a witch!" That confirmed to me that he was not a Christian. He had taken the cross to make himself accepted by King Alfred. "No, I war against the men north of the old Roman wall. I blood my young warriors and gain land."

We had reached the river and I pointed upstream to the longphort of drekar which lay three miles upstream. "I have a hundred and fifty ships. With those of Siegfried and Sinric, we will have another forty. If you have other captains who wish adventure and treasure then we can make the raid on Paris."

"The Franks know that you are coming."

"That is why I need overwhelming numbers."

"I still do not understand why you need to raid Paris. With so many ships the treasure you take will not be worth the effort."

"The Empire is large. I am no fool. With every Viking who ever sailed, I have not enough men to defeat them. Should their Emperor ever get off his fat backside he would realise that and he would bring his whole army and drive me back into the sea. I need to make him accept me as ruler of this land. To do that I need to hurt him so much that his choice is war or acceptance of our presence. The Bretons have, unwittingly, aided me. They now attack the west of the Empire."

"Then you would become Christian?"

"No, I would not. If the Emperor recognises me he will have to accept that I am what he calls pagan."

Guthrum shook his head, "That will never happen. It is the Holy Roman Empire. The Pope is the one who crowned the Emperor. There are many claimants to the crown. The Pope would simply choose another. If you are a pagan then you cannot rule in a Christian land. I know that."

Guthrum was a practical and pragmatic man. He knew more about the way the courts worked. Doubts began to assail me. Perhaps I would need to reassess my plan. "Thank you for your advice. I know it to be honest and I will think about this. It does not change my decision to attack Paris but I may have to consider defeating the Empire."

"You said yourself that is impossible."

I smiled, "You are talking to a man who sank to the bottom of the sea and was reborn. Many people would say that was impossible. I never use the word. I try to work out how to make the seemingly impossible happen."

"*Wyrd!*"

Guthrum told me that he had planned on staying until the start of Þorri. To celebrate his arrival, we held a feast. It was the feast of the winter solstice. It was days before the Christians celebrated the birth of the White Christ. That was deliberate on my part. I wanted our pagan feast to be bigger. I met some of the people Guthrum had brought over. One was a priestly looking man; he looked young. He sat down from us with the warriors of Guthrum's oathsworn.

"You say you are not a Christian yet you have brought a priest with you."

He shook his head, "He might be a Christian but he is not of Alfred's faith. This is a priest from Hibernia. Some of them refuse to take the path of Rome. He serves me but Alfred does not like him. He is offended by his teachings. It is another reason I came. I am gaining favour with Alfred by ridding his land of those who question his priests."

"Then you will take him to Hibernia?"

"He does not wish to return to that isle. He is young and wishes to see the world. I told him that this land would give him that opportunity. Perhaps he could voyage on your drekar. He is a strong young man."

"Perhaps. I will speak to him on the morrow when my head and eyes are clear. My grandfather was ill-served by some men. I am cautious about those I let reside in my land. What is his name?"

"He was born Aiden but when he was baptised he took the name Padraigh."

I shook my head, "Why do the Christians like to change a man's name? You will always be Guthrum! I know not Athelstan!"

That made him laugh so much that tears sprang from his eyes, "You of all people should not comment about names! You were Hrólfr Ragnvaldson, then Göngu-Hrólfr Rognvaldson and I have heard men call you Longsword!"

I could not help smiling. "The difference is that I was given those names by my family and my crew. They were not some perfumed priest with soft hands and treacherous intent!"

"Then you will find Padraigh a refreshing change. He has rough hands for he works in wood and wields a sword when he practises with my oathsworn. As for treacherous, he is the most loyal man I know."

I nodded. There was a sudden uproar. Siegfried and Sinric had risen. They faced each other. They were both drunk and their hands went to their daggers. My wife looked shocked. I stood and roared, "The first man to draw a weapon here faces me and they will not leave this hall alive! If you wish to behave like animals then go back to your drekar!" Although both were drunk they were not drunk enough to face the wrath of the Lord of Rouen. They sat. I saw Sven Blue Cheek stride over and sit between them. He caught my eye and winked. There would be no further trouble.

Bergil Fast Blade and his wife were speaking with Guthrum and my wife with Æðelwald of Remisgat. He did not appear to like the idea of Guthrum's priest. Bergljót had been a little unwell and Bergil had left her in his hall. I knew that his thoughts were with his mother.

I realised the Gefn was alone." Is this too much for you, mother?"

She patted my hand, "My son I am as happy as any here. I am just worried about Bergljót," She shook her head, "To think that I am at a feast with a King."

I laughed, "He is just Guthrum!"

"Do not scoff," she chided me, "Your father would have been proud to know that a King seeks your advice. It is known that kings ride in fear of you. I know you to be a gentle man but you care for your people and your clan in a way that makes you greater than any king. I am content but I confess that I do miss Bergljót and Hrolf. We were of an age. We could talk about what it was like when we were young. The world was a different place then. Why even young Isabelle is learning to read! Until you came none in our village could read. Yet now Bergil can read and, so his mother tells me, he can write. Who would have thought we would have lived to see such times?"

At heart, she was a simple woman. It was a pity that her husband was dead but I hoped that we had made her last years comfortable. Poppa was very fond of her and I was grateful to my wife and daughters for the attention they lavished on her.

There was no more trouble but I made certain I was the last to leave the hall. I do not think that either Siegfried or Sinric were happy with me from then on. They continued to follow my banner but they resented me. I had commanded them as though they were my subjects. Poppa was asleep when I reached our chamber and I almost collapsed into the bed. There had been a time when all I needed to think about was myself and then my drekar crew. Now I had a whole clan to worry about. I had to think about alliances and I had to keep the peace between those who did not follow me. Life had been simpler when I had lived in Norway with Gefn. As I fell asleep I could almost hear the Norns spinning.

I was awake early. I had had a restless night. The Paris raid was almost in my grasp and yet it still needed work from me. The servants had cleared the debris from the hall and were laying freshly cooked meat and bread on the table. Along with pickled fish and cheese, we would eat well. The latest brew of ale was there too and I tucked in. I had eaten sparingly the night before. That had been a time for talking. Now I could break my enforced fast.

I had just finished when Padraig entered. He almost turned around and left when he saw that I was alone. I waved him to me, "Come, in my hall we all share the same table."

He had a quiet, almost shy way of speaking but he looked you in the eye. I liked that. I waited until he had brought his food and his ale to my table before I spoke. "Guthrum says you wish to stay in my land?"

He looked at me, "I am sorry lord, but it is my custom to thank God for this food before I eat. I grew up poor. One of my brothers died of starvation."

"Do not apologise, Padraig. Here we do not question another man's beliefs so long as he does not try to impose his on us."

He shot me a surprised look and then nodded, "Lord God I thank you for this food and for the hospitality of Lord Göngu-Hrólfr Rognvaldson, Amen."

I smiled, "That was simple enough and I understood the words. When my wife's priest speaks it is in Latin. It is almost as though the priests are trying to hide something from their people."

He nodded, "That is one of the reasons my sect chose not to follow Rome. There are fewer of us these days. I could have gone to the island they called Bardsey for there is a monastery there but I wanted to see more of the world."

"So long as you do not seek to convert any of my people then I am happy for you to sail on my drekar or stay if you wish. You seem a pleasant young man and I can see from your hands that you are not afraid of hard work."

"Thank you, lord, but I fear that Æðelwald of Remisgat would not agree with you. He does not like me."

"And that speaks in your favour. I cannot stand the oily man. Stay with us for I am certain that a man such as you will have sage advice to offer us. I am a warrior. Running a town, let alone a county is alien to me. In return for allowing you to sail on my drekar, I would ask that you help me to see how to run this town efficiently."

"Efficiently, lord?"

"I can read and I can write. I know numbers; that is to say, I know how many men are on a battlefield trying to kill me but the squiggles which tell you how much tax a man should pay is beyond me."

"And you think that I could do this?"

I shrugged, "I know not but whatever you could tell me would be more than I know and for that, I would be grateful. Guthrum says you are honest and I believe him."

"You too are an honest man, lord. I will do what I can but I do not promise to know all."

"The man who says he knows everything is a man to be feared and shunned. No man can know everything for the world is too wide and the Allfather too powerful" He nodded. "You are the first priest who has not grasped his cross when I spoke the word Allfather."

"That is because it may well be the same god that I worship. We have different beliefs, you and I, yet we both believe in a supreme being, a single god who rules all. I will take that compromise."

Others entered. "We will speak more when our guests have gone."

Siegfried and Sinric had been offended by my manner. They considered it high handed. They came to say they would be raiding but wished to know when they should return for the Paris raid. They were leaving.

"By Haustmánuður they should have collected all of their taxes and crops. Everything will be gathered for winter. We will have more ships then, for few captains wish to raid in the depths of winter." I smiled. "That also gives you the opportunity to raid without me at the steering board."

They looked at each other and then gave the false smile I had seen in men who were foresworn. Perhaps I would not need the two Danes and their ships. The Norns were spinning their webs! "Then we will return with as many ships as we can gather. You need not large ships. Threttanessa will suffice."

"Aye, it is the warriors who man them who are important."

My hall had a better atmosphere once they and their men had gone.

Not long before Guthrum left a rider came from Lisieux to tell Bergil Fast Blade that his mother was close to death. Gefn wished to be with her friend and sister. I had my horsemen escort her in a wagon. If we had not had guests then I would have gone with them for Bergljót had been ever kind to me and I wished to be there when she passed to the Otherworld. I did not make all of my own decisions now. I was the ruler of a large land and I had obligations.

When Guthrum left he promised me as many ships as he could manage for our raid on Paris. Now that he knew it would be Haustmánuður he was confident that he could encourage more of his Danes to join me. He had chuckled, "It may raise my favour with King Alfred if I tell him that I am sending them to you because they are pagans."

I never saw Guthrum again. He died the next year. When he died he was vilified by Alfred and the Saxons as being a monster and by his Danes for his change of faith. That was unfair. He was dead and could not answer those who criticised him. For me, he was always Guthrum. I trusted him and he never lied to me. That is all that you can ask of a friend and a shield brother.

Bergljót also died. Gefn was with her at the end as was Bergil Fast Blade. They arrived a day before she died and Bergljót went to the Otherworld content. When she returned, I noticed a change in Gefn. She smiled more and she was ever attentive to me, Poppa and the girls. She seemed to enjoy every moment of every day. When one of my daughters had a tantrum then it would be Gefn who would seek to calm her. It was as though she had found inner peace and happiness. I had not been there when my mother had died, nor my grandmother and so I did not move far from Rouen for I feared the worst. She did not have long left to live. I had made sure that, from the time she returned from Lisieux I told her each night that I loved her and I had embraced her.

The Norns were spinning and they ensured that I did not get to say goodbye to her or to be there at the end. I rode, with my horsemen to the desolation that was Mantes. I wished to see for myself what the Franks had done. I bade farewell to my wife and adopted mother.

Gefn looked frail and she was tearful as she bade me goodbye. "Come back safely my son. There is no amount of gold on this earth which can replace you."

"I will mother."

I took Padraig to one side. The Irish priest had taken on much since he had joined me. Now I gave him another task. "I would have you watch over Gefn. She is old and she is frail. I would not have her go to the Otherworld alone. I would be here for her."

He nodded, "Then that is easy, lord."

"It is?"

He nodded and smiled, "Aye, do not go on this raid. That way you will be here with her when she passes."

"Would that that were possible but the spell has been woven and the Norns have spun. I cannot avoid that which was prophesied."

"Then I will watch over all of your family and pray that you return."

Padraigh showed his true character. Æðelwald of Remisgat refused to have anything to do with her for she was a pagan.

"Padraig, you have shown yourself to be a man I can trust. What have you learned about my town and how I can rule it fairly?" He had spent the last month and a half looking at my town and its finances.

He nodded, "Your people love you lord but they are not paying what they should for the protection you afford them." I nodded. That was good to hear. "If you wish I could assess each of those who live within the walls of Rouen and make a suggestion of how much they should pay."

"For that, I would be grateful." I paused, "What would be the price?"

He smiled, "One you could easily afford, lord. Allow me to build a small church outside your walls. I swear that I will not try to convert any of your people but if the men and women of Rouen choose to come to my church then I will give them comfort."

I was uncomfortable with this. It seemed reasonable but was this a way to insinuate himself into my land?

"You would swear?"

"On a Bible, if you wished but I suspect that you would wish something different."

I nodded. "Take my arm, look me in the eye and swear and then you may have your church."

He did so and when I looked into his eyes I saw no lie. That was one of the best bargains I made. He was fair in his dealings with my people and yet I was richer for it. He worked tirelessly and he helped to build his own church. Æðelwald of Remisgat was less than happy when some of those who used to attend the church in the town began to go to his humble little church which had neither bell nor tower. I was learning that the Christian church was not as simple as I had thought.

More drekar came. Their crews raided just upstream. The land between Rouen and Mantes became a wasteland. Those that could, fled and those that could not died. The Bretons were also not content with the border I had created. They sent numerous expeditions to try to reclaim what they saw as their land but each time they were repulsed by my lords. My leaders each now had twice the men that they had. Young boys had become youths and other Vikings had sought a home. I was lucky for my lords were all good leaders.

When it was Sólmánuður I sent messages to tell them that I would need their ships in the Seine by Tvímánuður. I had had another drekar built. *'Gefn'* was a fine drekar. Boasting twenty-five oars on each side she was the biggest ship in my fleet. My adopted mother herself launched her. Tears sprang to her eyes. The prow had been carved well by Sven the Ship. Although it was a dragon it had Gefn's features. It was *wyrd*.

There were other changes too. Bjorn the Brave had never totally recovered from his wound. He could not use both arms as well as he needed for the shield wall and I made him captain of her. My wife was with child once more. I made a blót in the river. I was alone when I did so. This was a sacrifice made to the gods by me alone. I slew a young foal. It was one of a pair of twins and both had been bred by Erik Gillesson especially for me. I kept the other and named it in honour of my grandfather, Hrolf. When Gilles became old then Hrolf would be my horse. His sibling died to ensure that my child was born a boy.

Before I left I spoke with my wife and Sprota. I would be raiding and I needed them both to make every effort to do all that they could to protect my unborn child. "This time you rest as much as you can. I would not lose another child. It matters not if it is a boy or a girl. It is of my blood and I would have them live."

"He will live. That I promise you."

"A boy? Have you dreamed? Are you a volva now?"

She laughed, "We burn witches! No, I have not dreamed but I feel that it is a boy. I will eat those foods which the women of your clan say will make a boy and I will rest. This raid is important to you for you have been told that it will help you have a son. Father Æðelwald has told me that if we pray to God he will send a son. I pray every day with him. While you are up the river we will do that which we can to make you a son."

A month before my ships were due I sent for William, my spy. I had seen him at Valognes when I had watched him guarding Bagsecg's back. He was still a warrior. "William, we are going to attack Paris soon."

"I know, lord. Men speak of little else."

"I would have you scout it out for me."

"You wish to know if Charles the Fat has made any changes."

"I do."

"I said once before, lord, that it was Count Odo you should fear. His wife and children were slain by Vikings ten years since and he hates all of you. Paris will not fall easily."

I nodded, "And when you are done I would have you scout the lands to the south and east too."

He looked surprised and that was the first time I had seen that emotion upon his face, "Burgundy, lord?"

"Aye. I hear it is a rich part of the Empire. If things go ill with Paris it may be that we can wrest some coin and treasure from that fertile valley." He nodded. "I would have you back here within a month."

"It will be hard, lord but I will try."

While he was away I visited the drekar captains who had been at the longphort for some time. A few had been there since Ýlir. They had been the ones who had raided locally. I told them when we would be sailing. They had been patient and the prize that was Paris was worth waiting for. That done I had my drekar hauled out of the water and cleaned of weeds and resealed. The waters of the Seine might be safer than the wild west seas but it paid to be prudent.

When William came back it was not with good news. "Lord, they have blocked the river close to Mantes. You cannot get upstream." I merely nodded. Count Odo knows that you are coming and he is ready."

"And King Charles?"

"He is in the east and seems unconcerned."

"Burgundy?"

He smiled, he was an old soldier. "Blissfully unaware of any danger. They have had a good harvest. They have plenty of wine and they do not keep a good watch on the river. They also resent Charles the Fat and there are rumours of rebellion."

"You have done well." I gave him five golden crowns. "And is there another way we can sail to Paris?"

He smiled, "Aye lord, down the Oise! I have heard that Vikings can drag their ships overland. It is just two or three miles between the rivers."

I smiled, "William you are the best of spies for you have the mind of a warrior, a Viking warrior!"

The Norns had spun and the Allfather had smiled upon us. I had a way into Paris. Now I just needed ships. The drekar of my men were already in my river. There were fifty ships in the longphort. We now awaited those promised by Guthrum. Siegfried and Sinric arrived first. They had with them two hundred drekar. Most boasted less than fourteen oars on each side but that was a good thing. It meant they had a shallower draught. The two leaders left their ships at Rouen while their fleet sailed upstream to join the congestion there. They both had smug looks upon their faces.

"We said we would bring us enough ships. Now we can raid eh, lord?"

I nodded, "You have done well. Are these the ships Guthrum promised?"

Sinric shook his head. "We brought these from Frisia and Denmark. We do not need Guthrum and his ships. We have enough."

"We do not have enough. The river is blocked upstream from Mantes. We will have to carry our ships overland to remove the blockage. We can never have enough ships. I command and we will await the arrival of Guthrum and his ships."

They exchanged a look and Sinric shrugged. "We will wait at the longphort but we leave at the start of Haustmánuður with or without you Lord Göngu-Hrólfr Rognvaldson."

Their words disturbed me. Had I made a pact with my enemies? Would this be like the raid on the Tamese all over again? My captains had still to arrive and I needed their advice. Bergil Fast Blade, Sven Blue Cheek and Bagsecg the Horseman arrived first. I confided in them.

"We have invited the wolf into our home. We are hurt no matter what happens, lord. If they choose to take over this raid we cannot stop them.

There are so many ships and they are upstream of us. They could do what the Franks could not. They could take our homes." I knew why Bergil Fast Blade sounded so fearful. He now had a family.

Sven gave good counsel, "Lord you are assuming the worst. That is not always a bad thing where Danes are concerned but they will be our allies until we have taken Paris. We think they will be treacherous and we watch for it." He patted Bagsecg on the shoulder, "We have something that the other ships do not. We have Bagsecg and eighty horsemen. We have eyes and ears which can scout out the land. They will report to you."

I saw Bagsecg swell with pride. "If my father brought his horsemen then we would double our horsemen!"

Shaking my head, I said, "Your father and Ubba Long Cheek need to guard the Cotentin. I know that King Alan is busy fighting the Franks to the south but when he realises that we have taken the bulk of our men to Paris he may try to take back what he thinks are his towns."

Ragnar the Resolute, Sámr Oakheart, Halfi Axe Tongue, Finnbjǫrn Stormbringer and my other captains arrived two days later and they were apprised of the situation. When Guthrum's fleet of eighty ships arrived, I was relieved. They were led by Karl Saxon Slayer. I smiled as he stepped ashore. With a name such as Saxon Slayer and with the hammer of Thor hanging prominently from his neck, he was not the kind of warrior Alfred would approve of.

He grasped my arm, "It is good to be in a land which is not overpopulated with praying priests! We are ready to hew heads, Lord Göngu-Hrólfr Rognvaldson."

I took him to one side. "Before you join us there is something that you should know," I told him of my fears.

When I had told him, he was not surprised. "They were close to King Guthrum at one time but both are ambitious men. The King fears that they are joining you to gain enough coin and men to take his throne from him." He grinned. "I will slit their throats before that can happen!"

I was reassured. We had one last night in my hall and then we sailed our ships down to the longphort. We had enough ships and we had enough men. We could sail up the Seine and Paris would reward us. I bade farewell to Poppa and my daughters. I said, "I pray that you are safe and this child, my son is born healthy."

I gathered Sinric, Siegfried, Karl and Sven aboard *'Gefn'*. "We sail tonight for Mantes. It will take time for the fleet to navigate this river. I know that my ship will be at the rear. That cannot be helped. The river is blocked some miles upstream from Mantes. There is a small village called Vaux. My scouts say that from there to the Oise is just a couple of miles. We will have our smallest ships carried overland to the Oise. They can sail down that river and attack those who defend the river from the rear."

Siegfried asked, "Who will command these men?"

I looked him in the eye, "You know the bulk of the captains better than I do. Whom do you suggest?"

He smiled and said, "Sinric and I will lead those ships."

"Good, then we are decided. Once we have removed the blockade then we take Paris."

When the two Danes had left us Sven Blue Cheek and Karl Saxon Slayer remained. "I like not this, lord."

"Nor do I Sven but I think this is the Norns at work. Our ships are here at the rear of this longphort. They will be the first to Paris. Let us see what web the Norns have spun."

Chapter 13

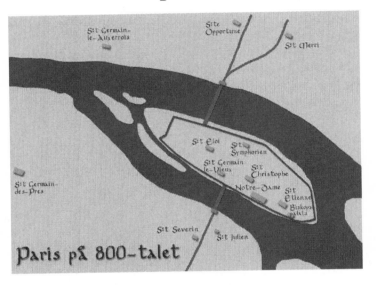

Paris på 800-talet

We passed Mantes and headed upstream. I had the largest crew I had ever commanded and we used a chant to make us one. The progress up the river was slow. The Franks would know we were coming. I knew this from Bagsecg's horsemen. They were on the south side of the river and they kept me apprised of what was happening ahead. They rode as far as the bridge over the Seine and told me that it was heavily defended on both ends. We rowed and we sang. To honour my grandfather and Bagsecg who had taken over his mantle we sang my grandfather's song.

The horseman came through darkest night
He rode towards the dawning light
With fiery steed and thrusting spear

Hrolf the Horseman brought great fear

Slaughtering all he breached their line
Of warriors slain there were nine
Hrolf the Horseman with gleaming blade
Hrolf the Horseman all enemies slayed

With mighty axe Black Teeth stood
Angry and filled with hot blood
Hrolf the Horseman with gleaming blade
Hrolf the Horseman all enemies slayed
Ice cold Hrolf with Heart of Ice
Swung his arm and made it slice
Hrolf the Horseman with gleaming blade
Hrolf the Horseman all enemies slayed

In two strokes the Jarl was felled
Hrolf's sword nobly held
Hrolf the Horseman with gleaming blade
Hrolf the Horseman all enemies slayed

The fleet stopped during the afternoon and I saw, ahead of me, men leave the ships to scramble ashore. All the men from the crews ahead of us left their ships to chop down a whole wood for its timber. It took a day to hew and trim the trees. Then they were laid like a wooden river and the threttanessa and other small ships were hauled from the water onto the trees. Each crew pulled their own boat and they all had their own chants. The air was filled with Viking voices. We saw not a single Frank and that gave me hope. If King Charles had an army nearby then this would be the perfect time to attack. With no Frankish warriors in sight then I knew that Paris and Count Odo stood alone. We waited until Siegfried and Sinric had left with the last of their drekar before we headed upstream. This time I led. We made our way through the throng of ships and headed towards the blockade. I had just one hundred and fifty ships with me.

It was dark by the time we reached the blockade. The Franks had tied ships together with a chain and they were across the river. They had the two ends protected by warriors and by hastily erected wooden walls. It was as I saw them that I realised we need not have transported our drekar to the Oise. We could attack the Franks and then dismantle the barrier. William had given me advice he thought was sound but he knew Franks. He had not seen us fight often enough to see our potential. We could destroy this barrier. We anchored just half a Roman mile from it. I summoned my leading captains.

"Sven, take four drekar crew and yours. Attack and capture the wooden wall to the south. I will take Bergil, Sámr and Ragnar. We will take the north end."

"Aye lord."

"Finnbjǫrn when the chain is unshackled, then the ships will drift downstream. Make sure there is a gap for them to do so. I want none of our drekar damaged."

"Aye lord." He laughed, "When we are in Paris before the two Danes I think that they will be unhappy."

Shaking his head Sven said, "Do not be too sure about that. They did not have far to go and the Oise feeds into the Seine. I would expect to see them when dawn breaks."

When they had left the four drekar I was commanding headed upstream towards the Franks. Nighttime suited us. We did not fear blades in the dark. Franks did. Leaving a skeleton crew on board we slipped ashore. This time I did use my shield and Sven's Vengeance. I did not wear my helmet. We were spotted almost as soon as we left the drekar. There was a cry of, "Vikings! Stand to!"

I pulled my shield around as hunting arrows came towards us. I began to run. I knew my long legs would outdistance my men but the closer I was the harder it would be to hit those behind me. I took a chance. The wooden wall which surrounded the end of the chain had been hastily erected. I did not slow. I hurled myself into the wooden wall and it shivered, cracked and then burst open. I barely kept my feet but I had surprise on my side. As I stepped through I swept my sword to the right and was rewarded by flesh. They reacted quickly and one sword smashed into my shield as another Frank lunged at my middle with his weapon. His sword scraped and scratched along my mail. I brought my sword back around even though he was too close for me to use the blade on him. My sword's hilt smashed into the side of his head. As Bergil Fast Blade and Sámr Oakheart led their men through the gap I had made I finished off the stunned Frank. This type of battle suited my men. It was close quarters and my men knew how to fight in such conditions. They used everything to kill and maim our enemies. Helmets, fists, feet and teeth; all were used.

We only knew we had won when we looked around, in the half-light of the tower, and saw only Vikings. "Bergil Fast Blade and Ragnar the Resolute, take your men and find fire. We will burn this tower. Make certain that there are no more Franks close to hand!"

"Aye lord."

"Come Sámr, let us release this chain."

We could hear the sounds of fighting from the south bank. Cutting through the post which secured the chain was simple enough but the Franks had also secured it to each of the ships. It was not enough to release the barrier from the bank, we had to release each ship.

Folki Fámrsson had an axe. The ships were all secured around their masts. "Folki climb aboard the ships and chop down the masts. Einar, go with him and release the chain. You will have to drift downstream when the last boat is released. Beach your ship and make your way back to us."

"Aye lord."

It was dawn by the time Folki and Einar waved to us as they drifted downstream. As we looked upstream Sámr pointed, "Look, lord, it is the other ships; the threttanessa. They are not coming here as you commanded. They are heading to Paris."

Leif said, "Perhaps they know that we have succeeded."

I shook my head, "The barrier is still there. The ships are moving but very slowly. Looking west, towards the dark, they would see it as a barrier. This was planned."

"Treacherous Danes!"

I nodded, "It does not change what we have to do. Back to the drekar!"

By the time the now wrecked ships had drifted downstream and our warriors had boarded our ships it was mid-morning. I could not see what the Danes had to gain by attacking Paris before us. By the time we reached the island city, the Danes had tied up to the north bank and the wooden bridge. Ahead of us, I saw the stone bridge which led to the south bank.

"Bjorn, head for the south bank. Keep us beyond arrow range." As we approached I saw that they had two towers. One was at the island end of the bridge and the other was on the south bank of the river. They were well made and were made of stone. They would not fall easily. As we tied up at the deserted group of houses I heard horses. I was about to draw my sword when Bjorn the Brave shouted, "It is Bagsecg, lord."

I jumped ashore. "What have you learned, Bagsecg?"

"That there are less than two hundred warriors on the island. There are many hundreds who will defend the island but they are not warriors."

I pointed at the towers. They need not be warriors. That bridge is a narrow killing field."

He nodded, "You are right, lord. They have stone-throwers on the two towers." He grinned, "They sent stones in our direction. We were too swift for them."

I saw that the bridge and the river were just thirty paces wide. They had a stone wall running around the island. I had good archers but there was no elevated position for us to use and the tower and the walls had a roof. We would have to take the tower and then try to take the far end of the bridge. It could be done but it would cost men. Was that the price I had to pay? Would the blood of my men buy a son?

I pointed to the church I could see, "What is that church?"

"Saint Germain-des-Pres."

"We will use that as our camp." My captains nodded. "Bagsecg, you have scouted upstream?"

"Aye lord. There are many churches and small towns without walls. We could raid there easily."

"Then tomorrow, when your horses are fresh raid as far as you can. Bring every animal and morsel of food that you can. Ragnar and Sámr, take your crews and help him. We will attack the tower and the bridge." I turned and saw a small abandoned fishing boat. "Come, Sven and Leif, we will sail across the river and see what our Danish brethren intend."

"Do we need more men lord?" Karl Saxon Slayer did not trust our two Danish brethren.

"If we take more men then there will be bloodshed. If I can I would achieve our ends peacefully. We have an opportunity here to become rich at the Franks expense. We can raid while we starve them out."

As we edged across the water, avoiding the end of the island, Sven asked, "Then we do not attack their walls and towers?"

"We do but we use machines to do so. I will not recklessly throw away men's lives. We know not what King Charles will do yet. We may need all of our men to fight him."

We could not get close to the bank and so Leif tied us to a drekar and we clambered over the side. Despite what Siegfried and Sinnic thought of me Sven and I were well respected by the warriors who followed them. We were cheered as we crossed to the land. The two Danes had already begun to build a defence. They had taken some of the stones from the river bank and had their men building a stone wall.

We walked close to them before we spoke and, when I did so, I spoke quietly. We had the largest number of warriors gathered since the great raid of a few years earlier. It would be foolish for us to fight each other. The two had been drinking. Siegfried smiled, "We have summoned the leaders of the Franks to a meeting."

I nodded, "Why did you not attack the blockade?"

He shrugged, "We knew you would overcome it. We thought it best to reach Paris first."

"I am leading this raid."

Sinnic shook his head, "You led this raid now the three of us lead this warband." There was a threat in his voice.

Sven leaned forward, his hand on his seax, "You are a pair of snakes. You would not even be here if it were not for Lord Göngu-Hrólfr Rognvaldson."

"He had the idea. We have the ships and the men. Would you fight us over this Sven Blue Cheek?" Sinnic knew that they had us. If we fought each other then the Franks would win and the prophecy would not come true.

I snapped, "No one will fight."

Just then one of Sinnic's men ran in. "Lord there are three men to speak with you. They came from the tower."

I saw that there was a bishop but he had a sword at his side. He was flanked by two warriors one of whom appeared to be related to the bishop for he had similar features. The bishop had a pugnacious face and was the most warrior-like priest I had seen. I knew that the two Danes spoke the language of the Franks. Both had female slaves that they used and they had been taken from the Franks. The Bishop spoke, "I am Gozlin, Bishop of Paris. Why are you here?"

Before I could speak Sinric made his demands. "We are here to sack your city unless you pay us four hundred livres in silver."

"We will pay you nothing. Leave us, pagans, before Almighty God strikes you down."

I admired his courage but the two Danes laughed. Sinric said, "And what is to stop us holding you hostage and selling you back to your people piece by piece.

The three men's hands went to their swords I said, "I am, Sinric. You summoned them to this meeting. They came in peace and they will leave in peace."

The man who looked like Bishop Gozlin took his hand from the sword, "From your size then you must be Lord Göngu-Hrólfr Rognvaldson." I nodded, "I am Robert, son of Robert the Strong. Bishop Gozlin speaks for Count Odo. We hold Paris for the Empire. I have heard that, for a barbarian, you are a fair man. I will give you some advice, Viking. Leave now while you can. Count Henry of Saxony is on his way here with an army."

Just at that moment, it began to rain. I held my palm uppermost. "And how long will it take him to march from Germany in this weather. How long will your two hundred warriors hold out then?"

They looked at each other in surprise. They did not know that I had that kind of information. Bishop Gozlin said, "Nonetheless we will trust to the Lord God Almighty and we will fight you barbarians!" He turned and led the others back to the tower and the wooden bridge.

I saw Siegfried's hand go to his sword. Sven suddenly thrust his dagger into Siegfried's ribs. "You heard what Lord Göngu-Hrólfr Rognvaldson said. I will gut you like a fish and think no more of it, Dane. My lord might have forgiven your failure to obey a command but I have not!"

Siegfried said, "This alliance is over. You fight from your side of the river and we will fight from ours! And the next time the Franks are foolish enough to step close to us then they will become hostages!"

As we sailed back across the river I said, "Perhaps we should just sail home, Sven Blue Cheek. The Norns have spun and I did not see this event."

"Lord, trust in the witch. We have not yet shed blood for Paris. It is a rich city. I fear not an army from Germany! They are just Saxons and we have beaten them oft enough."

"I will talk to my captains. I would not have men follow for the wrong reason." Because the two Danes had taken the more numerous threttanessa they had far more men than I did. They had a wooden bridge and we had a stone one. The odds were that they would take the island first and we would be left with nothing.

Our camp was defensible when we arrived. I gathered every captain around me and told them what had happened. The captains who had followed me stood firmly but five others looked unhappy. One of them who had come with Siegfried and Sinric, Snorri Folkisson shook his head. "I believe that nothing good will come of this, Lord Göngu-Hrólfr Rognvaldson. I would have happily followed you but I can see no good end from this raid. I will take my ship and we will sail down the river. We passed many places where I could raid."

"That is your choice. You are not oathsworn. Any who do not wish to stay may leave. I bear no grudges." I smiled, "Nor will I share the treasure."

The other four and a subsequent two more joined him on their raid. During the night another ten drekar deserted me. Sven organized the men ready for our attack the next morning but I contemplated sailing back to Rouen. There I would await my next child. I had done that which I was asked. I had attacked Paris. The witch had not said that I needed to take it.

I was gratified by the words of my men and the captains who had come from Guthrum like Karl Saxon Slayer. They swore to stay by me. I slept badly that night and I dreamed.

I saw my grandfather. He was riding Gilles. He was leading Bagsecg, Erik and all of my horsemen. They were charging a line of Saxons who stood on top of a hill. The first charge was repulsed and they rode down the hill. My grandfather lifted his helmet to show his men that he was alive. It was not my grandfather. It was my face but not my body. I led my men back up the hill and the Saxon levy charged down after us. We turned and slew them. We galloped back into the housecarls and all of them died. As I stood on top of the hill I heard my grandfather's voice, 'See the journey through. Trust your heart and trust your men.' Then all went black.

I opened my eyes and it was still night. I could not leave. I had to end this. It did not matter if we won or lost. So long as I tried then the prophesy and dream of my grandfather would come true. I could not let him down. He had journeyed for two years seeking me and I was willing to give up because of some faithless Danes. By the time Sven had awoken I had eaten, dressed and was prepared for war. He approached me cautiously, "Lord?"

"I am a fool Sven Blue Cheek! I expect Danes to behave as men! I should have known they would betray me. It matters not what they do. We will continue. Have stone-throwers built. There is no hurry," I clapped him on his back. "My son will not be born for some months!"

He shook his head, "I have followed you for years and yet your actions and thoughts are still a mystery to me."

When Bergil and Sámr took their men to raid I organised our men. Some improved our camp, others helped Sven to make his stone-throwers. We had captured some horses and I took two. Leif and I rode downstream so that I could see what the Danes were doing. Once we had passed the two small islands we could see the wooden bridge. The Danes were attacking the bridge with men. They were not building machines of war. I saw that they had some ships they were preparing. They were making fire ships! That was risky. We had nothing to do for a while and so we dismounted and we watched them. They lost many men attacking the two towers at the end of the bridge. The two leaders would not mind how many of their men fell. They would have less to share the treasure with. The defenders fought bravely. I saw the flames flicker on the three ships the Danes were using. Men rowed them. The current was against them as was the wind and only one struck the bridge. The other two sank and their crews floundered their way to the north bank. One ship struck the bridge and set it on fire. Their crew were not so fortunate. Half burned. The rest struggled ashore. The bridge was breached and it burned. I watched as the last defenders of the tower were slaughtered. The Danes had the north shore but how would they cross the bridge? We returned to our camp.

I told Sven, Ragnar and the other captains what had happened. Karl Saxon Slayer nodded, "They are reckless leaders, lord. They have lost men and yet gained little."

That night I inspected the stone-throwers. They were not finished but it would not take long to do so. That night twenty more drekar left us. They were all Danes. Some joined Sinnic and Siegfried but most headed downstream. I did not mind for I had my dream to comfort me.

Two days later and we had two stone throwers ready to assault the towers at the end of the bridge. Our men had returned with food, arms and booty. There were no warriors south of the river who could threaten us. We could attack knowing that our enemies lay on the island and nowhere else. The Danes belatedly began to make stone-throwers. They were still hewing trees as we dragged our stone-throwers into position. I had all of my men, except for Bagsecg and his horsemen behind the stone-throwers. When they destroyed the towers, we would be able to secure the southern end of the bridge. My horsemen would warn us of danger. The rain had ended and been replaced by biting cold. For those of us who had come from Norway, it was not a problem but three more crews deserted us before we managed to use the stone-throwers. I was nervous as the first stones were thrown. We had seen stone throwers but they were not regularly used by Vikings. It took a few practice stones but eventually, Petr Jorgensen got the hang of it and the towers began to be hit. With several hundred men ready to pounce once the towers fell I could sense the nervousness in the two towers. We had lost no men. The Danes had. We let the stone-throwers eat into the fabric of the towers. The left one went first and it was spectacular. Two stones hit it at the same time and a large section was demolished. The top half toppled into the river taking the defenders with it. The men in the second tower did not wait. They ran.

Sven led the men forward but the towers and the debris meant that the defenders made the island. We had, however, achieved one objective. We had one end of the bridge in our hands. I deemed that was enough for one day. We finished the demolition of the wrecked tower and placed the two stone-throwers on the bridge. Our plan was to attack the gates the next day. The Norns were spinning. It began to rain that night and continued for three days. The ropes became too slack for the machines to work effectively. We waited. We had food and we had shelter. The Danes did not. They had not raided and they were still trying to build their machines. When one of Bagsecg's horsemen rode in then I knew that the Norns had spun a fine web.

"Lord, Lord Bagsecg sent riders north of the river. There is an army of Saxons a day north of here."

"Can they cross the river and attack us?"

"No lord. They will attack the Danes."

I told my lords the news. We could do nothing about the attack. I guessed that the Danes would have their own scouts out and would know of the danger. They had more men. I was certain that they would be able to cope but part of me felt guilty. These were brothers in arms. We fought the same enemy, the Franks.

We heard the battle the next day. The sound drifted across the water. I sent men downstream to see if they could spy the battle but they could not. The next morning, when we woke my sentries reported that the Danes had sailed. Worse news was that ten more drekar, all Danish had followed them. I had less than ninety ships left and I was alone.

I met again with my captain. Halfi Axe Tongue asked, "Should we follow them? Perhaps there is a great Saxon army north of the river."

I stared north and thought again of my grandfather in my dream, "This desertion changes nothing. The only bridge across the river is this one. There could be an Imperial Army north of the river and we would be safe. When the rain stops then we will attack the gates. If any wish to follow the Danes then go now. I want men with me who have steel for spines."

None left.

I sent Olaf the Wanderer and ten drekar to the north bank. They would stop small boats supplying the people of Paris. This was now a siege. We had to starve the Franks. We would block ships sailing to supply them. When Olaf reached the other bank, he found forty warriors who had been abandoned by Siegfried and Sinric. He sent them across the river. Their leader told us what had happened.

"Lord Göngu-Hrólfr Rognvaldson, the Saxon army came but it was not as big as we feared. We served Tostig and Oleg. They were half-brothers and we were put in the front rank. The Saxons were brave but they fell like wheat. We had won when the Franks sent horsemen. We were surrounded for Siegfried and Sinric withdrew the rest of the army. We fought our way back to the river. Tostig and his half-brother died during the retreat to the place we had left our drekar. When we reached the river, we found our ships had gone. Had you not come then I know not what would have been our end. We would serve you, lord."

I nodded. You did not turn away men who had done nothing wrong. They had fought as ordered and their comrades had died. A leader did not leave his men behind. I was honour bound to take them. This had been my raid until the Norns had spun. This was another drekar crew and we needed numbers.

We settled into a routine. Each day we would collect stones and hurl them at the gates of the island. At the same time, we built willow hurdles and placed them on the bridge. Our archers used them for shelter and picked off men at arms on their walls. Each night they were moved a little closer to the gates. Bagsecg and his men kept us supplied as they ranged the land. They kept a close watch for the Franks. One Imperial army had been destroyed. When would King Charles send another? Olaf the Wanderer captured four small ships full of supplies. They were intended for the island. From the survivors of their crews, we learned that Siegfried and Sinric were raiding to the south of us, around Le Mans. I guessed that they had taken treasure from the churches north of the river and, perhaps, from the bodies of Count Henry of Saxony and his lords.

Drekar in the Seine

A month later and we were just twenty paces from the gates. Our stone-throwers had weakened them. We were now in a position to assault them. The Norns spun. Bagsecg and most of his men rode in. "Lord, there is a huge army coming from the southeast. It is led by King Charles himself. They outnumber us."

I sent for Olaf and his ships as I pondered the problem. I needed all of my army together. The captains who were not my lords all had the same suggestion. "We should head downstream lord. We cannot fight an Imperial army. We raid and then we leave."

I said nothing and I waited until Olaf the Wanderer and his captains arrived. It was then that I spoke. "I hear the voices that tell me to leave Paris and sail down the river like a whipped dog. It makes sense. We would have our lives. Yet in my heart, I do not believe that this is the right answer. Tostig and Oleg, along with many other warriors died. Siegfried and Sinric defeated one army."

A voice called out, "Aye lord and they left!"

I nodded, "And we stay. If they try to shift us from here they will leave a trail of corpses. We still have our ships. The river and the island protect one flank. My horsemen will protect the other. We make a shield wall and we let the Franks bleed upon our wooden wall. I am Lord Göngu-Hrólfr Rognvaldson and a witch prophesied that I would raid Paris. She wove a spell and used my hair and that of my grandfather. We do not follow the White Christ. We have magic that will help us. Fight one battle and if we are defeated then we sail down the river." I paused and looked at their faces. "We are Vikings. Let us show these Franks that we know how to fight and if we are to die then we will all be reunited in Valhalla!"

Sven and my other lords began banging their shields and chanting my name. When Karl Saxon Slayer joined in then I had them all on my side. We would fight!

We used the stones from the church to make a barrier and a wall to protect our right. I had Bagsecg and his horsemen hidden behind the church. I would unleash them when the time was right. The stone-throwers were placed behind our wall along with Petr and a hundred archers. The rest of us were arrayed in three long lines. Before us, we seeded the ground with stakes that were just the length of a man's arm. A warrior advancing behind a shield might not notice them. Then we waited.

The army did not come that first day. Bagsecg's scouts reported that they camped by the river. Boats put off from the island and sailed to meet with the King. We ate in shifts and slept in our lines. I was gratified that none deserted me. All the drekar were there as we woke to the cold, damp morning. The Franks liked their banners. They arrayed before us. Numbers were hard to ascertain. All that we knew was that they outnumbered us. I saw their priests walking along the front of their lines and making the sign of the cross. I did not see their King but I knew that he would be there.

Sven Blue Cheek and Bergil Fast Blade flanked me. I held Longsword in two hands with my shield over my back. I surveyed the men who would be advancing. In front of the main army were a hundred or so men armed with just a small shield and throwing javelins. They would not hurt us. They were there to absorb our arrows and protect the men who followed. The Franks used Roman tactics. The men we would fight followed them. They had shields and spears. This time not all of them were mailed. Many were but I saw that half were not. All of those in my front rank were mailed. Bjorn the Brave stood behind me. His wound meant he could not fight but he had my horn. Two blasts would send my horsemen to attack the Franks. Three would signal the army to fall back to the ships. If we fell back to our ships then I knew that many men would be killed. Three blasts would be a last resort. Petr Jorgensen commanded my two stone-throwers and my archers. He needed no commands. He knew distance and trajectory better than any man I knew. They would disrupt the attack.

Sven Blue Cheek turned to me, "If this is my day to die, Lord Göngu-Hrólfr Rognvaldson then I tell you that it has been more than an honour and privilege. I believe I was chosen, along with Bergil fast Blade and the others to follow you. Your name echoes around the world. Men will remember you and they will remember this day. No matter what the result of this battle, it is *wyrd*!"

There was a sudden cheer as the men around me heard Sven's words.

"You will not die today, Sven Blue Cheek!"

Then Sámr began banging his shield and chanting. Soon every warrior joined in and the words and crashes flew through the air to assault the Franks' ears.

Hrólfr and his Vikings march to war
See their spears and hear them roar
The Hrólfr and his Vikings with bloody blades

Drekar in the Seine

Their roaring means you will be shades
Hrólfr and his Vikings our best men
Hrólfr and his Vikings death comes again
Leading Vikings up the Breton water
They brought death they brought slaughter
Taking slaves, swords and gold
Hrólfr and his Vikings were the most bold
Hrólfr and his Vikings our best men
Hrólfr and his Vikings death comes again
Fear us Breton we are the best
Fighting us a fatal test
We come for land to make our own
To give young Vikings not yet grown
Hrólfr and his Vikings our best men
Hrólfr and his Vikings death comes again
Hrólfr and his Vikings our best men
Hrólfr and his Vikings death comes again

A Frankish horn sounded and the Franks advanced. There was no subtlety in their attack. They came in a column of men which was two hundred men wide and the Allfather knew how many ranks deep. All that we had to do was to kill those before us and keep on killing until either they were all gone or we were killed. It was as simple as that. Holding my sword above my head I did not believe that I would die. I did not think that I was immortal but I had an unborn child. Ylva and the Norns would let me die but only when I knew if it was a boy or a girl. If it was a boy then my life would have been worthwhile for the prophecy given to my grandfather might still come true. Petr's archers aimed their arrows at the men with javelins who advanced. Without mail and helmets, they fell. The handful of survivors turned and fled back to their army. As the Franks neared us so their lines became less organized. There were now dead bodies they had to negotiate as well as embedded stakes. When Petr's stones flew amongst them then carnage ensued. Mail did not protect against stones. Men fell. Gaps opened and I saw fear on the faces of the Franks who drew ever closer.

I have no doubt that when the attack was planned their King had thought that when they neared us they would charge. Certainly, some of the braver ones tried to do so but the majority approached at a walk. They saw the wall of wood and steel. They saw faces, some painted red and some tattooed. They saw plaited beards and moustaches. Some of the Danes had bones in their beards. They saw barbarians. They saw men who were not afraid to die. They were Christians. They had no Valhalla.

The ones who approached Sven, Bergil and me did charge. I ignored their spears as I swung Longsword. Sven and Bergil rammed their spears forward. There were spears poking from behind me too but I was exposed. My sword took the head of one Frank and knocked another over but a spear struck me in my shoulder. As the man who held the spear died it did not penetrate far but it drew blood. I ignored it and swung backhand. I soon found the rhythm which a Danish axe man enjoys. I was not even looking at the men I was hitting. I was seeking enemies beyond those who died as my figure of eight sword kept the three paces before me clear.

I could see that the stones and arrows of Petr and his men were having an effect. Gaps were appearing. Priests ran forward to tend to the wounded. Some fell to arrows that did not care if their target was a warrior or priest. As I glanced to my right I saw that men were pressing to get close to Petr. If the stones and arrows ceased we would be in trouble. It was time for my secret weapon. As Longsword sliced through the arm of an unarmoured Frank I shouted, "Bjorn, signal Bagsecg!"

The horn sounded twice. There was a pause and then it sounded twice more. My men knew what that meant. They intensified their efforts. The Franks before us thought that the horns signalled an attack by our men on foot. They braced for an attack that did not come. When Bagsecg and his horsemen appeared, it came as a complete shock to the Franks. They tore through the men on the Frankish left. Petr and his men were able to repulse the first Franks who had neared them and then they sent their stones and arrows deep into the heart of the Frankish army.

King Charles, or whoever commanded the Franks, sounded his own horn and the Franks tried to retreat. The bulk of their army achieved that but those whom Bagsecg had cut off were trapped. With horsemen behind and us before them, we closed the circle. Longsword was soon blunted and I drew Hrolf's Vengeance and my seax. We carved our way into the heart of them. I felt blood trickling down from the wound in my shoulder but I did not have to bear a shield. I had a seax and the wound did not trouble me. When the last Frank fell, my men all began banging their shields. Some hewed heads and held them high to wave at the Franks. Every byrnie was spattered with blood. I saw men nursing wounds. Others lay dead but we had won. Bagsecg reared his horse and

raising his sword shouted, "Lord Göngu-Hrólfr Rognvaldson! Mightiest
warrior! All hail, Lord Göngu-Hrólfr Rognvaldson!"

My men took up the chant.

The Franks withdrew back to their camp. Bagsecg and his horsemen
ensured that they did not make a sudden attack. We cleared the
battlefield. We took the mail and the weapons from the dead. Their lords
had treasure on them: rings, seals, silver crosses. We took them. Our own
dead were placed upon the Frankish fishing boats and knarr that we had
captured. They were set alight and sent down the river. They would
return to the sea. Even now they would be in Valhalla telling the
Allfather how they had defeated a Frankish army many times their size.
We repaired our defences and collected the stones we had thrown. The
Franks still had more than enough men to finish the job. As we sat
around the fire sharpening weapons we had our wounds tended. We had
brought no priests with us but our warriors knew how to deal with
wounds. Men who had had fingers and limbs so badly hurt that they
could not be repaired had them taken off and the wound sealed with fire.
Sven used a brand to seal the spear thrust in my left shoulder. It would
ache but would not stop me when we fought again.

My lords had all survived. Bergil Fast Blade had a new scar on his
face but it looked a worse wound than it was. It would frighten the
Franks when next we saw them. He said, "Will they come tomorrow,
lord?"

I laughed, "I am galdramenn now? I know not Bergil but if they do
then we are ready and they will be fearful when they do attack. I fear a
trick. We will keep a good watch this night. Let us see what the morrow
brings."

It brought rain. The fields over which we had fought became a muddy
morass and there was no attack. At noon, although as there was no sun it
was hard to determine the exact time, emissaries came from the Frankish
lines. I recognised Count Robert. I walked to meet him with Sven and
Bergil.

"King Charles would meet with you."

"Where? I am not so foolish as to walk into your camp and I doubt
that the King has the courage to walk into mine."

"In the middle then. We will bring six men. You may bring the same
number. I know that I need not remind you that this is a truce. You have
shown me that you are, for a barbarian, a man of honour."

I took Sven, Bergil, Sámr, Olaf the Wanderer and Bagsecg with me. We went bareheaded and without shields but we took our weapons. King Charles the Fat lived up to his name and his men had brought him a chair. I saw another bishop but not Gozlin. One man glared and glowered at me as we approached.

The King said, "I understand you speak our language."

"I do."

The man who had glowered at me snapped, "Say, Your Majesty, barbarian!"

"He is your King and not mine."

"Count Odo be silent!" The King might not have been a warrior but he was astute. "Half of your men have left you, Viking."

I nodded, "And they raid your lands around Le Mans. We did well enough yesterday. Can you say the same?"

I saw the hint of a smile on Count Robert's face.

The King nodded, "A fair point. Your men fight well. Become my subjects and you can fight for us."

Count Odo said, "They are pagans!"

"Perhaps they will convert."

I smiled, "And perhaps tonight the sun will set in the east. That will not happen. Just because Guthrum of the Danes did so does not mean that we will."

The King sighed, "What will it take for you to leave this land?"

Count Odo shouted, "You cannot buy off these Vikings. Did Bishop Gozlin, Count Henry and all the other men die just so that they could get what they wanted in the first place?"

"Either keep silent or leave!" He looked at me, "Well Viking?"

I confess that I had not even thought of a figure. We could not capture Paris that much was obvious but I had done that which Ylva wished. I plucked a figure from the air. "A thousand livres!"

I saw the shock on the faces of all but the King. He nodded, "That is too great a sum. Make it seven hundred livres and I will give your ships permission to raid Burgundy."

Count Odo said, "You would let them raid our own people?"

The King said, "The Burgundians have rebelled against us. Would you rather we have our men bleed? These barbarians will do that for us will you not?"

"I will not lead them but I am certain that there are ships that will happily raid Burgundy." I looked at those with me.

Karl Saxon Slayer said, "I will lead any who wish to raid, lord. You have led us well. I will try to do the same."

The King said, "It will take some time to collect the treasure. I have your word that you will not raid in the meantime?"

"How long do you need?"

"Five days."

"Then you have five days!"

We returned to our camp and I told the others what had been decided. The Danes and the rest of the fleet agreed to raid with Karl Saxon Slayer and Olaf the Wanderer. My men would return down the river with me. We had done that which was asked. Five days later and the silver was delivered. There was more silver than I had ever seen. I shared it equally amongst the captains after I had taken one hundred livres for myself. I would not have done so had not every captain insisted that I do so.

As we loaded our drekar Sven Blue Cheek laughed, "Sinric and Siegfried and all the other cowardly warriors will be cursing the day that they left. Had they had your courage then who knows what might have resulted."

"You think we could have taken Paris?"

"With the men that fled? I am certain. But this is *wyrd*. You have done that which the witch said and we can return home. I grow tired of this land and would be back in Caen."

I nodded and we loaded our drekar and sailed down the Seine. What awaited me in Rouen? What web had the Norns spun?

Epilogue

We were jeered by the people of Paris as we headed downstream. Karl and Olaf and their drekar were pelted with the rotting food of Paris as they passed the broken wooden bridge. I did not envy them their reception when they returned downstream. We did not have to row downstream. The current took us. We had lost warriors but my lords all lived. We had more treasure than we knew what to do with but that did not concern me. My child was due in a month. Had I done enough? Would it be a son?

My other ships sailed down to the sea. Some had a long voyage ahead. Saxbjǫrn, Finnbjǫrn, and Halfi would have the longest journeys. We had said our farewells when we had boarded our ships in the Seine.

When I reached my hall, I saw that Padraigh had organized all for me. He had spied my coming and taken it upon himself to have food prepared. There was no sign of Poppa nor Gefn. "Where are my wife and my mother?"

"I confined your wife to her bed. She is well but frets and fusses over you. The child, according to the women who know such things, is due. Gefn," he shook his head, "her time has come. She has hung on to say farewell to you, I think."

I went to Poppa first and the relief on her face was obvious. Her priest was by her bedside. "I do not need you, priest. I will speak with my wife." He nodded and left.

"You have been told of your mother?"

"Aye, Padraigh told me."

"He is a good man although he thinks that Gefn hangs on for you. I think it is this child she wishes to see."

"He will come when he will come."

She smiled, "You said, he."

"After losing men on the Seine then I hope that the bargain my grandfather made with Ylva will be fruitful, if not...?

I went to see Gefn. She opened her eyes and smiled as I entered, "Despite what they say, my son, I am not dead yet. Thank the Allfather that you live. And the raid?"

I waved a hand, "The raid went well but that is not important. Have the healers and priests done all that they can for you?"

She smiled, "I like Padraig. He does not try to make me change my beliefs. The other? I have told all to keep him from me. He reeks of perfume and has soft hands. He is not a man!"

I could not help smiling. She knew her own mind. "I am home now and soon my child will be born."

"I have made a blót to the Allfather that he sends you a son. If I am not here when he is born then know that my spirit will watch over him. I will be there for all time."

"You will watch him grow. I will not hear such talk."

She smiled, "And now I am tired. Let me rest."

I barely had time to go to my hall for refreshment when my wife's servant, Sprota, came running for me. "Hurry lord, your wife is about to give birth. You must come. I have sent for Æðelwald of Remisgat."

I roared, "No!" Drawing Longsword, I ran to my wife's chamber. I saw Æðelwald of Remisgat and Padraig hurrying too. I shouted, "No man enters this chamber." Padraig nodded and stopped. I stood before the door and barred it. I pricked the throat of Æðelwald of Remisgat who was still moving towards the door. "You cursed our family when you watched my brother being born. I will kill you before I will let another curse descend upon this family."

Padraig said, "Lord, this is not seemly."

"If you value your lives then leave this hallway now!"

Æðelwald of Remisgat put his hand to his throat where a trickle of blood could be seen. I had barely pricked him. Padraig put his arm around the priest and said, "Come we will pray for the Lady Poppa and her child."

After they had gone I did not move. I stood with Longsword in my hand. I listened to my wife's screams and moans. It was hard not to rush in and comfort her but I remembered the curse. Man was not meant to witness the mystery of birth. Eventually, it went silent and Sprota came to the door. "Lord, you can come in. You have a son."

I burst through the door. My naked son lay on the bed next to my wife. His eyes were open. I laid my Longsword on the bed and then hugged my wife. "I have a son! The prophecy can come true."

She gave me a wan smile, "And I am well. Thank you."

I kissed her, "I am sorry but grandfather gave his life for this." As I turned I saw that my son's hands were on the blade of Longsword. "See, he will be a warrior. He will be Longsword."

She nodded, "And could we give him the name of my grandfather? William."

Grinning I said, "Aye that would be *wyrd*. A Frank name married to a Norse one." I took a clean piece of linen and wrapped him in it. He did not cry but stared at me with the bluest eyes I had ever seen.

"Where are you going?"

"Gefn is close to death. She needs to see him."

I carried him down the hall. He was lighter than my sword. Gefn's servants were with her. Nanna, her closest servant, shook her head. Was I too late?

"Mother you have a grandson!" To my everlasting joy, her eyes opened and a smile appeared. I laid him next to her. A thin blue-veined hand reached over and my son grasped it. "This is William Longsword. Your grandson."

Her voice, when she spoke was thin and cracked, "I am Gefn and I swear that I will watch over you for all time."

Even as she spoke I saw the light leave her eyes. She died with a smile on her lips and my son's hand around her finger. It was *wyrd*. It is said that when the Allfather takes a life he gives one in return. I saw it in that instant. Others were sad but, in my heart, I was not. Gefn had done what she had desired most. She had seen her grandson. William had had two people make sacrifices for him. Both would be in the Otherworld watching over him. I was content. The Norn had said that my grandfather's blood would rule this land. I now had a son and one day he would be lord of a land greater than even the Emperor. It was wyrd.

The End

Norse Calendar

Gormánuður October 14th - November 13th
Ýlir November 14th - December 13th
Mörsugur December 14th - January 12th
Þorri - January 13th - February 11th
Gói - February 12th - March 13th
Einmánuður - March 14th - April 13th
Harpa April 14th - May 13th
Skerpla - May 14th - June 12th
Sólmánuður - June 13th - July 12th
Heyannir - July 13th - August 14th
Tvímánuður - August 15th - September 14th
Haustmánuður September 15th-October 13th

Glossary

Ækre -acre (Norse) The amount of land a pair of oxen could plough in one day
Addelam- Deal (Kent)
Afon Hafron- River Severn in Welsh
Aldarennaöy – Alderney (Channel Islands)
Alt Clut- Dumbarton Castle on the Clyde
Anmyen -Amiens
Andecavis- Angers in Anjou
Angia- Jersey (Channel Islands)
An Lysardh -The Lizard (Cornwall)
An Oriant- Lorient, Brittany
Æscesdūn – Ashdown (Berkshire)
Áth Truim- Trim, County Meath (Ireland)
Baille - a ward (an enclosed area inside a wall)
Balley Chashtal -Castleton (Isle of Man)
Bárekr's Haven – Barfleur, Normandy
Bebbanburgh- Bamburgh Castle, Northumbria. Also, known as Din Guardi in the ancient tongue
Beck- a stream
Blót – a blood sacrifice made by a jarl
Blue Sea/Middle Sea- The Mediterranean

Bondi- Viking farmers who fight
Bourde- Bordeaux
Bjarnarøy –Great Bernera (Bear Island)
Byrnie- a mail or leather shirt reaching down to the knees
Brvggas -Bruges
Caerlleon- Welsh for Chester
Caestir - Chester (old English)
Cantwareburh- Canterbury
Casnewydd –Newport, Wales
Cent- Kent
Cephas- Greek for Simon Peter (St. Peter)
Cetham -Chatham Kent
Chape- the tip of a scabbard
Charlemagne- Holy Roman Emperor at the end of the 8th and beginning
of the 9th centuries
Cherestanc- Garstang (Lancashire)
Cippanhamm -Chippenham
Ċiriċeburh- Cherbourg
Condado Portucalense- the County of Portugal
Constrasta-Valença (Northern Portugal)
Corn Walum or Om Walum- Cornwall
Cissa-caestre -Chichester
Cymri- Welsh
Cymru- Wales
Cyninges-tūn – Coniston. It means the estate of the king (Cumbria)
Dùn Èideann –Edinburgh (Gaelic)
Din Guardi- Bamburgh castle
Drekar- a Dragon ship (a Viking warship)
Duboglassio –Douglas, Isle of Man
Djupr -Dieppe
Dyrøy –Jura (Inner Hebrides)
Dyflin- Old Norse for Dublin
Ein-mánuðr- middle of March to the middle of April
Eopwinesfleot -Ebbsfleet
Eoforwic- Saxon for York
Fáfnir - a dwarf turned into a dragon (Norse mythology)
Faro Bregancio- Corunna (Spain)
Ferneberga -Farnborough (Hampshire)
Fey- having second sight

Firkin- a barrel containing eight gallons (usually beer)
Fret-a sea mist
Frankia- France and part of Germany
Fyrd-the Saxon levy
Gaill- Irish for foreigners
Galdramenn- wizard
Glaesum –amber
Gleawecastre- Gloucester
Gói- the end of February to the middle of March
Greenway- ancient roads- they used turf rather than stone
Grenewic- Greenwich
Gyllingas - Gillingham Kent
Haesta- Hastings
Haestingaceaster -Hastings
Hamwic -Southampton
Hantone- Littlehampton
Haughs/ Haugr - small hills in Norse (As in Tarn Hows) or a hump-
normally a mound of earth
Hearth-weru- Jarl's bodyguard/oathsworn
Heels- when a ship leans to one side under the pressure of the wind
Hel- Queen of, the Norse underworld.
Herkumbl- a mark on the front of a helmet denoting the clan of a Viking
warrior
Here Wic- Harwich
Hetaereiarch – Byzantine general
Hí- Iona (Gaelic)
Hjáp - Shap- Cumbria (Norse for stone circle)
Hoggs or Hogging- when the pressure of the wind causes the stern or the
bow to droop
Hrams-a – Ramsey, Isle of Man
Hrīs Wearp – Ruswarp (North Yorkshire)
Hrofecester-Rochester Kent
Hywel ap Rhodri Molwynog- King of Gwynedd 814-825
Icaunis- a British river god
Ishbiliyya- Seville
Issicauna- Gaulish for the lower Seine
Itouna- River Eden Cumbria
Jarl- Norse earl or lord
Joro-goddess of the earth

Jǫtunn -Norse god or goddess
Kartreidh -Carteret in Normandy
Kjerringa - Old Woman- the solid block in which the mast rested
Knarr- a merchant ship or a coastal vessel
Kyrtle-woven top
Laugardagr-Saturday (Norse for washing day)
Leathes Water- Thirlmere
Ljoðhús- Lewis
Legacaestir- Anglo Saxon for Chester
Liger- Loire
Lochlannach – Irish for Northerners (Vikings)
Lothuwistoft- Lowestoft
Louis the Pious- King of the Franks and son of Charlemagne
Lundenwic - London
Lincylene -Lincoln
Maen hir – standing stone (menhir)
Maeresea- River Mersey
Mammceaster- Manchester
Manau/Mann – The Isle of Man(n) (Saxon)
Marcia Hispanic- Spanish Marches (the land around Barcelona)
Mast fish- two large racks on a ship for the mast
Melita- Malta
Midden - a place where they dumped human waste
Miklagård - Constantinople
Leudes- Imperial officer (a local leader in the Carolingian Empire. They became Counts a century after this.)
Njörðr- God of the sea
Nithing- A man without honour (Saxon)
Odin - The "All Father" God of war, also associated with wisdom, poetry, and magic (The ruler of the gods).
Olissipo- Lisbon
Orkneyjar-Orkney
Portucale- Porto
Portesmūða -Portsmouth
Penrhudd – Penrith Cumbria
Pillars of Hercules- Straits of Gibraltar
Qādis- Cadiz
Ran- Goddess of the sea
Readingum -Reading Berks

Remisgat Ramsgate
Roof rock- slate
Rinaz –The Rhine
Sabrina- Latin and Celtic for the River Severn. Also, the name of a
female Celtic deity
Saami- the people who live in what is now Northern Norway/Sweden
Saint Maclou- St Malo (France)
Sandwic- Sandwich (Kent)
Sarnia- Guernsey (Channel Islands)
St. Cybi- Holyhead
Sampiere -samphire (sea asparagus)
Scree- loose rocks in a glacial valley
Seax – short sword
Sheerstrake- the uppermost strake in the hull
Sheet- a rope fastened to the lower corner of a sail
Shroud- a rope from the masthead to the hull amidships
Skeggox – an axe with a shorter beard on one side of the blade
Sondwic-Sandwich
South Folk- Suffolk
Stad- Norse settlement
Stays- ropes running from the mast-head to the bow
Streanæshalc -Whitby
Stirap- stirrup
Strake- the wood on the side of a drekar
Suthriganaworc - Southwark (London)
Svearike -Sweden
Syllingar- Scilly Isles
Syllingar Insula- Scilly Isles
Tarn- small lake (Norse)
Temese- River Thames (also called the Tamese)
The Norns- The three sisters who weave webs of intrigue for men
Thing-Norse for a parliament or a debate (Tynwald)
Thor's day- Thursday
Threttanessa- a drekar with 13 oars on each side.
Thrall- slave
Tinea- Tyne
Tintaieol- Tintagel (Cornwall)
Trenail- a round wooden peg used to secure strakes
Tude- Tui in Northern Spain

Tynwald- the Parliament on the Isle of Man
Úlfarrberg- Helvellyn
Úlfarrland- Cumbria
Úlfarr- Wolf Warrior
Úlfarrston- Ulverston
Ullr-Norse God of Hunting
Ulfheonar-an elite Norse warrior who wore a wolf skin over his armour
Uuluuich- Dulwich
Valauna- Valognes (Normandy)
Vectis- The Isle of Wight
Veðrafjǫrðr -Waterford (Ireland)
Veisafjǫrðr- Wexford (Ireland)
Volva- a witch or healing woman in Norse culture
Waeclinga Straet- Watling Street (A5)
Windlesore-Windsor
Waite- a Viking word for farm
Werham -Wareham (Dorset)
Wintan-ceastre -Winchester
Wihtwara- Isle of White
Withy- the mechanism connecting the steering board to the ship
Woden's day- Wednesday
Wyddfa-Snowdon
Wyrd- Fate
Yard- a timber from which the sail is suspended on a drekar
Ynys Môn-Anglesey

Maps and Illustrations

The Norman dynasty

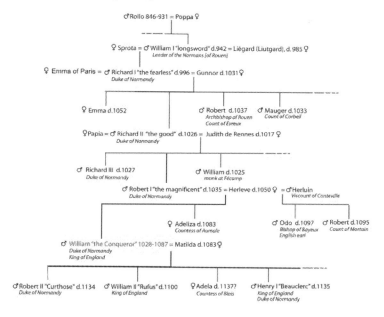

Courtesy of Wikipedia.

Historical note

My research encompasses not only books and the Internet but also TV. Time Team was a great source of information. I wish they would bring it back! I saw the wooden compass which my sailors use on the Dan Snow programme about the Vikings. Apparently, it was used in modern times to sail from Denmark to Edinburgh and was only a couple of points out. Similarly, the construction of the temporary hall was copied from the settlement of Leif Eriksson in Newfoundland.

Stirrups began to be introduced in Europe during the 7th and 8th Centuries. By Charlemagne's time, they were widely used but only by nobles. It is said this was the true beginning of feudalism. It was the Vikings who introduced them to England. It was only in the time of Canute the Great that they became widespread. The use of stirrups enabled a rider to strike someone on the ground from the back of a horse and facilitated the use of spears and later, lances.

The Vikings may seem cruel to us now. They enslaved women and children. Many of the women became their wives. The DNA of the people of Iceland shows that it was made up of a mixture of Norse and Danish males and Celtic females. These were the people who settled in Iceland, Greenland and Vinland. They did the same in England and, as we shall see, Normandy. Their influence was widespread. Genghis Khan and his Mongols did the same in the 13th century. It is said that a high proportion of European males have Mongol blood in them. The Romans did it with the Sabine tribe. They were different times and it would be wrong to judge them with our politically correct twenty-first-century eyes. This sort of behaviour still goes on in the world but with less justification.

At this time, there were no Viking kings. There were clans. Each clan had a hersir or Jarl. Clans were loyal to each other. A hersir was more of a landlocked Viking or a farmer while a Jarl usually had ship(s) at his command. A hersir would command bondi. They were the Norse equivalent of the fyrd although they were much better warriors. They would all have a helmet shield and a sword. Most would also have a spear. Hearth weru were the oathsworn or bodyguards for a jarl or, much later on, a king. Kings like Canute and Harald Hadrada were rare and they only emerged at the beginning of the 10th century.

The Vikings began to raid the Loire and the Seine from the middle of the 9th century. They were able to raid as far as Tours. Tours, Saumur and the monastery at Marmoutier were all raided and destroyed. As a result of the raids and the accompanying destruction, castles were built there during the latter part of the 9th century. There are many islands in the Loire and many tributaries. The Maine, which runs through Angers, is also a wide waterway. The lands seemed made for Viking raiders. They did not settle in Aquitaine but they did in Austrasia. The Vikings began to settle in Normandy and the surrounding islands from the 820s. Many place names in Normandy are Viking in origin. Sometimes, as in Vinland, the settlements were destroyed by the Franks but some survived. So long as a Viking had a river for his drekar he could raid at will.

The Franks used horses more than most other armies of the time. Their spears were used as long swords, hence the guards. They used saddles and stirrups. They still retained their round shields and wore, largely, an open helmet. Sometimes they wore a plume. They carried a spare spear and a sword.

One reason for the Normans success was that when they arrived in northern France they integrated quickly with the local populace. They married them and began to use some of their words. They adapted to the horse as a weapon of war. Before then the Vikings had been quite happy to ride to war but they dismounted to fight. The Normans took the best that the Franks had and made it better. This book sees the earliest beginnings of the rise of the Norman knight.

I have used the names by which places were known in the medieval period wherever possible. Sometimes I have had to use the modern name. The Cotentin is an example. The isle of sheep is now called the Isle of Sheppey and lies on the Medway close to the Thames. The land of Kent was known as Cent in the early medieval period. Thanet or, Tanet as it was known in the Viking period was an island at this time. The sea was on two sides and the other two sides had swamps, bogs, mudflats and tidal streams. It protected Canterbury. The coast was different too. Richborough had been a major Roman port. It is now some way inland. Sandwich was a port. Other ports now lie under the sea. Vikings were not afraid to sail up very narrow rivers and to risk being stranded on mud. They were tough men and were capable of carrying or porting their ships as their Rus brothers did when travelling to Miklagård.

The Norns or the Weird Sisters.

"The Norns (Old Norse: norn, plural: nornir) in Norse mythology are female beings who rule the destiny of gods and men. They roughly correspond to other controllers of humans' destiny, the Fates, elsewhere in European mythology.

In Snorri Sturluson's interpretation of the Völuspá, Urðr (Wyrd), Verðandi and Skuld, the three most important of the Norns, come out from a hall standing at the Well of Urðr or Well of Fate. They draw water from the well and take sand that lies around it, which they pour over Yggdrasill so that its branches will not rot. These three Norns are described as powerful maiden giantesses (Jotuns) whose arrival from Jötunheimr ended the golden age of the gods. They may be the same as the maidens of Mögþrasir who are described in Vafþrúðnismál"
Source: Norns - https://en.wikipedia.org

I have used the word town as this is the direct translation of the Danish ton- meaning settlement. A town could vary in size from a couple of houses to a walled city like Jorvik. If I had used ton it would have been confusing. There are already readers out there who think I have made mistakes because I use words like stiraps, wyrd and drekar!

The assimilation of the Norse and the Franks took place over a long period. Hrolf Ragnvaldson aka Rollo aka Robert of Normandy is not yet born but by the time he is 64 he will have attacked Paris and become Duke of Normandy. The journey has just begun.

Tower construction

Towers were made by constructing two walls with mortared dress stone and then infilling them with rocks. When I visited Penrith castle in Cumbria in 2017 I saw a partly ruined tower which demonstrates this. It helps that the dressed stone was red sandstone! You can see the width of the tower. This one is the 13th Century but the principle was the same in the 9th.

Drekar in the Seine

Author's collection

Viking Raid on the Seine

At some time in the 850s, a huge Viking fleet sailed up the Seine to raid deep into the heart of Frankia. Some writers of the period speak of over a hundred ships. The priests who wrote of the plague that they believe the Vikings to be tended to exaggerate. I have erred on the side of caution.

Greenways

I have used the term greenways in many of my books. We still have them in England. They are the paths trodden before the Romans came. Many of them became bridleways. I have taken a couple of photographs to show my readers, especially those in the US, what they are like. This first one is in the Lake District and runs along the River Eamont. It is like the one I use in Cantwareburh. The second leads to a hillfort.

Coutances and Saint-Lô

Both towns were captured by the Vikings in the late ninth century. Saint-Lô had all of the inhabitants massacred. During the latter half of the ninth century, the Vikings kept moving further up the rivers and further south. The great raid on Paris in 885 was the culmination of these raids and gradual encroachment into what became Normandy.

Isle of Man

The three legs of Man evolved in the late middle ages. Until then it was four legs; a swastika.

Guthrum, founder of the Danelaw

It is not known how Guthrum consolidated his rule as king over the other Danish chieftains of the Danelaw (Danish ruled territory of England), but we know that by 874 he was able to wage a war against Wessex and its King, Alfred.

In 875 the Danish forces, then under Guthrum and Halfdan Ragnarsson, divided, Halfdan's contingent returning north to Northumbria, while Guthrum's forces went to East Anglia, quartering themselves at Cambridge for the year.

By 876, Guthrum had acquired various parts of the kingdoms of Mercia and Northumbria and then turned his attention to acquiring Wessex, where his first confrontation with Alfred took place on the south coast. Guthrum sailed his army around Poole Harbour and linked up with another Viking army that was invading the area between the Frome and Piddle rivers which was ruled by Alfred. According to the historian Asser, Guthrum won his initial battle with Alfred, and he captured the castellum as well as the ancient square earthworks known as the Wareham, where there was a convent of nuns.

Alfred successfully brokered a peace settlement, but by 877 this peace was broken as Guthrum led his army raiding further into Wessex, thus forcing Alfred to confront him in a series of skirmishes that Guthrum continued to win. At Exeter, which Guthrum had also captured, Alfred made a peace treaty, with the result that Guthrum left Wessex to winter in Gloucester.

The Great Heathen Army

Historians provide varying estimates for the size of the Great Heathen Army. According to the 'minimalist' scholars, such as Pete Sawyer, the army may have been smaller than traditionally thought. Sawyer notes that the Anglo-Saxon Chronicle of 865 referred to the Viking force as a Heathen Army, or in Old English "hæþen here".

The law code of King Ine of Wessex, issued in about 694, provides a definition of here (pronounced /ˈheːre/) as "an invading army or raiding party containing more than thirty-five men", thus differentiating between the term for the invading Viking army and the Anglo-Saxon army that was referred to as the fyrd. The scribes who wrote the Anglo-Saxon Chronicle used the term here to describe the Viking forces. The historian Richard Abels suggested that this was to differentiate between the Viking warbands and those of military forces organised by the state or the crown. However, by the late 10th and early 11th century, here was used more generally as the term for army, whether it was Viking or not.

Sawyer produced a table of Viking ship numbers, as documented in the Anglo-Saxon Chronicle, and assumes that each Viking ship could carry no more than 32 men, leading to his conclusion that the army would have consisted of no more than 1,000 men. Other scholars give higher estimates. For example, Laurent Mazet-Harhoff observes that many thousands of men were involved in the invasions of the Seine area. However, Mazet-Harhoff does say that the military bases that would accommodate these large armies have yet to be rediscovered. Guy

Halshall reported that, in the 1990s, several historians suggested that the Great Heathen Army would have numbered in the low thousands; however, Halshall advises that there "clearly is still much room for debate".

The army probably developed from the campaigns in France. In Frankia, there was a conflict between the Emperor and his sons, and one of the sons had welcomed support from a Viking fleet. By the time that the war had ended, the Vikings had discovered that monasteries and towns situated on navigable rivers were vulnerable to attack. In 845, a raid on Paris was prevented by the large payment of silver to the Vikings. The opportunity for rich pickings drew other Vikings to the area, and by the end of the decade, all the main rivers of West Frankia were being patrolled by Viking fleets. In 862, the West Frankish king responded to the Vikings, fortifying his towns and defending his rivers, thus making it difficult for the Vikings to raid inland. The lower reaches of the rivers and the coastal regions were left largely undefended. Religious communities in these areas, however, chose to move inland away from the reaches of the Viking fleets. With the changes in Frankia making raiding more difficult, the Vikings turned their attention to England.

Invasion of England

The term vikingr simply meant pirate, and the Viking warbands may well have included fighters of other nationalities than Scandinavians. The Viking leaders would often join together for mutual benefit and then dissolve once profit had been achieved. Several of the Viking leaders who had been active in Frankia and Frisia joined forces to conquer the four kingdoms constituting Anglo-Saxon England. The composite force probably contained elements from Denmark, Norway, Sweden and Ireland as well as those who had been fighting on the continent. The Anglo-Saxon historian Æthelweard was very specific in his chronicle and said that "the fleets of the Viking tyrant Hingwar landed in England from the north".

The bulk of the army consisted of Danish Vikings, who, prior to the invasion, would have been raiding Frankia and Frisia. Some of the grave goods unearthed at Repton, where the Great Heathen Army spent the winter in 874, were of Norwegian origin, indicating that part of the army was likely to have contained elements of Norwegian Vikings, who would have been operating in Britain, raiding and conquering lands around the

Irish Sea. The Great Heathen Army would also have consisted of various independent bands, or liðs, coming together under joint leadership.

The Vikings had been defeated by the West Saxon King Æthelwulf in 851, so rather than land in Wessex, they decided to go further north to East Anglia. Legend has it that the united army was led by the three sons of Ragnar Lodbrok: Halfdan Ragnarsson, Ivar the Boneless (Hingwar), and Ubba. Norse sagas consider the invasion by the three brothers as a response to the death of their father at the hands of Ælla of Northumbria in 865, but the historic accuracy of this claim is uncertain.

Start of the invasion, 865

In late 865, the Vikings landed in East Anglia and used it as a starting point for an invasion. The East Anglians made peace with the invaders by providing them with horses. The Vikings stayed in East Anglia for the winter before setting out for Northumbria towards the end of 866, establishing themselves at York. In 867, the Northumbrians paid them off, and the Viking Army established a puppet leader in Northumbria before setting off for the Kingdom of Mercia, wherein 867 they captured Nottingham. The king of Mercia requested help from the king of Wessex to help fight the Vikings. A combined army from Wessex and Mercia besieged the city of Nottingham with no clear result, so the Mercians settled on paying the Vikings off. The Vikings returned to Northumbria in autumn 868 and overwintered in York, staying there for most of 869. They returned to East Anglia and spent the winter of 869–70 at Thetford. There was no peace agreement between the East Anglians and the Vikings this time. When the local king Edmund fought against the invaders, he was captured and killed.

In 871, the Great Summer Army arrived from Scandinavia, led by Bagsecg. The reinforced Viking army turned its attention to Wessex, but the West Saxons, led by King Æthelred's brother Alfred, defeated them on 8 January 871 at the Battle of Ashdown, slaying Bagsecg in the process. Three months later, Æthelred died and was succeeded by Alfred (later known as Alfred the Great), who bought the Vikings off to gain time. During 871–72, the Great Heathen Army wintered in London before returning to Northumbria. It seems that there had been a rebellion against the puppet ruler in Northumbria, so they returned to restore power. They then established their winter quarters for 872-73 at Torksey in the Kingdom of Lindsey (now part of Lincolnshire). The Mercians again paid them off in return for peace, and at the end of 873 the Vikings took up winter quarters at Repton in Derbyshire.

Drekar in the Seine

In 874, following their winter stay in Repton, the Great Heathen Army drove the Mercian king into exile and finally conquered Mercia; the exiled Mercian king was replaced by Ceowulf. According to Alfred the Great's biographer Asser, the Vikings then split into two bands. Halfdan led one band north to Northumbria, where he overwintered by the River Tyne (874–75). In 875 he ravaged further north to Scotland, where he fought the Picts and the Britons of Strathclyde. Returning south of the border in 876, he shared out Northumbrian land amongst his men, who "ploughed the land and supported themselves"; this land was part of what became known as the Danelaw.

Wikipedia

Rollo

I have used the name Rollo even though that is the Latinisation of Hrolf. I did so for two reasons. We all know the first Duke of Normandy as Rollo and I wanted to avoid confusion with his grandfather. I realise that I have also caused enough of a problem with Ragnvald and Ragnvald the Breton Slayer.

Rollo is generally identified with one Viking in particular – a man of high social status mentioned in Icelandic sagas, which refer to him by the Old Norse name Göngu-Hrólfr, meaning "Hrólfr the Walker". (Göngu-Hrólfr is also widely known by an Old Danish variant, Ganger-Hrolf.) The byname "Walker" is usually understood to suggest that Rollo was so physically imposing that he could not be carried by a horse and was obliged to travel on foot. Norman and other French sources do not use the name Hrólfr, and the identification of Rollo with Göngu-Hrólfr is based upon similarities between circumstances and actions ascribed to both figures.

He had children by at least three women. He abducted Popa or Poppa the daughter of the Count of Rennes or possibly the Count of Bayeux. It is not known if she was legitimate or illegitimate. He married Gisla the daughter (probably illegitimate) of King Charles of France. He also had another child. According to the medieval Irish text, '*An Banshencha*s' and Icelandic sources, another daughter, Cadlinar (Kaðlín; Kathleen) was born in Scotland (probably to a Scots mother) and married an Irish prince named Beollán mac Ciarmaic, later King of South Brega (Lagore). I have used the Norse name Kaðlín and made her a Scottish princess.

Poppa and Rollo

There is some dispute as to the true identity of the woman called Poppa. Most agree that she was the daughter of a Breton count but the sources dispute which one. I cannot believe that a legitimate daughter of a Count would have been left with a Viking and so I have her as illegitimate. More danico was the term used by the Franks to speak of a Danish marriage. The heirs were considered legal, at least in the world of the Norse. William was famously William the Bastard.

Rollo did make Jumièges his base and captured Rouen. My version is a fictitious one. The French king did put bridges across the Seine but it continued to be raided.

Louis the Stammerer

The story of King Louis is largely true. Poppa's words were spoken of the King. He brought an army from Aquitaine to rid Normandy of Vikings and he died. His army was defeated. I gave him a martyr's death.

The Siege of Paris

What follows are the actual events. I am a novelist and I have changed the time scale and some of the characters have been amalgamated. My purpose is to tell a good story. The facts have not been changed. The Vikings arrived in Paris in November 885, initially asking for tribute from the Franks. When this was denied, they began a siege. On 26 November the Danes attacked the northeast tower with ballistae, mangonels, and catapults. They were repulsed by a mixture of hot wax and pitch. All Viking attacks that day were repulsed, and during the night the Parisians constructed another storey on the tower. On 27 November the Viking attack included mining, battering rams, and fire, but to no avail. Bishop Gozlin entered the fray with a bow and an axe. He planted a cross on the outer defences and exhorted the people. His brother Ebles also joined the fighting. The Vikings withdrew after the failed initial attacks and built a camp on the right side of the riverbank, using stone as a construction material. While preparing for new attacks, the Vikings also started constructing additional siege engines. In a renewed assault, they shot a thousand grenades against the city, sent a ship for the bridge, and made a land attack with three groups. The forces surrounded the bridgehead tower, possibly mainly aiming to bring down the river obstacle. While they tried setting fire to the bridge, they also attacked the city itself with siege engines.

For two months the Vikings maintained the siege, making trenches and provisioning themselves off the land. In January 886 they tried to fill the river shallows with debris, plant matter, and the bodies of dead animals and dead prisoners to try to get around the tower. They continued this for two days. On the third day, they set three ships alight and guided them towards the wooden bridge. The burning ships sank before they could set the bridge on fire, but the wooden construction was nonetheless weakened. On 6 February, rains caused the debris-filled river to overflow and the bridge supports to give way. The bridge gone, the northeast tower was now isolated with only twelve defenders inside. The Vikings asked the twelve to surrender, but they refused and were all subsequently killed.

The Vikings left a force around Paris, but many ventured further to pillage Le Mans, Chartres, and into the Loire. Odo successfully slipped some men through Norse lines to go to Italy and plead with Charles to come to their aid. Henry, Count of Saxony, Charles' chief man in Germany, marched to Paris. Weakened by marching during the winter, Henry's soldiers made only one abortive attack in February before retreating. The besieged forces sallied forth and to obtain supplies. The morale of the besiegers was low and Sigfred asked for sixty pounds of silver. He left the siege in April. Another Viking leader, Rollo, stayed behind with his men. In May, disease began to spread in the Parisian ranks and Gozlin died. Odo then slipped through Viking-controlled territory to petition Charles for support; Charles consented. Odo fought his way back into Paris and Charles and Henry of Saxony marched northward. Henry died after he fell into the Viking ditches, where he was captured and killed.

That summer, the Danes made a final attempt to take the city but were repulsed. The imperial army arrived in October and scattered the Vikings. Charles encircled Rollo and his army and set up a camp at Montmartre. However, Charles had no intention of fighting. He allowed the Vikings to sail up the Seine to ravage Burgundy, which was in revolt. When the Vikings withdrew from France the next spring, he gave them 700 livres (pounds) of silver as promised, amounting to approximately 257 kg.

Books used in the research
- British Museum - Vikings- Life and Legends
- Arthur and the Saxon Wars- David Nicolle (Osprey)
- Saxon, Norman and Viking Terence Wise (Osprey)
- The Vikings- Ian Heath (Osprey)
- Byzantine Armies 668-1118 - Ian Heath (Osprey)
- Romano-Byzantine Armies 4th-9th Century - David Nicholle (Osprey)

- The Walls of Constantinople AD 324-1453 - Stephen Turnbull (Osprey)
- Viking Longship - Keith Durham (Osprey)
- The Vikings in England- Anglo-Danish Project
- The Varangian Guard- 988-1453 Raffael D'Amato
- Saxon Viking and Norman- Terence Wise
- The Walls of Constantinople AD 324-1453-Stephen Turnbull
- Byzantine Armies- 886-1118- Ian Heath
- The Age of Charlemagne-David Nicolle
- The Normans- David Nicolle
- Norman Knight AD 950-1204- Christopher Gravett
- The Norman Conquest of the North- William A Kappelle
- The Knight in History- Francis Gies
- The Norman Achievement- Richard F Cassady
- Knights- Constance Brittain Bouchard

Griff Hosker
April 2018

Drekar in the Seine

Other books by Griff Hosker

If you enjoyed reading this book, then why not read another one by the author?

Ancient History

The Sword of Cartimandua Series
(Germania and Britannia 50 A.D. – 128 A.D.)
Ulpius Felix- Roman Warrior (prequel)
The Sword of Cartimandua
The Horse Warriors
Invasion Caledonia
Roman Retreat
Revolt of the Red Witch
Druid's Gold
Trajan's Hunters
The Last Frontier
Hero of Rome
Roman Hawk
Roman Treachery
Roman Wall
Roman Courage

The Wolf Warrior series
(Britain in the late 6th Century)
Saxon Dawn
Saxon Revenge
Saxon England
Saxon Blood
Saxon Slayer
Saxon Slaughter
Saxon Bane
Saxon Fall: Rise of the Warlord
Saxon Throne
Saxon Sword

232

Medieval History

The Dragon Heart Series
Viking Slave
Viking Warrior
Viking Jarl
Viking Kingdom
Viking Wolf
Viking War
Viking Sword
Viking Wrath
Viking Raid
Viking Legend
Viking Vengeance
Viking Dragon
Viking Treasure
Viking Enemy
Viking Witch
Viking Blood
Viking Weregeld
Viking Storm
Viking Warband
Viking Shadow
Viking Legacy
Viking Clan
Viking Bravery

The Norman Genesis Series
Hrolf the Viking
Horseman
The Battle for a Home
Revenge of the Franks
The Land of the Northmen
Ragnvald Hrolfsson
Brothers in Blood
Lord of Rouen
Drekar in the Seine
Duke of Normandy
The Duke and the King

Drekar in the Seine

New World Series
Blood on the Blade
Across the Seas
The Savage Wilderness
The Bear and the Wolf
Erik the Navigator

The Vengeance Trail

The Danelaw Saga
The Dragon Sword

The Reconquista Chronicles
Castilian Knight
El Campeador
The Lord of Valencia

The Aelfraed Series
(Britain and Byzantium 1050 A.D. - 1085 A.D.)
Housecarl
Outlaw
Varangian

**The Anarchy Series England
1120-1180**
English Knight
Knight of the Empress
Northern Knight
Baron of the North
Earl
King Henry's Champion
The King is Dead
Warlord of the North
Enemy at the Gate
The Fallen Crown
Warlord's War
Kingmaker
Henry II

Drekar in the Seine

Crusader
The Welsh Marches
Irish War
Poisonous Plots
The Princes' Revolt
Earl Marshal

Border Knight
1182-1300
Sword for Hire
Return of the Knight
Baron's War
Magna Carta
Welsh Wars
Henry III
The Bloody Border
Baron's Crusade
Sentinel of the North
War in the West
Debt of Honour (May 2021)

Sir John Hawkwood Series
France and Italy 1339- 1387
Crécy: The Age of the Archer
Man at Arms
The White Company (July 2021)

Lord Edward's Archer
Lord Edward's Archer
King in Waiting
An Archer's Crusade
Targets of Treachery (Due out August 2021)

Struggle for a Crown
1360- 1485
Blood on the Crown
To Murder A King
The Throne
King Henry IV

Drekar in the Seine

The Road to Agincourt
St Crispin's Day
The Battle for France

Tales from the Sword I

Conquistador
England and America in the 16ᵗʰ Century
Conquistador (Coming in 2021)

Modern History

The Napoleonic Horseman Series
Chasseur à Cheval
Napoleon's Guard
British Light Dragoon
Soldier Spy
1808: The Road to Coruña
Talavera
The Lines of Torres Vedras
Bloody Badajoz
The Road to France
Waterloo (June 2021)

The Lucky Jack American Civil War series
Rebel Raiders
Confederate Rangers
The Road to Gettysburg

The British Ace Series
1914
1915 Fokker Scourge
1916 Angels over the Somme
1917 Eagles Fall
1918 We will remember them
From Arctic Snow to Desert Sand
Wings over Persia

Drekar in the Seine

Combined Operations series
1940-1945
Commando
Raider
Behind Enemy Lines
Dieppe
Toehold in Europe
Sword Beach
Breakout
The Battle for Antwerp
King Tiger
Beyond the Rhine
Korea
Korean Winter

Tales from the Sword Book 2

Other Books
Great Granny's Ghost (Aimed at 9-14-year-old young people)

For more information on all of the books then please visit the author's website at www.griffhosker.com where there is a link to contact him or visit his Facebook page: GriffHosker at Sword Books

Made in the USA
Columbia, SC
03 November 2021

48301984R00145